THE RING OF DARKNESS

T.R. Michaud

12/25/22

Happy Christmas & Merry Holidays!.
Enjoy & Safe Journey!!.

PAGE PUBLISHING, INC.
New York, NY

First originally published by Page Publishing, Inc. 2017

ISBN 978-1-64027-957-5 (Paperback)
ISBN 978-1-64027-958-2 (Digital)

Printed in the United States of America

ACKNOWLEDGMENTS

I would like to take a page to acknowledge those responsible for lending me aid and making this book a reality. Karen Alves, entrepreneur and owner of Design Principles, Inc., for both the cover sleeve artwork and the map of Kanaan; Laurie Bougas for transcribing my written words into type; and finally to those few who took the time to read and comment on this adventure before this story was told to you the reader. Thank you Carter, Auntie Pat, Tricia, and my little sister, Cherie.

In dedication to Mr. Earnest Gary Gygax and all those who worked for the gaming company TSR Inc. They both compelled others to tap into our imaginations. The creation of Mr. Gygax's visions and fantasies, along with the company TSR Inc, brought the role-playing game, "Dungeons & Dragons" to life, and for that I, along with millions, thank you!

To both Ed Greenwood and Jeff Grubb for giving us the continent of "Faerün" and its "Forgotten Realms," along with the heroes and villains that made up its inhabitants.

Finally, to my friends of times past; Trent R., Joey and Mario T., Randy and Kenny V., Adam and his dad Ben L., Seth H., Joe M., Joy, Chris, and Eric, whose heroes brought color and diversity adventuring throughout the realms. For giving so much of yourselves and your heroes during those adventures, along with sharing fantastic times together. This book is for all of you.

Safe Journeys!

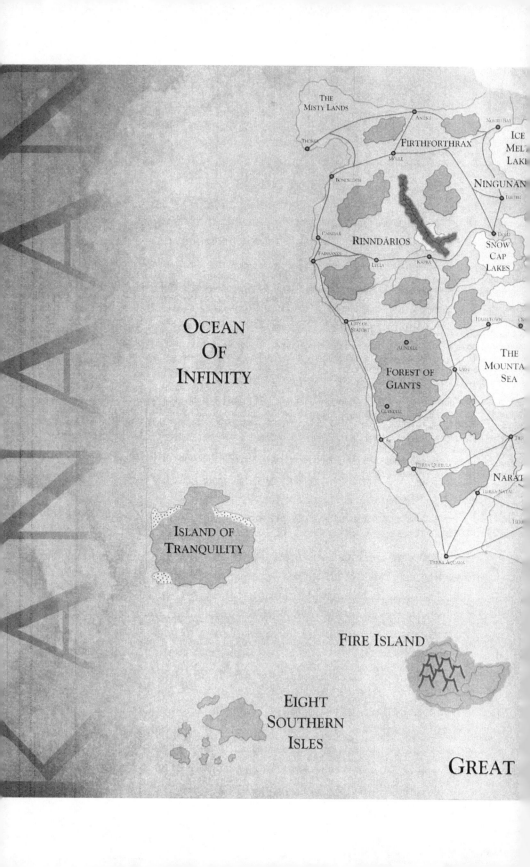

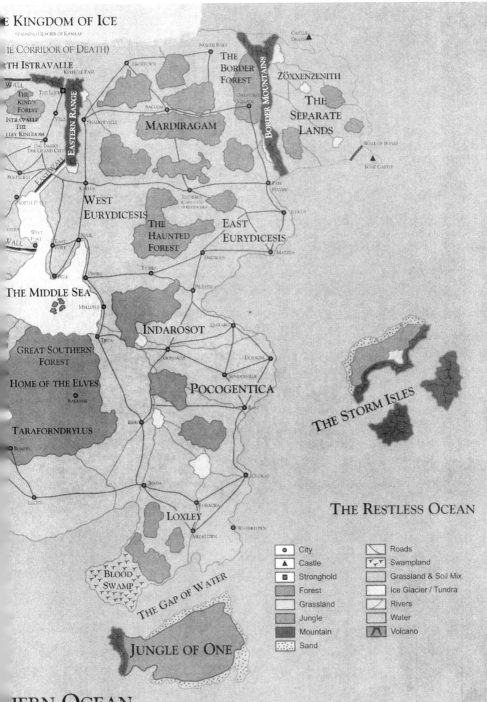

THE KINGDOM OF ICE

STAINING GLACIER OF KANAAS

(THE CORRIDOR OF DEATH)

NORTH ISTRAVALLE

KEYHOLE PASS

WALL
THE
KING'S
FOREST
ISTRAVALLE
THE
VALLEY KINGDOM

THE LOCK

VILLI

DAL BARRO
THE GRAND CITY

BOLFELKO

NORTH FORT

WEST
WALL

WEST
FORT

LISTEN

EAST
FORT

TELE

THE MIDDLE SEA

MELLOLI

GREAT SOUTHERN
FOREST

HOME OF THE ELVES

KADARIE

TARAFORNDRYLUS

RONDEL

ILLITH

EASTERN RANGE

EAST WALL

KISTA

NISSE

FOSSES

TIPTA

ESSU

JENDA

NORTH BAKO

FROSTTOWN

SACCONO

SHADOWVILLE

MARDIRAGAM

WEST
EURYDICESIS

THE
HAUNTED
FOREST

TIOTES

INDAROSOT

ADONSIALE

POCOGENTICA

LOXLEY

MEATOWN

FORACHA

BLOOD
SWAMP

THE GAP OF WATER

JUNGLE OF ONE

THE
BORDER
FOREST

OAKFOREST
VILLAGE

TZETOFELS
ELVEN CITY
OF EASTERN RANGE

FAIR
HAVEN

ILLOCUS

EAST
EURYDICESIS

MAERIA

ENDRIAS

PILETELE

QATARO

DUXXON

SUNDERVILLE

BAST

OLUKAY

WATERTOWN

BORDER MOUNTAINS

ZÖXXENZENITH

THE
SEPARATE
LANDS

WALL OF BONES

BONE CASTLE

CASTLE
DEATH

THE STORM ISLES

THE RESTLESS OCEAN

THE SOUTHERN OCEAN

⊙ City		▱ Roads
▲ Castle		⊤⊤ Swampland
▣ Stronghold		▱ Grassland & Soil Mix
▰ Forest		▱ Ice Glacier / Tundra
▱ Grassland		▱ Rivers
▰ Jungle		▱ Water
▰ Mountain		◣ Volcano
⠂⠂ Sand		

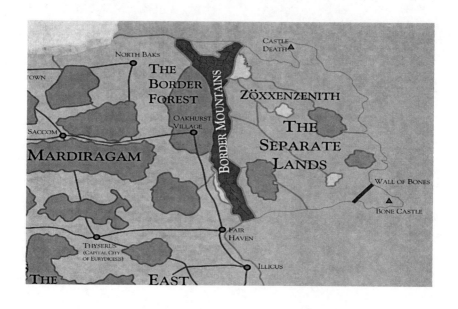

owner as the ambushers fell upon them. The night that had been calm and quiet was now filled with the sounds of snapping bones, ripping and tearing of chunks of meat, and the growling of blood thirsty beasts feeding on the donkey.

The old man, in a surprised and fearful panic, tried to quickly back away on hands and knees from the horrific carnage taking place only feet away from him. In the fear of knowing that he shared the same fate as his long-time friend Henry did, one thought crossed his mind, "It had been one of the nicest nights."

CHAPTER 1

Help Needed!
Adventurers Wanted!
Will Pay Finely!
Anyone Interested; Enquire
Within Tavern.

Reading the sign to himself, Calvin redirected his attention passed the sign to the small town and it's tavern that lay beyond. Being the first building on the right while heading into the town, the tavern stood two stories tall with windows on the second floor equally spaced into the structure. The building was built out of highly-plained material and being naturally stained took on a golden appearance. A farmer's porch was built on the front of the structure, and Calvin complimented how homey and different this entrance was compared to other taverns he had visited throughout the realms.

His attention was quickly brought back from his thoughts by the burning sensation in his eyes caused by the beads of sweat running into them. Rubbing his eyes and blinking away the watery vision caused by the salty intrusion, the stranger noticed a woman with child in tow look at him quickly, turn away, and then glance a second time before entering one of the other buildings in the small town.

Calvin pondered for a moment over the woman's weary glances, but then shrugged it off to his appearance. He was dressed in a shiny breastplate from neck to mid-thigh that reflected the light off of it like a mirror, and held the reigns of his large, muscular, white warhorse which stood behind his right shoulder. "Here we go again," he thought. "Cavaliers must be uncommon to these lands."

Around him, large, green trees reaching for the heavens flourished. Their full canopies casting shadows on the ground. It was the beginning of the summer months throughout the land, and already this late in the morning the sun baked down on it's inhabitants. The sounds of bugs humming and birds singing throughout the woods filled the air.

Again wiping away the sweat from his brow with the back of his hand, Calvin signaled to his mount with a couple of clicks from his mouth and both headed towards the tavern.

"We could both use a cold refreshing drink right about now," stated the cavalier in a soft tone while he glanced over his shoulder to his mount.

There were several people walking about or entering different structures on the one main road of the small town as Calvin lead his warhorse up to the tavern. Tie-down posts for animals, along with a couple of water troughs, were available in front of the porch. Lashing the reigns to a post, the cavalier double checked them making sure they were secure.

"Just as I like them," he satisfying thought as he looked up at his friend, who was dipping it's lips into the crystal clear water of the trough. The mount slowly raising its head from its refreshing drink and looking at its companion as if asking why he was still there. The warhorse's muscles rippled and flexed as Calvin patted his mount's shoulder. "I'll be back," he chuckled. Offering a snort, the animal lowered its head to take another drink.

Surveying the structure of the porch, the armored man ascended the stairs. "Very sound and strong," he thought touching a post. While climbing them, he also noticed several, small, round wooden tables accompanied by a pair of chairs at each dressing the porch. Glancing back to the entryway where a regular door would be, this tavern instead had a double-louvered swinging door at mid-body. "Different," he remarked under his breath as the cavalier swung the door inward walking inside.

The room was large and extremely spacious, and as soon as Calvin stepped into the room he noticed a long, wooden bar on his left that led to a staircase going up directly across from the entrance. In front were sixteen stools. Just like the rest of the tavern, the wood used to build this establishment, the bar, and the stools were crafted out of fine plained material. They were also stained golden as were the tables and chairs around the room.

"It looks more like a grand hall in here than a tavern," Calvin impressively thought as he also noticed a woman seated at the bar, the barkeeper, and a lone, hooded figure sitting at one of the tables. Before the cavalier could finish his mental inventory of the room, a voice grabbed his attention.

"Good day young sir, and welcome to my humble establishment!", came the friendly voice of the barkeep standing across from the woman patron. "Have a seat and I'll be right with you," he added turning back to a conversation he was currently having with the young woman.

Taking a quick mental note, Calvin quickly scanned the woman looking for any visible or concealed weapons. He didn't notice any, but the cavalier took note of her appearance. She was wearing buckskin pants with tan knee-high moccasins, along with a powder blue shirt covered with a buckskin vest. The woman had long, black hair that just grew past her shoulder blades and she wore it around her face hiding her features from the sides.

Making his way over to the nearest stool at the bar, the new occupant continued to survey the rest of the room. Across from the bar on the other side stood a beautiful, stone fireplace. Knick-knacks lined its mantle and inside it was clean with new logs waiting to be lit, but with the beginning of summer it would be a while before they were used. Curtains decorated the windows with a few puffing up as a light breeze blew through them. Beams spanned the ceiling, and Calvin could tell the tavern was strong and sturdy like the porch's structure. Beside the lone hooded figure seated beside the unlit fireplace the rest of the room's tables and chairs were empty.

With all his weight shifted onto the two rear legs of his seat, as he leaned backwards in his chair, the figure had his feet up on another at his table. The stranger wore a light cloak of brown color with its hood pulled over his head covering most of the stranger's face. If it wasn't for the fact that the figure brought a wine glass filled with golden, yellow liquid to his barely hidden lips under the hood, Calvin might have thought he napped. Continuing his observation, the cavalier checked the resting figure for any signs of weapons but none were visible.

"Probably concealing something," thought Calvin. "Could actually be a woman, but definitely an elf due to his or her really slender build," he added. Although whether a male or female mattered not at this time because suspicion radiated from this figure like rays of sunlight on a clear summer's day.

Turning back to the stool and taking a seat, an uneasy feeling ran through the cavalier's mind. Again, he wiped sweat from his brow as he looked for a mirror behind the bar but none existed. Calvin glanced out the entryway checking on his horse and the items it carried. He let his head rest in his hands and pondered the sign posted outside of the town. A second later he raised his head up from the cradle his hands had formed and waited on the barkeep.

Sitting with his feet on a chair, Devis heard the man about to enter the tavern while he was still outside. It's not that the man was loud, but with the hooded figures acute hearing, he could pick up the sound of the newcomer's first two steps on the stairs. Like all elves, Devis possessed sensitive hearing. Conversations that would appear to be a whisper to human ears, the elf could hear as clear as day most of the time; including most of the one being held by the woman and the barkeep across the room.

She had made a lot of small talk eventually inquiring about the sign on the outskirts of town. This peaked Devis' interest even though the barkeeper had told her the same story he had related to the elf earlier in regards to the village desperately needing help. What stood out to Devis is when the woman shared that she had skill and knowledge in natural healing medicine and herbs. She went on to add that she did possess some magical abilities also. The conversation quickly went dead when the armored man entered the tavern.

Barely moving an inch, the hooded figure inconspicuously looked the newcomer top to toe. The man wore traveling pants and boots but also a breastplate.

"Possibly a fighter for hire,..."-he thought- "...but where are his weapons?"

All the elf noticed was a dagger sheathed on the mans hip. Puzzled he added, "Maybe he killed or came upon the real owner's corpse, and took its breastplate."

Most importantly what Devis noticed that the newcomer had not, was how both the woman and the barkeep took a double glance before getting quiet.

Raising his yellow liquid-filled wine glass and partaking in a sip before returning it to the table, the elf stared at it for a moment. He loved the taste of Honey Meade. It always seemed to have a way of seizing his attention. "That's good," impressively he thought, but he quickly regained his current observations and focused them on the man starting to sit down at the bar. Once again Devis began to eavesdrop knowing that he might hear something of importance over the next dozen or so minutes.

～♌～

"What can I get you sir?", asked the barkeeper.

"An ale please kind sir," pleasantly responded Calvin.

"Uh yes, an ale. Coming right up!", as he grabbed a stein and filled it from a draft keg. "It is a hot one this day. Wouldn't you agree?", queried the bartender while sliding the stein in the cavalier's direction. Then he wiped his hands on a rag that stuck out of a pocket on his apron.

"How much do I owe you?", questioned Calvin as he pulled his money pouch out from under his breastplate somewhere down around his hip.

"Two copper sir."

Taking the two coins with his left hand, the bartender offered the new patron his other. "Name's Carl, Carl Hosgrove, and welcome to the Oak."

"I am Calvin Gaston," he greeted standing and clasping Carl's forearm. "Pleased to make your acquaintance."

Carl was a medium-sized man with a rotund stomach and a jolly disposition. He was middle-aged, roughly fifty winters old, and had a fair complexion. The barkeep wore a full beard that matched his short, salt and peppered hair. Carl's shirt sleeves were rolled up to his elbows and his forearms were thick from a lifetime of work.

Sitting back on his stool, Calvin lifted the sweat-covered stein to his lips and wet his parched mouth with a gulp of ale. A feeling of refreshment from the ice cold drink engulfed Calvin's tongue and throat. The feeling to keep guzzling the liquid assaulted his taste buds, but he knew that guzzling was not proper etiquette for a cavalier.

Removing the stein from his lips and returning it back to the bar Calvin savored the refreshment and coldness of the brew. "That's really good," he remarked. "How do you keep it so cold?"

"Thank a mage and a handy gnome for that," chuckled Carl.

After a brief moment, the newcomer inquired about the sign posted on the outskirts of town seeming to cause the woman sitting at the other end of the bar to rise from her stool and begin making her way over to where the cavalier sat. It was obvious to Calvin that she seemed to also be interested in the posting. Catching her movement out of the corner of his eye he stood to face her as she walked over in his direction.

"May I?", the woman asked while pointing to the stool next to his.

"Of course my lady," he bowed. "I would be honored," he continued pulling the stool away from the bar for her.

A smile dressed her face as she nod and sat down.

Calvin now got a good look at the woman's face. She was young and beautiful. "Probably twenty winters," thought the cavalier. Almost hidden by the young woman's bangs hanging in her face, her eyes seemed to twinkle like stars in the night's sky and her lashes were long and naturally curly. Her disposition was both pleasant and good-natured.

"I am Faith,…"-she pleasantly introduced herself while sticking her hand out- "…and I too was also asking Carl about the sign when you came in."

Taking her hand in his and gently placing a kiss on the back of it, he introduced himself. "I am Calvin Gaston, and we shall seek our answers together."

Faith smiled as she took her new seat at the bar next to his. After taking his seat, both turned back to where Carl stood, but he was gone.

❧

Looking past Calvin and Faith's introductions, Carl noticed the hooded figure seated at the table hold up a finger and beckon him over. Neither the man nor the woman saw the barkeep take his leave from his place behind the bar or heard him when he had excused himself.

Approaching the figure's table Carl questioned "Can I get you anything?"

"A refill."

"Is that all sir?"

The stranger only responded by nodding his head.

"Very well sir. I'll be back in a minute," came the bartender as he took the empty glass from the table and returned to the bar.

"I'll be right with you young folks," Carl stated to both Calvin and Faith, whom were awaiting his return and watched as he refilled the glass with the golden liquid for the lone figure.

❧

Taking up his place behind the bar after returning from delivering the glass to the stranger, Carl apologized. "Pardon the slight inter-ruption my lady, sir. You queried about the help the village needs." Pulling up a stool from a corner and taking a seat he continued, "The local law enforcement posted the sign nearly a month to a month and a half ago requesting the aid when people started disappearing and strange happenings began taking place at night."

Carl shifted his eyes between Calvin and Faith while they intently listen to him and his story.

"I had heard rumors about this village and the problem that plagues it lately throughout the last few taverns and bars I visited while I rode through their towns," confessed the cavalier. "This is why I chose to come here and maybe I can find out what is going on for myself and lend my sword."

Taking a sip of wine from her glass she had brought over with her, Faith thought the last statement Calvin had made sounded somewhat smug. "Like he was going to show up and take care of the town's problem with a swing of his sword," she thought, but quickly let that notion dissolve giving the cavalier the benefit of the doubt. Remaining silent she continued to listen.

"Is it true what they say about the shadows coming alive at night?", inquisitively asked Calvin.

"It is," replied Carl nodding his head in agreement. "In fact, the folk along with some travelers to the village have disappeared causing the local law to put a curfew into effect."

Again, Carl's eyes shifted from one to the other.

"Do you believe it to be ghosts or something unnatural?", query Faith.

"I don't know, but screams and loud cries can be heard most nights along with weird and unexplained events that have happened."

"Like what?", came Calvin's question.

"Well, just the other night the stable roughly twenty minutes outside of town,..."-explained Carl as he pointed with his thumb over his shoulder- "...had all the horses break out of the place spooked. Some ran through the town at breakneck speeds. Thank the gods no one was walking then or they would have found themselves under the animals!", he added in disgust. "It took poor Zeltax the next two days to round them all up."

"Jeez, as a matter of fact, this morning something weird took place," remembered Carl. "All the store front windows, except those with shutters, were discovered shattered by their owners."

Calvin called back to memory the windows of the tavern. There were no shutters on the second floor, but all the windows on the first floor had them, and they were stained to match the establishment.

For the next half hour, or so, Calvin and Faith listened intently as Carl shared some of the village's latest enigmas. To none of their knowledge did they know that the hooded elf listened attentively to their conversation. Devis did however mentally record several weary glances from a few of the town's people entering the place to order a drink or lunch.

Carl had just given his last bit of information on the unexplained happenings when Calvin swallowed his last gulp of his second stein of ale.

"Who do we speak with to sign up?", queried the cavalier.

"That would be Captain Woodrow," smiled Carl. "He's the head of the village guard."

Like a royal band drum roll, Calvin began to ask a series of questions. It actually sounded like he was interrogating the bartender.

"Does this Zeltax own the only stable in the village?"

"Yes sir, and may I add he's the best with horses and livestock," responded Carl. "The man has never had a mishap like the other night for years and years," he added.

"Where can we find Captain Woodrow?"

"The local guard have a tower just east of here past Zeltax's stable. You may have seen the pinnacle of the tower rising above the treetops, sir."

"Yes. I do recall seeing its summit," agreed the cavalier.

"Thank you Carl. You have been extremely helpful, but I hold two more inquiries for you," pointed out Calvin.

The barkeeper's eyes fixed on the young man in wait of the questions.

"How much do I owe you for my second ale and a glass of wine for Faith?"

"One silver piece," he answered with a chuckle.

"Finally, do you have a vacant room I could rent, and what is its price?"

21

"I have several rooms vacant, and the cost is a gold coin per night. That does include a wake up, if desired, and a breakfast plate," added Carl.

"Very well sir," agreed the cavalier as he slid both a gold and a silver coin across the bar.

Turning to Faith, Calvin added, "My Lady, a glass of wine for you to enjoy if you would please await my return?"

"Why thank you Calvin, but where are you going?", Faith asked smiling.

"To stable my mount at Zeltax's. I shall return, and we can talk more."

Standing and replacing his money pouch back to his hip under his breast plate, Calvin turned to Carl and explained he was going to retrieve his gear from his mount and place it in a room before going to the stable. The bartender nodded in affirmation while withdrawing a leather-covered ledger from under the bar.

~ 2 ~

Coming down the inn's stairs and stepping into the tavern, Calvin had placed his equipment in his room. Immediately he noticed the hooded figure was gone. Drawing Carl and Faith's attention to the empty table with an empty wine glass on it, "Did either of you see the person leave?", queried the cavalier.

"No," responded both in unison.

"Wow. That's spooky," added Faith.

Calvin walked to the swinging doors and stepped through them onto the porch. Sitting at a small, round table on the cavalier's left was the figure. The man with the hood still covering his head gazed down into his lap and had his feet on the second chair of the set. Again, a suspicious feeling arose in Calvin's stomach.

While looking up and down the only road that ran through town, Calvin wiped sweat from his brow and commented to himself, "Hot one this day. Thank the gods it be already mid-day."

He descended the stairs and unleashed his mount's reigns from the post. "Come on my friend," he suggested leading the warhorse away from the tavern and down the road. Calvin really didn't pay any attention to those walking and taking a glance at him only to turn away before quickly giving a second glance in his direction. His mind was focused on the enigma of the hooded stranger. The cavalier found himself pondering over this person.

Calvin's attention was finally brought back to the present with a snort from his warhorse. The cavalier patted his mount's muzzle as he led him out of town and into the trees that surrounded the road.

CHAPTER 2

The trees of the forest cast almost a continuous blanket of shadow on the road. Even though there was still little breaks in the canopy for sunlight to enter, it was much cooler. Birds chirped songs throughout the branches and dozens of squirrels and chipmunks scattered throughout the treetops or up their trunks.

Calvin, along with his mount had already passed a few farmhouses. They were scattered throughout the woods all around the town of Oakhurst Village. The walk was serene through the Border Forest, which was located west of the Border Mountains. The immense mountain range divided this quiet farming community from the cesspool of evil known as the Separate Lands. This village had been settled centuries ago and had never encountered problems from the Separate Lands, but the lack of this issue never prevented moms from threatening that land's evil on children misbehaving.

The apex of the guard tower could be seen through the breaks in the tree canopy. The outpost not only held the guards to police the local community but also doubled as a watch tower looking for any signs that evil from the Separate Lands was headed in their direction. It was true that most of the mountains were impassable, whether it be because of terrain, or wild animals, or monsters. The dwarves also had a couple of halls in the mountains. They were the first line of defense if needed and would use large, signal fires if Oakhurst Village was in any kind of imminent danger from beyond. The alliance between the Dwarven Kingdoms and the humans of the village was centuries old, and both prospered from this long time coalition.

Still not being able to see the stable through the trees, Calvin had a feeling it was nearby. The smell of manure drifted in the air and its aroma told of its close proximity. Its odor was slightly pungent considering this hot day.

"If this Zeltax keeps care of the place and its occupants as highly as Carl speaks of, then the stay will be one of rest for you my friend," offered the cavalier to his mount.

With its ears erect and listening, the warhorse just strolled behind in a rhythm as it walked with its tail swaying from side to side. The mount seeming to snort its affirmation.

Rounding a slight bend in the road, the face of the stable grew forth from the surrounding forest. It appeared to greet the companion and his mount. Just like the tavern, the stable was constructed of the exact same highly-plained lumber and had a natural golden stain. The face of the structure contained two large, double doors with a slightly angled ramp leading up to them. Their hinges black as night and rust free.

Above the double doors was a smaller version of them on a second floor. Loft doors the cavalier knew, and Calvin could see neatly stacked bales of hay as he got closer. Above the loft doors was a thick, solid beam with a large hook, a pulley, and thick rope hanging from it. Finally, in raised letters to both sides of the loft doors declaring this place Oakhurst Stables. The structure was both breathtaking and immaculate.

Behind the stable and to its left and right sides were wooden-fenced pens. One housed a small flock of sheep and horses could be seen grazing in the others. Two horses frolicked within another one of the enclosures.

Leading his steed towards the large, open, double doors, Calvin was astonished with this place. "This be not a stable, but rather a palace for horses! It looks as Carl wasn't exaggerating, and you may fancy this place, Thunder."

His mount snorted in acknowledgment.

Reaching the ramp and doors of the place, the cavalier could see stalls lining each side and a large, muscular, blonde man leading a beautiful looking horse out and equally sized opening on the other side.

Opening a pen the man spoke to the animal in a nurturing tone while removing its lead. "It's beautiful out today. Go get some fresh air while I clean your stall."

Entering the pen the animal broke into a gallop attempting to catch up to the two frolicking horses.

"Good day sir," greeted Calvin. His words seeming to carry on the day's breeze.

Closing and locking the gate, Zeltax turned to see the cavalier and his white horse standing across the stable from him.

"Good day to you," he replied wearing a smile as he started to walk towards the two. "How can I be of service sir on this beautiful day?"

"I am seeking to rent a stall for my friend here," motioning with his head towards his warhorse. "What is the fee?"

"For his size the cost is one silver coin per night but that does include food, water, a clean stall, and I personally like to groom the animal daily."

Zeltax offered his hand and introduced himself. Calvin returned the salutation.

"He sure is a magnificent and strong animal," complimented the muscular man. "May I?"

"You may. His name is Thunder."

"Here you go," offered the stable's owner as he pulled a feed apple from a pocket and gave it to the mount. Zeltax patted its muzzle before turning to Calvin, "Please, have a look around."

The cavalier walked side-by-side with the stable's owner through the structure. As Zeltax led the horse, Calvin glanced at all the stalls that lined both sides. The upkeep and care was impressive. He thought it looked and sounded to be worth the coin.

As the three exited the structure's rear, the cavalier really got a good look at the care take of the pens. One even had a field with oats growing in it, and Calvin was impressed as he turned to the warhorse and removed a belt holding a scabbard housing his blade. The cavalier buckled it on his hip with the sword hanging from his left side.

Looking up, Calvin started removing Thunder's saddle, but Zeltax stopped him.

"I've got that sir. Let me show you the rest of the place first."

"Very well," Calvin agreed accompanied with a slight nod.

Zeltax opened the gate to a pen and in walked Thunder. The animal strolled over to a water trough and lowered its head to drink.

Turning and leading the way, the owner was pointing out different aspects of the stable, all the while Calvin instinctively lifted the hilt of the sword clear of its sheath checking to make sure the sword would clearly slide out when drawn.

◆

"I'm looking for the tavern owner, or anyone who has any information regarding that sign out there!", came a loud, obnoxious voice yelling.

Breaking the silence and peacefulness of just about an empty tavern, Carl and Faith turned to look astonished at the figure standing in the doorway. They were the only two in the place at this time. The hooded man still sitting on the porch just shook his head. In the doorway between the swinging doors stood the perpetrator of the tavern's docile atmosphere; and a small perp he was.

"Helloo! Does anybody hear me?", loud and obnoxiously bellowed the gnome.

Both the bartender, along with Faith, and the patron out front knew this was like no gnome that either of them had ever met before. Gnomes are scientists creating weird contraptions and recording or blueprinting their findings. They are always involved in some type of technological breakthrough, or wander the realms with a life quest. Gnomes have a habit of speaking quick and running their words, sentences, and even paragraphs as one continuous statement. Obviously, not this gnome. This gnome was loud, obnoxious, and had a very irritating voice. Irritating enough to most likely chase any dragon away.

Stepping fully through the swinging doors and striding up to the bar the little gnome bellowed out, "Helloo, Kanaan to the Heavens! Is everyone deaf in here?"

"If we're not now, we'll soon be," Faith cracked softly. Carl responded in a low chuckle.

"I'm the owner of this here place, and welcome to the Oak."

"Great!", joyfully replied the gnome. "Since we've got that settled, I would like a mug of beer and some information about that sign. Oh yeah, and speaking of the sign, not all people are as tall as the height of the posting to that sign!", reprimanded the little patron angrily. "What did an orc hammer it up there?"

The loud mouth strolled up to the bar and stood next to one of the stools, which was twice as tall as he was. For a second he was quiet, but a second goes by quick. Throwing is arms up in the air, the gnomes voice filled the room again. "Not everybody is six feet tall! Is this place gnome proof, or what?"

"With a mouth that big and a voice that loud, you could have fooled me," quietly remarked Faith into her wine glass before taking a sip.

Suspiciously the little patron glanced in Faith's direction thinking he had heard her say something. She never returned his gaze.

Carl came from behind the bar carrying a frosty beer-filled mug with foam spilling over the sides. "I'm sorry sir. Everyone is welcome here, but truth be told, we don't get a lot of gnomes, or dwarves, or even halfling patrons," apologized Carl.

The owner pointed at a smaller table with a couple of chairs located near the wall. "You can sit there."

Looking at the set, the gnome scowled back at Carl, "What's that a kiddy table?"

A slight giggle escaped Faith's mouth.

"Take this!", he demanded handing his froth-covered mug to Carl. "Put it on the bar and help me get up on the stool."

After Carl completed the first step of the gnome's designed plan, he bent down and offered the little patron ten fingers. Stepping afoot into the fleshy cradle, the loud, obnoxious, arrogant gnome took a seat on the stool, of course with Carl's help.

Once again Faith giggled, but it was a little louder this time.

The little patron adjusted and gathered himself on the stool before taking a drink of beer and looking over at Faith. She sat only a couple of stools away from him. Using her peripheral vision she could see the gnome looking at her. Slowly Faith turned her head returning his gaze.

"Good afternoon, Miss," he greeted. His tone quieter now.

"It was," she thought but returned the greeting. "Good afternoon."

Turning back to Carl now, the gnome introduced himself. "The name's Moric. I would like to know the specifics regarding the information posted on the sign outside, but first there are a couple of things I must inquire about."

"Very well sir."

"I need to know how much for a room?",he asked before Moric continued while he motioned in Faith's direction with his head, "And how much for the whore?"

❧

After taking a quick tour of the stable and climbing an iron ladder connected to one of the walls, Calvin followed Zeltax to the rear of the loft. The loft was divided in half with the front full of bales of hay and odds and ends, while the rear half was not only an office, but doubled as Zeltax's quarters. Its contents included a table accompanied by two chairs, a wooden filing cabinet, record books, and ledgers. There was a bed and wardrobe chest along the left wall near the corner. On the right wall across from it, two food cabinets and a small table with a pitcher and wash basin stood. Instead of loft doors on the rear of the second floor of the stable there were two large, open windows. On one side of the windows was a small wood stove for cooking and heat in the winter. The windows presently were opened allowing the light breeze to blow through the loft.

"Very efficient and homey at the same time," remarked Zeltax.

"I see."

"Please, sit down," offered the blonde stable owner.

"Thank you," replied Calvin with an accompanying nod as he sat.

Taking up a seat across from him, the blonde man pulled out a ledger, along with a bottle of ink and a quill from the cabinet. "I'll be right with you."

Calvin recalled how clean and immaculate the place had been. All the stalls were clean with a fresh blanket of hay covering the floors. Two buckets, one filled with oats and one with fresh water, were the right heights for the stall's tenant's. Zeltax had commented that he had not got to two yet but assured the cavalier he would when the man left. At this particular time there were a dozen horses, not including Calvin's warhorse, a brown pony, and two goats sharing a stall. As for the flock of sheep, they freely roamed outside the stalls at night.

"Okay Calvin, how many nights would you like to house your horse?", queried the stable owner looking up from his ledger while at the same time breaking his silence.

"I have inquired about the sign posted heading into town with Mr. Carl Hosgrove at the Oak. He said, I need to speak with a Captain Woodrow at the guard tower, so I'm thinking for two nights now." Calvin continued, "Although, if I end up staying for several more days than I will need the horse housed longer."

"That will be no problem," assured the owner while writing in his ledger.

"Then it will be two silver for two nights, and I wait to hear from you the day after next."

Pulling his coin pouch out again, the cavalier slid two silver coins across the table to Zeltax. "Very good sir, and thank you."

"No. Thank you."

"While I am here, do you mind if I ask you some questions in regards to your troubles the other night?"

The large man put his quill down and gave Calvin his full attention. "Of course not sir, but please believe me when I tell you that that incident the other night was the only time anything like that has ever happened."

"Do not trouble yourself my friend, for you and your apparent upkeep of this place have already earned my business," assured Calvin.

"Thank you."

"Do you know who might have accomplished this mischief?", continued the cavalier.

"Unfortunately, I do not have a notion."

"Do you believe something haunts the village?"

"Not that I believe, …"-answered Zeltax sure of his opinion- "…but I do believe it or who is magical."

Perplexed Calvin queried, "What makes you believe that?"

"Because the only way to get to the locks on the stable doors is to be inside. I know both sets of doors were locked," the large man firmly stated.

"Have you heard any cries, or screams during the night?"

"I have."

"Were the cries animalistic?"

"Somewhat, I guess."

Calvin asked his last question. "Zeltax, what do you believe made those screams?"

"I don't know," was the only response he received from the blond man.

⁓

"Well watcha go and do that for?", yelled Moric at Faith as liquid ran from his head down darkening his shirt and pants. His clothes were soaked and a puddle quickly formed around his stool. Dripping liquid, the gnome looked like a drenched rat after the woman poured his full mug of beer over his head.

Carl tried extra hard not to laugh handing the wet gnome a dry bar wipe but burst forth in laughter when he couldn't contain himself any longer.

Even Devis, still sitting on the porch, softly laughed to himself after hearing the obnoxious question through an open window and witnessing the little man's dousing.

Faith was fuming! "You're lucky I don't know how to morph you into a fish and then throw you into a pond!", she yelled.

"Aren't we the feisty sort," retorted Moric while drying his face off.

The young woman huffed in anger and disgust.

"Did anyone ever mention to you that you might have an anger management problem?", sarcastically asked the gnome. "I just thought…"

"Well you thought wrong!", yelling her response while balling both hands and waving them in the air. Shaking both fists, the young woman huffed once again.

Turning and walking back to the original stool she sat on before moving closer to Calvin when he was present, the angry woman now at the end of the bar near the stairs apologized to Carl for the mess and ordered another glass of wine. Within a minute or two the bartender brought her another.

"Don't worry about it Hon," he assured her with a wink.

Moric turned his attention to the woman now sitting at the other end of the bar. "I hope you make enough coin at whatever it is you do because you owe me a mug of beer!"

The angry woman turned in the direction of the loud mouth wearing a scowl of disbelief.

Carl slid another full mug in front of the gnome and handed him another dry wipe. "You asked about the sign?"

"Yeah, that's right."

With Moric's undivided attention, the barkeep retold the same story and related the same events that he touched on earlier that day with Calvin and Faith. He gave the gnome the same contact information, although he never shared any knowledge of anyone else asking. Carl believed that others need not know someone else's business.

When the conversation between the two had ended, the gnome paid for only one mug of beer along with the rent for a room. The tavern/inn owner handed him the keys to his quarters.

Jumping down from his stool, Moric collected his dry pack and his sword, that was strapped to the top of his bag and headed for the stairs. The gnome stopped at the foot of the stairs and was about to say something again to Faith, but the woman stopped him before he could. She had never turned to look at him, but could sense his lingering presence.

"Just keep walking," she sternly advised.

Knowing better not to even attempt a word he proceeded to ascend the staircase and retire to his room.

~∽

It was late in the afternoon when Calvin had finished his business at Zeltax's and now followed the road back to town. He wiped sweat from his brow and was extremely glad the day would start to cool soon. A light breeze still blew.

The cavalier was lost in his thoughts as he tried to piece clues from both Carl and Zeltax together but there just wasn't enough information to form the whole picture. Unlike other rumors or tales he had heard, at least these stories didn't seem exaggerated although he knew that they were still only opinions.

Continuing his trek towards the town, Calvin's thoughts shifted to Faith and the mysterious figure. "Who was this woman and what service could she lend to help solve this mystery? Maybe she was a cleric, or a magic user, or even a psionist." His thoughts continued when the stranger came to mind. "What role does he or she play, and why the secrecy?"

Calvin could not find the answers he searched for, and they were soon replaced as he started to think about the several townsfolk that he saw glance twice at him. "It is like they have never seen armor nor a cavalier before." Letting the thought linger in his mind he continued, "Maybe they have not."

Before Calvin could ponder anymore on the townsfolk, or the town's problems, or any questionable patrons, a noise broke the silence as a couple of bushes off to his left rustled. With lightning quick reflexes he drew his sword free from its scabbard. Adrenaline pumped through his body as he looked all around and up into the trees preparing for an encounter.

A jack rabbit with a red fox in pursuit burst from the bushes and ran across the road, only to disappear on the other side. Neither the hunted nor the red hunter stopped or slowed down. In fact, neither animal had noticed the cavalier.

Waiting a few seconds more, Calvin returned his sword back to its sheath when he assessed there was no danger before continuing his walk towards the town.

❧

Faith was just about to head up the stairs when Calvin walked through the swinging doors and approached the bar. "Carl, may I please have a stein of ale?"

Nodding, Carl turned to retrieve the order.

The woman also turned from the staircase and headed towards Calvin as he sat on a stool. "I'm going to my room to rest and freshen up before I come down for supper."-continuing she asked- "Would you like to meet and share supper and small talk? I figured since we might partake in this adventure together then maybe we can get to know each other."

"That is a good idea," he agreed. "I would be honored."

"Say we meet before sunset."

Calvin simply acknowledged with a nod, as Carl returned with a stein of ale for the cavalier.

Faith was already on the first step to the staircase when she turned and started to point over her shoulder upstairs. "By the way, there is also this loud, obnoxious gnome here asking about the sign. Just thought that you might like to know," she added accompanied with a slight smile.

"Thank you My Lady."

Turning back, she disappeared up the stairs.

Returning his attention back to Carl and his ale, the cavalier took a drink. Carl was chuckling and he took several minutes to narrate the story between Faith and Moric. Both men really had a laugh when the bartender had finished.

Eventually finishing his drink, the cavalier rose to head upstairs to his room. "Carl, why do you think I keep receiving double glances from folk around here?" Is it because a man in some metal armor is rare in these parts?"

But before the bartender could respond, the hooded figure came in from the porch and stood just inside the entryway. To both men's surprise, he was the one to answer.

"Because of your skin."

"Show yourself and state who you are now stranger!", ordered Calvin.

Removing the hood of his cloak, the cavalier gazed upon light brown eyes that were almond in shape. The elf's face was slender matching his build and his long brown hair flowed on both sides of it and over his shoulders. "My name is Devis, and like you, I also am interested in the events of this village."

Four words, "Because of your skin.", was the answer. Finally, Calvin realized the truth behind this statement. The answer was so obvious; but contemplating over the trouble, along with the elf's mystery identity, and Faith, he had not even brought the fact that he is black to mind. The cavalier knowing that a black knight was not common amongst any of the realms. In fact, so rare that Calvin was the only black knight in all the lands.

CHAPTER 3

Faith shut and locked the door to her room. Checking the doorknob, she started down the hallway while dropping the room key into a small, leather pouch she wore tethered around her neck before tucking the cloth bag back into its resting place under her blouse.

The late afternoon sun still clung in the sky casting the rest of its light through the four hallway windows located two each on either end of the hall. The light was dim, but Faith knew it would get darker within the next hour or two.

Coming down the hallway, the young woman had a slight bounce to her step and was actually feeling lively and refreshed after washing up and taking a short nap. She had retired to her room earlier in the day and now wondered if anyone else had asked about the sign besides her, Calvin, and Moric. Just thinking of the obnoxious gnome brought heat to her blood. "Man he gets under my skin," she thought.

Her thoughts quickly vanished as Faith passed a door and overheard the occupant inside snoring extremely loud. "He's not even quiet when he sleeps," the woman thought amazed while shaking her head.

Reaching the stairs, the young woman paused for a moment and took in the aromas of freshly cooked food dancing through the air. The bustling sound of activity from the tavern below seemed to beckon her. Faith closed her eyes and drew in a deep breath absorbing as much of the mouth-watering smell as she could before slowly reopening them and starting down the stairs.

The staircase was wide enough for two people to pass comfortably with railings on both sides. It was also bordered on both sides with three glass-covered candlestick holders each holding a new candle. A young, blonde woman was in the process of lighting the fourth candle located near the middle of the staircase as Faith passed. Both her and the girl acknowledged each other with a smile.

Stepping down off the last step, Faith paused again looking around the tavern. Before retiring to her room earlier, she and Calvin had agreed to meet for supper so they could make arrangements for the next day's meeting with Captain Woodrow. They had both concurred that they could talk and become acquainted with each other over supper and now the young woman searched for him amongst the busy room.

The tavern was more than half full and only a few stools remained empty at the bar, along with most of the tables being already filled with townsfolk eating or waiting on their meals. In his normal position behind the bar, Carl was serving a hefty platter to a large, bulky gentleman. Steam rising from the food. Two woman wearing white aprons moved about the tables in the room like bees in a hive. Once again, she drew a deep breath and her stomach slightly ached from hunger pain.

Surveying the busy room trying to locate Calvin, Faith finally caught sight of him. A small smile creased her lips as she started towards him. He was sitting at a corner table near the unlit fireplace and it looked like the cavalier was talking to another at his table, but a fat man standing was blocking Faith's view of the other person.

As the young woman neared the table, and the obstruction sat down, she could see a slender person with long, brown hair sitting at the table. Upon seeing his pointed ears, Faith realized Calvin was speaking with an elf. Both men noticed the young woman at the same time, as she approached and stood in front of the them.

"Good evening," came the cavalier pushing his chair back and standing. He proceeded to pull her chair out from under the table.

"Good evening to you Calvin," she said sitting down. "Thank you."

Returning to sit in his chair, he introduced the woman and the elf. "Faith, this is Devis. Devis, this lovely lady is Faith."

"My pleasure," came the elf while bowing his head.

The woman smiled and gave a nod. Faith thought about how sophisticated Devis looked in a peach-colored, long sleeve shirt with ruffles at the cuffs. His face with his almond-shaped eyes and long, silky hair made him lovely looking. Faith was slightly taken aback by how handsome she thought Calvin looked wearing a royal blue shirt with ballooned, black pants and soft, black boots.

A serving girl came to the table at that moment. "Can I get you folks anything?"

"Yes please, an ale for me. A glass of wine for the lady," ordered Calvin looking at Faith with a questioning look.

"Yes," smiling and nodding she acknowledged.

The cavalier glanced at Devis questioning, until the elf stated, "A glass of Honey Meade, please."

"Very well," responded the serving girl. "I'll be right back." Turning, she headed for the bar.

⁕

Rubbing the sleep from his eyes, Moric sat up on the bed. His sense of smell waking him. The gnome's nose twitched as he looked around the room deeply breathing in the sweet scents of food that drifted through the air. A ruckus of noise also rose from downstairs accompanying the delectable aromas.

Rolling off the bed, the gnome's feet were the first to experience the weird, squishy sensation of his beer-soaked clothing on the floor. Moric's face quickly grimaced, "What the?!", but the memory from earlier flooded his mind. After entering his room shortly after the incident with that pissy broad at the bar, the gnome had stripped off all his wet clothing, not paying any attention to where he dropped them. Moric knew now though. Feeling sleepy, the gnome had curled up on top of the blankets and fell sound asleep in seconds.

His grumbling stomach brought Moric's mind back to the present, the thought of food, and the feel of the uncomfortableness under his feet. He kicked the clothes into the corner near the door

38

THE RING OF DARKNESS

and started for a small table with a wash basin and pitcher on it. Next thing he realized was the rooms ceiling when he ended up on his back. A victim of a small, liquid puddle, in this case beer, and hardwood floor.

"Son of an orc's mother!", the small victim yelled from the floor. Now he was fully awake.

Getting up from the prone position he was in with his stomach grumbling almost non-stop now, Moric made his way over to the table. He lifted an arm and took a quick sniff of his pit. "Whew!" The gnome's face contorted at the pungent body odor.

Looking up, the table was a little too tall for the little guy, but Lady Luck was on Moric's side this time. Under it was a step stool that he pulled out and stepped up on. Again, Lady Luck was with him because the pitcher was full of water, so he poured half of it into the basin.

Moric quickly washed his face, hands, armpits, and then splashed his hair. The sight was equal to that of a bird washing itself in a bird bath. Finally the gnome tried to smother his short, dark hair, but it only spiked up like quills on a porcupine.

Stepping down from the stool, he went to retrieve his pack. Dumping its contents onto the bed, the gnome selected a pair of forest green pants along with a mint green shirt. He was instantly interrupted once again by his grumbling stomach, but its declaration this time came louder. "Down boy," ordered the gnome rubbing his pot belly. Hastily, Moric dressed, grabbed his room key, and headed out the door. Speed walking down the hallway, Moric was on a mission!

❧

The serving girl stood holding a small tray as she daintily placed the guests drinks properly in front of each one. "There you are folks," she added with a smile. "Will you be dining tonight?"

"Yes," responded Faith with a smile of her own.

The girl took three menus from her tray and placed them on the table. "I will return after I've afforded you time to decide what you would like," she smiled one more time before turning and heading back to the bar.

Dispersing the menus, the three table guests scanned through them and after several minutes ordered their selections when the serving girl had returned. She gathered the list of dishes and quickly headed for the kitchen to place her order.

Calvin took a drink of his ale and turning his attention back to Faith and Devis, restarted their conversation. "I think mid-morning is a good time to go see this Captain Woodrow, and find out exactly what is expected."

"That sounds alright with me," agreed Faith.

"Also I," Devis accompanied his approval with a nod.

Leaning his right elbow on the table and placing his face in the palm of his hand with his index finger erect against his cheek, the cavalier queried with a thought-fulled expression. "I would like to know what the gnome plans to do."

Faith practically shuddered at the mere mention of the loud mouth.

As if on cue, the elf directed Calvin's direction to the bottom of the staircase with his eyes, "Here's your chance."

Turning, both Calvin and Faith peered in the direction of the stairs. The young woman turning her head back to the elf, "Great."

<hr>

Moric stepped from the stairs and headed to the bar quicker than an arrow can leave a bow. Both the cavalier and the elf witnessed a serving girl jump startled with both a surprised expression on her face and a vocalization to join it as the gnome crossed behind her. No doubt a pinch on the bottom got her attention. Devis only responded with a small chuckle.

Reaching the bar, Moric slowly started to wave his arms trying to get Carl's attention. This was to no avail right now due to the bartender being extremely busy waiting on two young men. Yelling over his shoulder to a swinging door towards the kitchen, he barked their apparent order.

"Hellooo back there! Yoo hoo!", jumped the gnome waving his arms more frantically now. "What's a guy got to do to get something to eat and drink around here?" Carl was still oblivious of the bouncing little man.

⌘

Watching the gnome at the bar jumping and waving his arms, Calvin rose from his chair. "I will invite him over to share in our discussion."

"Must you really?!", disgustedly asked Faith quickly grabbing his forearm.

"I feel it would be important to know what he plans, what he is about, and most importantly where he stands."

Releasing her grip she reluctantly responded, "Well, if you think it will help."

"I do My Lady."

Excusing himself from the table briefly, Calvin made his way through the other tables and patrons to the bar towards the gnome. Hearing the desperate tone in the leaper's voice, he tapped the other on the shoulder during one of his jumps. "Excuse me sir."

Turning to see where the voice and the touch originated, Moric looked up at a tall, bald, black man with a goatee. He wore a royal blue shirt, black balloon pants and soft, black boots.

"What?!", asked the aggravated gnome.

"My name is Calvin Gaston, ..." -introducing himself and then sweeping his arm and pointing to the table that both Faith and Devis sat at he continued- "...and my acquaintances and I would like to welcome you and ask that you join us for supper."

A small twinkle appeared in Moric's eye when he noticed the back of Faith's head, but as the dousing earlier came to the forefront of his mind that twinkle quickly fizzled out.

"It depends," he bargained.

"On what?", inquired Calvin.

"I plan on eating and drinking, and with this being my only set of clean and dry clothes I choose not to wear neither food nor beer!"

"I see,...", acknowledged the cavalier accompanied with a nod, "...and you did not happen to do or say anything that would trigger a reaction like that from earlier?" asked Calvin while raising the eyebrow above his right eye.

Moric stared a few seconds at him and in a normal voice never admitted any antagonizing statement. "Alright."

"Very good sir," approvingly came Calvin as he put a hand on the gnome's shoulder and they started to make their way back to the table through the growing crowd.

Outside the night had fallen on the village shrouding the town in a blanket of darkness. There was no moon in the sky shining only adding to the night's blackness. Above, shining stars pin-holing the dark canvass cast small amounts of light, although it proved not to be a big help to Oakhurst.

On the main road to the town there were five, seven foot tall posts each with a rugged-looking metal hook to hang lanterns from. These street lights usually illuminated the road and the surrounding building fronts, but ever since this mysterious chaos had begun in spring, the lanterns were non-existent. There were no porch lights, in fear they would be used to set the places they lit ablaze, and the town seemed deserted.

Inside the Oak, the place was just about dead except for the table of four, Carl, two serving girls, and the clinging, banging ruckus that came from the kitchen as someone cleaned up. As the time had passed, guests filtered out the doors until all the patrons had left within the last hour. Nightfall became imminent and the tavern closed and locked up till the morning. Two doors now stood barred hiding the double-swinging doors on the outside of the room. These doors had been swung open and latched against the inside walls allowing the access of the beautiful, summer weather during the day. Besides the doors, all the slatted window shutters were closed, but air and the night-time breeze flowed through the slightly open windows thanks in part to those slats.

Carl had been straightening up and putting away mugs, steins, and glasses at the bar. Now he was putting the stools on top of it. One of the serving girls was busy placing chairs on tables while the other stepped through a swinging door leading to and from the kitchen carrying a broom and mop in one hand and a bucket of water in the other. Obviously, the owner along with his help were getting the Oak ready for a new start in the morning.

Earlier in the evening, the four at the table shared in supper along with drinks together and they all seemed to start to bond even sharing a laugh or two. There were still some rough spots between Faith and Moric, but at least the gnome didn't say anything outlandishly rude to her. For supper all three except Moric had a full plate of mouth-watering venison with a side of mashed potatoes, green beans, and a warm biscuit with butter. The gnome had requested three thick links of sausage with a side of great northern beans accompanied also with a warm biscuit and butter.

The future companions partook in mostly small talk, but now that they had finished eating and the table had been cleared of all the dirty dishes, time had passed and they got down to business.

"Are we all in agreement that we go to the tower and see Captain Woodrow during mid-morning?", queried Calvin watching the others respond in the affirmative before he continued. "I believe it would help if all of us knew what talents and skills we possess that will benefit us completing this mission. I will go first," he offered. "I can offer my sword along with my knowledge of military strategy and battlefield tactics toward our cause. My experiences in quickly recognizing and adapting to other's combat tactics will come in beneficial, I believe."

"I also can lend my sword along with my bow," Devis spoke up. "Being an elf I possess a very good tracking ability and have excellent sight as well as hearing. The forest is our kingdom."

Leaning forward, Moric glanced from one face to the next. Being used to his loud, obnoxious tone, the other's were surprised when he spoke quietly just audible enough for them to hear him. "I have skills that allow me to move in complete silence, hide in shadows, and get my way through locked doors."

"You're a thief?!", shockingly questioned Faith. Her eyes wide open with surprise!

"Shhh!", quickly shot Moric before he sat back into his chair while drawing his mug to his lips. "I prefer to think of myself as a finder of lost goods and a damn good locksmith," he offered ending in a smile before taking a swig of his beer.

Taking a moment to compose herself, Faith shared with her future companions. "My skills are in healing with natural herbs and such. I do know which ones will help or speed recovery, along with which ones will poison you or cause death. I have also studied the art, but please sirs do not mistake my words, I have not made the progress to rival any mage who has studied their whole lives."

"Still a plus," interjected Calvin optimistically.

Caught up in their talk, the four never noticed Carl dismiss the two sering girls from any further duties. They had retired to bed, and the cook must have also, because no further noise came from the kitchen. Besides them, Carl was the only other in the tavern and his back was to the new companions as he mopped the floor.

"I believe now is a good time to retire," plainly stated the elf tilting his head towards the barkeep while rising from his chair.

"Agreed. We all meet here in the morning before leaving to see Woodrow," stated the cavalier.

"Good night Carl," Faith said walking passed him mopping as she headed for the stairs. Both Moric and Devis behind her.

"Good night folks. Thank you."

Calvin placed the four chairs onto the table and started for the stairs. Passing Carl he asked, "Do you need anything sir?"

"Nope. Just going to hit this area here, kill the lights, and to bed I go."

"Well goodnight Carl. The food was more than worth its cost."

"Well you'll have to tell Martha tomorrow, she's the cook and she'll love to hear that. Thanks anyway and good night son."

Calvin had just gotten to his room's door when a primitive cry broke the night's silence somewhere outside. He rushed to the stairs to see if Carl was alright.

Meanwhile upstairs, six other doors opened and the room's occupants rushed out into the hallway. One, who was Devis, had just closed his door. The elf ran to the double windows at the end of the hallway closest to him and peered out. Faith ran to the other end to do the same.

Standing at the top of the stairs and receiving an okay from Carl, the cavalier asked both the elf and the woman, "Do you see anything?"

"No, nothing," responded Faith.

"Nothing here either," confirmed the elf.

CHAPTER 4

Calvin awoke to the singing of birds from the trees outside his slightly ajar window. A hum from bugs vibrated the air signaling a hot day lay ahead. The curtains danced a little as a light breeze flowed through the open window. Rubbing and blinking his eyes several times trying to remove the sleep from them, a yawn escaped his lips. Grogginess still held a slight grip on the young cavalier.

Laying in the bed while staring at the ceiling, Calvin's memories of last night came to him. The primitive cry was fresh like he had just heard it only minutes before. "What was that?", the cavalier thought. He pondered on that notion for a minute before starting to climb out of bed. "Only one way to find out," he added.

After being one of the last to retire to his quarters last night, Calvin had sat at his room's window in complete darkness and gazed out. Looking out of it, he waited for another cry or maybe he would spot something, but neither cry nor movement ever came.

Sitting on the edge of his bed another yawn drifted to freedom while he spread his arms wide and arched his back in a stretch. Calvin rose and made his way over to the table with a pitcher of water along with its wash basin on it. The cavalier poured the pitcher's contents into the basin and proceeded to wash up.

Roughly a half hour went by and Calvin emerged from his room. He wore a white shirt, black traveling pants, along with his soft, black boots, and his sheathed sword hung from his left hip.

Removing the key from the door, he checked to make sure it was locked. Satisfied, the cavalier dropped the key in a pouch on the other side of his hip and proceeded down the hallway.

The light from the early dawn shattered the darkness in the room. Being used to waking up at daybreak and enjoying a sound sleep last night, Faith sat on the edge of her bed curling her toes into her feet a couple of times. She rose from her bed arching her back while reaching for the heavens with a cat-like grace to her stretch.

The combination of sunlight shining through her curtained window and her nakedness was breath-taking. The light appeared to radiate off her leaving her appearance celestial.

Faith started for her backpack and a little laugh eluded her, as she thought about what her mom always said while she was growing up. "The early bird is always the first at the dinner table!" Reaching the pack and opening it, Faith pulled out a leather-bound book before returning to the bed.

Jumping back into it, she sat with her back against the headboard and pulled the covers up to her waist. Drawing up her knees and placing the book in her lap, she turned to the first page to select and begin studying her spells for this day.

After roughly a couple of hours, the woman had studied her selections in the spell book and cleaned up. Faith dressed in a white shirt, a pair of brown pants, and her buckskin boots. Her accessories included two pouches near her left hip, a pouch tethered around her neck and dropped into her shirt, along with a dagger and a sheath on her right hip.

She closed the door behind her and locked it before putting the key in the pouch that dangled from her neck and placed it back under her shirt where it hung between her hand-sized breasts. Turning to the stairs, the young woman recognized Calvin coming towards her down the hallway, also on his way downstairs.

"Good morning Faith," he greeted as he reached and waited for her at the staircase.

"Good morning," she replied with a smile walking towards him.

When she reached the staircase also, they both descended together.

As Calvin and Faith took their last steps off the stairs and into the tavern, both spotted Devis already sitting at the table they had sat at last night. The man and woman started towards the elf, who automatically spotted them and watched them near.

"Good morning," greeted Calvin followed by Faith.

"To both of you also," responded Devis. He continued in a joking manner, "Are you guys twins, or did we have a dress code that I missed?"

Looking at one another, both finally realized that the color of their shirts matched.

"Well they say great minds think alike," wittingly came Calvin.

Faith smiled beaming with pride before the three broke into a laugh.

The cavalier pulled out a seat for the young woman and after she sat down he followed taking up one of the two left chairs at the table.

The tavern was extremely quiet this time of morning, and only a party of two sat at the bar. Instead of Carl being behind the bar there was a woman, who was just serving the two patrons each a steaming plate of food when she glanced at the table of three.

"I'll be over in a minute folks," she yelled to them.

Leaving from behind the bar, the woman walked over to the building's doors. She unbarred them and opened them latching them to the walls with small hooks. Then the woman proceeded to step outside and open all the window shutters on the porch. "One of the girls will get the rest when her shift starts," she thought to herself.

Making her way through the swinging doors back into the Oak, she approached the seated companions.

"Good morning lads and lass!", greeted the woman wearing a pleasant smile. "I'm Martha. Martha Hosgrove, Carl's wife."

"Good morning," responded Faith and Devis.

"Good morning Mrs," came Calvin rising up and offering a slight bow, before returning to his seat.

Martha was a pleasantly, plump woman of middle-age like her husband. She had shoulder length brown hair and brown eyes. Her skin was in between a rough and a fair complexion, and the three could tell that like her husband she was not afraid of work. Martha wore a white apron with an oak tree embroidered on it at chest level. There was a couple of wet spots near the pockets, along with a few splotches of stains about it.

"You must be three of the four folks that came in yesterday asking about the sign," she pointed out. "Where's the fourth?"

"Probably still sawing lumber," remarked Faith before adding, "The supper was extremely good last night!"

"Yes it was Mrs. Hosgrove," declared the cavalier.

"Oh, you sweet young folks. Thank you, but just call me Martha," the woman beamed with pride and appeared to have a mother-like personality.

"Can I get you some breakfast?"

"Yes please!", addressed a medium tone from behind her.

Turning her head, the four watched as Moric strolled up to the table and took the last remaining, empty seat.

"What's with you always showing up when we're discussing food?", asked Faith through a half laugh.

"Call it impeccable timing," Moric stated straightening himself up in the chair.

After sharing a brief laugh with the four, thanks to the gnome, Martha took everyone's order and retreated to the kitchen. She only stopped at the bar to check on the older man and woman before watching them leave the tavern through the swinging doors. Removing their dirty dishes, she disappeared into the kitchen.

"We shall eat breakfast and then meet with Captain Woodrow," declared Calvin.

A short time passed and Martha returned from the kitchen carrying a serving tray with food and drink on it. She dealt each of the companions a bowl with steam rising from the oatmeal it held, a small plate with two links of sausage, a glass of apple juice, and to all except Faith, a small cup of hot coffee. The young woman partaking in a cup of tea instead. Just the smell wafting up from the food was enough to make anybody hungry.

"Ooh, the sausage from last night!", excitedly shouted the gnome as he quickly cut a piece and brought it to his mouth.

Martha slipped the empty tray under her arm smiling. "When you folk are all done, I'll be back to clear the table." Then she turned to head back to the bar and kitchen.

"Why must you always be so loud?", disgustedly asked Faith while halfway through breakfast.

"What do you mean?", questioned Moric with a mouthful of food that he had been chewing on like a cow chews grass.

"Forget it!"

The cavalier and the elf both let a small smile crease their faces.

Confused the gnome looked amongst the other three, "What?"

⁂

Martha had been in and out of the kitchen a dozen times finishing preparations for the day. It was extremely slow this morning serving breakfast, only having one or two others come in. The pleasantly, plump woman never noticed the four companions finish their breakfast and leave the tavern.

Grabbing a dish bucket, she made her way to clear off and wipe down the table. As Martha started to remove the dishes and place them in the bucket, she noticed two gold coins laying in the center of the table. Picking them up and holding them in her palm while gazing at the currency, a serious thought crossed her mind, "I wonder if they realized they overpaid, really overpaid!" She slid the coins into a pocket of her shorts she wore under her apron, and continued to clear the rest of the dishes.

⁂

It was slightly before mid-morning as the four left the town behind and followed the road into the forest. They all shared in small conversations but none of them were regarding this trip too see Woodrow, or any recent problems the village was encountering. If anyone of them thought about it, none of the others had a clue.

The morning was beautiful and a slight breeze blew in from the southeast headed northwest. Small birds merrily sang and hopped from branch-to-branch, and occasionally, a squirrel skirted up a tree trunk or through its canopy. Again the air was filled with the humming of bugs warning of the day's oncoming heat. Shadows from the canopy shifted on the forest floor.

Devis had become more sociable and more conversational as he entered the forest. Calvin noticed it right away and credited it to the comfort of the plants and animals around them. Like all of Kanaan, he knew elves were at home amongst the woods.

Eventually, their walk brought them by Zeltax's stable, and the cavalier thought about stopping in but decided to wait until their walk back. He knew he would have to go settle his business and make preparations with the blonde man before the cavalier departed on this adventure.

Throughout their journey, Calvin noticed the tower several times through openings in the canopy and knew they were close now. A short time later the forest cleared into an open section and before the companions stood the local guard outpost. An immense tower reaching towards the heavens rose from behind the stone walls surrounding it.

"Wow!", came Moric astonished at the sight.

From their stand point a thirty-foot, smooth stone wall stood erect in front of them with the top bastioned. Three soldiers stood guard strategically placed on it looking for any signs of trouble. All four walls were dwarfed by the tower.

The smooth, stone wall of the tower matched the look and texture of the four walls protecting it, and the adventurers figured it had to be at least four hundred feet tall. A flag waved in the wind at the tower's apex, and there was no doubting that this structure along with its walls were dwarven crafted. Just the appearance left one breathless.

"Who goes there?", yelled a man from the wall.

"Four who would like to meet with Captain Woodrow regarding the sign posted on the road into town," responded Calvin after all four companions decided he would speak for the party.

"Proceed to the entrance."

The companions followed the road up to an opening in the wall that was guarded by a black, metal portcullis. Behind the large gate was another four men waiting their arrival. All the guards wore leather armor with the insignia of an oak tree upon their chests. Two men carried spears, which at this time were being held by their sides with the points facing up. The other two guards were empty handed but wore sword rings holding long swords at their hips.

"Word has been sent to the captain of your arrival and your request."

"My thanks," came Calvin accompanied with a nod.

After several minutes of quiet waiting a man dressed in leather armor, also wearing a sword at his hip, escorted a man donning chain mail and trailing a red cape behind him. The emblem of the oak tree was also upon his chest.

"You seek information regarding the request for aid?", queried the soldier wearing chain mail.

"Yes sir, that is true."

"Fitzgerald, raise the gate!", ordered the caped man.

"Yes sir!", responded a voice from behind the wall and out of sight.

Slowly the portcullis raised allowing access of the four companions before lowering back to the ground again.

"Please follow me," said the man wearing chain mail as he turned and led the four towards the tower.

Crossing the courtyard, the companions saw barracks for the guards. A total of three Calvin and Devis inventoried. They also took a mental note of two stables with a sheep pen in between both of them, and another pen housing pigs in the far corner. Behind the wall out of sight were two horse teams used to raise and lower the portcullis.

The entrance door to the tower was made of thick oak with four metal bands across it. Its strength and durability showed. Again, Calvin and Devis took note of the arrow slits throughout the tower's walls and its lack of windows.

The solider in leather armor, whom had escorted the caped man out of the tower, pulled open the door and raised his fist to his chest. Obviously saluting the man wearing the chain mail armor as he and the four companions entered.

Upon entering the tower and having the door closed behind them, it took a brief moment for all their eyes to adjust from the bright sunlight outside to the torch lit dimness of their new surroundings. As soon as their momentary blindness disappeared and the companion's sight fully returned, a set of circular, stone stairs rose on the right side around the tower's inner perimeter. Its first step placed right after the entrance.

"Follow me," directed the caped man walking forward.

They passed another small, gated door on their left. A wall of total darkness stood behind it. The walls on their route wore torch brackets and a dozen torches sizzled in them. The companions, escorted by the armored soldier passed several wooden doors on their left and right heading straight for a door at the end of the hall.

Reaching the door and opening it, the soldier stepped to the side ushering the companions to enter the room. "Please, after you," humbly requested the captain. He was the last to enter, closing the door behind him.

The room was big enough for the five people and its furniture, and only a bit more space remained. Only the wall the door was in was flat leaving the rest of the room's wall curved. Like the rest of the tower there were no windows in the wall and the only light source came from two standing candelabras.

Against the semi-circular wall stood five file cabinets arranged to mimic the curvature along with two bookcases. In front of the cabinets, more towards the room's center, was a medium-sized table utilized as a desk with papers and ledgers strewn all over it. A quill and two ink bottles also joined the mess. Behind the desk, between it and the files, sat a single chair with two chairs arranged in front of the makeshift desk. To the left of the table was a small, open-ended, wooden crate with several rolled up maps residing in it. Against the only flat wall stood a bed, and it was obvious to all that this room was both an office and the captain's sleeping quarters.

"Welcome to Oakhurst Tower," the caped man offered while heading to stand in front of the lone chair behind the desk. "I am Captain Woodrow. Please, at least two of you can take a seat," he added sitting down.

Moric quickly jumped into a seat like a child playing a game of musical chairs while Faith took up the other one.

Captain Woodrow was a medium-built man of slightly less than middleage and approximately stood six feet tall. He wore his light brown hair roughly shoulder blade length and was clean shaven with a square like jaw displaying a scar that ran from the outer corner of his left eye to just outside his mouth. The captain gave off a commanding-like aura.

"I have been informed that you are all here regarding the notice for aid. Correct?", he queried looking amongst the visitors.

"That is true," responded the speaker for the four companions.

"If you choose to accept, the pay is a gold coin per day and two when you return to report substantial news. All will be paid in full upon your delivered report." The captain continued after a brief pause, "The village will pay for any healing if needed but not resurrections."

"Well in that case, we better not die," interrupted the gnome.

The others just gazed at him for what seemed like hours to Moric. "What?"

After a brief pause Captain Woodrow continued "You can keep any spoils and treasure you find."

"What can you tell us about the information you have on what has been going on?", queried Calvin.

"I can't tell you anything because we don't know anything. All we know are folk are disappearing or being killed. I have no idea by whom or what, and I'm struck less of mind as to why. What I can tell you is, …" -continued the captain- "… I have sent out a patrol a ten day ago and haven't received any word from them as of yet."

"Do you believe they are dead?", questioned the cavalier.

"I think so, but I pray not."

"How many men?"

"Twelve in all."

"I wish we had more time, hell I wish we had more info, but night comes too fast bringing with it darkness on this land," flatly stated Captain Woodrow shaking his head several times. "Unfortunately that's all I can offer you folks."

Asking his final question, the captain looked from one adventurer to another, "What say you?"

Calvin looked to see the other three nod with affirmation. "We accept."

CHAPTER 5

The four sat at a table eating a late lunch while making a list of equipment they might need for their adventure. It had been slightly later than mid-day when the companions left the tower and started their hike back to the tavern.

They had made a quick stop at the stables to take care of matters with Zeltax. It appeared that Calvin was not the only one with a horse there, and the elf also had business to conduct. It seemed both Faith and Moric took two separate caravans from two different places, but then again that was how news and rumors traveled the realms making it into bars and taverns throughout Kanaan.

Before leaving the tower, Captain Woodrow gave them a hand-written voucher to the general store in town for equipment and some supplies. He also added that he would like them to take the rest of the day to straighten out any matters, but wanted them to return in the morning and be ready to go. They would also at the least have three others joining in the quest.

"Read back the list so far please," came the cavalier dunking some bread into a puddle of gravy on his plate.

"Okay. There's torches, flint and steel, rope, waterskins...", listed Faith, but she stopped when the gnome interrupted her while thinking out loud.

"Twelve," he quietly stated before continuing. "Twelve. I mean if twelve trained soldiers were no match for this, this whatever it is, then how can only us four stand against it?"

The table of four was both quiet and still for a moment until Calvin leaned toward the gnome and placed a hand on his shoulder.

"Do not trouble yourself my little friend but first you must conquer doubt and fear because when you do then you have already won half the battle," he assured. Removing his hand with a small pat to Moric's shoulder before he did, the cavalier turned back to Faith for the rest of the list.

❧

Later that afternoon, the companions had gone to pick up the supplies they had felt they would need for the adventure. They took their time making sure to purchase everything on the list that the four had drafted along with anything that wasn't on it that they believed might come in handy.

Upon returning to the Oak, the four had disappeared into Calvin's room to divide up the supplies equally among all before returning to their own rooms to pack for the morning. The companions also made plans to meet for supper later that evening.

Supper was uneventful and very little conversation took place amongst the four. Maybe it was due to mentally getting prepared for the journey that lay in front of them or just the fact that they all wanted to enjoy the last home-cooked meal before going into the wilds. Whatever the reason was, even Moric's loud cow-like chewing was non-existent.

At the end of their meal, a serving girl stopped at the four's table to remove all the dirty dishes. After she cleaned the table, the girl pulled a damp cloth from a pocket on her apron and wiped it clean. "Can I get you all another round of drinks?"

"One more please," responded the cavalier with the rest in agreement.

The serving girl took everyone's order before disappearing with the dirty dish pan back to the kitchen and the bar. Within ten minutes, she returned and set all the drinks in front of their respectable consumers. "Excuse me folks," she added before leaving to tend to another table. "Mr. and Mrs. Hosgrove would like to have a word with you all before you retire for the night."

"Excuse me miss!", came a man calling a second time from another table.

"Thank you," quickly spoke Faith before the serving girl smiled again and turned towards the voice beckoning for her.

"Coming."

There was a lull from the hecticness during supper and Carl along with Martha made their way over to the companion's table.

"Hi kids. How's it going?", cheerfully asked Martha.

Calvin stood momentarily, "Good evening Mrs. Hosgrove; Carl," nodded the cavalier.

"Food was very delicious again," came the melodious voice of the elf.

"I concur," agreed Faith.

"Yeh, and the sausages are great!", loudly declared Moric.

Martha giggled a little. "Thank you, I'm glad you liked them."

"We actually wanted to come over and thank you guys for your help," now spoke Carl. "Tonight's meal and your drinks are on the house along with the morning's breakfast," he continued.

An appreciative response found its way around the table.

"We would also like to store, at no fee to any of you, your unneeded belongings until your return," the barkeeper added.

Again, an appreciative response circled the young adventurer's table and Calvin stood and extended his hand to Carl. "Speaking for everyone, thank you Carl and thank you Mrs. Hosgrove also for all your hospitality."

"Don't forget the sausages!", Moric quickly inserted.

The owners of the Oak, accompanied by the other three companions, broke into a laugh. A laugh that lasted at least a couple of minutes breaking the seriousness of this night.

∾☙

The four companions appeared a small formidable force breaking the tree line while continuing to follow the dirt road towards the guard tower. The cavalier wore his shiny breastplate with a pair of plate mail pants. He carried his helmet in his right hand and a half-body shield in his left. The insignia on the shield was of a fiery phoenix. On Calvin's left hip he wore a bastard sword sheathed and a sheathed dagger on his right.

Walking beside him on his right side was Faith with Devis on her right. Faith wore a green blouse with her buckskin vest over it. She also wore her buckskin pants along with her knee-high moccasins. The young woman wore a dagger on her right hip with two pouches in front of it towards her stomach. On her left a whip was rolled with two pouches in front of that mirror-imaging the other side. A pouch hung under her blouse from around her neck.

The elf was dressed in brown, leather armor with a pair of soft, brown boots. His brown, hooded cloak was clasped under his neck and Devis wore the hood over his head. It hid the elf's face, although still some of his long hair flowed out. Being an elf, Devis had a slightly better tolerance than any other race on Kanaan to heat and cold. A long sword hung on his left hip and a sheathed dagger was strapped to the outside of his leg just under his right knee. Devis also carried his long bow in his left hand and a quiver of twenty arrows shared his back. Slung over his shoulder was his full pack.

Walking on Calvin's left, Moric wore black, leather armor with soft, black boots. Both outer forearms were adorned with black sheaths each housing a dagger. A short sword dangled from his left hip and the gnome wore a hard, square, small leather case on his right.

As a matter of fact, all the companions wore full backpacks containing the supplies they had purchased on the prior day.

"Who goes there?", a posted sentry on the wall asked.

"Calvin Gaston and friends to meet with the captain. May we pass?" he asked as the four got closer to the wall.

"Fitzgerald, raise the gate!", yelled the wall guard.

Passing through the opening for the third time in two days the companions were met by a leather-armored guard. "The captain has been waiting on you adventurers. Follow me."

They followed the guard passed the stationed sentries, who were now aiding in lowering the gate, heading towards the tower's door. Again their eyes had to adjust to the change from sunlight to torchlight when they entered. The guard led the four to one of the wooden doors before the one at the end of the hallway where they had entered on the day before. All that could be heard were the clinking of equipment, the footfalls, and lit torches hissing in their wall brackets.

The soldier opened the door inward and ushered the adventurer's inside, "Captain Woodrow will join you shortly," he added before closing the portal.

The chamber was illuminated by six evenly spaced torches housed in sconces on the walls. A square, wooden table surrounded with five wooden chairs was the centerpiece of the room and its only furniture. The room was really plain looking and Calvin knew instantly this chamber was an interrogation room. One occupant was the only addition in the chambers.

❧

Watching the companions enter the room, the very large man sat across from the door. He had a tanned complexion with a head full of red, curly hair that stopped just above his shoulders. He wore a bushy, red mustache, and even the curly hair on his large, muscular chest was red. Freckles dot his face and his eyes were emerald green. The man wore no armor, but instead had on a green vest that almost matched his eyes. The lack of sleeves revealed his thick, tree trunk-like arms. Rising to his feet, the mammoth wore a pair of buckskin pants with a large, hunting knife on his left hip. He stood at least a good hand and a half taller than Calvin, who was the tallest companion at just over six feet. The man's body was dense and extremely wide with muscles. It appeared that his muscles had muscles of their own. In the corner to the man's left stood a wooden staff.

"I'm Jericho," he pleasantly offered in a deep voice that sounded like the tolling of a bell.

Walking towards the mammoth and clasping forearms with the man, the cavalier was the first to introduce himself, "Well met. I am Calvin Gaston." When they broke the newcomer relieved himself of his pack placing it in the corner with Faith and Moric's.

Devis stated his name and nodded his greeting from where he stood near the closed door across the room.

Loudly came Moric hopping into a chair seated near Jericho, "You sure are a big one, as tall as a tree, and built like an ox!"

"I knew he couldn't keep quiet long!", ridiculed Faith. "Anyways, that's Moric and I'm Faith," continued the young woman as the enormous man took her extended hand and gently shook it.

"You young folk must be here to help," assumed Jericho while looking from one companion to the other.

Moric nodded with approval.

"Where are you from?", inquisitively queried Faith.

"I own a farm in the countryside southwest of here."

Before anyone else could continue, Captain Woodrow opened the door and entered the room followed by two young men wearing leather armor unlike the kind worn by the soldiers. Torches flickered from a breeze caused by a flow of air from the door opening.

"This is the McKinley brothers," introduced the captain after everyone was in the room and the door shut. "These two men will be the last joining you on this quest."

The two finding it hard not to stare in Calvin's direction.

The McKinley brothers were obviously twins with the only difference between the two being an obvious telltale. The one introduced as Harold wore his hair cut short while Edward had long, wavy hair. Both had the same build, and both had brown hair and eyes. Even the leather armor they wore matched, and if it wasn't for the difference in hair length then no one would be able to tell them apart.

Harold carried a javelin and wore a dagger on his left hip, along with an imposing, studded mace that hung from his other side.

Edward wore a dagger on his right hip with a crossbow bolt quiver dressing his left. A long sword was strapped to his back while he carried an unloaded crossbow.

"Thank you all for coming," graciously came the captain. "I have spoken with each one of you about what is required of you. I also explained about being paid in full upon your return with credible information. Are there any further questions that we need to address?"

Some nodded their affirmative and a few gave out a yes, but only Harold spoke up.

"Do we have a specific leader, and who shall that be?"

Surveying the assembly before him, Captain Woodrow offered his advice. "I've personally known Jericho for some time now and I know he is very familiar with the forest and the village so I believe he can help. Although I fully believe to avoid any trouble during this chaotic time you should appoint the knight as your leader," he pointed a finger at Calvin.

A gasp filled the room as everyone looked in the cavalier's direction. Devis wore a slight smile already knowing more about the knight than was revealed. It was apparent to the elf that besides him and the captain, the others knew nothing of their newly appointed leader. All, except Devis and the commanding soldier, were struck with surprise and awe at the revelation.

CHAPTER 6

It was mid-afternoon when the seven adventurers left the guard post. The sun had already reached its highest point in the sky and was now descending from the heavens. Evening was close with nightfall to arrive shortly after that and that was usually when hell broke loose in the Oakhurst region. Calvin knew the party wouldn't want to be caught exposed on the dirt road.

The seven had stayed within the tower for a little more time after Captain Woodrow revealed the shocking surprise. It appeared obvious that none of the others, besides the captain and the elf, knew or had any clue that Calvin was a knight. In fact, the only black knight in all of Kanaan. Not everyone listened to all the rumors throughout the realms or apparently believed them. Moric and Faith seemed more taken aback with shock than any of the others present, while Jericho expressed his admiration at the opportunity to meet a real knight. As for the McKinley brothers, they also were shocked at the revelation, and even a flicker of doubt sparked in Harold.

"How is that possible? All blacks throughout the realms are either servants or farmers, soldiers for hire or maybe even entrepreneurs, but none ever serve so high a rank in any royal army. How do we even know he is what he says he is?"

"He never said any words human, but the captain is correct. Calvin is a knight, a knight of the realm Tierra Natal," inserted the elf.

Quietness filled the room and only the hissing torches broke the calmness. Devis now commanded everyone's attention as all the occupant's eyes were on his brown, almond-shaped ones. His melodious voice broke the silence while looking from Calvin and then back to the others. "As you all are aware, we elves live a life longer than any other race on Kanaan. I have heard the full tale of the Black Knight told throughout my homeland, and although a recent story in itself, it is a saga about battling the odds and overcoming them. It is a tale of true friendship and honor."

Then as the elf told the account of Calvin's ascendence to knighthood the others listened attentively and seemed to be brought back to another time.

❧

"Calvin was born twenty-six winters ago as a servant's son to the kingdom of Tierra Natal. His mother, a kitchen maid to the king and queen of the realm, was a single mother. Calvin's father is not known. Growing up he spent all of his waking time with the king's son, who was born only months after him, playing and adventuring around the castle like children do. It is rumored, Calvin saved Trent's life on more than one occasion from an early demise and Trent would always defend his friend when status was questioned at court.

"Both boys did everything together until they reached their teen years when status and birth rank could no longer be ignored. Trent was the prince of Tierra Natal, and because of his birthright, he was expected to military service learning how to lead the realm's army. During the upcoming years, Trent would learn military tactics, field command, and strategies just to name a few. These years to follow would mold the prince into a leader and eventually the king of the land. As for Calvin, he was a servant and now was his time to learn how to serve like his mother. The childhood friends, who grew as close as brothers, would now be separated never to enjoy each other's friendship again.

"After a ten day of long nights and debates between the king and prince, Trent had won Calvin a chance to serve as his squire. The serving aspect appeased the king, and the childhood friends reignited their brotherhood for adventuring like they had growing up. Throughout the next couple of years Trent learned during the day and taught Calvin at night the use of weapons, proper etiquette, horsemanship, combat tactics, and even command. Although status and birthright meant everything in this world, it had no meaning between friends. When Trent's schooling ended, the prince along with his squire, and a small unit of five would patrol the countryside.

"One day on patrol the group was ambushed by ten mercenaries swiftly killing four soldiers from the patrol. The fifth fell to serious wounds but would not succumb to death. There was still a total of six mercenaries left and only Trent and Calvin remained standing. Both held their own against the six quickly dispatching two of them. Mounted, the prince found himself ready to face off against one of the ambushers on foot. In the blink of an eye, the man thrust his javelin into the prince's mount striking the artery in its neck. The horse reared and collapsed onto the falling heir's bottom half of his body pinning him underneath the dead mount. The animal's weight crushing Trent's hip and legs. The ambusher with the javelin moved in for the kill, but Calvin, on foot, intercepted the attacker and ran him through.

"Run brother! Save yourself!", pleaded the prince, but the squire outnumbered three-to-one would not leave his friend. *"Never!"*

"Taking a guarded posture over the pinned prince and assessing the three remaining mercenaries, Calvin was ready for the next attack. Even though the months of their late night training sessions were running through his mind, it was the squire's reaction that came into play as the first attacker came swinging his sword.

"Calvin quickly parried and stepped with the speed and grace of a tiger elbowing the attacker in the face. He followed that up with a slice from his sword across the merc's neck as the man reeled from the elbow strike. Blood sprayed into the air as the ambusher died while falling to the ground.

"Before the squire could absorb the sight of his own deadly work a second attacker was on him swinging a club. The reaction to block was slower this time, and the blow caught Calvin on his left shoulder knocking him off balance and stumbling to a knee. Shaking its effects off, Calvin was surely happy he wore plate mail armor although he knew his upper arm and shoulder would sport a good-sized bruise. The defender quickly located the club wielder.

The man came following another swing, and Calvin quickly started to stand to meet his attacker head on. The only difference was this time, he was ready.

"Behind you!", he heard Trent shout, and only for a split second took his eyes from the battle that approached to see the third mercenary throwing a pair of daggers at him. Calvin hastily dove to his right in a roll.

"When he came out of the roll, the squire swiftly found his footing along with his two attackers. The ambusher, who had thrown the knives stood with his eyes wide in shock witnessing the two daggers sticking out of the club wielder's chest. The unfortunate mercenary slowly dropping to his knees and then flat on the ground dead followed by his club.

"Calvin charged his last attacker ready for a melee, but all the fight was gone now and wouldn't come. Knowing he was on death's door, the last of the ambushers dropped to his knees begging for his life.

"Please! Please, don't kill me!", the lone man pleaded.

"I shall not kill you this day, although I will bring you to justice and you will be judged by the king," Calvin responded sternly while holding his sword on the prisoner.

"The squire bound the man's hands and feet so he could go check on the prince and the other fallen soldiers of the patrol. Trent was still pinned under his animal and had been rendered unconscious from the pain. Only one other soldier remained alive. The good news was that he could at least ride with the wounds he had sustained from the encounter.

"Next Calvin quickly assembled a litter out of thick branches and lashed them together. He used a couple of cloaks from the dead ambushers to form the couch and connected those to the branches. Using another thick limb, Calvin pried the fallen mount up enough to slide his fallen friend out from under.

"Hold on my brother," he added slightly above a whisper as he slid Trent free and onto the makeshift litter, before attaching it behind his mount.

"Within the hour of the successful defense, the squire bound the prisoner's lead to the saddle horn of the horse the soldier rode and then led both animals back to the castle. In tow, the captured mercenary along with his seriously injured prince lying on the litter.

"Calvin had taken inventory of the soldier and his injuries. The soldier was in and out of consciousness with a large gash on his head, while Calvin's upper arm and shoulder throbbed with pain when he tried to lift it over his head.

"Soon the beat up three and their prisoner were within sight of the castle. A small unit of soldiers rode out to meet them and escorted the survivor's back to the safety of the walls. Riding across the drawbridge, the king had rushed out as soon as word had gotten to him.

"*Oh no! My son!*", -he concerned- "*What happened?*", demanded the king.

"*We were ambushed my lord,*" stated Calvin. "*The prince's horse took a fatal blow and landed on him pinning him underneath. His legs and hip are in need of care. The soldier was hit on his head pretty good, and ...*"-Calvin pointing at the prisoner- "*...he is the only one of the attackers alive.*"

"*Take the prince to the clerics and the prisoner to the dungeon. I will deal with him later. Calvin, report to the healers also and we shall speak once they are done.*"

"*Yes my lord,*" replied the squire bowing his head.

"Three days after the prince came to, the king heard all the events that took place in the attack. He listened how the squire was the only man standing, and even though he was told to flee by his prince, Calvin had stayed to defend Trent after he was pinned by his fallen horse. Not only did the heir of the throne tell about the battle before he succumbed and blacked out from the pain, but the interrogated prisoner shared the same story of the events before being hung the next day.

"The king overwhelmed with gratification for protecting and rescuing his son did something at the crowded square, where everyone witnessed the hanging, that no one saw coming. Calling the squire to kneel in front of him, the king asked a soldier for his sword.

Laying the blade on the rescuer's shoulder he loudly decree, *"From this day forward let it be known throughout the lands of Kanaan that squire Calvin Gaston will not be known by that title any longer. He will be known and recognized as Sir Calvin Gaston, Knight of Tierra Natal and savior of its prince!"*

"Both childhood friends met each other's astonished gazes. A chant rose from the crowd, *"Sir Calvin! Sir Calvin!"*, and a kitchen maid, who was once a squire's single mother, had tears filling her eyes."

⤬

When Devis had finished recounting the tale as he heard it the rest of the adventurers still seemed to be in awe. The elf looked at Calvin, "I accept your appointment as leader and will follow you anywhere."

One by one the rest of those in the room agreed that the knight would be their leader.

The party was now on the road heading away from the tower. The small group walked in no particular order and no definite formation. They looked like an amoeboid from overhead.

The day went on the farther they walked until they arrived at the end of the road. Only forest stood in front of them now. "Let us take a break and eat a supper here, then I suggest we get out of the open and into the trees," offered Calvin.

The companions found places to sit on fallen trees or stumps while the remaining ones just sat on the road. Their dinner consisted of beef jerky and two of Martha's homemade biscuits. The party washed the food down with a couple of swigs of water.

After roughly a thirty minute break everyone collected their packs along with any other belongings and headed into the forest as dusk fell on Oakhurst.

Calvin had only two thoughts in the forefront of his mind as he entered the woods cautiously scanning the trees and the underbrush. The first was; "They had to find somewhere to set up camp." The second was; "Let us see what trouble nightfall brings with it this night."

CHAPTER 7

The canopy from the tree tops cast a shadowy shroud throughout the forest. It was obviously darker now in the woods then when the party had been eating their supper on the road. Light from the setting sun pin-holed the tree cover allowing only a minimal amount of illumination to dot the heavily wooded floor. Most of the forest's wildlife prepared to hunker down for the oncoming night and the bugs took an interlude from their humming until the next morning.

"We will set up camp here, …" -declared the party's leader- "… and set up a couple of lookouts here and here," he added pointing from one spot on a side to another place across the invisible perimeter. "I believe it will be better for the guard rotation to consist of three shifts. Jericho and I will take first watch. Devis and Moric the second, with Harold and Edward the last."

"What about me?", inquired Faith.

"You are the group's magic-user; therefore, I want you to be fresh when you study in the morning. We do not know what we are up against yet, and I believe we will definitely be needing your aid!"

The young woman nodded her affirmation.

"We'll start collecting some wood for a fire," offered Edward with Harold ready to go with his brother.

"That will not be necessary. Tonight, and probably most nights from here on out will be cold camps," stated Calvin.

"What's a cold camp?", asked Edward puzzled.

"No fire or light," Devis interjected.

"Why?"

"Because we do not wish to be seen, nor invite any unwanted visitors," answered the knight. "Now everybody on watch tonight, look alive."

Night fell quick on the land and the darkness caused any vision for the two on first watch to be very limited. At some points it seemed their eyes would pop out of their heads due to the strain. The hoots of an owl filled the air and nothing appeared out of the ordinary.

Back at the cold camp everyone slept; everyone except Faith and Devis.

"I can't believe Calvin never mentioned being a knight!", astonishingly spoke Faith into the darkness.

"Why would he?", questioned Devis before continuing. "Knights are an honorable type of people. They do not look down upon nor disrespect others. A knight gives respect to all and lives to defeat evil. His life is one of law, and with it a knight will defend those who cannot defend themselves. The code of ethics for a knight is one almost all folk in the lands cannot follow, never mind live by, but for a knight it is his way of life. A person like Calvin remembers where he comes from and that has instilled in him humility. He is a humble man no matter his title."

"I just can't get over that he had nothing to gain, and only his life to lose, yet he stayed to defend a prince even after he was told to flee."

"Honor and loyalty not only to the crown, but to his brother-like friend," came the elf looking towards the woman while raising an unseen eyebrow. It was too dark for Faith to notice any of his facial expressions.

"I guess you're right," conceded the woman.

Finding a slightly comfortable place amongst the forest floor to lay down and catch some sleep she added, "Good night Devis."

"And also you."

The elf sat on a log and within minutes he was the only one awake in the camp. He listened to the rhythm of the slumberer's breathing and concentrated. The hoots of the night time predator played in the background.

It was close to the end of the watch for the elf and the gnome when a cross between a primal cry and a bestial scream carried through the blackness of night. The companions were up, weapons at the ready, and all their heads on swivels looking around into the darkness.

"Stand fast guys, I'm coming into camp," cautiously stated Devis as his outline seemed to materialize from out of the dark.

"What do you see?", questioned Calvin. The others standing and listening eagerly for the update.

"I can't say for certain the origin of the cry, but I have seen bursts of lights in the distance ignite the night sky."

"Where?"

"To the southwest at least a day or two's journey from here," responded the elf to the leader's question.

Taking a moment, the party's leader formulated the group's plan." We will stay put here the rest of the night and on the morrow we will head in that direction. Harold, Edward, it's just about time for your shift. Go relieve the gnome, but any sign of something amiss sound the alarm."

The McKinleys went off in opposite directions to begin their watch.

"Get some sleep Devis," came Calvin patting the elf's back.

Shortly after, Moric walked into camp.

⟳

The rest of the night was quiet after the one cry, but none of the companions at the camp fell into a complete slumber. They all found themselves going in and out of consciousness, except the McKinley brothers on watch and the elf. Devis had made himself comfortable on one of the trees standing within the cold camp's perimeter and sat on a limb with his back against the trunk in a meditative state. Elves never slept, but instead they fell into a dream-like state they called the "Reverie". Within the Reverie, Devis was lost amongst his thoughts allowing him to focus, prioritize, and put those thoughts into perspective. The elf's mind was open and like a sponge just soaked up knowledge. Through this whole state, the dreamer never had to shut his or her eyes, and even though never seeming to appear in the minute, an elf never missed what was happening around them.

As the sun started to rise trying to pry the grip away from the night, new rays of light brightened the forest a little bit at a time. Faith started to rouse from her cat nap and slowly the woman sat up and took a look around. The others still seemed to snooze. Raising her arms up to the tree tops, she stretched and yawned in unison before taking another quick look here and there spotting exactly what she was seeking. Faith reached out and grabbed her backpack. Rummaging for a brief moment she pulled a leather-covered book from it. The early bird put the pack by her side while leaning her back against a log. Drawing her knees up, she placed the book in her lap and opened it. Before any of the others started to stir, Faith was studying her spell selections for the upcoming day.

Breakfast went by quick shortly after everyone roused, and with the start to the new day, the morning's light had finally broke the hold nightfall had held on the land. Already birds sang their welcome and forest life began its daily business.

During the companions' breakfast, Calvin felt secure that no attack would come, so he had the two brothers reeled back into camp to share chow with the party. The group ate the rest of the biscuits Martha had made with a slice of cheese and an apple, along with only taking a couple of swigs of water from their skins to wash it down. None of them had any idea how long they would be in the woods for searching for clues, but they all knew it was to their benefits to ration the only food they had. Although in a worst case scenario all the companions, some better than others, could hunt and live off the land if need be.

Calvin took the opportunity of everyone being together and taught them how to communicate in silence using only hand signals. Demonstrating and instructing them of their meanings before quizzing the party's comprehension on at least a dozen gestures he had displayed.

"What does this mean Moric?", asked the teacher holding up a fist with his elbow bend at a right angle.

"Stop!", excitedly answered the gnome confident in his knowledge of that one.

"Correct."

"What about this Edward?", quizzed Calvin using a repetitive salute-like motion chest high starting at his heart and extending his arm out in front of him.

"That's the sign to seize fire. Right?"

"Yes. Very well," came the knight pleased.

After the brief and informative lesson, the leader lined the adventurers up in a single file line. The elf with his keen eyesight and hearing accompanied with his tracking abilities took the lead. Following ten feet behind him came the knight followed by Moric. In the exact middle of the line was the magic user. Walking behind her was Jericho with Edward and his loaded crossbow trailing him. Lastly, came Harold watching the rear.

"This is how we are going to traverse through the woods for now," declared the leader. "It will cut down on any evidence of our passing."

Looking to Edward while pointing at the loaded crossbow, Jericho said with a little concern in his voice, "Be careful with that thing. I don't want to end up like a spitted pig."

"I will," Edward responded hoping to ease the big man's worry. "It does have a safety mechanism."

The companions, with Devis in the lead ten paces in front, moved out for the day's trek.

⁊❧

The day was again summery, but the shade cast from the tree cover made the temperature a little cooler on the forest's floor. Everyone was thankful for the slight reprieve, but then again Devis would have not been affected if the heat had remained. The elven ability to tolerate a slight inflection caused by the temperature would have left no influence on his comfort. The low prolonged sound of humming filled the air.

Throughout the day, the party encountered a numerous amount of wildlife activity including the chattering from some squirrels raising an alarm caused by the line's intrusion. The companions also passed several farmhouses dotting the landscape throughout the woods. Jericho seemed to know all of the farms and their residents but the brothers only knew a couple of them. No doubt due to the age differential between the big man and the McKinleys. On a few occasions the group stopped to inquire about any information concerning the events of late when the landowners took notice of them, especially their giant companion.

During a stop at a farm owned by a man named Smithers, the group stayed a bit and enjoyed an early supper known in these parts of Kanaan as Country Breakfast. Smithers' wife made scrambled eggs with onions, peppers, and tomatoes fresh from their gardens, along with maple-flavored oatmeal, and a chicken-flavored gravy poured over potatoes and a fresh biscuit. To drink, everyone enjoyed a cup of milk.

Shortly after the meal, Calvin decided the evening was approaching and the need to find a place to camp before it got dark was imminent. The adventurers thanked the Smithers for their gracious hospitality before rejoining their hike. The activity by the wildlife had slowed just a bit, and the temperature dropped a couple more degrees as most of the day was gone now.

The burning sun started to set and give way to the night again. It painted the sky auburn in the dimming light and was still mostly blocked out by the canopy of leaves. Still not totally dark in the woods yet, the group could only barely see. Blackness had started to creep slowly under the trees.

Little words were shared amongst the seven and a thick tension, that one could cut with a dagger, filled the atmosphere. They knew they needed to find a decent place to set up camp for the night. One, they might need to make a stand at because they were a day closer to the light bursts and the possible origin of the cry they had heard last night in its wee hours.

The adventurers moved through the woods and the underbrush as quietly as possible. Even the gnome, whom was usually loud, moved in complete silence. Moric actually seemed quieter now than the others in line. On several occasions Calvin lost sight of Devis, only to see him reappear a few feet further away. Devis was an elf, and blending into the forest along with moving silently through the underbrush was an elf's specialty.

Darkness fell even thicker now causing Calvin to stop when once again he lost sight of the elf walking the lead. The leader held up a closed fist. The signal used by the companions to stop. A second hand gesture had the group sinking into the underbrush. Calvin gazed at the last place he had seen the elf before glancing from left to right of that spot. Moving his hand to grasp the hilt of his sword, the knight slid up the blade an inch or two making sure it wasn't stuck in its scabbard.

Moric simultaneously unsheathed the daggers on each of his forearms while surveying his surroundings. "What's wrong?", he whispered to the knight.

"I know not yet," Calvin responded over his shoulder.

Everyone in line was on high alert.

Reappearing out in front of Calvin, Devis crouched down as he waved the party to him.

Quietly, Calvin moved the line forward to the elf's position.

"What is it?", questioned the cavalier, as the companions slowly and cautiously reached Devis' crouched position.

Pointing passed the trees and brush the elf whispered, "A clearing ahead, but something doesn't feel right. It's too quiet."

That's when the silence which had eluded Calvin during his search for the elf became apparent. The surrounding forest had fallen deathly quiet giving him the impression that he had gone deaf. The knight also noticing the tall grass across the clearing move like it had shivered in the wind, but no breeze blew. Grasping the hilt of his sword, Calvin heard the solid whack behind him. The woods were no longer quiet and the sounds of weapons being drawn and shouts quickly filled the silent void.

Looking to his left, Jericho saw the brush move seconds before the goblin leaped at Faith. Standing straight up, pivoting his hip, and sliding both hands closer to each other, the big man swung his staff over the crouching woman's head. The blow landed a direct hit across the leaping attacker's face causing a dark, greenish, black blood to spray out from the goblin's crushed head covering the bushes and the tree trunks. It was dead before landing on the forest's floor.

Now a dozen goblins with canines bare and saliva running from their mouths dripping to the ground popped up from the surrounding brush or came out from behind trees. Even the clearing became alive as eight goblins rushed into it howling.

Devis quickly knocked an arrow and let it fly striking a rushing goblin coming across the clearing in its throat. Its bestial scream going mute as it instantly dropped.

"Into the clearing!", ordered the group's leader. "We shall make a stand there!" He knew there was no room currently for any of the adventurers to swing their weapons, but the opening offered the space they would need to attack and defend themselves against these foul beasts. Pointing towards the clearing he yelled, "Devis!"

"I'm on it!", cried the elf as once again he let loose another arrow striking the upper thigh of another charging goblin. Its run abruptly halted as the shot brought the beast to the ground.

Calvin dashed passed Devis into the field towards the oncoming rush. Shield in his left hand while waving his bastard sword in his right, the knight roared a battle cry all his own. Moric followed Calvin into the field, both daggers at the ready.

Grabbing a hold of Faith's vest as she began to stand up, Jericho helped her out of her crouch as they moved forward. Both erupting out of the bush and into the clearing before the dozen goblins could descend upon them.

Four of the twelve beasts were closing fast on the brothers. Firing his crossbow at point blank, Edward struck a goblin between the eyes dropping the adversary. Hastily he drew the long sword sheathed on his back while letting the unloaded crossbow hang from a tether on his hip.

"Watch out Eddie!", warned Harold thrusting his javelin over Edward's right shoulder blocking a goblin's downward sword strike with the weapon's shaft.

The elf attaining an extensive knowledge of one of his mortal enemies knew that six goblins to four favored his companions in the clearing. Devis spun to see how the brothers faired. Having an arrow already knocked on his bow, he took aim and fired striking one of the three remaining beasts attacking both Harold and Edward from their left flank. The arrow struck its ear.

Dropping its sword, the goblin howling in pain grabbed its split ear seconds before Harold ran it through. The brothers and the elf making a fighting withdrawal backing into the field. The remaining goblins were in pursuit of their prey.

❧

Calvin blocked a studded mace blow with his shield and then came down on the goblin's shoulder with his own sword strike. The beast howled in pain and lost its mace as the knight's blade cut through its shoulder cleaving into its chest cavity. Dark greenish, black blood sprayed the air. With no other beasts confronting him, the leader quickly surveyed the battle evaluating the situation.

Devis along with Harold and Edward were protecting the rear as the remaining goblins burst from the trees. A quick count of the beasts gave them ten. To the front was a total of five standing and one on the ground with an arrow in its leg. Two were fighting Jericho, and Moric had just dropped one decreasing the count now to four.

"Faith, support our rear!", cried the leader.

❧

The goblin opened its mouth to scream, but no sound ever came out. Going to help its pack members against the extremely large man, the beast had paid no attention to the gnome skulking up behind it. Moric thrust both of his daggers into the goblin's back puncturing both its lungs. The beast shuttered forward; dropped to its knees, lost its sword, and fell face first into the dirt.

Committed to its sword thrust, one of the attacking goblins that faced off with Jericho overextended its strike. The big man side-stepped the thrust, and with both hands on his staff, brought the weapon across his body vertically to block the goblin's arm. When the staff made contact a snapping sound like a twig breaking could be heard and by the instant howl coming from the beast, Jericho knew the snap was its elbow breaking. As the shocked goblin released its grip on the sword and grabbed its broken limb while howling in pain, the giant gracefully stepped back with his right foot and thrust the butt end of the staff into the other attacker's stomach. The blow lifting the goblin off its feet before it dropped to the ground gasping to refill its lungs with air.

Turning back to the goblin howling in pain, Jericho took hold and twisted the beast's head in his immensely large hands breaking its neck. Replacing his second hand back on his staff, the giant man spun back around bringing his cudgel down across the base of the goblin's skull while it was on all fours attempting to catch its breath. The beast's arms folded underneath its body causing it to slap off the ground. The enemy laying still never to move again.

Faith heard Calvin's order and turned to help the elf and the brothers against their wave of foes. Devis with sword drawn, was now in hand-to-hand combat fighting alongside Edward and Harold. The three had already cut four more goblins down.

Reaching into a pouch at her waist, the young magic-user pulled out two arrowheads. Faith whispered some words causing one of the arrowheads to dissolve into mid-air. Raising her other hand and pointing at her selected target, a golden, magic arrow flew straight into a goblin's chest sending it sailing through the air and into some bushes. Smoke rose from the charred corpse.

Again Faith called upon her magic to aid her and the second arrowhead dissolved. This time her target was a thick, dying tree limb to a half-fallen tree. For a second time Faith pointed her finger and a golden arrow took flight hitting its target. A loud-popping break was heard, but before any of the enemies could react, the dead limb came down landing on the heads of three goblins. The remaining two beasts fighting were dispatched swiftly now by the rear's three companions.

❧

Calvin heard the beast's footsteps rapidly approaching from behind him. Spinning on the balls of his feet and catching the goblin by surprise with a heel kick, the leader followed that strike with a punch from his shield causing the goblin to fall backwards dazed.

A second adversary tried to stop by digging its heals into the ground but it couldn't stop in time. Thrusting his sword forward, Calvin watched as the goblin skewed itself when it ran onto the cavalier's blade. The knight kicked the beast off his sword as he pulled his weapon free.

Directing his attention back to the prone goblin, Calvin spun his sword in his hand so the blade was pointing downward, and drove it through the beast's chest.

Dispersing this last adversary, the group's leader turned to check and see how the rear was holding. He witnessed Harold running a beast through with his javelin while the other brother slashed its back, and the elf was presently running his sword through the last one.

Scanning the clearing, Calvin took in the sight of the small opening littered with goblin's corpses and puddles of blood. Moric kneeled on the back of the beast still alive with the arrowhead in its thigh. The shaft lay snapped on the ground near it.

"What do you want to do with this one, question it?", the gnome offering the answer to his question while holding his daggers against the back of the pinned goblin's neck.

"Yes, but bind him up first and let's make it quick! Night is just about on us," stated the leader pleased with the parties performance in its first skirmish as a team.

CHAPTER 8

"Liar!!!", yelled Devis planting a kick into the captive's chest. The blow knocking the bound goblin backwards off the log.

"Take it easy elf!", cautioned Calvin before reaching down and helping the beast by its shirt lapels back to its seat on the log. Glancing from Calvin back to the beast, the elf started his interrogation again.

"What are you up to around here?!"

"Can't tell you," the goblin answered in a scared voice.

With a high level of agitation, Devis asked the question again emphasizing every word. "WHAT ARE YOU DOING AROUND HERE?"

"Grum can't tell you," the beast stated a second time. It groveled as the elf threatened it with a slap across its bald head. "No! No! Please!", the goblin winced.

"Than you better start talking," the leader interjected.

"We found this," interrupted Moric.

Turning his attention to the gnome, Moric handed Calvin a rolled up map and gave an assessment of the body searches he and the others had performed.

"The map here is of this village, the tower, and the surrounding forest. We also found of some interest from the corpses, a small bit of jewelry and more coinage than most goblins carry. Then of course the usual stuff: dice made from bones, various shaped and colored stones, and a goblin's delicatessen; rancid food," Moric updated. "Most of the weapons were normal goblin weapons, but the mace was most likely from the missing soldiers. I'm also sure that the map belongs to them as well."

Looking at the rolled up map in his hand, Calvin kept asking himself the same questions in his head over and over; "What happened to the missing unit?; what are the goblins doing here?; and where did they come from?" The answers eluded him and nothing seemed to add up.

"Good work you guys," complimented the leader to the group. "Someone bring me the mace."

Turning back to Devis, Calvin took over the questioning of the captive. "Where is the human patrol?"

"Grum know not!", fearfully answered the goblin shaking its head.

"Liar!!!", again yelled the elf.

"No! No! Please! Just let go," begged the beast. "I not hurt any of you. Pretend I never saw any of you."

"You would skew any of us if given the opportunity," hissed Devis moving to once again assault the interrogated captive. "Especially me!", he added.

Calvin laid a hand on the elf's chest intercepting him before he beat Grum. "Take it easy my friend. I have this."

"One more time, where is the patrol?"

"Grum not know."

"Did you kill them?"

"Yes," it answered quickly followed by "No." The change up causing the companions to glance at one another momentarily before returning their attention back to the prisoner.

"What are the goblins doing here, and where are you from?"

As if the mere mention of the plural goblins awoke an act of defiance in Grum, the beast's facial expression changed from one of fear to one of intimidation. It smiled and hissed out its declaration. "More goblins come."

"And we shall rid this countryside of any infestation as we have you and your pack!", the knight confirmed. Calvin nod to Devis and turned to accept the mace the gnome had brought to him.

The one time smiling face of the captive turned to a face of horror, "No! No!", it pleaded before the elf ran his sword across Grum's throat. The beast gurgled as its lungs fought for the night air.

"We need to get well away from this clearing and find a place to stay for the night," declared Calvin. "Form a single line again and put one hand on the person in front of you. We do not need anyone getting lost in this darkness."

When all the companions affirmed that one hand was filled with a weapon while the other was on the person in front of them, Devis led them away from the field. Another benefit of those not human is being able to see in the dark.

The party silently hiked through the dark woods away from the scene of the skirmish with the goblins. Not a word was spoken amongst them and they tried to be extremely quiet with each of their footsteps, but only the elf and the gnome's footfalls were completely silent. On several occasions one of the sight inhibited companions snapped a small fallen branch or rustled a bush during the traverse. The need to create distance between them and the clearing seemed almost desperate as they searched for a campsite. Only the hoot of an owl carrying on the night's air seemed to follow the group.

The forest's darkness took on a murky, bluish air with its objects like trees and brush a solid, detail less black. The companions, except the two demi-humans, could only make out the solid onyx figures of their surroundings and each other. The tree canopy was still mostly continuous with areas here and there allowing the passage of light from the stars in the sky. There radiance from the gaseous, celestial bodies were almost completely obscured by the beautiful, lush landscape of the Border Forest; although, enough light was allowed to pass the plant life blockade letting the elf and the gnome see as clear as a cloudless day.

The demi-human races of Kanaan including, but not limited to elves, some half-elves, halflings, dwarves, and gnomes had the ability to see in the dark. This inherent characteristic worked in a couple of different ways all depending on if any type of light source existed. If a minimal light source was present a demi-human's retina is made extra sensitive to this illumination causing it to see at night just as clear as a cat. The second way, one was able to see in complete darkness with no light was again another function of the eye's retina. This time the lack of any illumination caused the eye to distinctively signify any and all patterns of heat like that of a viper.

The group came to a stop roughly three-hundred yards from the field when Devis reached a point in the woods that looked to be an ideal spot to rest for the remainder of the night. The site had three large trees all growing rather close to each other, and a dead, broken giant rested in pieces behind them, along with what appeared to be a continuous, full-grown bush in the darkness. The bush consisted actually of smaller shrubs, and the whole plant life scene gave one the impression of a solid wall.

"This sounds like a good place to set up for the rest of the night," offered Calvin after receiving the elf's opinion on the sight. "I would have liked to have been a little further away, but it is late and we all need some rest. Tonight we run two watches each with three men set in a triangle," advised the group's leader speaking into the night's shroud. "For the first half of this night's watch will be; Jericho, Moric and I with Harold, Edward, and Devis relieving us for the remainder."

Before splitting up Calvin shared some praise regarding the companions performances on the battle with the goblins. "Good job people back at the clearing! Way to handle ourselves and watch each other's backs. Now everyone on watch look alive."

The three headed off in separate directions not too far outside of the cold camp while the rest tried to get some shut eye. Finding his spot to set up for his shift, Calvin unconsciously wrapped his hand around his sword's pommel and lifted the blade only inches clear from its scabbard before letting it slide back in. If need be drawn, the weapon would be ready. Soon the howls from wolves joined the throaty cry of the night's bird of prey. Calvin knew the dog-like predators had found the goblin corpses.

***

Faith had just shut her spell book and returned it to its original spot in her backpack when Jericho began to stir. The large man sat against an oak with his staff across his thighs, as both hands gripped the weapon. A mighty yawn fled past his lips and he blinked his eyes four or five times. Removing one of his hands on the staff, Jericho brought the other up to his face and rubbed his eyes using his thumb and index finger trying to remove the sleepiness from them. Again, another giant yawn escaped before he noticed Faith watching him.

"Good morning," he greeted.

"Good morning to you also," she chirped. "How well did you sleep?"

"Off and on," was his answer while reaching for his pack and digging out a garlic biscuit for breakfast with a slice of cheese.

"Jericho, you mentioned that you were a farmer back at the tower, right?"

"Yes that's right."

"What do you grow?", inquired the young woman.

"Well I don't actually grow anything," he responded in between bites of his snack-like meal. "I'm a dairy farmer. I supply most of the village with milk and cheese."

"Oh!", surprisingly came Faith. "How many cows do you own?"

"Thirty cows and a dozen goats. Not everyone drinks cow's milk."

"I see, but if you're here who's tending your farm now?"

"My wife and I have four sons. Our two oldest handle the daily chores and upkeep mostly," answered a pride-filled Jericho.

The answer left Faith a little perplexed. Puzzled, she blurted out the only question now on her mind. "If you have a family and own a farm, then why did you volunteer for this quest?"

"To deal away with the evil that has infested Oakhurst before I too find it eventually at my farm's doorstep."

"A valiant cause," chimed in the knight, who neither of the two noticed woke up.

The gnome still lay curled in a ball sleeping.

⁓⁓

Small waves of smoke emitted from the end of the lit cigar protruding from a mouth hidden behind a bush of brownish, red facial hair. Removing the stogie with his thick, stubby fingers and blowing a cloud of smoke into the air, the dwarf took a second to gaze at it as he held it between two of his digits. "I love these things my old friend," he proclaimed to his mount while smacking his lips in enjoyment between his thick mustache and even thicker long beard. Then like a flash caused by a lightning bolt, the dwarf's anger erupted like a volcano. "By the Great Forger and his brother the Quarrier, if you want something done right then you have to bear the load yourself!"

Sticking the cigar back into his mouth, the dwarf started to mutter as he spoke out the side of it. "I should've played stupid! Hell, I should've never let the chief know where I was going to start with!", he complained. Speaking directly to his mount, actually his only true friend on Kanaan along with being the only living, breathing creature that could put up with a dwarf's grumpiness and moodiness, he added, "The problem with this younger generation is no responsibility! They should've been born those lazy-ass elves instead of responsible, hard working dwarves!"

The cave bear he rode just roared its support.

The dwarf forgot about the nice day surrounding him and even forgot about the cigar he was enjoying as his mind drifted back to the spring night almost a month ago.

He had taken a well deserved vacation for a ten day and had come out of the Border Mountains to visit a tavern shadier than a moonless night. Drinking, singing, sex, and fighting were the four main attributes of this place with drinking and fighting tied for its highest two.

The dwarf had been sitting at a small table in the establishment while waving a tankard of ale in the air and singing along to a lively song that he knew for over a century and a half. His cheeks were red and rosy matching his facial hair and his long, brownish, red hair flowing from the his head. A thick, hairy arm was wrapped around a whore decorating his lap, and he knew they would be sharing a bed later that night. What the vacationer didn't know was that this bliss-fulled night was about to sober up real fast.

Entering the shady establishment and looking around the rowdy, rambunctious room, the two dwarves heard the bellowing voice of the singing recipient to their message. Looking at one another as each wore an expression of anxiety written upon their faces, the two deliverers cautiously approached the tankard swinging dwarf after noticing him with the woman. Both remembered one key description given by Chief Stonechin; "Hammerstone is as ornery as a rattlesnake sun-bathing on a rock."

Walking straight over to the table where the thick, dense dwarf waving his tankard in the air, singing, and sitting with an arm wrapped around the prostitute seated on his lap sat, apprehensively stood the two dwarven messengers both ill at ease. "Mr. Hammerstone? Thorin Hammerstone?", one inquired.

Looking over at them, Thorin's expression became one of disbelief before lowering his tankard of ale to the table. "What do you want lads?"

"We need to speak with you outside. We carry a message from Chief Stonechin."

"You've got to be joking right?"

"No, we're not."

Pulling his arm from around the woman and whispering in her ear that he'd return, Thorin got up from the table and followed the two outside. Already his blood began to boil.

Stepping outside the tavern and around a corner the recipient looked from one messenger to the other. "What's this about?", he gruffly inquired.

One of the two dwarves pulled out sealed scroll case, marked with Stonechin's stamp, from inside his cloak and handed it to Thorin.

Breaking the seal and opening the tube, he dumped the parchment into his thick, meaty hand. Unrolling and reading the message, Thorin became more and more ornery as his eyes shifted from left to right. "Tarnish!", was the only word that erupted from him, but it was enough to startle the two messengers, who both took a quick step back.

"Chief Stonechin wants you to see why the hall hasn't received any gems from Millen Fireheart's outpost in over a month," revealed the messenger, who had handed him the correspondence.

"He does, does he?", harshly questioned the dwarf, who had been in good spirits up till the time these two had shown up. "Well you go back and tell the chief that when I'm done running his little errand we're going to sit down and have a long talk," angrily threatened Thorin.

Leaving the two dwarven messengers standing outside the bar, the agitated Thorin went back to the table he sat at. Unfortunately, a new patron had laid claim not only to his seat, but also the whore who now took up residence on his lap. Shaking his head back-n-forth in disbelief and lousy luck, Thorin exited the rowdy establishment.

Looking up and down the street for the two messengers, the agitated rattlesnake wasn't surprised when he couldn't find them. They had hastily left as soon as he had gone back inside the bar and neither of the two were anywhere in sight. Shaking his head with an added expletive and putting swiftness into his own steps, the dwarf started down the street heading for the town's surrounding woods and his mount.

Returning to the present, Thorin noticed his cigar was ready to burn out. He pulled a new one from the bandolier across his chest and used the old one to ignite it. Taking a few puffs from the stogie to get it going, Thorin added with pure agitation in his voice to the bear he rode, "By the gods! They could have at least displayed some common decency and let me finish the song."

His mount only blew a couple of short huffs in acknowledgment as the two continued on their route for the dwarven stronghold.

CHAPTER 9

"How about you?", asked the gentle giant. "I mean where are you from? You asked about my reason for volunteering, but why did you decide to come here and help?"

"I don't know if we have enough time, or if Calvin wants to move out," reasoned Faith while looking between Jericho and the group's leader.

"We will give the gnome a little bit more time to sleep before moving out," confirmed the knight. " Please, proceed my lady," he added.

Looking from one companion to another, the young woman began her tale. " I was born twenty-two winters ago in the small, coastal town south of here, Fair Haven. My father was a savvy merchant, who owned a fish market near the docks, and my mother helped him in the mornings with the daily running of the place. During the afternoons, she would open up her herbal remedy and apothecary shop. Other than my father, this was my mom's real love," she shared with the two all the while smiling as she reminisced of a time past.

"My mother, her name is Joy and my father's Douglas, were loved by the town's community. They performed a lot of charity work for the poor and under-privileged. It could be anywhere from my father giving out fish at the end of each store day that hadn't been sold to my mother offering her knowledge and assistance in caring for the sick with medical aid.

"As I grew up both of my parents would take me to my father's market in the morning and my mother and I would leave for her shop in the afternoons. They both included me in all their charity works and I really enjoyed lending help to others."

"That explains why you're a kind person," interrupted Jericho.

"Why thank you," she smiled with her cheeks slightly blushing causing her to pause only a moment before returning back to telling her story.

"I'm sorry, please continue."

"Well I really respected my father's trade, but it was my mother's profession, along with magic, that peaked my interest. I started following any magic-user that came to town and I remember asking them hundreds of questions," -Faith let out a giggle before continuing- "Anyways, a woman probably a little older than my mother began coming by my mother's shop to purchase herbs on a regular. She shared small talk at first, but not long later it seemed like the three of us were carrying on conversations. Sophia was her name and when her and I got on the topic of the art I became really intrigued. I didn't know it at the time, but Sophia was a spellcaster herself, and she offered to show me some magic. After some days of persuasion, my parents allowed me to visit Sophia at her house across town where I eventually would become her student in magic.

"As the time passed, I began spending more and more time with her until I no longer visited my father's market nor my mother's shop daily. I was very fortunate to gain the support from both of my parents while Sophia trained me in the knowledge of spells, along with their components and the incantations that would bring the spells to life.

"One night tragedy struck and Sophia's house caught fire and burned to the ground. Unfortunately, she was still inside and died," -somberly spoke Faith gazing at the ground- "No one knows how it caught fire or exactly how she died, but since then I go by her grave and the sight where her house stood every year to place some flowers and pay my respects."

"I am sorry for your loss my lady," offered Calvin shortly followed by the giant's sympathetic words.

Looking up from the ground and trying to smile her depressing thought away, Faith acknowledged the two. "Thank you."

"Well I heard about the problem up here and decided to come and see if I could help," she added while smiling and slightly tilting her head. "So here I am." "Well I for one am glad you did and thank you," praised Jericho.

Finally, the gnome, who had been sleeping in a fetal position began to stir as the other three companions on watch made their way into camp.

ॐ

The day was hot and no breeze blew making it a little worse than yesterday on the group as they trekked through the woods. Even the elf, although not uncomfortable, felt the change in degrees rise a bit. Once again the forest canopy teemed with wildlife.

The day went by uneventful for the most part and the party only stopped a few times when they rested for a lunch or came upon the place where Devis estimated the burst of lights had been the night prior. The group also stopped and visited a farm owned by Jericho's friend, Jacob, warning him of the goblins' presence in the woods before the companions left and continued on.

The party stopped and set up a camp for the night before the sun passed its reign of the sky to the quarter moon and the stars. With it still being early evening and the falling orb still casting light down on the land, Calvin decided that a campfire and a cooked meal would suit all the companions just fine this evening. Devis, with Lady Luck on his side, was able to kill and bring back to camp three rabbits while Edward was able to bag a couple himself. The two hunters were most welcome by their companions as they sat down and skinned the evening's meal.

During the meal, the party shared in small talk but always stayed alert for any signs of trouble. Once, a pair of squirrels chased and played with each other among the branches causing a small ruckus that had all the companions up and weapons ready for another skirmish. Eventually, they had settled back down and continued their discussions only when they were satisfied that a battle was not imminent.

All of the companions seemed to share the same apprehension and it had been the one major topic of the discussion all throughout supper and leading up to the time the fire had been extinguished just before night had fallen. Not one person could give the answer to the question asked, "Where exactly are we supposed to go?"

⁓

Sitting with his back against a tree and finding an excellent hiding spot behind some brush, the gnome stayed to the shadows. Moric had relieved Jericho of his watch only hours ago, and only the hooting of an owl broke the silent peace throughout the woods. The little thief finding it somewhat relaxing.

Looking around the tree back towards the cold camp where all the companions slept except for him and the elf, who also was on watch, Moric couldn't make out any of their bodies through the thick plant life around them. He then lifted his eyes to the tree limbs searching for any view of Devis, but again was unsuccessful spotting any signs of the elf. Turning back around, he stuck a palm-full of dried fruit with mixed nuts into his mouth.

Another hour passed and the night was still quiet and peaceful. With no excitement going on, Moric's mind drifted bringing him back to the time when he had first joined the Thieve's Guild in the city of Seaport.

Located on the western seaboard of Kanaan, the city was one of the largest places in all the realms. Whether in the regular market or on the black one, anything and everything could be purchased in this mighty metropolis. Its two biggest suppliers; the fishing industry and the guild.

Moric joined the guild shortly after his thirteenth birthday. In human years, that would be equivalent to just over five winters. He had never been interested in a gnome's way of life while growing up an orphan on the city's streets focusing more on his survival. Instead of desiring to journey on a lifequest, a young Moric craved gold and riches. "I'm going to be rich one day!", he would say over and over to himself.

No one in the guild practiced his trade as hard as Moric did. Day and night he would work at fighting and efficiently using two daggers in combat. The gnome constantly trained in moving silently and hiding in the smallest of shadows. He seasoned his lock-picking ability until no secure door was any match for the up and coming thief. The gnome never cared that society labeled his profession shady and unlawful, and it never bothered him that others called him immoral. The only thing that mattered to Moric was Moric, and his obsession with being rich! What the gnome didn't know yet was that all that was about to change.

The little thief had been training with a series of locking mechanisms going from the easy ones to some really advanced ones. A few were even trapped but with nothing that would cause serious injury to the gnome. Taking a knee in front of a locked door, Moric closed an eye and used the open one to sight the lock. His tongue hung out of his mouth and would move back-n-forth while the thief attempted to disarm the mechanism's trap and unlock the door. In front of Moric's bent knee was a square, hard, leather pouch containing all of his lockpicks. "A little bit more," he thought just about to overcome the obstacle when his one open, concentrating eye caught movement from his side. Opening Moric's shut eye and quickly looking in the direction of the movement, he was enchanted into an awe like stare by the gorgeous woman gnome standing there watching him.

The woman gnome was standing with her weight shifted onto one leg with both her hands on her curvy hips. Her hair was short, roughly shoulder length and wavy, and its color black like an onyx. A long strand of her bangs had a tendency of hiding her right eye behind it. The woman cast him a smile and her mouth was filled with snow white teeth. They, in unison with her face, radiated a beauty that Moric hadn't seen before today. The black leather pants with a royal blue blouse and soft, leather boots only accentuated her beauty.

While Moric was caught in rapture a small bing-like noise filled the room causing his eyes suddenly to open as wide as gold coins. "Ouch!", cried the practicing thief while quickly pulling his hands away from the tripped trap of the lock. His two lockpicks tumbling to the floor as a needle point stuck out from the keyhole of the door.

The gnome nimbly jumped to his feet with his pricked finger in his mouth and was about to start yelling and screaming at the woman, but before he could she let out a small giggle.

"Sorry about that hon. I just got interested in the way you had contorted your face and was moving your tongue around," she apologized. "People call me Blü."

Something about her really touched a chord in the little thief's heart, and he eventually chuckled a bit at her explanation before introducing himself. "Hi, I'm Moric." There was no obnoxiousness or loudness in his tone.

From that day on, Moric and Blü were an inseparable team, and all the jobs they performed, the two did together. No one could ever find one of them by themselves no matter what time of day it was, and the two thieves were not only best friends but in a short time became lovers.

Blü had explained how she was originally a solo act until a rival guild of Moric's had pushed up on her and had initiated the soloist into their guild. The woman thief spent a couple of winters representing the guild in their entrepreneurship throughout the city and against their rival guild; his, but eventually a falling out occurred between her and them. It took place during a night time job she and one of the guild's founders were performing on the estate belonging to the city's mayor. As fate would have it, the chief official was also the number one realtor in Seaport. He possessed not only a small treasure but also some very important land grants. One permit title was for a lot next door to the secret hideout for the guild and the mayor had planned on selling the lot, which most likely would have put a damper on the guild members' comings and goings.

The founder, along with Blü, were only going to take some money and some deeds to land around Seaport when the mayor accidentally walked in while the two were in the middle of their heist. A small clash between the thieves and the mayor's four bodyguards ensued. Three of the security had been killed and the city's official ended up losing a leg.

Blü had dispatched the fourth bodyguard after taking a bolt in the thigh from a crossbow shot. She was left behind by the guild's founder as collateral damage, but would escape. From that moment on the old saying, *"There is no honor among thieves."*, stuck with her. The woman thief being lost in the man's betrayal, snuck up behind him one night and slit his throat. That night, she became an enemy to her thieves den.

Within two winters of meeting Blü and becoming lovers, Moric grew bored with the metropolis and its ways only craving adventure along with the promises of riches. His yearning had made him decide to leave Seaport. Moric begged Blü to come with him traveling through the realms chasing the dream of distant treasures, but the woman thief stayed rooted in the city. Finally the day would arrive when the two thieves, friends, and lovers separated and went their own ways.

Moric missed Blü a lot and his eyes filled with water causing a tear to roll down his cheek as the gnome felt a hollowness in his heart. Wiping the secretion of water from his eyes, the party's thief saw some taller grass roughly ten feet in front of him move. He brought a signal whistle to his lips and was about to raise the alarm when two small animals walked into view. The invaders were a pair of mask-wearing racoons foraging the forest's floor for something to eat.

Dropping the whistle from his lips and letting it dangle from a leather cord hanging from his neck, this night Moric really missed Blü.

❧

Devis sat perched on a tree limb with his back leaning against the trunk of one of the forest's mighty oaks. Like a predator surveying the ground for any type of movement, he was ready to swoop down on his prey. The elf was right at home in a tree spending most of his life so high above the forest floor. His was the only race on Kanaan that called these giant plants not only their friends but also more importantly their homes. From this vantage point, Devis had a much better view of his surroundings.

Taking a drink from his water skin, the elf had witnessed several of the night's nocturnal creatures going about their business of foraging or hunting. Nothing appeared out of the ordinary.

Drawing another sip of water, Devis' thoughts turned to Faith's magical execution against the goblins. Even though the magic-user was still of a young age, he was impressed by her coolness under fire and her intelligent decision-making. To use one dead limb from the deceased tree to take out three enemies was notable in his book. The elf knew and could foresee that Faith had the makings of a powerful mage, and as long as her disposition didn't change that would be a benefit for the realms in the fight against evil.

❧

Thorin leaned against a large boulder just off the path winding its way through the Border Mountains. With a small campfire a few feet away from him, the dwarf looked imposing as the firelight danced off his plate armor and his weapons laying beside him. Only his dwarven maul was inclined on the boulder off to his right side. Its head in the dirt. Also resting on the ground were a double-bladed axe and a loaded crossbow. A dagger decorated his right hip, and across his thick barrel chest, Thorin wore a bandolier full of his favorite cigars.

The dwarf had just been nodding off for his nights rest when the battle axe in the grip of his right hand started to vibrate. Just barely opening his eyes and stealing a glance at the pommel of the bladed weapon, the emerald in its base gave off a green glow.

With his eyes barely open, the dwarf scanned the rocky mountainside with its scattered tree line coming to an end around this altitude. Thorin noticed a small group of eight pairs of glowing, red eyes staring at him from inside the darkness of the disappearing plant life. The dwarf had two aspects in his favor against these ambushers; first his magical weapon had warned him of their approach, and second his ability to see in the night. Thorin knew goblins had nothing but evil intent.

Laying still and pretending he had no clue to the beasts presence, the dwarf baited them forward. A quick question entered his mind, "Where's that damn bear?", but swiftly left when he first saw the eight goblins doing their best at skulking out of the tree line towards him. "Stupid beasts," he thought as they were within sixteen feet now.

With the speed and accuracy never seen by a dwarf before, Thorin quickly took his hand from his axe placing it on his loaded crossbow, raised it up and aimed it, then fired. Its bolt hitting one of the first beasts between the eyes. The goblin was dead even before the others looked to see what had happened. Turning back to the dwarf, the ambushers gave a primal scream as they rushed forward teeth bared and their primitive weapons at the ready. Thorin rose to his feet, double-bladed axe in hand.

Placing both hands on the weapons handle and lifting the axe over his head, the dwarf heaved it at the closest onrushing goblin. The blades twirled end-over-end throughout its flight until the double-bladed missile sunk into its target's sternum lifting the beast into the air. The power drove the onrusher backwards into another beast also knocking it down. The axe protruding from the dead carcass. Thorin quickly turned to grab the handle of his dwarven maul leaning against the boulder, but one of the goblins swung its sword hitting him on his left, upper arm and knocking the dwarf off balance into the boulder.

Slapping off the large rock, Thorin was able to regain his footing while lifting his two-handed hammer in a defensive position. The beast, along with a second one, pressed its attack.

The original attacker swung its sword from right to left in a slashing motion while the second beast brought the sword it had downward trying to strike the dwarf's head. Again, with speed not common amongst dwarves, Thorin sidestepped the downward attack creating not only distance between him and the slashing sword strike coming from his left, but also used the second goblin to shield himself from the other's attack.

A painful howl erupted into the night as the first attacker's sword bit into the side of the second beast. The second goblin in pain dropped its weapon instantly. Thorin, a seasoned fighter, saw the opportunity and swinging his maul into the wounded one's back drove it straight forward into the boulder. The combination of crushing bones along with a sickening, wet splat came from the goblin as it bounced off the solid, immovable object and fell on its back. The beast's face covered in greenish, black blood and reduced to a pulpy, broken mass.

The first attacker snarled its rage at the dwarf but hesitated in its attack. Thorin was pointing the top, flat end of his hammer at the goblin's face while muttering the command word that would call on the maul's magic. The ruby attached to its pommel glowed casting a red light shining from the dwarf's plate mail armor making the seasoned fighter take on a look of evil.

The goblin raising its sword to press its attack was met in the face by a flaming sphere erupting from the top of the hammer's head. The ball of fire blew the beast's head clear off its shoulders. Seconds later the smoldering, headless corpse slunk to the ground.

Thorin turned to face the remaining four ambushers, who were now huddled together ready to attack. Teeth bared, they slowly advanced. The dwarf now stood holding his maul in both hands across his body beginning to let out a low-pitched growl that rose to a loud, roaring type yell.

Suddenly the four beasts halted their advance on the battle yelling dwarf and began to tremble in fear. Behind Thorin, towering over his display of intimidation, standing on its two hind legs, was a massive-sized cave bear joining the dwarf's battle roar with one all its own. The petrified goblins cried out in fear before turning and breaking into a mad dash for the tree line they had earlier rushed out of.

"Pussies!", shouted the dwarf to the backs of the fleeing four.

Thorin turned around when he felt the vibration on the ground of the bear dropping down on all fours again. Its jaws clapping while it huffed out the side of its mouth in aggression. Walking forward it listened as the dwarf addressed the animal.

"There you are! It's about time you showed up!", reprimanded the dwarf. "I almost had to finish taking care of those no good, waste of air, dumb beasts myself," he confidently added. "Well you might as well be getting after those things before they suck all the breathable air out of the sky."

The bear seemed like it was taking Thorin's advice as it started its pursuit into the woods after the animal's prey. The dwarf knew it wouldn't be long now for the remaining four.

Pulling a cigar from his bandolier, Thorin touched a small, twig-like branch to the campfire until it caught. Bringing the burning twig to the end of the cigar protruding from his hidden lips, the fighter puffed as the stogie lit causing him to toss the small wooden lighter back into the camp's blaze. Two cries of death from the unfortunate goblins broke the night.

Taking a couple of puffs and removing the cigar from his lips with a "V" formed from his index and middle finger, Thorin blew out some smoke as he gazed into the star lit sky. "I ain't seen goblin in these parts in over a century. I wonder if these vermin are the reason behind Chief Stonechin not receiving any gem shipments from Fireheart lately," he wondered speaking softly to himself. Drawing another inhalation from his stogie and exhaling, Thorin added to the night, "Looks like we may be dealing with a pest infestation here."

Another death cry interrupted his brief contemplation.

CHAPTER 10

Faith jumped as the blood curdling scream awoke her from her slumber causing her hand to automatically go directly for her dagger. The young woman's head on a swivel seeking out trouble in the night's darkness. All the companions were quickly awakened with a start, and the sound of weapons being drawn and at the ready carried throughout the cold camp.

"What was that?", anxiously questioned Edward.

"Easy people," softly commanded Calvin. "Can anyone see anything?", he continued.

One by one the companions answered in the negative.

"Can anyone see Moric or Devis?", was Jericho's query.

"Just stand down everyone," ordered the leader. "There was no sound from either signal whistle so they shall return."

Moric was the first into camp behind an issued warning stating his intent to safely enter. "Is everyone alright?", he questioned before continuing, "I could make out a little light somewhere back from where we passed but not much with all the bushes obstructing my view."

Still being the dark hours of the night, the scream had brought everyone on their guard. Adrenaline flowed through everyone's bodies and even though they slept only minutes ago the chemical release had them wide awake with no signs of grogginess hampering them. Their solid, black forms were all any of them, except the demi-human could distinguish from the blue night air around them.

"Where is Devis?", tensely asked Calvin.

As if the knight's question conjured him, the elf seemed to materialize out of the darkness. "I'm here."

"What could you see?"

"There is a bright light roughly two miles back from where we came," the elf reported. "The scream sounded more human than animalistic."

"Did you two see anyone or anything approach?"

"Nothing," responded the elf followed by the gnome confirming the negative response. "Nothing Calvin."

At that moment, another scream like the first ripped through the night.

Calvin knew they needed to at least investigate and possibly face an upcoming battle. With the light, from whatever source caused it, the group would at least be able to see. Waiting for further instructions, Devis was the first to speak.

"I wait on your word Calvin."

"Moric, you shall lead all of us through the night to the source of the light," ordered the leader. "Elf, you go ahead but don't get caught in any trouble. The rest of us will be there as soon as possible!"

With the leader's orders given, Devis disappeared running into the night-covered brush. His destination; the source of the illumination and its accompanying scream.

Devis ran quickly through the brush hurdling bushes and logs, along with any other small obstacles he encountered. Noticing a fallen tree leaning against another at just the perfect angle, the elf ran up it and took to the trees. He nimbly ran from limb to limb covering a greater distance faster. Devis had no problem keeping his balance and never slowed tree-walking or running for it was second nature to an elf like breathing involuntarily was to the inhabitants of Kanaan. His vision adjusted as he got closer to the brightness caused from the source of the light.

Stopping in a tree and hiding behind the leaf-filled cover that the oak's limb provided, the elf gazed upon the clear section of land in front of him. A farm house along with its barn and accompanying chicken coop were on fire blazing out of control. Devis cautiously looked back over his shoulder before surveying the surrounding grounds. Unfortunately, he recognized the burning structure and knew exactly where he was. The lumber from the house and the barn cracked and groaned as it burned, and both building's roofs insulated with thatched hay snapped and hissed in the blaze. By the looks of the area, a massacre had taken place.

The ground was littered with mutilated livestock and a numerous amount of footprints caused from all of the blood shed covering the farm's clearing. A dog with blood-stained spots where three arrows stuck from its body, lay dead in between a child and a mauled goblin's body. It seemed apparent to Devis that the canine had died defending the child the best it could. Again, the elf surveyed the area and knowing the rest of the party was on their way dropped to the ground just inside the cleared perimeter.

Landing with a cat-like grace and barely making any noise upon contact, the elf cautiously dropped to a knee. Drawing his sword while constantly scanning for any signs of enemies, Devis made his way over to the child and her defender. Dropping to a knee as he reached the little girl, the elf had just met her yesterday. It was Jacob's youngest daughter Veronica of only six winters old. She wore a white night dress covered in her own blood caused by a slit across her throat and the child's hair was stained crimson red. Veronica's eyes stared unblinking at the night sky still filled with horror. Taking two fingers and lightly brushing the girl's eyes, Devis closed them saying a quick, silent prayer for her innocent soul to the gods.

Turning his attention to the child's friend and defender, the elf commented softly while giving the dog a couple of pats. "Best friend and loyal companion to the end." A loud crash stole his attention as the roof to the farmhouse's porch collapsed.

With his acute hearing picking up a low cry from the far side of the burning barn, Devis crept low to the ground with his sword on the ready for action in the direction of the noise. He started to pass the farmhouse and noticed a pair of boot marks interrupted by two straight drag lines in between them. The elf's tracking knowledge telling him that two people dragged another. The tracker continued to follow the boot prints and the drag marks.

Staying at a safe distance from the burning structures in case they collapsed, Devis stalked low to the ground, head on a swivel, and sword in front of him at the ready. On his way to his new destination he recognized a man sitting against the base of a tree. "Jacob," thought the elf realizing the wounded man was the origin of the initial noise he had heard. The tracker abandoning the marks momentarily as he made his way over to Jacob. Taking only three steps, the elf suddenly caught a glimpse of movement from the corner of his eye causing him to direct his attention as he took in the sight of two goblins hovering over a prone woman. Their backs to the elf.

Laughing at the naked woman lying on the ground, the two goblins never heard nor saw Devis sneaking up behind them.

Looking up at her attackers, the woman witnessed a sword's blade erupt and stick out of the chest of the beast standing on her right side above her. Its eyes rolled back into its head and its smile disappeared. The attacker's laughter ceasing forever.

Devis swiftly withdrew his blood-covered sword while pushing the dead body's left shoulder forward. The dispatched beast dropping to the ground dead. In an instant, he used the arm that he had just shoved the corpse with, to elbow the startled goblin on his left in its face. The force of the blow breaking its nose and causing the beast to stumble backwards before it could comprehend what had just happened. A sword swing later the goblin's head rolled from its shoulders and its decapitated body fell backwards to the ground.

Dropping to a knee on the side of the prone, naked woman, her savior slightly flinched at the gruesome horror caused by the two beasts. Laying in a puddle of her own blood with her stomach cut and ripped open, Devis recognized Jacob's wife. Their unborn baby had been torn from her womb.

"They took all my babies! Please help my babies!", she softly gasped while reaching for her savior.

"I will," promised the elf grasping her bloody hand in his. Devis knowing that even though he attempted to comfort the woman in her last moments of life it was all in vain. For on this night she would be joining all of them in the after-life from the looks of the carnage about.

"Please elf, save my babies from those monsters," was the last words from the dying woman.

"I will," repeated her avenger.

It was the last words she had heard before passing from this realm to the next.

Devis used his fingers to close her water-filled eyes. "At least Jacob's wife got to witness some type of vengeance handed down upon her family's transgressors," he reasoned before offering a prayer to the gods for her.

Scanning the area while rising to his feet, Devis quickly made his way back to Jacob sitting against a tree. Upon reaching him and kneeling by his side the elf placed his index and middle finger onto the side of the man's neck attempting to feel for a pulse. He did, but it was a slight one. The elf then placed his index finger under Jacob's nose and felt him softly breathing.

Devis was once again startled but this time it was as the group burst into the clearing from the surrounding woods.

"Over here!", he yelled to his companions causing the wounded man to open his eyes. The fire's light reflecting back off his teared up eyes.

Suddenly, a loud crash filled the wee hours of the morning as the burning house and the barn collapsed in on themselves.

CHAPTER 11

Jericho automatically knew the collapsing structures and where he was before he heard Devis call to the party. Rushing over to where the elf kneeled next to the injured man the giant man recognized the bloodied and battered face of his old friend Jacob. "Oh no, Jacob!", he concerned.

Taking a knee next to the dying man, and laying his staff on the ground near him, Jericho captured the man's gaze. "I'm here old friend," speaking as softly as his deep voice allowed.

Both men had grown up as friends, and spent all of their lives in Oak hurst. In their younger years, Jacob and Jericho had played together as children. When they were in their teens, the two spent their free time away from their parent's farms either fishing, swimming, or chasing the girls of the village. Now they were both in their early forties and had inherited the family businesses from their folks, raising families of their own. It was not uncommon to see one or the other helping his friend out around either of the places.

In their down time, both families would enjoy each other's company and their children played together often. Once in a while, Jacob and Jericho would take a day to visit the local pond spending the day fishing together like they had done when they were teens. Now it was obvious that those shared good times would be coming to an immediate ending.

"Jericho, my old friend. How it favors me to see a friendly face on this night," came Jacob in between shallow breaths.

"What happened here?", the big man asked while trying to disguise his fear of the inevitable.

"We were all sleeping when Rex began barking and going frantic. It woke me up, and as I started downstairs to check out the commotion all the while thinking a family of coons or a fox was about causing mischief."

Suddenly Jacob was interrupted by a cough causing him to spit up some blood.

"Take it easy Jake," consoled Jericho while uncorking his waterskin and offering Jacob a drink.

"Thanks," -the dying man took a gulp then continued- "When I arrived downstairs I went to peak out the window and I was met by a pair of red eyes peering back in at me."

A cough interrupted him a second time and again he spit blood onto his chin. Using his blood stained bed clothes, Jericho wiped his mouth and cleaned his face. Jacob's breathing seemed to become slightly more shallow and his eyes began to glaze over, he tried to continue, "All hell broke loose as the goblins burst through the door and the windows. I tried fighting um but there was just too many for me to take. It was a matter of seconds before I was overrun.

"It's alright. Just calm down," spoke Jericho trying to relax his friend. "How's Florence and the children?"

Jericho glanced over at Devis, who was still kneeling near the dying man and somberly shook his head answering the big man's unasked question.

Turning back to Jacob, Jericho's eyes met his friend's death gaze. The man had passed from this realm onto the next. The giant sunk his head into a hand trying to fight back the tears while Devis brushed Jacob's eyes shut and for the third time tonight offered a silent prayer to the gods.

"Have you seen his wife?", queried the man raising his head from his palm.

"Over there," softly replied the elf while tilting his head in her direction.

"It's bad Jericho," he added.

Grabbing his staff while standing up, the giant man walked over to the dead woman's body. Jericho was taken aback by the scene of heinous violation. Anger and sadness combined as one as tears flowed freely from his watery eyes. Bowing his head, he said a prayer.

The rest of the companions witnessed the tough events unfold and could easily tell by Jericho's body language that he was hurting. All the others felt somber, and the air was thick with a terrible sadness about the place, even though the companions had just met Jacob and his family on the day prior. Everyone of them could tell they were good people.

"You guys,…" -addressed Calvin- "…go and secure the perimeter. We do not wish to get caught unaware if they should return."

Walking up to the elf as he was rising from the ground, the knight commended his companion. "Good job Devis. Are you alright?"

"I just wish I was here earlier," he somberly responded. "At least for the woman's sake."

Both companions approached Jericho while he stood over Florence's body. "We are truly sorry," offered both of them.

"Me too," was Jericho's sad reply. "We must burn the bodies."

"We know my friend. The elf and I will help you," offered the group's leader.

♒

None of the companions could sleep after collecting and burning Jacob and his family's bodies. The group even threw the loyal, family companion into the funeral pyre to join its masters and lifelong human kin. Only the crackling and popping from the burning ruins filled the somber atmosphere in the woods. The party gathering around the big man offering their condolences and support during the sad cremation.

"A whole family massacred in minutes," disbelievingly stated Jericho while watching the fire's dancing blaze and shaking his head in utter disgust.

"Didn't they have three more children ?", softly inquired Faith.

"Yes, but there's no signs of there bodies out here," Jericho responded. "Most likely caught in the fiery house and its collapse."

"Oh," sadly came the young woman. "I really am sorry."

After some time had passed, the rest of the companions left Jericho to mourn his loss in front of the dying pyre. The sun was beginning to rise from behind the Border Mountains declaring a start to a new day. Like the mornings past, the birds started to sing their merry tunes rivaling the feelings of the saddened group of adventurers.

Calvin had ordered the McKinleys to watch over Faith as she found a spot to study her spell selection for the upcoming day. The leader had also instructed Moric to guard a border of the clearing while the elf looked for any clues that would tell which way the beasts headed after leaving this place. Calvin also took watch on the other side of the disastrous spot.

Soon after, Jericho approached Calvin's position. "What are your instructions Calvin?", inquired the giant.

"How are you doing my friend?", answering Jericho's question with a query of his own.

"I'm sad but I'll be alright. This is not the time to mourn their losses, for there will be a fitting time later when we rid this village of those monsters that did this!"

"Very true my friend," confirmed Calvin, but before he could continue both men watched as the elf hastily approached.

"I believe the children live!", proclaimed Devis with a certainty in his voice. "I have found tracks from the beasts, along with three sets of bootless, human footprints leaving here and traveling east into the forest."

Faith had finished her studying and committed the chosen spells to her memory. At any time throughout the next twenty-four hours, the magic-user could call upon their aid. The woman with both brothers walked up to the three companions already engaged in conversation.

"Show us," came Calvin responding to Devis' inspiring revelation. Jericho, who only moments before knew sadness and loss in his heavy heart, now felt the spark of hope ignite in its darkness.

"What's going on?", asked Faith as the elf led the two men across the scene of last night's tragedy.

"Devis found some tracks left by the children going through the trees," answered the big man. "He believes they live!", he added before all six of the companions started for the only traces left of Jacob's surviving family.

As the six reached the spot of the telltales, the elf quickly dropped to a knee and began pointing out the differences in the tracks. "Here are the booted marks of the goblins, ..." -he pointed to them- "...but these three tracks here are all human prints. These are two larger prints probably belonging to the boys we met here yesterday while this set here most likely belongs to the child, Katherine." The elf looked up at the others.

"They live!", excitedly expressed Jericho.

"Good job," confirmed the leader as he patted the elf on the shoulder.

Looking into the forest the knight gave his next orders to the five other companions present. "We pursue the goblins and rescue the children!", decreed Calvin. "One of you go get the gnome."

Now the party had a definitive answer to the one question that puzzled them earlier. They knew where they were going now and they would be chasing their prey east. The companions would be hunting goblin.

⁓

The early, morning sun bathed Oakhurst in a pinkish hue of light. Wildlife had started to wake and stretch off the cobwebs of a night's slumber. The canopy's green leaves rustled with the soft blowing of a northern breeze. The upcoming day appeared to be slightly cooler so far but the summer weather could deceive one's guess.

Embers from the fire that consumed the farmhouse and the barn stilled burned sending a cylindrical column of smoke rising into the air. It was carried like a slithering snake across the treetops by the blowing breeze. The area still had a somber atmosphere hovering above it, but the news that three of Jacob's children possibly still lived lifted everyone's spirit.

The ground was soft from the blood of a handful of dead goblins along with the butchered livestock strewn about it. Already, a pungent odor had begun to emit from the corpses and after several minutes of discussion amongst the companions they decided to collect the goblin's bodies, stack them up, and burning them. The party came to the agreement that wild animals would eat the slaughtered livestock corpses or they would just decay fertilizing the ground, but the dead goblin bodies could possibly pass some type of disease to the village inhabitants starting a plague. No one wanted that scenario! The companions sought to help Oakhurst, not damn it!

After throwing the bodies onto the smoldering remains of the barn and assiting them to ignite creating a goblin-made bonfire, the adventurer's used water from the farm's well to clean up and refill their waterskins. The party swallowed a snack-like meal of nuts, fruits, and bread with cheese before moving out in a single file line into the forest. The tracks as their guide.

❧

Throughout the day the temperature stayed cool thanks to the breeze blowing out of the north, but even though they were grateful for the slight reprieve, each individual was covered in a sheen film of their own sweat, with the knight wearing his plate armor being the worst of the bunch.

What most likely would have dropped any others hours ago appeared to have very little, if any, effect on Calvin. He had trained for years now, both mentally and physically, in plate mail and his endurance in that heat was unrivaled throughout the realms except in his southern homeland of Tierra Natal. Rivers of the salty body fluid freely flowed from under his helmet running over his face but it seemed not to slow him down. Taking another gulp from his waterskin, the knight still seemed grateful for the short rest in their pursuit.

The hunters had switched from walking to jogging throughout the day but unfortunately had never caught up with their quarry. It appeared their prey was somehow moving at a rapid pace even with the three captive children. Instead of gaining ground, the party was slowly falling behind.

Leaving his companions taking a breather, Devis went on ahead to scout out the area. Taking a knee, the tracker studied the trail of prints looking for any changes in direction, the amount of impressions, and even their size, but found none. All the while he constantly kept a weary eye out for any type of ambush.

Silently stalking through the woods, the elf's eyes darted from left-to-right, front-to-back, and up in the trees waiting for an attack at any minute. His acute hearing not only caught the leaves rustling in the summer breeze but the wind seemed to carry the animalistic grunts along with a type of ripping or tearing noise through the forest. Devis quickly dropped to a knee and scanned the trees looking for an aerial vantage point.

After finding several limbs low enough to assist him in getting into the leaf cover, the tracker selected one and started for its tree's trunk. The elf utilized a short burst of speed and leaped towards the plant's wooden stem placing a foot on it about four feet off the ground. Using it to push off of, Devis bounced with a quick acrobatic-like spring launching himself in the direction of the limb he had earlier chosen to be his ingress into the tree. The airborne tracker grabbed the branch and swung his body onto it softly landing on the bough with a cat-like grace in a squatting position. The tree-walker had took to higher ground.

The elf felt a sense of security now that he could see further, along with knowing he possessed a superior bonus against any grounded adversary. With the cover of the full oak limbs, Devis tree-walked in the direction of the sound. His silent foot falls were graceful and the elf's passing was noiseless.

Standing on a limb and gazing about ten feet away, Devis discovered the answer to the mysterious sound. On the forest's floor below was a large, black bear feeding on a man's dead body. The corpse wore brown, leather armor.

The tracker led the group to the spot of his horrific find roughly a hundred yards away from where they had rested for a breather. The sight of the area was gruesome and the scent of baking decay hung in the air. Most of the companions were aghast as they came upon the location, quickly using their shirt sleeves or whatever they could find to cover their noses from the offensive odor. Blood had soaked into the ground around the body leaving the soil stained and paw impressions formed a chaotic collage in it. Pieces of meat, along with leather armor, were torn away from the corpse's torso and right thigh, with its right arm totally missing from its glenhumoral joint.

"Set up a perimeter people," instructed the leader. "We do not want any scavengers coming in unexpected."

The party broke apart and took up guard at six different points in a circular fashion.

Calvin made his way over to the deceased for a closer look. Flies buzzed in a feeding frenzy all over the body and the corpse, or what was left of it, wore brown, leather armor with an oak tree symbol upon the chest. A sword lay on the ground near to where his missing hand would have been if still there. Four sword slashes were evident upon the dead.

"It appears we unfortunately know what happened to at least one of the patrol's men," softly spoke Calvin to no one in particular. The count seemed to increase with Harold confirming another find.

"There's a body here also Calvin!", shouted the McKinley brother with short hair. "By the gods of Kanaan, I almost stood on it."

In the brush lay another corpse decaying, and like the first one discovered it had also been chewed upon by some type of animal. The only difference was its limbs were still intact. The body was wearing brown, leather armor with the oak tree emblem upon its chest. By its side lay a crossbow along with a quiver holding a dozen bolts.

"Another one lay here," added the gnome, but that would be the last of the patrol men any of the party would find in this vicinity.

Calvin spent roughly fifteen minutes looking over each corpse. Finding nothing of interest that might help the group, the knight whispered up a prayer to the gods and ordered the companions to move out. "We would give the bodies a proper burial but the living are more important at this time. We need to keep moving for their sake."

Again the party was on the move following the goblin's tracks with the three human footprints through the wooded terrain. They had continued to lead east towards the Border Mountains, home to a couple of dwarven clans. It was later in the afternoon and evening quickly approached.

The adventurers moved with haste in their steps, for time needed to be made up, ground needed to be covered, and distance needed to close between the hunters and the hunted. Somehow, their prey constantly stayed ahead of them and eluded them. Devis, like a cautious hound dog locked onto the trail, was followed by his companions ten feet behind.

Slightly concerned, the elf took several glances at the sky beginning to overcast. He knew rainfall was shortly on its way and with it eventually nightfall. Darkness would fill the sky and his human companions would be limited in their vision. Apprehension kicked in more and more as Devis thought about the rain and the restrictions it would offer to the trail along with his tracking ability.

It was true that all elves, some better than others, possessed the knowledge and required skill needed to track; although on Kanaan no one or no races' ability could rival the proficiency to track like a ranger. A ranger could detect just the slightest imprint or the minute marks of a sought after telltale. Their skill covered any and all types of terrain and the climate was barely a factor in their pursuit of a trail.

Devis was no ranger, and the possibility that the rain could wash away the existing trail was now dangerously imminent. Catching up and retaking Jacob's children could potentially take a turn for the worse. For the next couple of hours, the party pushed themselves to the limit.

No fire was lit and the darkness surrounded the camp. Tonight's cold camp was wet and miserable as a light, consistent rain fell on the land. It had begun to fall shortly before the party had set to hunker down for the night, and the sound it produced drumming off the leaves along with Calvin's armor created a type of tranquility amongst the night's air. Eating a quick fireless meal, most of the party fell right off to sleep exhausted while both Calvin and Jericho took up first watch.

Calvin had been on watch when loud rumble-like booms and bright flashes of light broke the peacefulness of the rainy night. At first he mistook the atmospheric vibrations and the sky's illuminations as a thunder and lightning storm, but within mere moments realization imbedded in his perception. This wasn't a storm but instead a battle, and its bright lights were caused by spell discharges.

Within minutes, all the slumbering adventurers along with Jericho, who was drawn by his amazement away from his position on watch, stood side-by-side gazing at the night's sky brightened by flares of light. Somewhere at least a day's travel away from where they camped, a fight was in progress; a battle of magic.

CHAPTER 12

The six men slumbered in the rainy darkness of this night and had earlier chosen this small clearing hoping the stars and the quarter moon would cast some brightness helping them to see better without a campfire. The overcast sky along with the rain put a damper on those plans as it fell upon the land and the men at a steady rate.

Four of the six men were dressed alike wearing chain mail shirts and leather-armored pants with a banded-armor crossing. Their helmets lay on the ground off to one side of their prone bodies and the warriors' swords laid hidden on their weapon hand sides. Accompanying them were two other figures wearing hooded, brown robes covering their heads to their ankles. Underneath the robes both men wore leather armor.

The camp was peaceful and besides the slumbering bodies the only evidence it was a site was a rock-ringed, extinguished fire pit. Several small logs rested there but any signs of smoke rising from a lit fire were long gone.

Staring out from behind the bushes and trees were a dozen pair of red eyes. The goblin ambushers preparing to fall upon the sleeping, unsuspecting six. Behind them, standing guard around the three captive children were another nine beasts. Three captors stood with their hands clamped over the scared captives' mouths menacingly. To the right of the trio stood a hooded, black-robed figure with his arms crossed in front of his stomach and his hands hidden inside the sleeves of the other arm. If not for the darkness of the night, one would be able to see the magical ruins on both sleeve cuffs. The robe's hood hid his face.

The twelve waiting ambushers surveyed the site carefully looking for any signs of more people or a trap. After assessing that only the sleeping six were present, the lead goblin turned to the figure as if asking for his permission to attack. The beast's ability to see in the dark of night allowed him to watch the robed man withdraw a hand from the sleeve of his other arm and point a thin, black finger in the slumberers' direction and nod the affirmative.

With the permission they waited for given, the ambushers began to stalk towards their unaware victims. Their mouths dripped saliva with the thought of chaos and murder in their mists. Leaving the tree line and exposing themselves in the clearing, the goblins were taken by surprise as one of the prone, hooded, robed targets lifted an arm pointing it at the lead beast. Three golden arrows materialized out of thin air and closed on their mark. It was too late for that goblin to even share a cry of horror as the magic missile fire slammed into it killing the ambusher.

The other brown-robed figure waved his hand in the direction of the camp fire logs. A magical light illuminated the site like a bright torchlight while the six jumped to their feet swiftly ready for battle. The four had their helmets on and a long sword in hand. The robed figure, who lit the logs, pulled his hood off and readied his sword. The other brown-robed figure left his hood on and drew his blade. A battle roar erupting from the six at the same time their trap was sprung.

Slowing the eleven goblins for a couple of seconds as their sight adjusted to the sudden illumination, the ambushers started their charge covering the remaining distance. A primal growl all their own. The four warriors standing in front of the two robed figures stood their ground as the magical light radiated from behind them highlighting their silhouettes. Swords ready and waiting for the oncoming rush.

Again, the hooded, brown-robed figure with sword in his right hand, pointed the index finger of his left hand at a charging goblin. Three golden arrows took flight a second time lifting the creature into the air and propelling it backwards into an oak. In a bone shattering smack it bounced off the immense plant falling to the ground.

Weapons clashed as the warriors and goblins came together meeting in hand-to-hand combat.

A warrior confronted by two of the beasts parried a spear thrust by moving his sword across his body perpendicular to the ground while turning his hips allowing the spears point to go past his body on the right side. His return strike was a slash from his sword leading with his left elbow across the beast's chest. Somehow, the goblin ducked away from it. The second beast brought his sword strike in a downward motion causing the human warrior to dodge to his right. The blade biting into nothing but air.

A second warrior was swarmed on by three beasts. He blocked the first goblin's sword swing and parried the second ambushers attack but the third attacker caught him square in the left part of his chest with a blow from its mace. The shot knocked the warrior back stumbling, but before this third goblin could press its attack on the warrior, the robed man, who had removed his hood from his head earlier, intercepted the beast with a series of sword slashes. It never knew what hit it because the ambusher had concentrated on the reeling warrior. The goblin would never get the chance to make the same mistake again.

The third warrior was confronted by two beasts positioned to his front and almost his left flank. The one in front of him slashed his sword from left to right aiming at his head. The warrior quickly jumped back to dodge but unfortunately for the defender he leapt right into the path of a spear thrust. The strike hit home as the spearhead entered just below the man's ribs. Screaming in defiance, the warrior grabbed hold of the spear and swung his sword in a backhand fashion. The tip of the blade just missing the goblin's neck. The beast tried to run the spear into the fighter's body deeper and finally succeeded when the warrior dropped to his knees from the initial injury.

The fourth fighter in the formed defensive line in front of both of the brown-robed men took an onslaught of the creatures. Three ambushers all carrying swords teamed on him and pressed their attack. The fourth man was so busy blocking attacks that he never was able to at least get a chance to go on the offensive.

Nine more goblins rushed from the trees to join the fray.

"Let's see how the wizard and cleric like these odds," thought the hooded, black-robed figure.

With the fourth warrior being overrun and killed by the three creatures there was no one in front of the hooded, brown-robed defender to help defend his position. Quickly, the wizard-warrior called upon his magic to aid him in his defense. Waving his sword-free, left hand back-n-forth around his chest height and starting to expertly twirl his blade in a figure eight motion from side-to-side, he watched as the eyes of the three goblins glazed over while locking their sights on the moving sword. The beasts' were so fascinated by the swinging weapon, they never paid attention as the wizard-warrior approached their stuck positions. Over the shoulders of the hypno-tized three, he watched as nine more goblins erupted from the woods.

"Be prepared brothers!", the wizard-warrior shouted the warn-ing. "Another wave attacks!"

Seeing the reinforcements come running out of the woods, the cleric-warrior offered a prayer to his deity and pointed at one of the goblins attacking the second warrior. The beast preparing to strike at the fighter turned its attack on its ally. The other creature surpris-ingly cried out as its pack companion brought its sword down the other's face and body driving the beast to the ground dead.

The commanded goblin stood in horror over its ally's body after the spell released it from its effect. The beast never saw the warrior's swing that seperated its head from its body. The removed head roll-ing into the grass.

The first warrior still had two of the ambushers confronting him. One of the attackers used its spear thrusting forward and the fighter made what appeared to be a wise move side-stepping the stab to the beast's left. It provided a wide open shot on the spear wielder and put the attacker in between him and the other goblin leaving it with no chance of any type of sword strike. As the warrior lifted his own sword above his head preparing to bring a blow downward, a bolt of lightning struck him dead center in the chest. The fighter was thrown backward along with his free blade. When he hit the ground, smoke rose from the burnt hole in his chest.

For a matter of seconds all melee between the three defenders, the four attackers, and the charging goblins came to a halt. The realization that another magic-user entered the battle provided different reactions from both sides. The warrior, the cleric-warrior, and the wizard-warrior were jarred by the new and devastating spellcaster's introductory. As for the goblins, they were excitedly inspired by the reality in knowing this addition was in their favor.

"Jhessail!", wailed the cleric-warrior with a worried tone.

"I am aware Brother Titus!", was the only response Jhessail could find at this moment.

Another lightning bolt tore from the tree line flying past the charging goblins towards the remaining warrior.

"Look out Percival!", warned Brother Titus.

Percival never winced as the bolt approached. It was not favored by his god and believed to be thought cowardly if one cringed at battle or the death it brought. Standing in acceptance, he waited for a blast that never came.

Watching the second magical attack birth from the woods and head directly for Percival, the wizard-warrior had to react swiftly. Jhessail called on an abjuration while uttering the spell's incantations and waving his sword-free hand. Before the jagged lightning bolt could find its mark, the evocation spell was dispelled by a protective one. Particles of energy shot past the warrior like dust in the wind.

Quickly Jhessail summoned an evocation spell from his arsenal of magic before the four closest goblins and the nine closing beasts were upon him and his companions. He slowly passed his hand in front of him tapping an unseen source of power as a wall made from fire appeared in front of the three separating them and their attackers.

"What is your plan Brother Jhessail?", asked Brother Titus while the burning wall held the beasts at bay.

"I will hold off the wizard and the goblins while you two return to the temple and retrieve help."

"But the temple is all the way in Fair Haven!", surprisingly came Percival. "No, I shall stay with you and battle these creatures to the death!"

"No. You will return and inform Brother Talon of the illness that plagues this peaceful village and its forest," assertively reprimanded the wizard-warrior.

"As you wish brother."

"We will meet again brothers. Now go!", ordered Jhessail.

Both Percival and Brother Titus ran for the cover of the forest. Sweat running off them even now in the light rain. As they made the trees, both gave a quick glance in the direction where they had just come from taking in the sight of the wall of fire blinking out. Obviously the magical flames dispelled by the rival mage. Alone stood Brother Jhessail prepared to defend his friend's getaway and buy them some time. Brother Titus offered a prayer to their deity; Guerra, the god of war.

Watching the wall of fire blaze in the darkness, the hooded, black-robed wizard felt the burn of impatience ignite in his body. He grew bored and tired of this game. "It ends now," he snarled his decree to the goblins restraining the children.

The wizard walked out of the woods towards the flaming wall. "Everybody back!", he shouted the order and began to gesture with his recently exposed hands toward the magical barrier. Words came from his mouth and suddenly the wall was gone. Standing behind it was a hooded, brown-robed figure. Smiling under his black hood to himself, he knew it was the wizard-warrior.

"This is between you and I wizard!", firmly stated the wizard-warrior. "You think you can control your pack of mangy mutts?"

Laughter escaped from under the hood of the black-robed wizard. "This fool is mine, and mine alone! No one touches him!", he shouted the order.

Removing his brown hood while returning his sword to its sheath, Jhessail spoke as he revealed his identity. His hair flowed long down his back and it was both straight and chestnut brown. His eyes were almond-shaped and matched the color of his hair. Jhessail's face lacked any scars and he would have been one of the most handsomest humans anyone would have probably seen throughout all of Kanaan, but the fact that he was only half man could not go unnoticed. On the sides of his head were the pointed ears of an elf. Jhessail was a half-elf.

"I am Jhessail Silverleaf. Humble worshiper to the god Guerra and my face shall be the last one you see before you know death."

The hooded, black-robed wizard laughed and clapped his hands. "And you call these beasts mutts you half-breed?", he mocked while sweeping a thin, black hand towards the goblins waiting on an order to kill.

"It disappoints me that you are not all elf, half-breed," flowed the derogatory statement while the figure removed his hood. "I want you to know who kills you."

Pulling the hood from his head, long, white hair fell upon the wizard's back and covered parts of his thin, black face. His eyes were like midnight surrounded by a small amount of white. His lips turned up in a snarl.

The worshiper of the god of war came face-to-face with the worshiper of chaos and pure evil. The half-elf's adversary was none other than the realms most-hated, wicked, darkest of races. In front of Jhessail standing almost twenty feet away stood a drow.

Already prepared with a spell, the half-elf was through with introductions. He recanted a few words and a bolt of lightning roared from his hand racing towards the evil wizard. As the magical energy approached the drow, an invisible barrier brightened as it absorbed the raw energy.

Now the drow took the offensive muttering a spells incantation. Pointing all ten fingers in the half-elf's direction, web shot forth at him. The sticky, magical substance was also absorbed by Jhessail's defensive barrier.

"Impressive half-breed," snarled the drow.

Again, a bolt of electricity shot forth from the half-elf's right palm. Its target was different this time causing a concussive blast when it hit the ground in front of the dark elf. The blast throwing the drow backwards knocking him to the ground. Jhessail pressed the attack.

Speaking the incantation to his next spell, the drow could feel his body start to stick where it was. Knowing the enemy wizard was trying a hold spell, he quickly spoke the phrase to dispel the attempted magic.

From the ground the wizard called upon his retaliating spell, as Jhessail was approaching on the run. He watched as the half-elf began to lose his balance and slipped leaving him open to attack.

Waving his hands around trying to catch his balance, he never saw the three, black, magical arrows until his defensive barrier flared absorbing the energy. The brightness had placed light spots in his eyes and the half-elf knew the protective magic was used up.

In between falling and the hardship with his vision, Jhessail caught sight of his adversary's hand movements. The drow released another bolt of lightning and this time he had the half-elf dead in his sights, but the wizard-warrior did something that not only his enemy never expected but never saw coming.

Jhessail, seeing the beginning of the bolt let his momentum from the slide combined with his forward progress send him into a roll toward the downed drow. The lightning bolt flew over his body slamming into an oak across the small clearing sending splinters of wood into the sky. During the roll across the grass, the quick think-ing half-elf drew a dagger closing on the grounded, drow wizard.

When the acrobatic move ended, Jhessail was almost on top of his adversary. Scrambling quickly, he pinned the black-robed wizard down holding the dagger to his throat.

"No! Wait!", the panicked drow begged. "Over there, the children!"

The brown-robed man only looked when a girl child cried out because the goblin restraining her began to twist her frail arm. That second was all the drow needed as he unloaded three, black, magi-cal arrows into Jhessail. The concussive blast propelled the half-elf through the air carrying him about ten feet. Smoke rose from his wounds.

Rising to his feet, the dark elf started to laugh a sinister laugh. "Almost you thought, half-breed."

Jhessail lay on the ground slightly moaning.

Pointing his hand at the prone wizard-warrior, the black-robed wizard called upon his magic a final time. A cone of cold-killing ice blasted into the grass where the half-elf once laid. Jhessail had disappeared.

CHAPTER 13

Laying on the forest's floor still wracked with pain from his previous magical battle with the drow wizard, Jhessail looked up into the tree branches. Waves of smoke rose from his body where the black, magical arrows had found their mark. The half-elf's face grimaced at the throbbing ache coming from his torso. "Possible broken ribs,", he thought. "At least bruised ones," he added to himself.

The casting of the teleport spell that had brought him a hundred feet away from the small clearing saved the half-elf's life. Now the spot that Jhessail and his small group had stopped at for supper earlier in the evening before moving on to the clearing, became a sanctuary for his battered body. Around him were trees and bushes.

The half-elf preferred lying still for some time due to the pain being just too much to move. He thought about two major questions over and over while he rested. "Had he provided enough time for his companions to get away?"; and "What were goblins and a drow doing with children prisoners?" No matter how much he searched, Jhessail couldn't find the answers. They might have been there somewhere but the pain stole his thoughts. Closing his eyes, the wizard-warrior slipped into the peacefulness of unconsciousness.

Rain pounded the land along with its inhabitants. The forest was dead quiet with all its wildlife hidden away in their nests, dens, or whatever it was they called home. The falling water pounded and ran off its initial location, whether it be plants or leaves littering the ground, forming puddles and thin, running streams. Nothing was immune on Kanaan to the rain goddess, Lluvia.

It was mid-afternoon on the third day of their trek through the Border Forest and all the companions experienced a dreary, wet camp last night. With the consistent light rain all morning leading up to the downpour only minutes ago, the party was soaked to the bone. The feeling of gloominess left all the pursuers miserable.

Kneeling near the disappearing tracks, Devis rubbed his temples using a thumb and index finger. The feeling of disappointment due to circumstances he had no control over frustrated him moment by moment.

"Are you alright elf?", questioned the concerned leader standing next to his kneeling companion.

Devis responded while wiping some water off of his forehead. "I'm fine Calvin. It's just that this damn rain is washing away the tracks, and I may lose the trail."

"Easy my friend. You will do fine," assured Calvin.

"But I told Jacob's wife before her spirit left her body that I would return her children to safety," a tone of both anger mixed with frustration filling his response. "Besides, what about Jericho and what it means to him."

"Calm yourself elf. We are all trying our best including you," reinforced the knight. Rain pinging off his armor. "That is all Jericho, the children, and Jacob along with his wife would ask," pointed out the group's leader. "Like courage wins over fear, rationality and calmness defeat emotional reactions all the time. You are doing real good Devis," he complimented placing a hand on the elf's shoulder.

"Thanks knight," responded the elf with a renewed resolve to his spirit. Determined to figure out what direction to go, Devis returned his attention to the disappearing prints and the plant growth around him.

"Everyone take a break but look alive people," instructed Calvin.

The companions either leaned against wet trees or tried to find somewhere dry to hide from the constant soaking they were receiving. Due to being tired and miserable the brief rest was quieter than the others had been so far. Jericho was silent more due to his anxiousness in getting Jacob's children back, but then again what could they really come back to. The big man already knew beyond a doubt that he would shelter and raise those kids like they belonged to him and his wife, but all the time knowing the reality was their real family was dead.

After some time of stealing a rest, Devis' announcement broke the silence of the quiet companions. "I have found it Calvin! We remain east on this path," the elf confidently announced.

"Are you sure?", queried Calvin. "How do you know?"

"The stupid beasts left a sign for me. It took some searching along with time to find it but I did."

"Show me."

Leading the knight a little into the brush in front of them, the tracker pointed out the semi-hidden telltale. Mostly concealed, but still visible to the searching eye laid the sign. A pile of partly-covered goblin skat lay in the grass.

The group had spent all day hiking through the wooded terrain east towards the mountains. The rain had stopped but the dark sky was still overcast and gloomy. Unfortunately, the downpour had washed away the remaining tracks, and Devis had to inspect the greenery for any tells of the passing goblins. This was harder than following a laid, definite trail, but the ends justified the means to the adventurers.

Pressing on, Devis stopped and bent down holding up a closed fist with his elbow bent, signaling the party to stop. Calvin added the "get down" hand sign, and the group lowered themselves to the ground. Their heads on a swivel seeking anything that didn't look right. The knight checked to make sure his sword, if needed, could be easily drawn.

Ahead the trees opened into a small clearing. Surveying the open site, the elf counted three dead bodies, along with a figure in a hooded brown robe. He appeared to be collecting the bodies and laying them near each other. Using the silent language of hand signs, Devis motioned the party to his location. Quietly approaching the squatted elf, the party found refuge hiding behind the humongous plants and existing bushes. Silence hung in the air.

❧

After regaining consciousness this morning, Jhessail had offered up a prayer to his deity and cast a few healing spells to mend his beaten and battered body. When the half-elf's wounds had fully healed, he rose to his feet and inspected his weapons along with his armor. The wizard-warrior's belongings were still in the clearing.

"At least my armor held up," he softly commented to himself while feeling the spots of his torso where the magic shots had hit. "I have to go back and see how bad the damage is in the daylight,..." -he thought- "...or should I say rain."

Deciding to walk the hundred feet instead of teleporting, Jhessail started out for the clearing.

The site was littered with the three bodies of his fellow worshipers, who had died in battle last night. Their bodies searched and the small camp ransacked. Some of his belongings were scattered here and there. After collecting his pack, along with some of his other personals, the half-elf got busy at work. Jhessail was going to perform an offering of the bodies to the afterlife. Those who follow the way of the war god believe their bodies accompanied their warrior spirits to the battlefield of Guerra where they happily served him fighting.

Jhessail was just placing the corpse of the third warrior in the line with the other two fighters when his magical alarm spell silently alerted him to the presence of others at the small field. Scanning the tree line around the clearing, the half-elf drew his sword and prepared for another fight. "Show yourselves, for I am aware of your presence!", the wizard-warrior announced yelling into the forest.

The companions searched all over to see if anyone else was with the hooded, brown-robed figure but didn't catch sight of any others.

"I said show yourselves!"

"I am coming out, but know I mean you no harm nor ill-will!", Calvin shouted from his place of concealment. Motioning for the others to stay put, the knight rose from his hiding spot and proceeded to walk into the clearing exposing himself. He stopped five feet after revealing his presence.

"State your business."

"I am in pursuit of a pack of goblins who have taken three children captive, and by the looks of the scene before me you and your friends have encountered them," offering his perspective of the cryptic background.

Never taking his eyes off the armored man, Jhessail searched for any others that might accompany the stranger from under his hood.

"You have guessed correctly. They did pass this way last night, but to prove your offer of no harm or ill thoughts have the others with you reveal themselves. Then, and only then may we speak freely."

"How do I know you yourself are here alone and do not try to deceive us?", swiftly queried Calvin before the companions gave up their hiding spots.

"You have my word!", Jhessail responded while sheathing his sword. The half-elf then removed his hood so all could gaze upon his face. "The solemn swear of Jhessail Silverleaf."

Never turning away from the robed man, Calvin called the rest of the group to him. "Come on out you guys and show yourselves."

※

Watching the fire consume the dead from the edge of the clearing, the companions waited for Jhessail to finish his prayers over the fallen's souls. They shared talk amongst themselves over the events the half-elf shared with them from the previous nights encounter with the goblins and their drow wizard leader. The whole time keeping their eyes on the look out for more trouble.

"He's coming with us?", Faith asked Calvin while motioning with her eyes towards the pyre's flames.

"Yes. He wishes to avenge his fallen brothers," replied the knight. "He said he has a score to settle with the drow," the cavalier added.

"The right question is, do we trust him?", chirped in Edward concerned.

Calvin pondered the question before giving his answer. "I can't say that I'm fully sure yet, but in his favor, he has upheld his word so far."

"Well just keep an eye on my back! Okay Jericho.", came Moric shouting in his concern.

The big man smiling at his littlest companion.

"I believe we can trust his word," confidently offered Devis.

"Why because he's half an elf?", someone asked.

"Exactly," replied the elf to the question. "Whether full-blooded elf or half-blooded, the despise from both races towards the drow is close to being equal." Devis continued to enlighten the party on the history of the evil dark race of Kanaan.

"In the beginning of the elven race our people had two gods, Taradryll and his sister Thaisia. All loved the brother and sister, but they both possessed different outlooks and opinions on how their people should live their daily lives. Their biggest dissimilarity was the two's dispositions and personalties.

"The god Taradryll believed in the greater good, not only in life, but in his elven people. Their heart, like that of his own, illuminated the benefit and happiness that accompanied this favorable quality. Taradryll instilled in them the conviction of goodness, and bestowed on them a life longer than any other race on Kanaan. The god intended an elf to fill one's being with enjoyment and knowledge. Not live to work, but only work to live.

"Thaisia on the other hand had no time for order, but instead found enjoyment reveling in chaos and mischief. Her trickery and deception was unrivaled by the gods. Thaisia found evil as a better way of life enjoying using the elven race to further her diabolical schemes and gain pleasure from the mortal's unruliness. She would find pleasure watching from the Heavens her people's pain.

"Growing weary one day of her wickedness, Taradryll confronted his sister and her wrong doings. He had planned to seize all control of the elven race from her, and punish her insolence with a threat of banishment casting her down to Kanaan making her walk the land as a mortal. In her fear, Thaisia used trickery and was able to deceive her brother by swearing her wickedness would end. Forgiving his sister her wrongs, Taradryll embraced his sister in a hug. This is when the bitch god struck.

"In the embrace, Thaisia drove a poisoned dagger into her brother's back whispering in his ear a pledge to cast down evil and chaos onto his people. As Taradryll's godly body succumb to the effects of the poison, he fell into a deep slumber. How long the slumber lasted, one does not know for sure, but it is said to be at least two winters.

"The elven race for that duration of time only knew chaos and darkness. Unrest ran rampant throughout the realms and evil gave birth to new and horrible tragedies. Races were almost wiped out to extinction due to wars, all the while the queen of darkness watched down from her place in the heavens. A content smile of evil dressing her face.

"Finally the other gods had sat back and witnessed enough wickedness and the blackness it brought with it. The gods of goodness needed to act and together formulated a plan in an attempt to aid Taradryll, by magically defeating the poison that plagued his body. It was not an easy task, but after several unsuccessful tries, their combined efforts worked leaving the god in a deeply unconscious state.

"For months after, the gods concealed the elven deity from his sister's evilness, allowing Taradryll to regain his strength. Soon the day came when his presence was unsuspected and Thaisia's plan at domination was foiled. Her shock at his revelation was enough to drop her to her knees trembling in fear. Her trickery and deception lost from her grasp in the goddess's surprise.

"Instead of killing the evil Thaisia or casting her down from the Heavens, the gods allowed Taradryll to hand punishment down upon his sister. The elven god bequeathed on Thaisia the skin shade of blackness to match the color of her heart. He also seized control of his good people, and bestowed on those that worshiped her the punishment that would limit her people to a subterranean life dwelling under Kanaan. They would never walk in peace in the sunlight that shone down brightening the land, but would dwell in the deep darkness of the underground. All of them would only know the sun as their enemy. From that day forth the race of chaos and evil would be known to all as the drow. The dark elves," he finished.

Plumes of steam rose from behind Jhessail as he approached the party members whom had listened to the history of the drow's creation. They had been waiting for him, and watched the half-elf use a magical cone of ice to extinguish the dying funeral pyre. Seeing all the companions staring in his direction, Jhessail felt slightly compelled to speak. "Wouldn't want to cause the forest to blaze out of control. Right elf?"

With the day coming to an end and the dreary, overcast night approaching, the party and the new addition left the clearing entering the woods. The hunt for evil began again.

CHAPTER 14

"Leave em alone!", shouted Katherine crying out the command to the goblin kicking her older brother, who had been lying on the wet ground exhausted trying to sleep.

"Get up human scum!", it ordered the boy laying on his side in a fetal position holding his ribs. The prisoner's hands lashed in front of him at the wrists.

The goblin she had yelled at started towards the smallest of the three captives. As it approached, the beast raised its hand and swung the back of it at the girl. Katherine shut her eyes and winced from the threat as she anticipated the blow and the accompanying sting it would bring with it but it never came. Instead, the child opened her eyes when she heard a loud slapping noise that sounded like some of the hand's bones snapped. The pain-stricken cry from the goblin ensued as it had made full contact with some sort of invisible barrier.

Cradling its hurt hand with its other one, the goblin caught the blow against the side of its bald head causing it to reel from the strike. The beast quickly looking up and meeting the irate stare from the drow wizard. The black-robed mage's own hand ready to deal another blow.

"Do not conceive the misleading belief of your importance nor your need for attendance here," growled the dark elf. "You are expendable and can be replaced in a blink of an eye. Never again will you attempt to damage that which does not belong to you, or I shall not hesitate to show you a slow, torturous demise," he threatened. "Know your place beast. Am I understood?"

Looking at the wizard while feeling both pain and total fear, the goblin still clasping its wounded hand slowly backed away. "Yes Master! Sorry Master!"

"Now get up boy," demanded the wizard captor changing his gaze from the sniveling beast to the pack's commander.

"We move into the mountains tonight," he stated. "Our hastened travel is necessary."

"Will you be using more of the enchanted dust?", asked the goblin in charge.

"Not yet commander. With this constant rain and its treacherous conditions under foot, I do not want avoidable injuries to plague us nor slow our ascent."

"Prepare to leave!", the commander shouted the order amongst the resting beasts.

Katherine looked up meeting the gaze of the dark elf. "Thank you for helping me and Junior from those monsters."

Snarling at her display of courtesy, the drow spoke at the child. "We will see how gracious you are when I deliver you to Wizard Zebbulas and he puts you to toil. Do not think in that little mind of yours child, that you are too important," he added while poking the girl on her forehead with his black finger. "For if you, or those brothers of yours, ever birth a notion that you are too important than I swear your demise on Kanaan will be hastened."

Cowering away from the captor, Katherine tucked her head into her shoulders. The facial expression from the combination of annoyance from the drow's finger poke and her fear waved over the frightened child. The words, "I'm sorry," spoken barely audible and practically automatically drifted from her lips followed by a final, "Thank you," as she dropped her head staring at the water-logged ground.

"Are your preparations to leave finalized?", queried the wizard to the goblin commander.

Knowing to never respond in a negative fashion or he would suffer repercussions he replied, "On your orders Master Wizard."

"Very well,", he sinisterly smiled. "We leave now," decreed the dark elf heading towards the direction leading into the mountains.

"Move it scum!", ordered another goblin shoving one of Katherine's brothers.

Soon the captors, with their captives, started up the slight, inclining topography on their way leading to higher elevations. No one, especially the goblin that had kicked Jacob Jr., ever noticed the muddy piece of ripped bed clothing left under three, small twigs forming an arrow. Its direction pointing east into the Border Mountains.

The rains poured down relentlessly on the Border Mountains leaving finger-like rivers rapidly flowing down its slopes. The destination of the wild, running waters was the lower elevations. Over a dozen ponds formed in rocky recesses creating natural reservoirs. At least it was the beginning of the summer, and the rains were warm and somewhat refreshing at first, but now the land's population had had enough of the drenching.

The land could not soak up all the water from the constant liquid bombardment and the muddy ground was common here above the tree line making any type of passing laborious. Even Thorin's great-sized cave bear had problems as it trudged through the soft, wet terrain.

A combination between the bear's instincts, the dwarf's natural, race trait with stone and other earthen materials, and Lady Luck's good fortune helped Thorin find a huge cave that he and his mount could hunker down in and rest for the night. Most importantly it let the two take refuge out from the down-pouring rains.

The natural shelter had a stone ramp leading up to a platform large enough to allow access to enter the cavern while still having room for a campfire. Above the stone's ramp, was an outcropping of rock overhang similar to the cover of a roof over a porch. The cave bear, who the dwarf suitably named Mountain, slumbered inside the natural hospice. Its stomach full of unlucky goblin. Meanwhile, Thorin sat on the platform eating bread and a type of salty, beef jerky. Looking into the gloomy, wet, starless night for more signs of goblins, the drenched dwarf commented to himself about the three encounters he had with the pests over the last two nights. "Yup, I'm sure of it now. We got a god darn infestation here in these mountains. I can't wait to hear Fireheart's plan of remedy now." Thorin drew a large drink of dwarven spirits from his skin as he continued his silent vigil into the darkness.

～⚬～

The grand, bedroom chamber was the biggest, private quarters throughout the whole dwarven stronghold. Tapestries depicting battle scenes between dwarves and dragons decorated the stone walls. One of the woven textile, wall hangings pictured a dwarven king standing with his double-bladed axe buried into the skull of a large, red dragon. A pile of treasure rose to a cavern's roof in the background.

There were half a dozen, five candle-holding, candelabras scattered amongst the rooms and were usually used to fully illuminate the large chamber. At this time, only the small one on a large table off-centered from the room's entrance, burned. The ample, wooden structure stood only four feet tall and its borders were lined with carvings of fire-breathing dragons. The legs of the table were sculptured to resemble those of the large serpents with two like chairs making up the set.

The quarter's only door was made out of thick oak and reinforced with three, metal bands evenly spaced and running horizontally. Not only was there a keyhole present, but the only entrance into the room could be barred from the inside.

Across from the barrier, lining the far wall were eight, wardrobe closets. They contained everything from majestic dwarven robes, to shirts and pants, to both soft and hard boots. The last one in the furthest corner from the entrance held a suit of dwarven, plate mail armor with a helmet. A golden crown adorned the head protection. The suit matched the one being worn by the king on the tapestry pictured with the dead dragon.

Roughly three feet to the right of the door stood an ivory, soaking tub with its feet fashioned into four claws. The fixture was long enough and wide enough to accommodate a dwarf or small human the chance to relax. There appeared no possible way to fill or drain the vessel, so one would have to believe that the water occupying and emptying from it was done magically.

Against the right wall, stood a large, canopy-style bed accompanied on either side by two wooden, drawered, night stands. At the foot of the room's main piece of furniture rested a seated, bed chest made from wood. The front of it was etched with a heart ablaze and inside the heart, the design of a solid, black symbol of a dragon with an emblem of a pick and hammer underneath the creature decorated it. This was the hall's coat of arms. An egg-shaped rug lay in front of the bed chest while two others dressed the floor on both sides of the canopy bed. A seethrough veil covered all sides of the large piece of furniture, and its headboard was carved depicting both the dwarven gods, the Forger and the Quarrier, watching over any sleeping occupant.

Presently on the large bed were two drow entwined in a dance of sex. Moans carried from the female's mouth as her lover rose and fell into her opened body. The covers responding to his moves. The male's mane of long, straight, white hair hanging down from his head slightly covering the female's profile while looking up and contorting his face into a grimace. Underneath the drow, his female lover sinking her teeth into his bare, ebony chest leaving a bite mark before letting go to gasp for another breath.

The dark elf's long, black hair matted all over the bed's pillow as she arched her back pushing her breasts into the air while meeting his thrusts. Her hands grasping and pulling at the sheets. Sheens of sweat covered both lovers in their pursuit towards the final beat of ecstasy, and the smell of perspiration and sex lingered filling the room's air. Bedding followed his lead as the male drow horizontally danced faster now. His breathing matching the rhythm of each plunge. The female drow's moans came quicker and louder now until both partners grunted out their rapture in the imminent explosion of sexual bliss.

Rolling off the female and onto his back, the dark elf slightly exhausted and catching his breath laid staring at the ceiling. The last hour of the extracurricular activity left a small smile on his and her face.

"Who would have known you'd be a worthy lover, wizard?", she complimented instead of more than asked while trying to catch her breath. "I'm never disappointed nor dissatisfied with your performance."

"Thank you priestess," he humbly accepted her compliment while secretly thinking about how many times he had frolicked in the sheets with her own mother. The thought prompting his next question.

"How is the matriarch? Does she seem pleased with our progress here?"

"My mother is fine," she slightly snarled her answer. "I believe she is satisfied for now, but know this Zebbulas, very soon I shall take my mother's place as matriarch of House Zexthion and when I do we will move up in rank within drow society," she added confidently. Still staring at the ceiling from her back, the priestess continued, "You know I will require the assistance of a good house wizard. Will you serve me like you have served my mother?" Turning she gazed at Zebbulas.

The wizard knew that any telltale, whether it be a physical give-away or the inflection of his answer, could be perceived as a lie. It wouldn't matter if he spoke falsely or truthfully, a female's perception of a male in drow society was all that mattered. The females were at the top of the food chain and their goddess had made certain of that. Thaisia had not only created them in the likeness of herself to be both beautiful and irresistible, but the females were slightly larger and stronger. In essence tougher than any of the males. It was a matriarchal race and they called all the shots.

Turning his head sideways and meeting the priestess' unblinking stare, Zebbulas responded with the only answer that would save his existence. "Why of course priestess. I would be honored."

A smile broke through her serious gaze creasing her lips as she remained gazing upwards. "A wise decision."

Rolling up onto his lap and placing her hands on the wizard's chest, the priestess smiled down. "Shall we continue a new round?"

The companions hiked through the forest until finally arriving at the base of the Border Mountains. There were large oaks still dressing the topography as they began up the slope. It had been a full day and a half since encountering the half-elf at the field preparing to cremate his three warrior brothers.

The rain had finally stopped sometime yesterday afternoon, but the ground was still saturated and various size puddles formed everywhere. A good size pool of dirty water had developed at the mountain's base forming a miniature moat defending the grounds rise from where they stood. The disappearing rains gave way to a melodious tune from the singing birds, along with the climb in heat.

At this time, there was no doubt from any of the party's members that the captors were somehow being magically hastened in their escape or whether they sensed they were being followed. Right now the most important question was figuring out which way the hunted had gone. The drow wizard along with the goblins and Jacob's children had put a great deal of distance between them and the group leaving the hunters at least a day and a half behind.

Pushing themselves in their tiring pursuit, the companions were somewhat relieved when Calvin called the quick break for a lunch. Being famished they all dug into their packs for something to devour and then tried to find a dry spot to take a seat. Like those they followed, the group was eluded again when it came to locating any of those areas to sit.

Jericho, who was the most anxious about getting the children back, needed the opportunity to refuel his large body. Looking up from his backpack, the largest of the group watched the elf searching high and low for any signs that would tell him which way the goblins traveled.

"Take a break and eat something Devis!", Jericho shouted out his advice.

"Got to try and find something that lets us know which way they went."

"What are you going to do when you finally catch up with them? Mystify them when you fall out from hunger and malnutrition,…" -the big man attempting to stress a valid point in between bites- "…

137

or do you plan on dropping on the way there and becoming more of a burden than a help?"

That question struck a sensitive nerve in the elf. Taking his eyes from the ground and staring at the big man, Devis allowed his emotions to take over and control his rising, inner anger. "Listen farmer, I'm planning on rescuing those kids with or without you! I gave my word to a dying mother and I will not break those vows!", angrily retorted the elf. "Just two days ago, they were all you could speak on; although by the looks of it, your stomach has won over your heart."

Throwing his quick lunch of jerky, bread, and the rest of his cheese down on his pack, Jericho bellowed while jumping off his damp seat on a small boulder-like rock, "Let me inform you of something elf..."

Witnessing the heated, verbal argument about to blow out of control at any second now, Faith started to stand and interrupt the two combatants, but Calvin stopped her laying an armored hand on her shoulder.

"Jericho is right. Devis needs to eat first and he has not all day," calmly came the knight.

"But they're about to come to blows."

"No one will let that happen," he reassured her. "They both need to let out frustration. Have not you been witness to the two's pent up anxiety since we left the scene of the brutal attack the other morning?", softly asked Calvin.

"I want those kids back more than anyone else! They are my best friend's children and are like family to me and my wife." Sweeping his hand from oak to oak, Jericho added in a lower tone, "Your home may be in the trees Devis but this is my lifelong home."

Turning and reaching to gather his scattered lunch laying on his pack before taking his seat back upon the rock, Jericho added one more request. "All I'm saying is, please take a brief rest to come and eat Devis. You will be no good to anyone, especially them kids, if you fall when they need you most."

Staring at the big farmer and regaining his composure, the tracker realized the man was right. The thought of letting the children along with his group down when they needed him and his skills the most doused his internal frustration and anger. A look of acknowledgment filled his eyes where only moments ago they watched heated words flow from his mouth. The elf spoke in a normal tone directing his words to his one time verbal adversary. "The elves have a saying used to explain why my kind are soft spoken and very patient. The god Taradryll has given us two ears but only one mouth so we can hear twice as much more than we can speak. Your words were only words of help and concern while all the while mine were those of misjudged anger and frustration. I hope that I have not caused harm with my tongue and ask humbly for your pardon. I am sorry my friend."

"There is no harm done," assured Jericho. "Just take a quick break to rest and eat and then I'll help you the best I can."

The elf gave his large companion a smile followed by a nod before walking over to a forked tree and placing his pack in the middle of the split. Rummaging through the bag and pulling out an apple, Devis took a bite of the fruit then chased it down with a mouthful of some water. Stealing another gulp from the skin and glancing down at the tree's base to stare at a twig he had just stepped on, the elf tried to recognize the object lying on the forest's floor.

"What's that?", piped up Moric while pointing at something near the elf's foot.

Squatting down to get a closer look, recognition filled the tracker's eyes. "Jericho, come look at this."

Approaching his crouching companion, the big man looked over Devis' shoulder. Taking a few seconds to stare at the dirty object and the stick figuration, an awareness instantly hit him. "Well I'll be a son of an orc!", he smiled in amazement.

CHAPTER 15

For most of this day, along with a full day yesterday, Katherine and her two brothers, Jacob Jr. and Thomas, plodded up the first of several, small alps through the mountains led by their goblin captors. The ground was still wet from the drenching the land had received about two days ago causing their hike to be a treacherous one. At any moment, any one of them could slip breaking a bone or badly spraining an ankle. Two of their captors had already made a footing mistake and paid for their clumsiness with injuries; one a bad sprain and the other possibly a broken foot. The lames fell to the rear with their inflictions eventually causing them to lag behind. There was no slowing down for the misfortunate.

Trees and shrubbery still covered the slope here, and little Katherine was glad several times for that. The prisoner's hands were untied to help in their ascent, and on a couple of occasions, the child slipped only to be saved when her tiny, nine year old hands reached out grabbing a hold of one of the plant growths in her vicinity. Her brother Thomas had been grabbed during one incident before he tumbled down the slope, a quick slap to his head accompanied the rescue. The children had been captives for three days now.

Getting close to reaching the small mountain's apex, the drow called a halt to their trek and turned to speak with the pack's leader. Soon after, two others were being ordered to scout ahead. Rushing amongst the oaks and bushes, they were both lost from view as they disappeared into the forest inspecting for a safe passage.

"Rest!", shouted the commander.

The children were wrangled up and corralled together during the rest. It was easier for their guards to keep an eye on them while they were huddled in one spot. Katherine and her brothers searched for a dry place to sit, but again those were almost impossible to find on the tree-covered slope. With their small bodies wracked with tiredness and being completely dirty in their bedclothes, or in Katherine's case her night dress, and looking like homeless vagabonds, the three finally decided to take a seat on the damp ground. A goblin guarding them passed a waterskin for them to share in a drink. The wetness quenched their thirsts along with the prisoners dry mouths and as soon as all of them were done partaking in the liquid, the goblin moved off to join some of its pack already busy at a game of dice.

With no beast directly in the area and the commander speaking with the drow further up the slope, the children were able to sneak some talk amongst themselves. The closest guard sat roughly twenty feet away and all the captors knew the three had nowhere to run. If one or all even tried to escape they wouldn't get far. Katherine remembered what the drow wizard had said to her and her fear from those threatening words stuck in the forefront of her young mind as she spoke with her only living kin.

"Are you guys alright?", queried Junior concerned for his two, younger siblings.

Both affirmed with a quiet "yes."

"What are we going to do Junior?", Katherine quietly asked her older brother. Fear radiating in her voice.

"I'm not sure yet and I haven't come up with an escape plan," Junior looked around.

"Escape!", disbelievingly whispered Thomas.

"No! You saw what they did to mother and father!", interjected Katherine, her voice slightly louder than before.

A goblin stole a quick glance in their direction when it thought it had heard something. The three prisoners sat quietly hoping they hadn't drawn any unwanted attention to themselves. A moment later it was back engrossed in some kind of conversation with two others.

"Shh. You have to keep your voice down Kat or we'll be in a lot of trouble if they hear us," warned her oldest brother.

Taking a quick look around and checking to make sure the coast was clear, Junior continued where he had left off after warning his sister to lower her voice,

"I'm sorry."

Junior offered his little sister a smile. The little girl seeming to brighten her spirits a bit from her brother's facial expression.

"Don't worry guys, I'll think of something to get us out of this," swore the oldest boy.

"Really?", Kat asked a little excited at her brother's words.

"I promise and Tommy is going to help me."

Thomas looked at his brother, a spirit of confidence in his inclusion of Junior's plan. He looked up to his older brother being only four years his senior. None of the captors witnessing Junior give a big smile and hug to his two, younger siblings.

"We'll be alright," he added

≈≈

An hour and fifteen minutes had passed after the two scouts had returned to camp and the trek had begun again. The band had finally reached the apex of the first, small mountainside, and like the climb prior, the rest of the ascent had been dangerous, and several more slips had taken place. As for the two lame goblins, they were both still on the mountain's slope trying to reach it to the top. Trees and bushes still covered the elevated terrain and still no one could see what laid in front of them down this side due to their canopy. Like the ascent to the summit, the descent was just as hazardous with the ground being in the same kind of condition.

Traveling for at least the rest of the hour, the goblins stopped to set up camp. Lashing the prisoner's hands together in front of their bodies like earlier, the beasts allowed them to sit near a lit campfire. Precautions had been taken and now three blazed casting their light and warmth during the night. Junior knew they were more for the captives' benefit then theirs because all of the captors could see in the dark. Katherine was still afraid and in fear of the beasts' glowing, red eyes.

The drow wizard along with the goblin commander sat near one of the fires by themselves obviously discussing their plans for the upcoming day.

"By the end of tomorrow we should be in the valley," flatly stated the drow. "We'll set up camp there like usual and then two days later we shall arrive in Bright Star Hall; stronghold of the drow."

Having just finished the small quails that the beasts' hunters had caught earlier, the commander just responded nodding his head in an affirmation while he picked his canine teeth with a small animal's leg bone.

"Your manners goblin are unrivaled throughout Kanaan," he sternly added before stealing a glance over to where the children sat around the fire. "Did any of your group feed those three?"

"Not yet," the pack's leader replied as it tossed the marrow-empty bone into the fire. "If you are through with me then I'll feed them myself."

"Very well. We move out at dawn," advised the wizard while watching the commander rise to its feet.

"On your orders master," it added before walking away to feed the prisoners.

Wizard Zolktar watched the back of the goblin as it left to perform its duties while his thoughts focused on the commander's service to him. "The goblin would make a good leader for his own personal army one day, but first, I need to rid myself of House Zexthion's lap dog, House Wizard Zebbulas."

The campfire snapped and popped in front of him as he stared right into it looking at nothing but the dancing blaze. One would think he was watching a scried vision, but Wizard Zolktar had one thought running through his mind over and over, "Soon. Very soon."

❧

It had to be somewhere near the middle of the night as the group's climb up the mountain's slope continued. Above the tree canopy, the sky was clear with a third of the exposed moon and its joining star-filled night shining down on the slightly damp land. The brightness it cast was only a fraction more illuminating in the mountain's tree cover compared to the forest below, but it mattered very little in tonight's trek. The diminishing, perilous, terrain's darkness gave way to the radiating light breaking through the blackness.

After luckily finding the piece of torn bed clothing under the makeshift stick arrow an emergence of hope solidified the determination throughout the band of pursuers. Jericho and the elf had automatically forgot about the heated argument they breached right before its discovery, while the others shared in a brief rejoicing. None of the children knew any one of them were attempting to save and rescue the hostages, so what possessed one of them to attempt to leave some markings of a trail? The companions had discovered two more telltales during their climb up the slope. The only reasonable solution the party's members could come up with is when the half-elf had informed them about him seeing them and vice-versa at the battle with the drow wizard. The children must have some type of hope that Jhessail followed the goblin pack to avenge his fallen comrades.

A unanimous vote at the base of the small mountain now had the group pushing on through the night's darkness. A magically shining, hand-sized stone casting light allowed the human companions to see and ascend at a swifter pace. Calvin had proposed the idea to make aware every dangerous obstacle in concert with planning the party's defensive strategy if an attack should fall on them.

Edward carried the magical stone allowing his brother, Harold the ability to use his javelin and Jericho his staff to assist them in their movement. The benefit; their weapons in hand. The leader was positioned directly to Edward's left. Climbing and centered behind the two came Faith with Jericho to her right rear and the other McKinley, Harold to her left rear. Forming a triangle around the outskirts of the humans were the three demi-humans taking up their positions on the borders outside the magic light's perimeter. The three's night vision was by far their most important ability at this time. On the left flank ascended Jhessail with the stealthy, little thief on the right flank. Moric was small and talented enough to disappear into the shadows cast by the surrounding plant life. Finally, still walking point, but doing it in the tree's branches was Devis. He would make sure the companions would not find themselves walking into any traps. Besides with his bow, the elf was the party's surprise, aerial attack or defense, whichever the situation called for. All the demi-humans carried signal whistles tethered on leather straps hung around their necks.

With the time left in the day, along with the will and determination to keep going into the late hours of the night, the group's leader called for a halt when the magical light had faded out of existence. The three demi-humans converged on their companion's location.

"Are you guys alright?", queried Devis into the darkness.

"We are fine," assured the knight. "This would be a good time to rest and get some sleep especially since the rock's magic has run its course."

"Sorry guys, …" -apologized Faith- "…but I never studied for a light spell yesterday morning. I don't know if Jhessail's got anymore illumination spells left he can cast."

"I can if you guys need me to," the half-elf affirmed the woman's last statement. "Unlike humans or some other half-elves, I have inherited my father's elven ability to cast spells without the need to study my spellbook," Jhessail informed the others.

"No, that shall not be necessary. We all need a little food and water, along with a brief sleep before we continue on tomorrow," Calvin advised the others before their opinions to push on flooded the night-time darkness. The leader had to call a halt to their verbal wishes.

"Okay, let us say we push on; we are still some distance from the goblins but now we all require an adequate time to rest and anytime we have made up will be lost. Or maybe we do encounter the beasts, but are so tired and rundown that our fighting is sloppy, and our magic-users become ineffective due to their exhaustion. What use are their spells to us if they slur their words? We will be of no use and all our efforts will have been futile. What then will our dead spirits be able to accomplish in aiding Jacob's children?"

"Calvin is right," confirmed the wizard-warrior. "Let's rest for whatever the duration you determine knight, and before we depart in the morning I will pray to Guerra to bestow on us a good meal and some more water."

"That's a plan!", jumped Moric into the conversation. A little loud and a lot excited of the mere mention of food.

"Very well," agreed the party's leader. "We need to get an early start on the morrow, so let us set up watches for the remainder of this night."

"That will not be necessary. I can cast an alarm spell like I did when we met back at the clearing. It will let me know if anyone or anything approaches, and this way everyone can be fully rested when we continue our pursuit," Jhessail offered his companions.

"Good idea," complimented Calvin. "Now everyone get some rest, you all did good today."

The party had no way of knowing that their quarry was now only a day away. They had closed the gap in distance by a half of a day.

*

Hours later the two lame goblins limped into the beasts' camp. Besides the watch, they were the only two still awake. Unknown to them, the drow wizard just feigned his sleep. Like the elves, the dark elves possessed the race trait of the Reverie.

Finding and open spot amongst the slumbering bodies, the wounded misfortunates laid down to rest and within minutes their exhaustion overtook them causing both goblins to fall into a deep slumber. The last thought crossing their minds was the early hardships they would face at sunrise.

*

Earlier in the night after finding a spot to rest for the evening, the dwarf kept replaying the events of the encounters with the goblins that he had experienced throughout the last four days. Taking a drag from his cigar, Thorin addressed his large, furry companion laying on the floor of the cavern across from where he sat in the dark. The only light besides the third of the moon and the stars in the sky was from the slow-burning glow of his stogie.

"Tomorrow we're going to have to go back down into the tree line and head for our cave in the valley before going to Bright Star Hall."

Taking a puff and exhaling a small cloud of smoke into the air he continued, "It should take us about two to three days to get there, and then another to get to Fireheart's place."

The prone cave bear lay there watching Thorin with his smoking cigar in the semi-bright night while running its tongue over his massive teeth exposing an intimidating view of its canines. The animal yawning as it listened to its little friend's travel plans while Mountain's eyelids began to slowly close.

Taking another drag, Thorin watched the bear start to fade towards sleep. Exhaling the breath, the slightly perturbed dwarf asked, "What am I boring ya?" His question going unanswered.

"Sometimes bear, I feel you're an ingrate," came an ornery Thorin.

The animal never hearing the dwarf's words as his deep, rhythmic breathing filled the cavern's air.

CHAPTER 16

The wizard along with the pack's commander stood in the cover and the offered safety of the tree line gazing upon the open valley in front of them. A roaring waterfall dominated the air here with the sound of crashing water filling up a large circular pond. Spray from the rushing liquid falls cast a rainbow image in its misty aura. A wide river, roughly twelve to thirteen feet and splitting the open area in half, flowed from the pond leading out of the valley and into its surrounding mountains. On both sides of the running border, a carpet of soft, dark, green grass covered the ground dotted with bright, yellow dandelions, and a wooden bridge decorated with carvings spanned the gap of the watery obstacle.

The sun had made a daily appearance in the sky for roughly four days now heating and drying the land, and its rays sparkled off the crystal, clear pond. It also made for a safer descent down this side of the small mountain. Only one other goblin joined the two lames' fate when it was bit by a viper. The beast's arm had already swelled up twice its original size and began to blacken. The third lame kept stumbling as the snake's venom went to work in the goblin's body.

Taking a little extra time to survey the area, Wizard Zolktar and the commander searched the open canyon for anything out of the ordinary. Nothing stood out of commonplace and the coast looked clear, but still an uneasy feeling rented space in heads of the whole pack. They all knew this was the killing zone. Even Jacob's children could feel the anxiety and its tenseness coming from their captors.

Jacob Jr. had overheard two of the beasts briefly discussing the feeling of uneasiness they had about the place on the way down the slope. It seemed to him even though they had been switching back-n-forth between the common tongue and the goblin's native language that the beast had been falling prey to something in the field or overlooking the open ground. If they knew exactly what it was, Junior couldn't tell.

Turning to the pack's commander, the wizard dictated the plan for the exposed crossing. There seemed no quicker way around the valley and the captors knew they would have to tread hastily to get to the other mountain's slope.

"I will use the rest of the magical dust on all of us, excluding the three wounded. It will allow us to cross the ground within the day lowering any possible casualty rate," informed the drow. "When we reach the other side, set up camp for the night and I will teleport back to announce your future arrival to House Wizard Zebbulas."

"As you desire master," agreed the lead goblin.

"Now bring everyone together, except the prisoners, so I can use the dust."

"Not the prisoners master wizard?", puzzled the commander.

"No not the prisoners. Two of your pack each will grab an arm lifting the children off the ground enough to carry them across the field, over the bridge, and to the other side," revealed Zolktar.

"As you wish."

⇜⇝

Three pairs of red eyes watched the pack of goblins along with their three unfortunate prisoners being led across the first field by the hooded, black-robed figure from behind the cascading waterfall. The combination of the falling liquid and the mist-covered rocks covered the entrance of its cave. The goblin's looking all over, including to the sky, searching for any sign of the predator killing them off.

Upon the unmistakable recognition of the children captives, one of the cave-dwelling beasts snarled and started forward almost exposing its hiding spot until a second grabbed its upper arm halting its progress.

"Stand down Nathaniel. Now is not the time," it ordered the other.

149

"We're just going to let them go?", angrily asked the enraged cave-dweller.

"They have a wizard with them."

"So what?"

"So, we don't stand a chance is what!"

A third cavern dweller piped up, "If they're pattern continues then we should be having another pack of them beasts coming back this way soon."

"Correct, but if they have a wizard escort then we'll have to be ready to change our plan of attack," the second informed the third.

"We have to do something!", the first, enraged dweller pleaded its case.

Patting the first's shoulder, it assured the other watcher, "Oh we will, but not this time."

Before starting back into the cave, the second declared in a determined tone to the other two watchers from behind the wall of water. "Let them pass but keep me posted if anything changes. The goblins might have some stragglers for us to deal with."

Turning back to the black cave and starting down it, the cave-dweller's eyes glowed red.

⚶

"Wow! Look at the magnificent beauty of this valley," admired Moric with his mouth slightly ajar.

All of the companions seemed to be caught in awe at the splendor of the natural sight in front of them. It was hard to believe that the gods could bestow such wonderful beauty anywhere on Kanaan. Even Devis was taken aback by the view.

"This must have been like what father had told mother and I about," inserted Jhessail.

Glancing at the half-elf, Devis quickly acknowledged that Jhessail's father must have been speaking about ancient, elven lands of times past.

Returning his gaze, he joined the others as they soaked in the tranquility of this place. The elf had only recently witnessed some type of parallel line tracks reminding him of the ones he had found

150

at Jacob's. They had started at a point further back heading down the slope and now he watched the drag marks disappear into the lush, grass carpet.

Surveying the open field in front of him, and being glad that the sun set in the west behind him, the elf could make out two limping goblins dragging a third one in tow. Squinting a bit to really focus his sight, Devis estimated the distance between them and where the party stood in the tree cover.

"Hey guys, take a look there," getting the other's attention and pointing at the three lame beasts.

"Must have met with bad luck back on the mountain," guessed Jhessail.

"Hey Faith. You think one of those magic arrows will reach em?", queried Moric.

"Hold fast magic-user," interrupted the leader. "Save your magic. We will meet up with them in the morning."

"Or not," Harold stated while the companions witnessed seven other goblins approaching from in front of the three lames.

Ducking out of a normal reaction behind some plant life, no one in the party expected to witness what happened next.

Limping from a possible broken foot and assisting Delp dragging their unconscious pack member behind them, Sitar was the first of the two perspective lames to notice seven goblins approaching them. They were jogging across the field, and Sitar could at least see three of them carrying what appeared to be javelins. The others seemed to be unarmed, except for their swords bouncing at the beasts' sides. For some reason that seemed lost to it now, Sitar took heed of the torn, brown clothes they were all wearing.

"Looks like we finally have some help," reasoned the goblin glancing at Delp. "The commander must have sent them here back for us."

Glancing all around the valley and looking up towards the sky as the two hobbled along, Delp noticed the assistors getting closer and closer. "Why send others back for us now?", it asked.

"What do you mean?", puzzled Sitar.

"Delp was told this is the valley of death. They say many goblins disappear in these fields, never to be seen again, and that a monster swoops down from the sky," he informed the other lame.

"Who are they?"

"Who are they?", Delp repeated the question before looking over to Sitar, who was currently staring at the other with a puzzled look upon its face.

Before Delp could attempt to answer the other handicap's question, the small group of seven goblins stopped in front of them roughly ten feet away.

"It's about time the commander sent some help for us," stated Sitar in the goblin language.

The beast appearing to be the seven's leader tilted its head as the other's words went unrecognized.

"Oh great! A goblin who doesn't understand the goblin's tongue," alleged a frustrated Sitar. It continued but this time speaking in common. "Well since the commander finally sent you to help us, why don't you lend a hand?"

"Because your commander never sent us to help any of you," sternly stated the beast, who only seconds ago tilted its head. "In fact, we came on our own wretched creature."

Both Delp and Sitar looked over to each other before sharing their last words. "That's not brown clothes they're wearing. That's torn leather armor!", shouted Sitar.

"They're not from the pack?", baffled Delp.

Five of the seven armored goblins started towards the two lames dragging their unconscious load. Delp and Sitar cried out in horror as they dropped their lifeless companion and desperately tried to run. Both were cut down instantly and massacred while the unconscious beast lying on the ground got its throat slit.

In a matter of minutes, the small blood-bath was over and six of the seven armored goblins carried the three lifeless bodies, two beasts to a corpse. One had its arms while the other its feet. Their destination; the burn pit.

The sky had a purple hue to it as the sun started to drop over the horizon. A large shade had already consumed more than half of the valley, and the confused companions, who had just witnessed the slaughter stood in amazement. The group watched the seven goblin victors carrying away their three dead prizes until they eventually became smaller and smaller and disappeared out of sight.

"What do you think that was all about?", finally asked Faith directing her question at no one in particular.

"Maybe a gambling debt," slightly chuckled Edward. "Remember all the dice we found when we fought them that first time?"

"No, that's not it at all," offered Devis while still staring into the field. He gave his opinion basing it on his knowledge and understanding of the elves life-long enemy. Taradryll's people learned as much as possible about one of their most hated adversaries; goblinkind. "I believe we might have just found ourselves in the middle of a pack war."

Turning his attention towards the group's leader, the elf continued to offer some more advice. "We should be putting at least three on every watch tonight Calvin. For all we know now, these woods could be crawling with a whole nother problem."

The statement seemed to cause the rest of the party to begin surveying their wooded surroundings a little more closely now. No one wished to be taken by surprise from behind.

The elf added before turning his gaze back to the killing field, "We also have to come up with a plan to still get across."

At that point, all realized one obvious issue they had overlooked up until now. There was no hiding in the open once they began their crossing and it would leave them exposed to anyone or anything watching.

It was dark when the seven goblins stood over the earthen pit located at the other end of the valley not far from where the river's running waters flowed into the mountains. They watched the newly lit fire start to consume the three victim's corpses. Their eyes glowing red as they witnessed the flames start to dance in the night.

The leader of the seven, satisfied that the bodies would burn and the fire would eventually extinguish itself like it had on several prior occasions, gave the order to move out. "Let's head for home gentlemen. There shall be more to burn tomorrow, but for now we need some food and rest first."

"Yes sir," was the only answer it received as the other six beasts replied in unison.

Starting their slow jog, the seven goblins were somewhat glad a third of the moon and the stars brightened up the valley this night. Their nighttime vision assisting them in their home bound return even though all knew one realization; it would be the wee hours of the next morning before the seven would reach the cave hidden behind the waterfall.

⁂

That night after Jhessail, with Guerra's graciousness, magically whipped up another meal and drinks for the party, the companions assigned watch shifts amongst themselves. Calvin had decided that each shift would be made up of two humans set up at a right and left flank closer to the valley's field, but still being located in the cover of the tree line. These positions would allow whomever was assigned to that watch the ability to utilize the light from the night's sky to assist them in keeping an alert eye to the open ground while still guarding the flank from any attack coming from the side.

A demi-human, with his ability to see in the dark, would take up a place at the rear of the camp. This spot should protect the party from any ambushers directly behind them, and the watcher would be able to see some of both sides of the southeast and southwest of the rear flanks. The group believed these three locations guarded all access to the remaining companions sleeping.

It was also determined that Moric, Jericho, and Calvin would take the first shift. Harold, Edward, and Devis the second, with Faith, Jhessail, who had limited night-vision, and the leader, who would be taking a second watch for the night, on the last.

"Look alive people," ordered Calvin before leaving to take up his position on the beginning watch.

The goblin pack led by the drow wizard had hastened through most of the valley earlier in the day and was now setting up camp on the next mountain's base slope. All were glad they had made it across the open field without even a sign of an attack by whatever it was that had been taking goblins throughout the last month. Maybe the hazard had only stopped here in this place while it migrated to some other destination, or maybe something had killed it. Whatever the reason for the pack's smooth crossing, the superstitious beasts thanked their god for the tree cover again.

Katherine along with her two brothers sat on the ground watching the movement around the rest stop for the oncoming night. Their arms and shoulders hurt and were tired from the constant lifting and pulling on them by their captors throughout the day. Tears of pain made Katherine's eyes moist and red.

"What's the matter Kat?", Thomas asked his sister with concern when he noticed her slightly crying.

Upon hearing the question, Junior moved closer to his little sister.

"Don't worry Kat. It'll be alright," Junior tried to reassure her. "We'll get out of here."

"No we won't Junior. Who even knows we're here?", she asked while starting to cry. "Father and mother are never coming back so they can't help us! They even hurt Veronica and Rex. Nobody knows Junior. Nobody." Her words and the hopelessness of the situation causing her to more tears by the minute.

"No. No. Sis don't cry," pleaded Thomas. "Someone has to know and will come get us, right Junior?"

"That's right Thomas."

"Who?", the little girl asked while trying to fight back her tears.

"Maybe the wizard will come to rescue us," hoped Junior.

"Who, this wizard here?", Thomas asked his older brother while pointing with his chin in the drow's direction.

"No. Not that wizard," he responded with a little agitation in the tone of his voice accompanied by the thought of cupping his sibling alongside his head if his own hands weren't lashed together. "Remember the one that fought the drow at the clearing in the forest about four or five days back?"

Both siblings acknowledged his question with nods from their heads but were not sure if they completely understood.

"Do you think he's trying to follow us?", again Katherine asked another question.

"I'm not sure, but I've been leaving pieces of clothing and other signs to let him know what way they're taking us if he is.", smiled Junior finally revealing the beginning of some type of rescue plan.

The oldest brother's grin must have been contagious because soon after the little girl's face also wore one. Thomas seemed pleased with the sound of hope in Junior's plan.

"You're the best, oldest brother a sister could have!", complimented little Katherine while putting her bound wrists over her brothers head and embracing him with one of her hardest hugs. The girl added, "I love you Junior."

"I love you too," Junior responded kissing his little sister on the top of her head as she snuggled into his chest.

⚓

Hours passed and the two youngest children slept in the semi-quiet camp. They had fallen into sleep sometime before a new group of at least twenty or more goblins had come in to join the returning pack.

Sitting up in the darkness outside the fire's light with his hands lashed behind his back for the night, Jacob Jr. watched and counted the arrival of the new beasts. He wasn't fully certain but he thought he heard its leader say they were on their way to the village. No wizard was leading them so he hoped the townsfolk would kill the beast before they too grabbed more hostages.

He never saw the drow wizard, who had led the pack that had taken him, his brother and sister, leave. Junior seemed to be lost in his own thoughts.

Looking into the darkness of the leafy, tree branches, a tear ran from his eye as he said a silent prayer to the heavens begging aid from any god who would hear him and listen.

"To whichever god answers my plea for help. I will forfeit my life in exchange for your aid in freeing Thomas and Kat. This I swear to you."

Trying to remain strong for the sake of his siblings, another tear rolled down his dirty cheek. The teenage boy hoping that his prayer would not go unanswered.

CHAPTER 17

Following the rushing river on his left upstream, the dwarf mounted on his bear emerged from the forest and into the shadowy part of the valley. Only the field half past the watery boundary and the eastern slope of the mountains on his immediate right were bathed in the morning's rays. The rocky landmass housing the dwarven stronghold, Bright Star Hall, blocked out this entire half of the valley's field from the rising orb's sunlight. Its shaded tree cover only leading halfway up the massive alp. The valley's bottleneck opened to a large expanse of lush, dark green grass with a wide river separating his position from that of the brightened clearing. Half a day ahead was a crystal, clear pond being fed by a large, running waterfall. The cave behind the wall of water was Thorin's destination. Smoke rose from a crater thirty feet in front of the dwarf and his mount.

The bear let out a deep, throaty moan as its head was tilted back and the animal took short sniffs. Something didn't smell right to the large mammal.

"What's the matter bear? Pick up a whiff of those pesky goblins?", asked Thorin looking around for more of the pests. "I don't see anything, but that smoking hole in the ground ahead," added the dwarf as he and Mountain headed for the crater.

As the bear lumbered towards the cavity, the gritty dwarf darted his eyes to the tree line in search for anything amiss. He knew the running waters on his left protected their flank and they would have no problem seeing any attack coming across the clearing or from the giant plants on their right before it actually got to him and the bear unless it was missile fire or magic.

Upon reaching the medium-sized crater, the dwarf jumped down from his mount to check out the oval-shaped void. Both his dwarven maul and his double-bladed axe formed an "X" on his back thanks to a special type of sheath that was made to hold the two weapons. A dagger dressed Thorin's hip, and a bandolier holding his last two cigars crossed over his breastplate.

Slowly and carefully approaching the hole's edge, the gritty warrior looked down inside. At the bottom of the cavity smoke rose from three, freshly burnt goblin corpses laying on the remains of other bones. The dwarf quickly withdrew his gaze from the stink rising into the air.

"Well what in the name of the Gods of Kanaan do we have here?!", he queried grimacing from the smell as he took a quick look towards the trees. "I ain't never come across no burial or pyre pit, or whatever the hell it is, in all my life that stunk as bad as this one!", Thorin stated while meeting the bear's gaze. "Besides, since when on Kanaan did goblins start burning their dead?"

Starting towards the animal to mount up again, the dwarf issued the next set of directions, "Stay close to the water bear keeping a distance from them there trees, and head for the cave."

Resting its head on its front paws, the bear tilted forward giving the dwarf access to mount. Pulling himself up, Thorin took his position while grabbing for the hanging crossbow and bolt that hung from a leather harness allowing him to tether the weapon along with its ammo to the custom made saddle.

Rising to its feet and beginning to lumber its way in the direction of the cave, the bear gave a deep, throaty moan followed by a couple of huffs. It was obvious to anyone who knew anything about the omnivores that Mountain was already slightly agitated.

"Yup. You're right my old friend," -the dwarf agreed while loading the missile-fire weapon- "I'm going to light me a new cigar when I'm done here with this thing. I definitely think Fireheart has gone and got himself into some type of trouble, and by the looks of things, it's got those pests written all over it!"

The morning sun painted the sky pink as it rose in the east up from behind the large alps. The open area closest to where the companions had camped for the night bathed in its light and warmth causing the lush, dark, green grass to seem as if it stretched up trying to soak in as much of the orb's rays as it possibly could.

Calvin had to keep to his hiding spot so the brightness of his armor wouldn't radiate sunlight off of it like a flashing beacon saying, "Here we are!" The knight, who had been up more than anyone this past night taking the first and third watch, felt free from any grip tiredness might have on him. He had spent the last shift formulating a plan to cross the open area undetected, and the leader knew the party would be needing their available magic-users to pull this off.

Calvin understood Faith's limited ability with magic would force everyone to rely on Jhessail's talent with the arts, but the knight had also realized over a ten day ago that her spirit and heart were hard to rival. No matter what, the woman was part of this team. The one most important difference that he knew of between Faith and Jhessail was her need to study spells for casting while the half-elf could just summon what he needed at that particular time. Calvin made the decision that the woman's spells would dictate the half-elf's selections.

He had formulated a plan and was going to share it with the party over a prompt breakfast within the upcoming hour, but for now he just patiently waited for the young woman to finish her morning studies. She would let him know when she was ready.

Once again the half-elf prayed asking his god for the offering of food, and once again Guerra bestowed him the magical sustenance. Jhessail knew in his heart that his god was not happy with how his worshipers were killed, and the deity wished to see the wizard-warrior dish out vengeance.

As the companions came together and swiftly tore into their breakfast, Calvin shared his plan with the rest of the group.

"We as a whole have some idea of what each one of us is capable of at this time. It is of no surprise that we are young, and with youth comes the lack of experience. Our magic-user is the same as you and I," -spoke their leader while sweeping his right hand from one to the

160

other and then finishing by using a thumb to point at himself- "The best, and safest way to win a confrontation is to avoid the encounter if possible. Jhessail, can you make the party invisible?"

"I can make everyone invisible by casting a spell on an object, but that object will need to be carried and we will be limited to stay within the affected area of the spell's range," the half-elf explained.

"How big is the area you speak of?", queried Calvin.

"Roughly ten paces side-by-side by ten paces front-to-back, but more in a spherical shape though," informed Jhessail after taking a moment to think about his answer.

"What about casting two or three of those on these?", questioned the knight while opening his left fist and revealing three stones.

Shaking his head briefly, Jhessail shared his opinion, "Yes, I think it will work."

After the half-elf explained to the rest of the group exactly how the spell will work and how long its duration would last, Jhessail cast two spheres of invisibility on only two of the rocks. He made everyone clear that to work they would have to stay within the spell's affected area, and if anyone of them attacked then that person would instantly lose the benefits of the magic.

"Even while still in the area?", asked Edward.

"Yes."

Jhessail went on to notify the party that they will not be able to see each other when inside the sphere so everyone needs to stick close to the bearers of the enchanted stones.

"How exactly will we know where to step, or if we're still inside the,… what did you call it?", Moric shook his head attempting to remember the spell's name along with the magic's effects and its limitations that had been explained.

"The spell will only effect you not being seen. It will however; still allow others to hear any noise, or see any boot prints, or even the imprints made while stepping on the field's grass," revealed the half-elf.

"That's it. Does everyone have it or is there anything else?", Jhessail turned to ask.

The rest of the companions shook their heads.

Before leaving the trees, the wizard-warrior cast an invisibility spell on himself. It functioned separately from the rocks and only he was affected by the spell's magic.

The companions were now crossing the first half of the open field leading to the waterfall and its pond. None of them had seen any goblins thus far, and everyone just wanted to cross the valley with no trouble. Jacob's children at the forefront of their minds.

～❧～

Both separate packs of goblins split from each other as they departed from the camp they had shared last night. The smaller of the two groups heading up the slope to one of the entrances leading to Bright Star Hall. The larger, continued with the village of Oakhurst its destination. The bigger of the two packs crossing the valley's shaded field, their eyes darting in all directions on the lookout for whatever was killing their kind during the open area's crosses.

～❧～

It was almost the middle of the day as the cave-dwelling goblins watched from behind the wall of water the large, advancing pack headed towards the bridge connecting both fields separated by the pond and its existing river.

"How many did you count Nathaniel?", inquired the leader of the dwellers.

"Roughly thirty sir."

"Hmm, that big," sounding more sternly and determined as it formulated a plan for a quick strike. "That's the biggest raiding party we've seen so far heading to the village."

"What do you want to do sir?", another asked from the cover of the cascading waterfall.

Before the leader could respond with the question's answer, the sudden appearance of seven others from out of thin air took not only the cave-dweller's, but the large, goblin pack by surprise. Eight of the beasts fell instantly.

 ◈

The invisible companions watched the thirty approaching goblins while they crossed the river's bridge.

"The spells are about to run their courses Calvin. Do you want me to cast two new ones that will carry us passed this obstacle ahead?", whispered the wizard-warrior from somewhere off to the knight's left.

Before the group's leader could answer, Jericho quickly spoke in a low tone, "We can't let them get to the village. Imagine all the chaos and death they will cause."

The knight knowing the art of surprise favored the party, although the numbers didn't, took a quick census of everyone's thoughts on the matter. The invisible companions agreed to make a stand here and now.

The first eight goblins would never see the melee attacks coming that did them in. They were only startled for a brief moment when half a dozen bladed weapons appeared in mid-air before the blackness of death overtook them. The remaining pack jumped back in fear when the seven blinked into existence. The half-elf remained still under the guise from his separate invisibility spell that allotted him one more unseen attack.

Giving a battle cry while advancing, Calvin offered the first startled beast a shield punch knocking it to the ground. The knight followed that with a downward slash opening the next pack member from face to abdomen. The beast appearing to almost be cleaved in half.

Spinning from the fallen goblin he just disposed of, Devis' blade caught the next unsuspecting beast across its throat. Grabbing at its neck with both its hands, the beast fell to its knees. Rivers of blood flowing out from behind its fingers.

Jhessail became visible after the half-elf's sword thrust skewed a beast leaving it stuck on the end of his weapon. Pulling the blade out of the goblin's chest cavity while dislodging it with a kick, the wizard-warrior took the battle to the next available adversary.

Faith's dagger stuck out of the falling pack member's brow while she glanced from side-to-side making sure there was enough room between the scattered party members and herself. Instantly the sound of a crack from her bullwhip entered the noisy chaos. She had decided to hold onto her spells until needed.

Using his size and strength, Jericho used both hands swinging his staff like he was cutting down a tree. The unfortunate goblin catching the strike alongside its face was launched airborne several feet into the air. The beast's face bones shattered upon impact and it landed in the grass unconscious leaking greenish, black blood.

The gnome ran forward armed with both daggers, and before the startled creature knew it, Moric was on it slashing it with both blades. A cry of pain-fulled surprise escaped its mouth when the party's thief sliced the beast's femoral artery with one blade and followed the strike with a thrust that hit its mark when it met the goblin's genitals. "That must have hurt!", mockingly yelled the gnome.

Letting his javelin loose at point blank range and witnessing it go clear through the startled goblin's body, Harold quickly pulled the slipknot loosening his swinging weapon at his hip. The young farmer looked menacing with the studded mace in hand. His former adversaries body hanging limp from the javelin sticking up from the ground.

Attempting to close the small distance between him and the goblin, Edward's footing slipped and the McKinley brother stumbled forward planting the palm of his open hand on the ground. Promptly realizing its advantage, the club-wielding beast he was going after closed the gap bringing its bone weapon down scoring a hit on the unlucky one's head. The blow leaving Edward laying in the grass with no signs of consciousness.

❧

The cave-dwelling goblins witnessing the surprise attack from behind the waterfall, took several moments before actually comprehending what was happening. Realizing the goblin pack in the field outnumbered the brave adventurers, the cave-dweller's leader shouted an order to the other eight while running out of the hidden entrance behind the wall of water, "Aid the party against the beasts!"

A roar different from the gallons of water dropping over the falls reverberated through the valley as nine goblins erupted into the field running towards the battle.

෴

Standing over the unconscious, human body, the goblin raised its bone club over its head preparing to bring down its skull-crushing blow. Suddenly the beast's body seemed to twitch forward followed by its eyes beginning to roll in its head and blood dribbling out from its open mouth. Slowly lowering the blunt weapon while slightly rocking forward and backward on its heels, the goblin fell over the prone body towards the river's bank. A crossbow bolt sticking out of its back. The focused beast never seeing the armored dwarf with the smoking cigar protruding from his mouth fire the weapon while running towards the fight.

෴

It only took the startled goblin a dozen seconds to recover from its initial shock of surprise before raising its sword and attacking the knight. Coming with a hard swing from the beast's right side, Calvin was able to block the strike with his shield. The force of the blow vibrating up the cavalier's arm.

The initial goblin he knocked with a shield punch still sat on the grass shaking the stars from its eyes.

The elf in his blood lust for the beast's body fluid was confronted by two at a time. The first goblin's sword strike was an overhead-downward swing causing Devis' sword to ring as it deflected the blow away to his right. The block left the attacker wide open, but before the elf could capitalize on the defenseless goblin, the second lunged at him thrusting its bladed weapon. Moving with the fluidness of a dancer, the elf rolled off the first goblin's back like water from a duck.

Jhessail quickly stepped to his left just side-stepping the spear thrust from his first of two attackers when the second goblin, thinking it saw an opening, swung its sword at the chest level of the half-elf. Nimbly, the wizard-warrior rolled under the weapon's strike coming out of the move into a fighting stance as he prepared to retaliate.

Three of the beasts were held at bay by the movement and cracking of Faith's whip. The goblins stalked in a circle looking and waiting for an opening.

Out of all the companions, Moric was the luckiest right now only being confronted by one adversary. Both combatants walked in a circular pattern while the goblin feigned an attack. Finally not locating a clear opening, the beast pressed forward swinging its bone club. The gnome dodged the attack watching and biding his time for the right moment.

Two of the beasts rushed Jericho at the same time with their swords raised high, but the big companion stood at the ready. One of the goblins closed first and found itself extremely over-powered when Jericho side-stepped its strike while getting a part of its upper arm with his staff. Using its momentum, Jericho guided its body into the way of the other oncoming beast foiling the second goblin's attempt at an attack.

Harold had his hands full with the two on him. Swinging his mace across his body, Harold was able to block the first one's sword strike. The second beast almost scored a direct hit with its sword, but twisting his upper body sideways, the young farmer was lucky to get only nicked from the thrust. Small drips of blood beginning to flow from the cut on his right forearm.

Swinging across his body from left to right leading with his right elbow, Calvin's sword was blocked by the snarling goblin's blade. "Do not fool yourself beast! You are no match for me!", cried the knight. His peripheral vision catching the other starting to rise from its seat on the ground.

Spinning to take up the position behind one of his foes, Devis delivered a right elbow to the back of the beast's head following through with a backward swing from his sword. The blade bit deep into the forward falling goblin spraying its blood into the air and slightly onto the elf's face. "One down. One to go," he proclaimed to its partner.

Jhessail noticed Harold in trouble from the two that had attacked the farmer. Knowing the boy had very little experience in melee, the half-elf decided to even out the playing field for the young man. Pointing his empty hand while uttering the proper incantation, three, golden arrows soared across the field finding their mark. The goblin, that Harold was able to block its attack earlier, flew sideways from the three direct hits. Its corpse smoldering as it lay dead on the ground.

Harold flinched back in surprise when one of the foes he had been in melee with was lifted from its feet and flew sideways through the air. Making a speedy recovery, the McKinley swung his studded mace at the second goblin, but the beast was ready for the strike blocking it with its sword. At least now, for the young man's sake, it was a one-on-one fight.

The gnome attempted a one-two combination following his backhanded slash with a downward strike from his second knife. Unfortunately for Moric, the beast was able to back pedal away from his attempts. The party's self-proclaimed locksmith's foe stood ready to launch its counter attack.

The big man feigned a right swing with his staff and with both his hands roughly a foot apart at the center of the wooden weapon, Jericho was able to surprise one of the goblins with a left strike to its head. The biggest farmer simultaneously pushed his left hand forward while pulling his right hand into himself extending the staff for the strike. The beast's knees buckled and it came crashing to the ground. The hit causing it to slumber instantly.

The second adversary realized it was now alone against the farmer and slowly started to back away glancing one way and then the other seeking aid from another of its pack. Obviously it was intimidated by Jericho's massive size.

Faith, still surrounded by the three stalking beasts outside her swinging whip's perimeter, swiftly looked over her left shoulder when she heard the loud, wet, bone-crushing smack from behind her. Thinking it was one of the creeping goblins making a move towards her, the woman was surprised to see an armored dwarf cave the beast's right side of its head in with a blow from his maul.

Facing back to her other two adversaries, her whip barricade started to falter, and slow down. Faith's eyes grew to the size of gold coins as she slowly stepped back ever so gingerly. Fear had limited her movement. The young mage accidentally backing up into Thorin's open arms.

The two beasts watched the cracking of the whip start to die out, as the woman started backing away. They had somehow scared her, and the goblin's were ready to charge, and tear Faith limb from limb.

Looking at the ground before charging the woman, one of the goblins wondered why a large shadow covered it and the grassy carpet around it. Where there was sun casting all around the beast only moments ago, something now was eclipsing the light. The goblin began its slow turn to see what the solid obstacle was. Its eyes widened and a cry of pure fear left its mouth as behind it, standing roughly twelve feet tall towering over the petrified beast, stood a massive, cave bear.

✑

Thorin freed his maul from the special dwarven sheath on his back holding both the large hammer and his double-bladed axe. The dwarf checked on the unconscious lad first, then headed straight to assist the woman wielding the whip being circled by three goblins.

One of the beasts, the one behind her, never saw the dwarf approaching. Thorin swung the two-handed hammer catching the unsuspecting victim square on the side of its head. The loud, wet, bone-crushing smack lifting the beast off its feet before it crashed to the ground.

The dwarf watched the bear raise up on its hind legs, standing over one of the two goblins preparing to attack the woman whose cracking whip defense began to falter as she backed away right into Thorin's open arms. Surprised by the dwarf's touch, Faith's head spun in his direction.

"It's alright lass," Thorin assured the startled woman. "He's with me."

~~◈~~

"By the gods!", shouted one of the cave-dwelling goblins running to the aid of the outnumbered party. They had watched the bear run across the field from behind the presently engaged pack in hand-to-hand combat. All of them had not seen the dwarf dismount the animal before it staged its own ambush by circling around to the rear of the fighting goblins.

"Fifty more strides men!", informed the leader of the onrushing dwellers. "There looks to be another entering the battle so be ready!", it added.

~~◈~~

Staring up at the large animal standing in front of it, the goblin tried to break away from it. As the beast turned to run, the cave bear roared while swinging a massive, clawed paw striking its prey straight in the face. The animal launching the goblin ten feet to the bear's left. The prey's neck clearly broken as it hung half torn from its body. Roaring into the air for a second time, there was no doubting who owned the field of battle now.

~~◈~~

All the combatants took a step back from each other and turned their attention to the huge animal now commanding their focus. The goblins, now almost outnumbered and deathly afraid of the bear, instantly broke into a chaotic run for their lives throughout the companions.

Not knowing the bear was actually an ally, Calvin shouted his next order, "Take as many goblins down as we can then prepare to defend against the bear!"

Seeing his opportunity to strike, Moric rushed at the goblin he fought when it turned to see where the roar came from. Turning to face the gnome before it broke into a chaotic panic, the beast took a dagger thrust into its left eye while the gnome's other attack landed under the right part of its jaw. Moric jamming the second blade up as hard as he could. The little thief's adversary fell to the ground twitching.

This time the strike from Harold's studded mace landed against the panic-stricken goblin's back knocking it to the ground. Without a moments hesitation, the young man pummeled the beast into oblivion. Harold ran to check on his fallen brother when the beast stopped moving.

The last of the three goblins that Faith had held at bay with her whip, turned to run before the bear dropped down onto all four paws. Watching as the animal started after the beast, Faith launched an attack at the goblin striking out with her whip. The leather weapon wrapping itself around the fleeing beast's ankles and causing it to fall to the ground. Within seconds it screamed as the bear fell on it with open jaws. Faith pulled back her untangled weapon.

"Come on lass!", excitedly cried the dwarf never losing the smoking cigar between his lips. Pulling Faith by her arm he added, "Your friends don't know my bear's one of the good guys."

The two goblins, who had just witnessed the half-elf's roll followed by the magical attack aimed at aiding his companion, made a sound decision to withhold their attacks on Jhessail and run after witnessing the arrival of the cave bear. Almost in unison, the two began to flee towards the nine cave-dwelling goblins quickly approaching. They would soon find out that that run would be their last.

Devis took advantage of the temporary lax from the beast that was left against him. With no love lost between the two races, the elf pressed his attack reciting an inaudible phrase. Devis' sword swings and attacks came so fast that the goblin blocking as many as it could wasn't able to keep up with the blur they made. It took several slashes across its arms and face until finally a clean hit separated the beast's head and its body. The elf hearing Calvin's shout looked to the bear mauling another goblin.

The intimidated beast backing away from Jericho only needed to hear the roar before turning to run as fast as it could. Recognizing two of its pack members fleeing towards nine more goblins dressed in torn, brown leather, it ran in the same direction.

Coming down with a sword swing of his own, Calvin shoved the blocking sword back into the goblin's forehead. The knight's sword following the futile attempt of a defense as it bit into flesh and bone driving the dead beast down to the ground.

Turning to locate the one that was starting to rise after it got dropped by his shield punch, Calvin only saw the back of the fleeing creature. The knight turned all of his attention back towards the newly commanding presence on this field of battle now; the bear.

⁓◦⌒

Looking up from his last goblin kill and seeing the members from the adventuring party ready their weapons, Mountain felt threatened. Standing on his hind legs and reaching an intimidating twelve feet tall, the bear once again filled the valley with a roar of defiance. The animal informing the others of its readiness to fight.

"Now hold on a second lads! Before you all go getting yourselves into trouble by biting off more than a dragon can swallow this here is my bear!", informed Thorin pointing at his companion. "Lower your weapons now," he added from around his smoking cigar.

"He's telling you the truth!", pleaded Faith. "Both the dwarf and the bear came to my aid."

Looking between the two she offered, "Thanks."

The dwarf gave a quick nod while the bear, still towering over everyone, glanced at the woman giving a short, deep, throaty moan followed by four puffs from the side of its intimidating muzzle.

"I'm telling you, lower em lads," seriously advised Thorin.

"Stand down!", Calvin ordered lowering his sword. The rest following his lead.

Taking a moment and making sure the threat had passed, the bear dropped down on all fours. The dwarf softly pat the animal near its ear before removing the cigar stub from his mouth. Faith's shorter rescuer introduced the two.

"The name's Thorin. Thorin Hammerstone, and this big fella's my bear, Mountain."

"Wow! That's a big bear mister!", loudly came the gnome.

Directing everyone's attention to the newcomers with a point from his chin, the dwarf queried, "Friends of yours?"

The party looked over in time to watch nine, leather-armored goblins slaughter the beasts, who took off running after the bear's arrival.

"Calvin, over here!", yelled Harold kneeling at his fallen brother's side. "Eddie's bleeding and is out cold! He needs aid!"

CHAPTER 18

Harold kneeled over his prone brother lying on his stomach face down on the grass. Blood ran down the sides of Edward's head leaving his long, wavy hair wet and matted. The hurt McKinley brother's eyes were closed and his breathing was slow and deep. If not for the flowing blood caused by the gruesome dent in the back of his skull, one would think Edward slept peacefully instead of slumbering from a mace blow knocking him unconscious. Both of the brothers were fortunate that Thorin had intervened probably saving Edward's life before the goblin, laying dead only inches away, could have dealt the prostrate companion a final death blow.

"Calvin over here!", yelled Harold. "Eddie's bleeding and is out cold! He needs aid!"

Calvin swiftly stole a glance over to his farming companion near his fallen brother before turning back to the nine approaching goblins that had seized his attention. The knight knowing both issues required his directness.

The rest of the group stood weapons in hand and at the ready waiting for the start to the imminent confrontation approaching them. Their chests moving in and out with every inhale and exhale as they tried catching their breaths. Weapons ready to clash again in combat.

"Know that you are not leaving this field of battle today!", swore the elf still in his lust for goblin blood and waiting on the knight's orders to continue the beasts' demise.

173

"Stand down soldiers!", ordered the leader of the cave-dwelling goblins. "Check on your wounded. We shall not attack you," it added reassuringly while the other eight beasts lowered their weapons.

Cautiously, the party's leader glanced over to Jhessail standing at the ready. "Go check him out and ask your god to aid him," he wearily stated full of a questioning speculation if the half-elf was not only a wizard-warrior but also a cleric. The companion fell back and quickly moved to Edward's side.

"We mean your party no harm," the goblin's leader offered the dwellers' positions.

"Then what are you doing here?", queried the cautious knight.

The companions stood on guard waiting for an attack as their eyes darted across the field searching for anyone or anything attempting to try and sneak up on their position. A feeling of unrest took hold of their bodies as a fear of being caught in the middle of a pack war gripped them. The party scanning the area for more armored goblins.

"Killing as many as those wretched beasts as we can, and trying to slow their siege on the village," replied the leader of the nine.

"Do not be fooled by their trickery Calvin!", warned Devis. "They are just trying to save their lives and be allowed to leave so they can warn others!", the concerned elf added his angry proclamation. "The others lay in wait somewhere."

"That's not true!", defended a slightly larger goblin holding the shaft of a spear. Its tip driven into the ground.

"Stand down Nathaniel," ordered its leader.

The knight wore a puzzled look on his face. To him something was not right, nor was any of it expected. Calvin knew something was definitely different.

"The numbers do not favor your pack so you'll say anything to avoid death now. Anything in order to leave so you can return with more goblins and try to kill us!", the enraged elf firing out statements of accusations.

"You are wrong this time elf," responded the goblin leader. "We are the only ones, and we come to you in peace as friends not as enemies."

"Goblins will never be friends of mine, nor my people!", shouted Devis. The elf was through with talk and began forward, his intentions clear; death needed to be dealt.

⁓❧

During the face off between the nine and the companions, Calvin was perplexed with several characteristics that held a questioning doubt at the forefront of his mind. Something was definitely different about these goblins, but what? Maybe the previous skirmish kept the obvious solution covered, but whatever was behind the reason for his uncertainty seemed to elude him. The group's leader desperately needed to find the answer to his puzzled deliberation.

Pulling up all the memories in his mind's eye from the time the nine goblins entered the field of battle up until now, Calvin sorted through them seeking the concrete answer to his unresolved feelings. He found himself questioning their actions. "Why have they shown aggression to the other goblins they had slaughtered but had not displayed any combative acts towards them? Why have they not shown any type of racial hatred towards their longtime enemy, the elf, like others had in past encounters?" The differences seemed to constantly assault his thinking as he sought an explanation.

"These goblins communicated and appeared to act in a more military-styled fashion than any others previously had, and they used names uncommon to the goblin race," -he thought- "How come the nine...", but the question trailed off as a realization finally exploded in Calvin's mind. His mental eye revealing the one obvious clue he needed to finally place the missing piece into the puzzle making it whole. Glancing in the direction of the nine wearing torn, brown, leather armor, the knight reached for and grabbed the elf's shoulder as Devis started forward towards the beast.

"No Devis! Stand down!"

⁓❧

Watching the elf start forward, all nine goblins took a step back, with the slightly larger one pulling its spear point from the ground.

It prepared to defend itself. The beast's leader barking out its last command, "Stand down Nathaniel!"

∽⌒∾

Kneeling down and joining Harold at his unconscious and bleeding brother's side, Jhessail lay his sword in the grass while starting to inspect Edward's head wound. The back of the young man's skull was crushed inward causing blood to flow out of two grotesque lacerations. The McKinley's respiration slow and deep.

"Is he going to be alright?", panicked Harold.

"I need to try and heal him now if he's going to have a chance," calmly informed Jhessail laying his hands on both sides of Edward's skull just behind the young man's ears. The half-elf lowered his head and closed his eyes. Words of prayer to his god left his lips carrying over the prone body and into the valley's air.

Harold hopefully looked on.

Jhessail's hands started to take on a dim, blue aura that built and built in both brightness and size until a brilliant azure light radiated the air around Edward's unconscious form. Blood that only moments ago had flowed out from under the half-elf's fingers stopped and the two cuts began to slowly close magically healing the wounds. The McKinley brother's skull, which only minutes ago had been broken and dented inward, repaired itself to a wholeness.

As the healing started to come to an end, the blue aura started to fade out of existence until finally blinking out a minute later. Removing his laid hands from Edward, both Jhessail and Harold watched the young man's head roll to one side as he opened his eyes.

"What happened?", asked the groggy McKinley.

"Just rest for a couple of minutes my young friend," directed the half-elf touching Edward's shoulder.

"Eddie! You're back!", relieved Harold. "Thank the gods!"

"No Harold. Thank Guerra," Jhessail informed the happy brother while rising to his feet with his sword in hand. "Have him rest for a couple of minutes before he gets up."

Jhessail's attention quickly stolen away from the moment of relief upon hearing Calvin's order to Devis.

Turning on the knight and staring with fire raging in his eyes, Devis growled the statement followed by his question through gritted teeth. "Let me go Calvin! Why do you defend these beasts?"

"Because, they are not what they appear to be," answered the group's leader. "Look closely at their torn armor."

Glancing at the nine goblins in front of him and staring at their torn, protective clothing, the elf missed the obvious sign due to rips and tears or just plain dirt and grit. "What Calvin?"

"Look closely. They wear the symbol of the oak tree. These beasts are not beasts at all, instead they are the nine missing patrolmen wearing the guises of goblins."

Upon closer inspection, the companions realized the truth in their leader's words.

A smile seemed to crease all the missing, nine patrol's faces at the same time as Calvin recognized them for who they really were. The companions still somewhat caught in awe over the surprising revelation watched the leader approach Calvin.

"Well done," complimented the commander of the soldiers. "We didn't think anyone would ever figure out our mystery."

Sticking out his goblin disguised hand to the knight, the patrol's leader offered his name and rank. "Sergeant Douglas Piner, sir. It is both my pleasure and gratitude to meet you," shaking the hand of the party's leader.

"Sir Calvin Gaston. Knight of Tierra Natal."

"I am sure glad you recognized us or we were going to have a battle on our hands that neither my men nor I really wanted."

"My companions and I found three of your soldiers back in the forest," Calvin revealed before sympathetically adding, "I am sorry."

"As am I. Those were really good men and it's a shame their lives seemed a waste at the end, but they died defending those they took oaths to protect," mournfully reflected Piner. "Those men were not just soldiers, but our brothers in arms."

"What happened?", concerned Faith.

"We were investigating a disturbance in that area when a large pack of goblins led by a drow wizard and drow priestess ambushed us," -narrated the sergeant- "They happened to kill three of my men in the fight, but the wizard found it more amusing to morph us into those disgusting beasts and be shunned by those we have sworn to protect."

"What are all you doing here?", queried Faith.

"Well since we couldn't return to the village or my men and I would've taken a chance on being killed, the nine of us decided to kill as many of these creatures as we could before making their way into Oakhurst. Unfortunately, it doesn't appear to be making too much of a difference," the sergeant remarked. "The valley seemed like a good place to hide out and stage these attacks."

"And where exactly have you and your men been hiding, sergeant?", the question inserted into the conversation by Thorin.

"See that waterfall over there?", pointed the patrol's leader. "Well behind it is..."

The commander's words trailed out of existence when the dwarf removed the smoldering, cigar stub from his mouth and finished off the sentence for him. "My cave?"

The disguised, goblin sergeant blinked his eyes in astonishment. "Uh, yes dwarf. A cave."

Darkness had just closed its grip on the valley as the companions accompanied by the nine, disguised soldiers reached the roaring waterfall. The two groups had made the decision to take the goblin corpses to the fire pit at the other end of the fielded canyon and burn them. The later half of the sunny day passed and now the group decided to follow Thorin to the cave so the dwarf could retrieve some things. What exactly it was only Thorin knew.

A plan was formulated on the way to and at the pyre site. The companions, which also included the dwarf and his bear now, would stay the night in the shelter of the cave and the vicinity of the fall before crossing the remaining field to begin their climb into the mountains on the morrow. Thorin was going to be their guide on the slopes and their rocky alps. They had also decided that the patrol would go with them but the bear would stay to watch over the valley. The animal wouldn't let anyone or anything through that didn't belong there.

Tonight however, the design called for the bear to patrol the valley along with the field's tree line. The village's disguised soldiers would set up a cold camp outside the cave's entrance while the companions would get a sheltered rest this night. A repose, that after almost ten days since the companions had entered the forest, they all could desperately use.

The group, led by the owner of the cave, disappeared behind the falling water rushing to fill up the crystal, clear pond at its base. The dwarf had warned the others of the hazards caused by the mist-sprayed, slippery rocks covered by the cascading liquid. Before entering the cavern, Thorin pulled his dagger with the blue sapphire on its pommel and held it up uttering the command word that would free its magical aid. A bluish glow lit the black void of the cave's channel.

The stone hallway was roughly seven feet high and almost five to six feet wide. Large enough to allow the bear easy access through it. The passage's walls and ceiling were more arch-like and very rounded and smooth. The tunnel gave the impression of being magically created, instead of one of Kanaan's natural creations, but some of the party knew the stone's smoothness was the handiwork of the dwarves. Most of them automatically assumed in their minds that Thorin had a hand directly in its appearance.

With the benefit of a light source, the companions walked down the passage nearly thirty feet. The winding path led to a lone room in the back of the cave, and the sound of the loud, continuous roar caused by the crashing of gallons upon gallons of water diminished. Eventually the reverberation would die out as the nine companions were now at the end of the tunnel. Before them stood the opening to a large, rocky chamber.

The natural cavern was relatively good size with a high ceiling to the room. Jericho guessed at least sixteen feet, but no matter the actual height, he knew the bear would be able to stand up and still have a little space above its head to spare. Against the far side of the cave was a small, straw-bedded platform. Obviously, Thorin's stone-made sleeping area. Two open, wooden crates lined a portion of a wall on the left and a small campfire pit sat off more to the right rear of the natural shelter with a pile of wood six feet from it. The rocky chamber definitely big enough for all of them to rest.

"By the gods," came Thorin breaking the silence of the quietly amazed occupants entering the room. "These guys ate all my rations!" Suddenly his eyes opening a little larger as the dwarf rushed to the back of the cave. "My cigars better still be there or they're gonna have a problem bigger than those guised looks of theirs!", the dwarf announced.

The other companions just watching him in his anxious haste.

Reaching one of the walls near his straw-covered, stony bed, Thorin used his hand to search for something on its surface. Quickly locating the hand-sized pressure plate more from habit than from finding its whereabouts, the dwarf applied the right amount of force pushing the hidden, square segment inward. He knew if the pressure used was either too much or too little then he would set off the concealed, cache's trap. Smoothly it depressed causing a two foot wide by one foot tall section of stone to slide open off to his left about shoulder height. A small burst of air jettison a cloud of dust as the hidden enclosure was revealed.

Inside the secret cubbyhole was stored two leather pouches each appearing full with girth and a twelve inch by six inch metal container covered in black leather with gold inlaying. Two small gold latches secured the artistic box.

Removing the leather covered container from the cache and placing it on the solid mineral deposit furniture, the dwarf unlatched the fasteners keeping the box sealed. Opening the top and gazing at its undisturbed contents, a smile dressed Thorin's mouth hidden under his long, red beard and mustache. His stubby fingers selected one of the twenty cigars it housed bringing it up to eye level.

"Now that's a work of art."

The others just stood baffled as they gazed at the dwarf.

Turning back to the eight party members, Thorin asked, "What are you all standing around for? Get a fire started or do I have to do that myself too?"

Blinking while trying to comprehend what exactly just happened, the group of eight started in different directions. The McKinley's were the first to the small, wood pile.

&

Shadows danced on the rocky walls of the cavern emitted from the light thrown off by the flickering of the fire's flames. Its smoke seemed to disappear as it rose to the cave's ceiling instead of hanging and filling up the room's air. The chamber gave everyone a sense of security from being in the enclosed area.

Weapons, gear, and their owners were strewn about the place as they consumed another meal provided by the wizard-warrior's god. All the adventurers, who had embarked on this mission back in the village, were more than thankful again for the magical sustenance since only trail mix remained in the group's packs. Together the nine companions shared any and all knowledge they had about the goblin and the drow's presence. The patrol's leader was present to share in the debriefing.

"What we have found out so far within the last month, give or take, is that the goblins with their drow leaders have been using the dwarven stronghold in the mountain there as their base of operations," informed Sergeant Piner.

"Well that goes and explains why Stonechin hasn't received any shipments from Fireheart," reasoned Thorin. The rest of the party gazing in his direction lost in his audible self-revelation. "I'm sorry sergeant. Continue," he added once he realized all eyes were stuck on him. Their owners clueless to his words.

"The wretched creatures have been raiding the village not only to spread chaos, but they are returning there with captives from Oakhurst. To do exactly what, I'm not sure."

"They took three children with them several days ago and we've been following them ever since. Have you seen the three I speak of?", asked Calvin.

"Yes knight," replied the patrol's Sergeant Piner. "Only yesterday they crossed the valley. My men and I didn't do anything because the pack was accompanied by a drow wizard leading them and they seemed to somehow be hastened in their travel," he informed the others in the chamber.

"Magic," offered Devis.

"I agree elf," came Jhessail nodding his head in acknowledgment.

"We have to get those kids back!", desperately interjected Jericho.

"We will," assured Faith. "We will."

Calvin stared at the dancing flames concentrating on bits and pieces of the debriefing conversation. His thoughts roaming in his mind from question to question until Edward grabbed his attention with the directness of his inquiry.

"What's the plan Calvin?"

Looking up at his companion, the group's leader gave him the only response he could at the time while shaking his head. "I know not Edward. At present a plan eludes me."

A hush fell over the group and only the snapping and popping from the crackling fire could be heard. The large cavern was quiet for a time as everyone's eyes roamed from one to another. It was the knight that finally broke the moment of silence.

"For now everyone get some rest. We shall need our strength on the morrow," he advised while gazing into the dancing flames.

CHAPTER 19

"You're an Incompetent Fool!", shouted the figure from the darkness sitting behind the desk of the shadowed room. "Do you not have any common sense in that head of yours? Even a little?", the voice added sharply.

Standing in front of a piece of the room's furniture, Wizard Zolktar timidly responded to the voice coming from the shadows. "My apologies House Wizard Zebbulas. I was not aware that the goblins were not expendable to our cause."

"They are, but what is the reasoning behind allowing more than half of the beasts given to you to perish when the need does not call for it?"

"House Wizard, if you pardon me saying, we came upon a group of the war god's followers and we..."

Zolktar's words were cut off by House Wizard Zebbulas slamming his fist onto the desk, "Enough!"

"Yes house wizard," he replied with a bow.

The room was silent for a moment before a sudden knock on its door.

"Enter," ordered Zebbulas.

Both drow wizards watched quietly as a dark elf priestess came into the shadowy chamber. Closing the door behind her, the priestess walked towards the seated house wizard while watching Wizard Zolktar offer a bow to the woman out of respect for both her position as a holy follower of the goddess of evil and her higher status in the social order of the dark elves. He knew the pains and penalties he would be forced to endure if his actions were viewed as disrespectful in their matriarchal society with death being the better way to exit this realm.

House Wizard Zebbulas quickly rose to his feet, "Priestess Xarna, how can I be of service?", he wondered.

"House Wizard Zebbulas, are you aware that Wizard Zolktar has delivered to us three children?", she asked pleasantly while leisurely finding a paper-free spot along the corner of the desk to half lean against and half sit on.

"I am priestess."

"And are you also aware that the guards found this on one of the newly acquired boys?", Xarna asked tossing something onto the desk.

At first neither of the wizards could make out the balled up object.

Zebbulas was the first to reach for and pick up the soft enigma.

Opening it up to look at, he held up the item in front of him taking in the sight of the piece of bed clothing. An expression of puzzlement replaced the mask of humbleness that he had been currently wearing.

Seeing past the item to the house wizard, whose lips had now begun to form a snarl matching the one worn by the priestess, Wizard Zolktar could feel his own panic begin to creep in and take root. "What is it house wizard? What's the matter?", his voice wavered with fear.

"Do you know what this is?"

"A bed shirt," he answered unsure.

"And this here you idiot?", Zebbulas pointed out before ripping the shirt from the other's grasp.

Wizard Zolktar's eyes widened with acknowledging fear when he finally noticed the torn away pieces of clothing. In a sudden panic-stricken heartbeat, he took a step back.

Zebbulas threw the bed shirt hitting Zolktar in the chest.

"Were you followed you fool?", barked the priestess.

"I...I don't think so," stumbled the drow over his own words.

"So now you think!", shouted the house wizard.

The panicked Zolktar found himself unable to react as he crashed to the ground on hands and knees. The veins in his neck bulging from the strain he felt pushing him downward. It was like the mountain was pressing down against the drow trapping him under all its weight and he couldn't move.

"You're lack of competence and the excuses that accompany it are both taxing and tiresome to this operation. Its design to accomplish and sustain a safe passage through these mountains bringing utter destruction and tyranny in the name of Thaisia to these lands are above one person. Especially a foolish one as yourself," snarled Zebbulas.

"But no need to worry because you can still be of assistance towards the greater cause," added Priestess Xarna while her stiletto-healed boots struck the ground as she made her way behind Zolktar. He desperately struggled on all fours against an unseen force holding him vulnerable to her delight.

"No! No wait!", pleaded the panicking, prone mage.

"Your display of begging is disgustingly amusing," laughed the priestess standing behind him.

A hissing filled the room and Wizard Zolktar's robe tore violently from his body. The magically ripped in half material softly landed on the floor around him exposing his thin, ebony-colored back to the punishment he was about to receive. Zolktar's long, white mane falling over both sides of his face. The dark elf knew what followed.

Cutting through the room's air, only filled with a hissing, the scourge cracked when it lashed out at the prone drow. The real pain wasn't just the whip itself, it was the three pairs of needle-like fangs biting into Zolktar's back from the three viper heads at the lash's end. The magical weapon of the dark elves priestess' was designed to punish those for their wrong doings against the god or any of her female worshipers, but in a chaotic society what might be viewed today as right may be looked upon as wrong a minute later. The only good thing for drow males was their natural born immunity towards any type of snake or spider venom.

Again the magical weapon of punishment struck the dark elf's back. Its six fangs biting into the skin of its victim and removing pieces of the ebony organ. Blood began to flow from the wounds as Zolktar winced and his fingernails on his black, slender hands dug into the rocky floor leaving scratch marks. The wizard held in every cry of agony because the drow male knew better than to let one escape from behind his quivering lips.

The whipping continued and the pain seemed to come faster and faster now. After the first dozen times, Wizard Zolktar lost count and would eventually succumb to the blackness at the corner of his eyes. The drow went limp when he passed out from the pain. Tears had filled his eyes and in silence ran down his cheeks falling to the stone below. Zolktar never heard Priestess Xarna's order to the two guards standing outside the door ordering them to take him to the slave pens.

⁓⬥⁓

Katherine sat huddled in a corner next to her two brothers with her knees pulled up to her chest and her chin resting between her knee-caps. A look of fear was written across her face as her brown, doe-like eyes took in her bleak surroundings. Every muscle in the little girl's petite body involuntarily shook from knowing only dread.

The child was in a large cavern somewhere located within the hall of the dwarves. Makeshift holding pens surrounded her and occupied anywhere from two to fifty people at one time. The barred enclosures appeared full of both the dwarves that lived here and some of the townsfolk from her village. The captives' clothes were dirty and hung from their underfed frames causing some who were so thin to look like animated skeletons. Katherine awoke from her terror-filled trance when she heard her brother call her name.

"Kat. Kat. Are you alright?"

"I'm scared Junior," she softly replied glancing over to her oldest sibling.

The shirtless boy put an arm around his little sister's shoulder and pulled her into him. Junior could feel her trembling as she wrapped both her arms around his torso. With his other hand, the oldest of the three reached out and took hold of his brother's shoulder while smiling at Thomas. "We'll be alright," he offered but somewhere behind his feigned smile the oldest boy really wasn't sure.

186

Jacob's children suddenly looked at the cage's gate to see what was causing a commotion amongst the others locked in the pen with them. At the entrance stood two drow warriors supporting a third dark elf, who was bare from the waist up and hanging limp. The elf's head hung loose on his shoulders with his gaze remaining transfixed on the passage's floor.

"Get in there," snarled one of the guards shoving the prisoner into the open doorway. The other warrior closing and locking the gate before he spat on the falling drow. Both laughed as they walked away.

Katherine noticed streaks of blood crisscrossing the wounded drow's body as he crawled to a spot near the wall just inside the barred gate. The dark elf sat back cautiously against the stony partition with his knees drawn up to his chest and his head resting on his bent limbs. The drow's full, white mane, streaked crimson red, flowed over his legs.

"What do you think happened Junior?", inquisitively asked Thomas.

"I don't know."

"He looks hurt," offered Katherine while looking up at her older brother.

"Well whoever it is, they probably turned on him," declared Junior. "Deserves him right!"

Katherine actually found herself sitting and watching the still drow. Her one time terror seeming now to be replaced with curiosity.

❧

Pain wracked his back and he could feel the dried, caked up blood all over the rear of his torso. At least Zolktar was a drow, and had the natural born race trait of immunity to snake and spider venom. He could actually feel his body battling the affects of the viper's poison. The wounds from the weapon of choice of all the dark elves priestesses burned as if they were on fire, but now the injuries were the least of his problems. He needed to find out who exactly he was.

Zolktar knew his name and was fully aware that he was a drow, but as for everything else that defined him, it was lost to the dark elf's memory. He desperately needed to find out who exactly he was and how his life became one of a slave. The drow not knowing if he was born into his social pitfall or how he had come to be there. The bigger problem was the more Zolktar searched his mind for the answer, the blacker the void was to the solution. It seemed all his memories were tightly knotted up and all paths to the truth ended in roadblocks. He thought maybe it was due to the constant, burning pain keeping the dark elf from fully concentrating, but whatever the reason, Zolktar knew one definite characteristic about himself; he was a slave at the present time. The drow's eyes staring into his lap closed as the notion to get some rest might aid him in discovering who he was and how he had become forced into the servitude of his society. The one time mage attempted to get some sleep.

Zolktar had nodded off but he wasn't sure for how long before a pair of guards, with a couple more standing outside the cage as reinforcements, entered the holding pen. The two just snarled at him while they walked by heading straight towards where the frightened children sat on the room's rocky floor.

"Come here boy!", commanded one of the dark elves reaching down and pulling the shirtless boy to his feet by his upper arm.

Both surprise and fear were present in Junior, but the boy's face hid the feelings as he tried to stay calm for the sake of his siblings.

"No!", cried Thomas and Katherine at the same time. "No Junior!"

"Leave him alone!", screamed Thomas grabbing the drow's arm that was trying to lift his brother up. The dark elf responded by forcefully shoving Thomas to the ground. "Stay down boy," he rasped.

Even a couple of the other prisoners started to come to Junior's aid, but were stopped short when the other guard drew his sword. Their response to retreat was due to a fear shrouding the prisoners rational thinking of the fact that they possessed the greater numbers against the guards.

Tears flowed from Katherine's eyes as she desperately tried to protest between sharp breaths. She watched her brother being pushed out of the cage's gate. The little girl ran over to the closing and locking entrance way not far from where Zolktar sat witnessing the whole event. "Junior!", she cried.

Looking back at her from down the passageway, Junior could barely see through all the guards' bodies. "It will be alright Kat! I love you guys!", he yelled.

Silently turning from the gate's bars, Katherine's doe-like eyes met the black pupil eyes of the dark elf, who had been sitting and watching the little girl.

"Come on Kat, Junior will be okay," offered Thomas wrapping his right arm around the girl and escorting her back to the spot they had squatted at.

The drow followed the child with his eyes and then placed his head back on his knees. For some reason all he could see in his mind's eye over and over was the little girl's doe-like gaze.

CHAPTER 20

Junior was shoved into the dark room by one of the guards, who had pulled him from the slave pen a short time ago. He caught his balance before the force of the push sent the boy crashing to the floor. Straightening himself upright, it took a few blinks for his eyesight to adjust to the darkened chamber.

The boy could only make out a desk with a chair in front of him. Seated behind the desk was a dark form, but with the lighting so dismal Junior couldn't really tell who the blackened figure was. The room's corners were totally hidden from the boy's vision.

"Please, sit down," offered a woman's voice from the darkness behind the desk.

"No thank you. I'd rather stand."

The unseen voice giggled. "It's okay child. I'm not going to hurt you." A dim light blinked into existence allowing him to see the desk clearly and the speaker seated behind it. "I'm sorry, is this better?", softly asked the dark elf. Junior stood in awe captured by the drow woman's beauty.

She had long, jet, black hair that spilled over the back of her chair. Her face was slender with a pair of prominent cheekbones under almond-shaped black pupil eyes and flecks of purple sparkled in them when the light hit them at just the right angle. The woman's lips were smooth and their violet color matched the highlights in her eyes. Her smallish, pointed ears accentuated the symmetry of her perfectly beautiful face.

"I'm Xarna," she said standing to greet the boy.

Junior's awe turned to outright amazement watching her rise from the chair. His own gaze locked on the drow roaming from her face to below her neckline.

Xarna's neck and shoulders along with her navel and most of her back were left uncovered and exposed by her black, leather top. A pair of firm, round breasts were only three quarters concealed by the article of clothing leaving the drow woman's chest and cleavage also visible to Junior's admiring gaze. Xarna's ebony skin seemed to glisten its softness and the boy couldn't find one flaw in its smoothness.

Captivated, he watched her walk around the desk. The drow woman wore tight, leather pants emphasizing her curvaceous hips and firm, circular ass. Xarna's stiletto-healed boots ticking on the stone floor as she strolled over to where he stood.

"Oh please, I insist have a seat," seductively she offered as a smile dressed her face.

Junior seemed almost in a trance, hypnotized by the dark elf's beauty and sexiness. Xarna watched as the boy slowly lowered himself into the seat. His eyes only leaving her for a split-second making sure he didn't miss the chair. "If you insist," he said.

The priestess giggled again as she knew that the boy was at the proper age where he would become more and more interested in girls, especially a sexy, older woman as herself. Junior seemed to grin out of a slight embarrassment at her little laugh. The drow woman kept playing him like a harp.

"I noticed you when you first came in with your sister and brother. Junior right?", making sure she had his name correct.

"Uh yes. How did you know my name?"

"I learn everybody's name who catches my eye for one reason or another," the woman half leaning and half sitting on the desk in front of him. Her pubic bone was now at his eye level as the priestess put a foot on his seat between Junior's parted legs.

"Your muscles are pretty big!", feigning her wonderment while pointing at one of his biceps.

Looking to his arm, Junior involuntarily flexed it and stuck out his chest as the boy adjusted his posture sitting erect in the chair.

"I do a lot of work on our farm with Thomas and ...", his words trailing off to silence. Softly he finished the statement, "...my father." Raising his eyes to hers, the boy asked, "Why did you kill my family and burn our farm, and why are me, Kat and Thomas here?"

"Oh no honey," compassionately crooned the drow. "Those no good goblins we sent to ask you to come here so we could borrow your muscles did." Xarna moved her stiletto-healed boot up on the chair brushing it against Junior's inner thigh. "When I found out about it I punished their leader and had all those monsters involved executed."

"Then why do you guys have all those people including Kat and Thomas in that cage?", he questioned her motives. "And why have you all been stealing village folk for the last couple of months now, if you just needed some help with something?"

A brief silence cut into their conversation. The priestess' nice act seemed to run its course as she dug her fingers into the boy's bed shirt behind her back. With the lightning fast speed of a snake strike, Xarna's foot, still on the inside of Junior's thigh, reeled back and kicked out hitting him square in his bare chest. The force of the kick knocking him and the chair backwards onto the chamber's floor. Shock and fear covering his face after he landed and met the dark elf's penetrating gaze.

"What's this?", she snarled throwing his shirt at him and hitting him in the chest.

"My. My!"

"What is it?", interrupting his answer while still fumbling for its words.

"It's, it's my bed shirt!", hastily answered Junior as terror gripped his body openly displaying in the tone of his voice.

"Who's following you?"

"I don't know!", he quickly confessed. "Probably no one!"

Reaching down, the priestess helped him to his feet by his neck. "Who's following you?", she yelled slapping the boy causing Junior's bottom lip to split. Blood trickling from the cut.

"No one!", he cried.

"Liar!", she screamed. "I want to know who you left a trail for by tearing pieces of your clothing so they could follow you," demanded the priestess more sternly this time.

"No one Xarna."

Slapping Junior across the face with the back of her hand and then pushing him to the floor, the woman snarled at the panic-stricken boy. "It is Priestess Xarna to you boy. Let us see if you still find favor in lying after this." A sudden hissing filled the room's air.

Junior's eyes went wide with horror and the boy scrambled to get up and run.

Priestess Xarna only laughed aloud at her frightened target. The scourge coming down to strike. Screams of pain accompanied the hissing in the room and it overflowed through the closed, wooden door and carried into the corridor. The three viper's biting into the boy's back and side.

"Who's coming?", yelling her demand.

"No one! Please!"

Again the whip cracked, and again the vipers sunk their fangs tasting human flesh.

"Who's coming boy?"

"No one!", he cried out in excruciating pain. "Please stop!"

Another crack filled the chamber.

❧

Two drow warriors carried the boy's broken, limp body out of the now quiet room. Blood still trickled from the multiple whip and puncture wounds on his body. Water trails covered his cheeks. Slamming the door shut behind the guards, Priestess Xarna felt somewhat sure that no one had followed the captives and their prisoners, although she wasn't fully convinced of it.

She had ordered the two guards to throw the boy back into his cell before sending them to warn the goblins at the mouth of the cave's entrance to stay on the look out for any unwanted visitors. Dead or alive it didn't matter to her what the beasts did to anyone who followed.

"What do you think house wizard?", she asked one of the dark corners in the room.

"I think you have made a very wise decision priestess," he answered with a slight bow of his head while materializing out of the shadows.

"You always know what to say to a lady Zebbulas," proclaimed the dark elf with hungry eyes. "All this sexiness and punishment has put me into the mood."

"Yes priestess. It was quite…"

"Shut up!, Xarna demanded. "Get over here and find something better to do with your tongue," she devilishly smiled while starting to untie the laces on the front of her leather pants.

⌒

Jacob Jr. had been gone a while now. Both his siblings sat in their spots unmoving and watching the gate for his return. The only time Katherine seemed to look from the locked entryway was to steal a glance over at the drow captive. If he happened to look up, she would quickly divert her prying eyes.

The little girl couldn't understand why he had stayed instead of casting magic that would free the dark elf. Katherine knew the prisoner was the same wizard who had seemed to help her with the goblins on the mountain. "Was that the cause behind him being a captive now?", she asked herself.

Movement at the cage's gate grabbed her attention as she watched two guards carrying the limp body of her brother enter the enclosure and drop him off just inside the bars. One of the two gave the seated drow a quick kick in the shoulder knocking him into the rock wall.

"Junior!", cried Katherine and Thomas getting up and running to their brother's unconscious form. The little girl began to cry when she saw her brother's back torn and bleeding. "What did they do to him? Why can't they just leave us alone?", her questions coming through tears.

A dwarf accompanied by two villagers approached the children. "Let's see if I can help lass," came the dwarf prisoner. "First we need

194

to get him over there and away from this one," he remarked casting a glance over to the seated drow prisoner.

The two villagers grabbed the limp boy's arms and legs carrying him over to a spot on the far side of the cavern's cell. They softly placed the unconscious boy on its floor while Katherine and Thomas hovered over the kneeling dwarf at their brother's side.

Beads of sweat formed across the wounded's face as he began to mumble incoherently.

"What's wrong with him?", asked Katherine with sheer panic in her question.

"I'm not sure lass, but I believe he's been poisoned," informed the helpful dwarf.

"Poison! From what?", came Thomas' query.

"From the priestess' snake scourge," the little man replied.

"What are you going to do?", came Thomas rapidly firing a second question at the dwarf.

"All we can do for now is comfort him and hope the boy didn't envenom too much," optimistically offered the dwarf.

❧

The dwarf introduced himself to the two children shortly after preparing a more permanent resting place for Junior. Now that the boy was as comfortable as he was going to get, the dwarf at least wanted to try and calm down both Katherine and Thomas. Their tears flowing like streams over their cheeks.

"I'm Drü Slopewalker," the chubby dwarf gave his name.

Drü was as rotund around as he was tall. Black, curly hair seemed to cover every part of his shirtless body except the dwarf's head. His beard and mustache were well groomed even considering the circumstances. The little light illuminating from a handful of torches mounted in their wall brackets throughout the holding pen seemed to shine off of his bald head when he turned it just right. Only his pants seemed dirty. Reaching out his small, pudgy hand and taking hold of Katherine's, he gently shook it. For a dwarf he sure had a soft, soothing tone to his voice.

"I'm Katherine," the little girl introduced herself blinking her wet eyes.

Drü repeated the process acquainting himself with Thomas.

"What happened here?", queried the boy.

"Well you see lad, during the beginning of spring a couple of the hall's lookouts noticed some goblin activity taking place further up one of the other slopes. They were making their presence known, but us dwarves didn't know at the time they were doing it deliberately, so our king decided to send a large patrol out to evict the oncoming nuisance," -swallowing to wet his throat before continuing- "What King Fireheart, nor anyone else knew, was that the group of beasts were working for the evil race of dark elves. Just like that one there," he pointed in the direction of Zolktar.

"Anyways, the patrol of unknowing dwarves went out to meet the goblins and were taken by surprise by the drow that night. All the hall's men died in the ambush, but unfortunately that wasn't it for them. The ambushers used their black magic to turn all the dwarves into undead zombies. The dark elves using their evil creations of blasphemy to make it look like the patrol returned with prisoners."

The chubby dwarf focusing his thoughts before he continued with his narration. "The drow didn't stop there. Somehow they located the river running through Bright Star Hall and poured some of their poison into the waters upstream. The sleeping affect it had put most in a deep slumber since the river is the hall's main source for drinking. Before anyone could figure out what was happening it was too late. The evil race used water breathing spells to follow the flow in and took those who had not succumbed to the poison's effects, or the battle with the undead and the goblins at the gate, by surprise. None of us stood a chance," Drü softly added while dropping his head looking at the floor. "Many were unfortunately massacred."

"What do they want all of us for then?", puzzled Thomas.

"Because the drow plan on using Bright Star Hall as a passageway, or bridge so to speak, to bring the evil and chaos from the Separate Lands through the Border Mountains and into the realms spreading their darkness throughout the free lands."

"But what exactly do they need us for?", Thomas was still a little baffled to the reason for their capture.

"I'm sorry child," apologized the dwarf forcing a meek smile. "They need us to continue to mine the one thing that gives this place its name; precious gems." Drü's smile faded into a look of concern as he added, "We are to be their circle of slaves in the drow's ring of darkness."

CHAPTER 21

Nine pairs of eyes and nine red sets of two peered out of the tree line surveying the rocky terrain of the upper mountain's slope. Large stones and boulders littered the land's topography and its grade slightly steepened a bit as its natural incline rose higher and higher. A small herd of sheep wandered amongst the mountainside.

"That's a good sign lad," pointed out the cigar-smoking dwarf to the group's leader.

"Why is that?", puzzled Calvin.

"It means there ain't no goblin about," he answered but quickly corrected the statement. "Ain't none except these here but they're not exactly goblin kind."

"We're also down wind," revealed the patrol's sergeant.

"Good point," added Devis.

The other's keeping their eyes on the rocky land and watching the grazing herd slowly wander off seeking every nook and cranny of the ground for food.

"The entrance tunnel is about half a day up after a stone bridge that crosses a deep chasm," informed Thorin. "If we don't encounter any of the beasts then we can leave the safety of the trees and make our way up the slope, where we will surely risk being detected the closer we get. We won't come to the structure until late tonight, or if we camp, in the morning sometime."

Looking at the group of eighteen he added, "It's your call knight."

Calvin seemed to silently hang sitting and pondering on the dwarf's words. The party quietly waiting for his decision as it took their leader several minutes before arriving at a plan.

"If we push on with only the light shining from the night sky it may not be enough to guide all of us over this unforgiven terrain. Us humans will not be able to see clearly, and even though some of you can see in the dark, the advantage will go to the goblins and the drow," warned Calvin. "But if we set up camp within the safety of the tree line using it for concealment this night, and leave here at the right time on the morrow, then we could take the bridge and meet our enemies at the hour that not only hinders them but favors us and our numbers; sunset," he revealed.

"I don't understand Calvin, why sunset?", queried Faith.

All the demi-humans knew the answer and after a brief pause Devis answered what was obvious to them, but not to any of the humans except the group's leader. "Because all who have the ability to see at night have their eyesight hampered at two times of the day. The hour of early sunrise and the hour of sunset."

"Provided the god Sol wins his battle with the rain goddess, Lluvia, then he will be setting the orb in the west at our backs causing it to still be shining into the eyes of those beasts we fight," added Calvin.

The party along with the nine accompanying patrol soldiers seemed impressed by the knight's plan up to this point.

"How are we going to get by them though?", inquired Harold.

"I am not fully sure yet, although I will come up with something before then."

"I like the way this guy thinks!", praised the gnome. "He'll come up with another plan that will work."

❦

"Calvin! Calvin! Wake up!", whispered Sergeant Piner while slightly shaking the leader's upper arm. Within an instant the knight reached for his sword and scabbard. Calvin opened up his eyes and blinked a couple of times recognizing the glowing, red pair meeting his.

"Calvin we've got some trouble."

199

"What is it Sergeant?", curiously asked the cavalier.

"My lookouts have spotted a goblin patrol coming down the mountainside, and they seem to be looking for something or someone," reported Piner.

"Wake the others quietly."

"My men do so as we speak," he confirmed.

The companions and the patrol decided that a four man watch would rotate three times this night taking advantage of so many with the benefit of night vision. It was decided that three of the soldiers along with one of the demi-human companions would make up a box-shaped watch. No one was taking any chances especially considering the group found themselves deep in enemy territory. It was the middle of the night and the sergeant with two of his men accompanied Moric on the second lookout shift.

Within minutes, the warning had been passed through the unlit camp and the eighteen formed a side-by-side line just inside the tree's perimeter. A plan was quickly formulated and passed amongst them as they lay in wait baiting the patrol of goblins down the slope and closer to their position. All eighteen had quietly drawn their weapons, and the rescuers' hearts thunderously beat in their chests while they anxiously waited. One could cut the tension-filled, night's air with a dagger.

"Remember no magic unless we really need its assistance," ordered Calvin. "I don't want to give away where we are with a light show." His message conveyed throughout the line to the party's magic-users.

"Moric, you stay and guard Faith when the fighting begins," the group's leader softly whispered to the gnome beside him.

"Got it," dutifully affirmed Moric.

The order had just been relayed when the first three goblins stepped out from behind the rocky obstacles covering their descent down the slope. In mere seconds more appeared behind them. Laying still, the ambushers patiently awaited for all the beasts to show themselves fully.

The dozen, goblin patrol passed into the opening roughly twenty feet away from where the group lay in wait. Suddenly one of the beasts froze in its tracks causing the others following its lead to instantly stop and look into the darkness. They scanned the trees and the stony mountainside.

"What is it Gentl?", cautiously asked one of the patrol's pack members.

"I smell something," it answered in a guttural tone while sniffing the air.

The ambushers held their breath wondering if their scents betrayed their hiding spots. Did the goblins find them before they could surprise their unsuspecting prey? It was all they could do to hold their concealed positions as the companions felt the urge to rush forward. All of them waited on Calvin's orders. Mere seconds seemed like hours as everyone hoped they wouldn't be spotted by the beasts, but Lady Luck seemed to be on their sides as the night's moon and stars gave off enough light to hold the goblin's eyesight to that of nighttime vision instead of their infravision that would allow them to see in complete blackness. Even Thorin could feel the vibration coming from holding his double-bladed axe. The dwarf tried his hardest to keep the greenish glow from the emerald in its pommel covered.

Again the pack members inquired Gentl about the scent as they sniffed the night air. "What do you smell?"

"Sheep," it responded gazing in the direction that the small herd of hoofed mountain climbers had gone. "There was some food here earlier. Come on let's go," it added to the eleven others. The search patrol again starting its descent down the slope towards the waiting ambush.

Calvin knew the twelve goblin's eyes were about to adjust from the light illuminating from the bright shining third of the moon and the night sky's stars to the deficient obscurity of the tree cover. He quietly gave the order when the search patrol was within fifteen feet.

"Now!"

An arrow flew striking Gentl straight in the center of the throat. Its force driving the beast backwards and off its feet.

The night sky seemed to be filled with a small volley of missile-fired and hurled weapons.

A crossbow bolt soared into the abdomen of another as a thrown javelin stuck from the goblin's chest sending it to the ground.

Another bolt found its mark in the mouth of one of the pack's members. It had opened it to sound a warning cry that never came as the missile's point located the back of its maw.

The soldier, Nathaniel, hurled his spear with such bull-like strength that the force from the blow took a goblin from its feet as the weapon's point flew right through it. The flying goblin struck a second knocking the beast down with it.

The rest of the companions and the morphed human patrol charged the remaining search party when the missile fire attacks began. They swarmed on the remaining ones still alive and in seconds cut the life from them. None of the beasts in their surprised state had time to howl out a warning in the quiet darkness. Anything or anybody listening had no warning that the large group was coming.

❧

"Take the bodies and dispose of them," ordered the knight speaking to the patrol's sergeant. "We will cover up all the blood stains on the ground leaving no impression that anything took place here."

"Very well," agreed Piner before turning to inform his troops of their valuable night mission.

"Sergeant."

"Yes sir."

"Make sure all of you come back," advised Calvin concerned about their welfare. "Safe journey."

"Yes sir," replied Sergeant Piner with a hint of a smile crossing his lips.

Within minutes, the goblin-disguised patrol made off with some of the bodies searching for a safe place away from the camp to dump the corpses.

Once again watch replacements were appointed and the new lookouts took up their positions at their assigned points around the cold camp's perimeter. Both Jhessail, who had previously been obligated to the last shift and Devis, who had already taken up his post on the first detail, were accompanied by the two

McKinley brothers on this substituted watch. The two humans scanning the open mountain terrain with the benefit of the bright, night sky.

The other five companions worked diligently kicking dirt and stones over the dark, blood-stained ground. Together they hid three of the goblin corpses in the tree line as they awaited for the patrol to return and take the bodies to their final resting place. After most of the group dozed off, Calvin still lay awake thinking and trying to formulate a plan that would get them at least over the stony bridge. Soon sleep consumed him.

CHAPTER 22

Katherine nervously jumped awake at the sudden intrusion caused by the four, drow guard entering the slave's holding pen. The fatigued, little girl trying to wipe the sleep from her blinking eyes as she swiftly sat up from the slumber that she had eventually succumbed to. Dirt covered every inch of her body from head to toe, except for her cheeks that had been streaked earlier from tears. Even the little girl's long, brown hair was totally messed up and stood out of place. Her frazzled appearance causing her to look like one stricken with madness. Katherine's heart pounded as it raced so fast that it felt to her as if it was about to leap from out of her tiny chest.

"Get up you scum!", yelled one of the dark elves while cracking a whip against the stone floor. "Form a line!"

Another one of the guard's kicked the seated Zolktar awakening him from his reverie. "You too!", sternly stated the drow.

The dark elf prisoner fighting his pain as he slowly rose to his feet. His face wearing only a grimace.

Katherine stole a glance over to where Junior lay on the stone floor. A water mark stain surrounded the fevered boy and beads of sweat formed about his face and forehead running and trickling down onto the ground around him. Drü knelt by his side monitoring the boy for any signs of progress.

"Is he getting better?", she heard Thomas ask.

"No signs yet,…", dejectedly responded the dwarf, "…but it appears that his body is fighting the venom," he added trying to sound hopeful for the sake of the boy's two siblings.

"I said on your feet!", the guard with the whip screamed at the little girl while grabbing a handful of her disheveled hair and pulling her up.

Katherine cried out in both pain and terror.

"Leave her alone!", cried Thomas running to his sister's aid, but a quick crack from the drow's whip to his ankle stopped his approach instantly. Thomas dropped to the ground screaming in pain.

"Don't ever forget boy who's in charge," the guard snarled while still gripping Katherine's hair. "Now stand up!"

Thomas gingerly rose to his feet.

"That's enough please," begged the dwarf rising from the fevered boy's side. "They're only children and they're scared."

"They should be," advised the dark elf releasing the girl's hair. "Now for the last time, everyone line up!"

❧

Thomas and Katherine, along with the large group of slaves, had spent half the day so far mining for gems in the extremely vast cavern. Now they were relieved to at least get a little break to rest their tired and weary bodies. The two were also somewhat at ease that their captor's at least allowed the dwarf, Drü Slopewalker, to stay and take care of Junior. His younger siblings wracked with anxiety over their brother's poor condition. Both Thomas and Katherine had already lost so much.

"Do you think mother and father will look down from the heavens on Junior and help him to get better?", the dirty, little girl inquisitively asked looking at her brother.

"I believe so Kat," Thomas answered smiling at the girl. Both the question and the answer seeming to bring each a sense of hope.

Before the two could continue their discussion a curly, red-haired, dwarven woman with freckles underneath her dirt smeared face brought them both a mug of crystal, clear water. "Here children. Drink up," came her caring voice.

Katherine grabbed a hold of the mug with both hands bringing the drink up to her lips. With her throat being both dry and parched from all the earlier days work, the little girl gulped a couple of long pulls she took from the metal, drinking cup causing her to breathe heavy in between the swallows.

"Slow down child," the woman laughed. "I've got a little more," the dwarven woman smiled looking to the pitcher she carried on a tray.

"What about him?", Katherine questioned looking over the rim of her mug before taking another gulp.

The dwarven woman turned to look at who the child was asking about. Her gaze taking in the drow slave seated on a rock. No one within two dozen feet of him.

"He's one of them child," softly spoke the lady changing the discussion back to the water. "Would you like some more?"

"Please," the girl responded while holding out the mug for a refill.

The dwarven woman topped it off with the liquid before refilling Thomas' cup and starting for the next slave taking a chance to rest. "I've got to go for now," she added with a smile.

"What is it with you worrying about that dark elf, Kat?", inquisitively asked Thomas after he had finished his drink. "He's the same one that helped the goblins back at our house."

"I don't think he was there with them because I didn't see him, and remember Thomas, he helped me when they starting bullying me on our way here," she convincingly relayed her belief.

"I'm telling you Kat, he's no good. Stay away from him," warned Thomas. "You and I only have each other and Junior."

Just the mention of his name had Katherine wondering about her older brother. Concern for his well being flooded her thoughts. "He'll be alright, right Thomas?", she asked.

"Yeh. Junior will wake up and be fine. He's tough you know," replied her brother not only trying to sound convincing for his little sister's sake, but also attempting to assure himself.

The little girl went back to eyeing the dark elf prisoner.

Junior laid still in his comatose state with a sheen of sweat still beading up on his forehead as his body fought the internal battle against the weapon's snake venom. The boy's dirty bed pants and hair were soaking wet with perspiration, and the collection of the body's natural cooling liquid stained the stone floor both underneath and around him. Junior still lay in the grip of his fever while his spirit to live fought a battle between life and death.

Drü kneeled beside him with both his hands placed on the overturned child's back. The dwarf's eyes closed while his mouth uttered words barely audible. Both Drü and Junior were the only two in the slave pen and the dwarf was glad as he offered a prayer to his gods asking aid to neutralize the poison. The clerical spell would give Junior the immunity against the venom and its affects. The cleric knew he couldn't delay the toxins any longer, but he was also aware that he couldn't rush the boy's healing either or the dwarf would risk the chance of being caught, and like all the other clerics of Bright Star Hall, Drü would end up facing the same fate they had; death.

✥

Sitting on a rock and taking a brief rest, Zolktar tried to unravel and clear his thoughts. The dark elf still wasn't sure who he really was or how he had become a slave. Images and memories of his previous life seemed gapped and left out every time the drow tried to concentrate and remember past events. Zolktar's brain seemed to knot with almost every deep thought, but somehow the little girl's doe-eyed face kept popping into the dark elf's mind. "Why, and who was she?", he found himself continuously asking, but before he could gather up anymore thoughts and ideas on that which escaped him, Zolktar raised his eyes from the ground in front of him. The child in his mind's eye stood offering the dark elf a mug filled with water.

"What do you want child?", growled the ebony-skinned slave.

"This is for you," softly she replied offering the cup.

Zolktar's glance went from the mug to Katherine and back to the cup before he asked, "For what?"

"Because you didn't get any," innocently pointed out the girl. "I thought that you might need some." Katherine presented the cup to Zolktar offering him to take it.

The dark elf's pride didn't want to accept anything from a human slave, especially a little child at that, but both his mouth and throat were dry and parched from the labor the drow had performed creating an internal struggle between his haughty behavior and the need he had to quench his body's desire for the cup of liquid. Zolktar pointed at a spot on another semi-flat piece of stone. "Put it there."

Katherine placed the mug of water down and turned back to the seated slave. Their eyes met and for a moment stared at each other. Again, the child's doe-like eyes fired up the curiosity in Zolktar's tied up mind, but he still couldn't figure out who she was. Suddenly, the dark elf was pulled out of his brief wonderment by the mocking of another's voice.

Looking up to the small rise of stone overlooking the area of the quarry, two, drow guards stood ridiculing the scene below them.

"Oh, isn't that nice. Zolktar's made a friend," came one of the taskmasters. The other joining him in laughter. "Don't forget to say thank you to the human child."

Zolktar clenched both hands into fists while sneering up at the two before dropping his gaze on the girl who had just made the dark elf a laughing joke to the guards. The amnesiac now adding mockery to his list of plaguing ailments.

Katherine recognizing his anger slowly and cautiously withdrew back to Thomas' side. Her slightly older brother meeting her with open arms accompanied by, "I told you Kat."

The group of companions with the disguised soldiers cautiously made their way up the mountainside. The slope's rocky terrain, along with the hazards caused by it, made the ascent a bit slower at this elevation. A steep, dirt road was always present, but now according to the dwarf, it had never been littered with this many obstacles. Large boulders now blocked up most of the way and some potholes were strewn about. On more than one occasion, the party of eighteen even had to climb and hurdle small, stone barricades caused by rock slides. It was more than obvious to Thorin that all these impediments were the makings and doings of drow and goblin.

The combined groups moved methodically with their weapons drawn as much as they could be, but sometimes the party would have to sheath them to free up both hands when needed. The group also had to keep their eyes on the lookout for danger or posted goblin sentries. The eighteen had decided to stop for a quick rest before they would be exposed when the stone cover ceased to exist roughly three hundred feet from the hall's entrance. Calvin would also go over the plan one more time debugging it because the knight knew that if they were going to gain access into the stronghold then the large group's performance needed to be flawless.

❧

"Where? Where am I?", groggily asked Junior looking around the cavern trying to focus his eyes. "What happened?"

"Gods be praised," softly stated the bald dwarf at his side holding the boy down. "Take it easy lad and rest."

"Who are you?"

"The name's Drü Slopewalker, and I'm a friend of both Katherine and Thomas'."

A slight panic overtook Junior when he heard his sibling's names. He tried to rise up on an elbow but the dwarf held him in place.

"Take it easy lad. Don't go getting yourself anymore hurt than you are already," he advised the boy. "Both of them will be fine. They're just in the quarry working at this time."

Junior felt dizzy and although he had slept in a comatose state, the boy still seemed exhausted. Laying back down on the dark-stained floor on his stomach, the weakened child asked again, "What happened?"

"By the looks of you the last half a day or so, you seem to have had a run in with the priestess and her snake scourge."

The memories flooded back into the boy's mind and the recollection of the meeting's events washed over him. "That bitch!"

Junior's name-calling brought a smile accompanied by a chuckle to the cleric in hiding.

"Stay here and rest. I'll go see if I can find some stashed food and water for you," advised the dwarf rising and leaving in an attempt to locate the scarce products.

What both lone figures in the cavern failed to notice was the hand-sized, furry, black spider on the side of one of the holding cell's rocks watching both the slave's actions. Its multiple eyes taking in the sight of the unknown cleric healing the feverish boy only moments ago.

CHAPTER 23

A fading brightness bathed the cave's entrance leading into the dwarven stronghold, along with the rocky terrain at this elevation's height. Within the next few hours, the blazing fireball in the sky would surrender its position to the slightly growing third-sized moon and its stars that would light the night. Good fortune favored the group of rescuers and even the sun god, Sol, positioned his burning orb at their backs. It almost seemed to most like he was on their side.

The two groups stopped and hid behind a couple of large boulders along with some rocky outcropping roughly three hundred yards from the stone bridge crossing the mountain slope's chasm. The rescuers quickly reviewing and going over the leader's plan designed to take back the entrance and grant access into the dwarven hall. Everyone fully understanding their chance of survival diminished if even one mistake was made. With the bright sun setting behind them their shadows cast on the ground in front of each of them, but in all there was only fifteen shady apparitions. Three were missing.

Squinting into the radiating brightness, the goblin sentry watched the surrounding nine beasts lead the elf and the captured human prisoners towards the stony crossing. Upon seeing its deeply hated enemy with the four men and one woman, the lookout's excitement grew causing a devious smile to cross its face. "Elf will be on the fire tonight," it thought devilishly humming before licking its lips.

"So there was someone following the last pack of marauders!", the beast thought surprised by the drow's intuition.

The disguised goblin, that was really Sergeant Piner, at the head of the group responded the affirmation. "They were correct."

"I see you lost three from your pack," stated the sentry.

"No thanks to this one!", the sergeant added with a push to Devis' head.

The bridge's guard growled a soft rumble. "I'll inform the others that you're coming."

"That won't be necessary."

With a look of puzzlement, replaced by the sudden expression of pain, the goblin's body lurched forward. Its mouth starting to protest the sneak attack it had just received. One of the morphed patrolmen quickly slapped a hand over the sentry's opening so no warning would pass the beast's lips. Behind the dying bridge guard materializing from out of thin air stood Moric. The gnome's daggers puncturing both its lungs.

The disguised soldier heaving the dead beast into the chasm.

"Good job Moric," complimented Calvin. "Now hurry up and fall in."

With phase one completed it was now time to move on to the plan's second part.

"Thorin, make your way around towards the cave," the knight addressed in the direction of the invisible dwarf. "Wait until it is clear before taking up your position. You will know when to act."

"Okay knight. I'm gone," came the gruff voice out of nowhere.

"Jhessail, when we're over the bridge make it invisible and cast an illusion of the structure over the chasm," Calvin added to the unseen half-elf following the group pretending to be captured.

"You've got it Calvin."

Without giving up the false pretense of captors and captives, the band of rescuers swiftly made their way across the stone structure. As soon as they were safely on the other side, the bridge disappeared and the copy cat image appeared five feet away from the invisible crossing.

❧

Thorin ran as fast as his dwarven legs would carry him across the remaining hundred and fifty feet of rocky ground to the cave's entrance. He knew he had to get into position before the next phase of their plan started. Thorin was a battle hardened warrior, who had been on Kanaan for a little over two centuries now, and had fought not only by himself but also under dwarven clan chiefs. The gritty fighter finding himself impressed with Calvin's plan.

Looking back and seeing the bride disappear moments before another materialized out of thin air, the dwarf knew he had to pick up his pace. Glancing around, Thorin noticed there appeared to be no goblins outside the entrance into the cave, but their lair was alive with loud chanting and growling. The beasts seemed to be focused on whatever it was they were doing, and a pungent odor wafted from inside. "Only a few feet left," he thought.

❧

An invisible, floating disc appeared from out of nowhere loaded with the captives hidden weapons. Taking a quick second, the five humans and the elf retrieved and armed themselves. Still none of the cave's beasts even had a clue that the rescuers had crossed the bridge.

"You think the dwarf is in place?", inquired Devis while nocking an arrow.

"Let us hope so," optimistically replied the group's leader. "Everyone, onto phase three. Time to get some goblin attention."

❧

"What's that?" perplexedly asked one of the beasts rolling some bone dice with two others. Turning to look at the opening to the lair, it missed one of its opponents turn the die the beast had just cast to another side. Over a dozen of the goblins also heard the yelling accompanied with the clashing of the weapons somewhere outside, and were now glancing towards the mountain's opening.

One of the beasts squinted as it observed nine goblins battling five humans, a gnome, and an elf. It yelled its discovery throughout the cave, and rushed to grab a weapon to help. "Gentl's caught something and the pack needs some help! Come on, he's got himself an elf!", it shouted in the beast's native tongue.

213

The lair became alive as others rushed to grab their weapons and aid the battling members of the search party outside. Over twenty of the beasts erupted from the mouth of the cave.

～ର

The dwarf hugged the rocky wall outside the cave when the twenty beasts started their downhill run to aid their other pack members. When the last had just run past him, Thorin decided to look in and see how many where left.

Being invisible, none of the remaining beasts saw him, or even smelt him over the terrible smell coming from two, large, cooking pots sitting over fires. The warrior knew he had to try and get most of them out of there.

Within seconds he devised a plan to evict more of the unwelcome residents. Pulling the dagger from his hip, Thorin spoke the command word shooting a magical web at the farthest of the two pots. The sticky substance hit the cookware just above the lit fire underneath it and instantly ignited causing a thick, heavy smoke. Thorin offered the blaze another shot before swiftly ducking back out of sight leaning against the rock on the side of the cave's mouth. Unfortunately for the gritty fighter, he materialized back from his invisible hiding spot and now hoped he wouldn't be noticed by any of those about to birth from the now smoking hole in the mountain.

The dwarf slipped the dagger back into its sheath while looking to the companions and the disguised goblin patrol faking their skirmish for the next part of the plan. The reinforcements a little more than seventy five feet away from the rescuers.

"I hope this works," he softly said to himself.

～ର

Calvin watched as the goblin reinforcements started their rush down the rocky slope towards the mock skirmish between the companions and the morphed patrolmen. They had gotten roughly sixty to seventy feet away and he witnessed some more birth from the cave's mouth. Thick, heavy smoke driving them from their residence.

"Now Jhessail!", ordered the knight.

A loud, deafening roar broke the noise caused by the charging goblins and the clash of weapons from the staged battle. Instantly all the reinforcements along with the ones fleeing the smoke looked to the attention-commanding, sky-shaking, reverberating bellow. Panic and terror washed through the goblin's body and their faces wore the look of sheer fear. Hovering in the sky, before landing in between the beast and the dwarven stronghold's entrance, was an enormous, red dragon. Horror-filled screams and cries replaced any and all feelings of helping out the battling search patrol. The goblins, who had one time been consumed with the feelings to maim and murder had them superceded by the survival instinct to run.

❧

Thorin watched as an adult, red dragon in all its majestic splendor set down on the rocky slope. The monster's scales going from a bright red to a pale yellow and white belly. Its leathery, red wings folding against its body's side with ivory-colored bone protruding into claws at its tips. The dragon's massively, thick legs connected to claws with talons thicker than some trees and sharper than any sword known on Kanaan. The creatures were unarguably the masters of the realm and the reds were at the top of the food chain.

A chuckle erupted from the dwarf. "Half-elf, you really did one hell of a job with this one. Now let's see if I can do your illusion any justice."

Thorin charged into the rear of the realistic image with his maul facing into the sun towards the goblin reinforcements. He called upon its magical ability, and a sphere of fire erupted from the head of the magical hammer. Its destination, a large pack of dismayed goblins in the presence of terror.

❧

The rescuers only took a second to watch the sphere of fire enter the chaotic scene of the panicked goblins. All of them seemed to be awestruck at the dragon's presence, but another deafening roar woke them from their terror-filled trance. Some of the fleeing beasts even seemed to be frozen in their places.

"Excellent job Jhessail!", yelling the compliment over his shoulder to the visible half-elf. "Everyone, stay away from the drop off! Moric guard Faith!", ordered Calvin. "Attack!"

Another roar followed by another sphere of fire erupted from the image of the red dragon. The companions and the patrol rushed to deliver the killing blows and take back the mountain's rocky slope.

"Attack men, and leave none alive!", yelled Sergeant Piner.

⤳

The goblin stood frozen by the sound and the sight of the red. Only the wash of terror was broken when the creature roared a second time erupting the grounds into a scene filled with chaos and frenzy. The beasts in their hysteria ran to and fro looking for a place to hide or a route leading to a possible getaway before they were devoured. Some had their sights pinned straight on the bridge, and over a dozen broke hoping for an escape.

A stampede of the goblins made their way to the stone structure while other petrified beasts ran to nowhere in particular. Upon arriving at the crossing another thunderous bellow filled the mountainside, but none of these beasts were about to look back. They rushed out onto what they thought was the bridge. Instead of crossing over the route of escape they had chosen, the goblins found themselves plummeting into the slope's chasm. Their screams and cries were not enough to stop others behind them as more running at a mad dash fell into the ravine.

Within mere moments, the frenzied goblins were swooped down upon by the eighteen rescuers. The beasts would meet death today, one way or another.

⤳

Calvin charged into the frenzy swinging his sword. The blade biting deep into a panic stricken foe. Greenish, black blood sprayed into the air, as it instantly dropped.

Another scared goblin charged straight into Harold's javelin thrust. The run-through beast just wore an asking look of surprise as it fell. The short-haired McKinley would bury the weapon into the fallen's body two more times making sure it would never get up again.

Moric was charged with Faith's safe keeping, so the two decided to team up on one of the attempted fleeing goblin. With her whip, the magic-user entangled the beast's feet dropping it to the ground. The gnome jumped on the fallen goblin jamming both daggers behind the prone beast's ears. Its body would twitch a couple of times before finally resting still.

Devis' blood lust took over his body, and the elf ran into the chaotic frenzy armed with both his sword in his right hand and his dagger in his other. The dagger's blade protruding from the little finger side of his hand. Running past a frightened foe, Devis struck out with his left hand and the blade easily sliced a goblin's throat open. Blood flowed out under the beast's hands clasping its neck as it stopped running instead dropping to its knees as the elf continued on to another.

Edward and one of the goblin soldiers converged on one of the fleeing beasts. It had no chance of getting away as both hacked it down with their swords.

Jericho took a slash across his upper arm from one of the goblin's set of fingernails. The five deep scratches drawing blood. The panicked beast fighting to get away from the red dragon, more than any other reason, had its head smashed in by the big man's swing from his staff. The strike, so hard, that its force almost separated the goblin's head from its body.

Taking advantage of the situation, Sergeant Piner smashed a goblin over the head with his mace that had been returned to him back in the valley by the companions. He was more than grateful to swing the weapon again as he took another swing becoming reacquainted with the affects of the solid, metal bludgeon.

Shock covered the faces of the goblins getting beat down and hacked apart by the soldiers of the morphed patrol. They couldn't understand why their pack members turned on them.

Again the dragon added its reverberating roar and stepped forward. A cry of terror rang from the fleeing beasts. Their panic so bad four tried to run across the dissolving illusion of the bridge. Their echoing screams fading out the further they fell into the ravine.

The invisible, stony structure materialized out of thin air. Two goblins noticed it as it came back into existence and started for it running over Faith and practically the gnome. The woman was having none of that as she called upon her magic to aid her and an arrowhead that she had been carrying in her left fist dissolved into smoke which escaped through her closed hand. Pointing with the index finger with her right hand still clenching her whip, a golden arrow shot forth. The goblin, who had knocked her over was struck between its shoulder blades launching it forward. Waves of smoke rose from its burnt carcass.

Moric, who had just avoided being trampled, threw a dagger sinking a blade into the goblin's calf. It dropped the beast instantly. The panic stricken offered a cry as it yanked the dagger out and threw it to the side. Knowing it couldn't support its own weight, the beast tried to crawl to the bridge, but the goblin's back arched from the driving force of Jhessail's sword pinning the beast to the ground.

Calvin had just stunned one with a shield bash knocking the goblin to the ground. Turning, the knight could see the mad dash by the remaining beasts to the real stone structure. "Block the bridge!", he shouted causing the eighteen group of rescuers to converge and take up their positions in front of the stone bridge.

Suddenly he was knocked backwards to the ground. His sword flying in the air. The stunned adversary had collected himself and now pressed its attack on the knight. The goblin used its long claws as weapons against the downed leader, who currently found sanctuary under the defense of his shield, but for how long? His foe swinging both hands with a speed that he could barely keep up to.

Grabbing the ends of Calvin's shield, and attempting to pry it away from him, the goblin never noticed the knight unsheathing a dagger that was housed on his side of the defensive hand-held armor. The fallen leader let the beast fling the shield aside. Turning back to Calvin, it never expected the thrusting dagger that plunged into its right eye. It howled in pain until the bladed weapon was pulled from its bloody eye socket and run across the beast's throat.

Pushing the goblin off of him and quickly retrieving his shield and sword, Calvin watched as both the dragon image faded away and the remaining outnumbered goblins were slaughtered. He headed for the rest of the party taking up a defensive position in front of the structure.

"Is everyone alright?", inquired the concerned leader as he approached.

Everyone confirmed their well being, although taking a rough inventory of the combined group's injuries, the mental note had most with some cuts and bruises from the chaotic frenzy and one of the soldiers had a severely sprained ankle. Two others helped to support his weight.

"Jhessail. Faith," the words grabbing their undivided attention. "Patch everyone up and heal what you can and who you can. Some of you come with me. The rest get rid of these bodies. Throw them into the chasm," added Calvin.

Glancing from one companion to another and then to the smoking cave's entrance, Calvin made a proclamation that seemed to lift all their spirits while the victorious rescuers caught their breath. "Today, after months of being under evils grasp, we have retaken this field of battle. Now we will retake the dwarven stronghold and forcefully take back our most precious to us; our people,..." -pausing before finishing his declaration, the knight's gaze fell upon Jericho's- "...along with Jacob's children."

The big man could feel his spirit to fight rise inside of him.

CHAPTER 24

Faith quickly covered her nose and mouth with her hand. The strong, pungent odor burned her nostrils and her vision blurred as her eyes welled up full of tears. The thick smoke that had billowed from out of the cave was just about gone now replaced by a heavier stench that filled the air. The young magic-user, who had performed or witnessed many chemical mixtures while growing up in her mother's herbal shop along with studying the art, was overcome by the smell emanating from the two, steaming, cooking pots. Using her free hand to wipe some of her tears away, Faith felt nauseous.

The others also tried to defend their attacked sense of smell by covering their noses with their free hand or hiding their nostrils in the bend of the arm at the elbow. Some even tried pulling their leather, armor shirts over their noses, but no matter what the group tried, it was to no avail. The extremely horrible aroma laid siege to their olfactories.

"That smells terrible!", Moric stated the obvious. "What is that?"

"Shh gnome!", scornfully demanded the young woman. "Do you want someone to hear us?"

"I'm just saying!", defended the gnome while glancing at a couple of the others and throwing a dagger-filled hand that he wasn't covering his face with into the air.

The stone entrance leading into Bright Star Hall was arch-shaped with the passage's highest, curved apex at roughly sixteen to seventeen feet tall, and its walls were semi-smooth like the ones in Thorin's cave. Scattered upon them were rough sketches and paintings depicting goblin life. All the way from what appeared to the companions as hunting parties and past hunts up to the beasts' god vandalized the dwarven stronghold's ingress. Even some of their weapons and other objects made from bone material littered the cavern's floor.

All the rescuers kept their eyes peeled open looking for anymore of the wretched beasts, but the only things moving in the cave were the dancing flames coming from hissing torches held by black, iron, wall sconces. The brackets were housed into small, square recesses in the wall every fifteen feet.

The two cooking pots over the simmering fires seemed to hold the three farmers' attention.

"What do you think is in these things?", perplexed Edward still covering his nose with the bend in his folded arm.

"I don't know," Jericho replied with a small shrug from his cannonball-like shoulders. "Let's get a look," he curiously added noticing the cauldron's cover half open. The metal top balancing on most of the rim while a large, wooden spoon-like utensil rose from the uncovered side of the pot.

"Do we really need to know guys?", Moric agonizingly inquired. "I mean in case you haven't noticed, it smells really bad in here."

"Here hold this for a second," Jericho gave Harold his staff as the big man reached for the mixing spoon.

The cauldron's vapors seemed stronger at the pot when the three stepped up to it. A thick, creamy, grayish-brown gruel bubbled within and flies buzzed and hovered over the goblins' smelly mix. The largest of the companions began to use the wooden utensil to slowly stir and turn the mixture. Suddenly, a whole human hand and a severed foot attached to its ankle floated to the top.

Quickly releasing his grip on the stirrer, Jericho jumped back in horror. "By the gods!", he shockingly remarked.

Both McKinley brothers also retreated from the startling revelation swiftly turning away in disgust from the scene.

"We need to keep moving," Calvin broke in. "Someone will need to stay behind and make sure no one sneaks up on us."

"I agree," acknowledged Sergeant Piner.

"I believe a small force of people can move not only quicker, but also owns a better chance of going undetected."

"What is your idea Calvin?", inquired the sergeant.

"You and your men remain here to guard the hall's entrance. The rest of us will follow the tunnel and free our people along with any of the dwarves. Thorin knows these halls so he shall lead."

"Very well," agreed Piner. The sergeant still in goblin guise saluted Calvin with a fist over his heart. "Good luck and watch your backs!"

Returning the salute, the knight responded. "You also."

"Everyone let's move," he ordered. "Thorin has the lead."

Watching the party disappear down the tunnel and out of sight, Sergeant Piner turned to his eight, morphed men. "I want two lookouts posted past that bridge and down the slope to where those rocks are that we quickly stopped at before coming here. I also want, two of you down that tunnel," he ordered. "No one is going to sneak up on us either way!"

"Yes sir!", responded the two turning and heading out the mouth of the cave quickly followed by two soldiers heading down the stony corridor to take up a position a hundred feet away.

Looking at the two, black, cooking pots before turning to the largest of the patrol, Sergeant Piner gave his last order for now. "Nathaniel, you and the rest of the men put out those fires and when the cauldrons cool down, get rid of that shit!"

"Yes sir!", smiled Nathaniel.

Dear, House Mother Xanthiaz

Matriarch of the House Zexthion

I pray to Thaisia that this letter finds you in good health and well being upon its arrival. Upon receipt of this note, you should be receiving the second shipment of gems from our newly, acquired outpost. I

hope like the previous goods, you are both happy and satisfied with their conditions and amount.
   I would also like to put your mind at ease with the news that...

House Wizard Zebbulas' attention was quickly pulled away from the brief letter he wrote to the house mother when one of her daughters, Priestess Xarna, threw the door to his office open in her haste. The drow woman's eyes ablaze with anger and her body language seemed to seethe with wrath as she tramped right into the room. As she slammed the wooden portal shut behind her, Zebbulas discreetly slid his partly-written transmission under some other blank parchments.

Laying the quill down near the bottle of ink sitting on his desk, the wizard watched Xarna take the seat across from him. Placing her feet up onto the piece of furniture, the priestess crossed her stiletto-healed boots as she sat back in her chair.

"How may I assist you priestess?", he pleasantly inquired knowing that at anytime Xarna could take out her anger on the wizard.

Staring into his eyes, the drow woman squinted as she prepared to speak. One query seemed to hang on her mind, "Was the wizard attempting to patronize her with the tone in his inquiry?"

"House Wizard, did I or didn't I make myself fully clear when I gave the order to kill all, not most, of the dwarven clerics?", she asked while still holding her composure.

"Yes priestess," he nervously answered. "Your directions were clear."

"Then maybe you can explain to me, why my ever watchful eyes witnessed a dwarven cleric healing the boy I whipped earlier?", snarled the enraged woman.

"Are you sure that's exactly what happened?", jittery inquired Zebbulas.

That question was the one extra gold coin that sunk the merchant's ship. Priestess Xarna with the speed of a striking viper dropped her feet off of the desk's top and lurched forward. Her anger lashed out at the male, dark elf and the hissing from her snake scourge filled the room. "Will you still enjoy to mock me with your questions, wizard?"

The startled drow pushed his chair back out of a natural reaction before anxiously responding, "No priestess! Please accept my humble apologies," he fearfully begged.

Staring at the shaken wizard for a moment, the woman lashed the magical weapon back to her side and resumed her seat. "I will allow this little meeting to continue, but do not mistake my show of meekness to be a sign of weakness. I may choose to whip you for your insolence later," she warned.

"Thank you Priestess Xarna. Again, I humbly apologize!"

"Stop groveling house wizard," Xarna advised in disgust. "It is not becoming of your rank."

Trying to change the subject of their conversation back to when she had first barged into the chamber, Zebbulas acknowledged what Xarna had said. "You say you know of a dwarven cleric in our midst?"

"That is correct. He healed the boy earlier," she coldly confirmed. "How do you think we should address this situation House Wizard Zebbulas?"

Rising from his seat and straightening out his robes the dark elf extended a hand towards the room's door. "After you priestess. I am sure that you would like to hear what the dwarf has to say, especially if my hunch is correct, and you have to beat it out of him."

The woman rose and a devilish smile dressed her face. "Again, you solidify the reasoning I have regarding keeping you around as my house wizard after I have removed my mother from the picture."

Zebbulas closed the wooden door behind him as he followed Xarna out of the room.

⚜

The stone room was dark as night with the only ray of light shining in through the small, barred, four inch by six inch slot in the wooden door. The cell was only a ten by ten foot space with a long chain hanging directly in the center of the chamber and a large metal hook ornate its end. Connected to the far wall was a complete set of shackles, and previously they held the room's only occupant by both his wrists and ankles. The prisoner was a beaten and battered dwarf.

The captives long, fire-red hair hung down over his face and shoulders. It flowed mid-way to the dwarf's back and was high-lighted with streaks of gray, and the prisoner wore a beard and mustache that matched in color. Bloody lash marks crisscrossed all over his emaciated body leaving dried blood caked on it. The dwarf's shirt laid on the cell's floor torn and tattered causing one to guess that it had fallen from his body instead of being removed. His brown pants were ripped in several places down his left leg and his small feet were shoeless. The captive's head hung from his neck and his gaze seemed to be locked on the floor below.

Outside the wooden door stood two drow guards with their eyes always on the lookout down both sides of the hallway. The sentries looked like normal male dark elves and both wore magical, subterranean armor of their homeland. The adamant, chain shirts radiated a soft, purplish hue and both of them wore pants and boots of black leather. Hanging from their hips, the drow were armed with two scimitars each. Only the dark elves could proficiently fight using a weapon of equal size in each hand. A hand-held crossbow, another weapon exclusive to the drow race, hung from one of the guard's belt tethered by a leather strap. A bandolier of darts crossed his chest, and knowing the dark elves, the small, hypodermic missiles were no doubt poisoned.

The companions followed Thorin down the cavern's passageway roughly three hundred feet on their way towards Bright Star Hall. The tunnel's width and height remained the same and the square recesses still lined the walls every fifteen feet housing burning torches. Their flickering flames produced dancing shadows on the enclosed, stony surfaces.

The group of rescuers walked in a single line and their footfalls were the only noise in the corridor adding to the crackling and popping of the burning wood from the tunnels only light source. Their eyes constantly on the lookout for any forms of trouble. The dwarf led the way followed by Calvin, Moric, the half-elf, Faith, Jericho, the McKinley brothers, Harold and then Edward, while the elf guarded the rear.

All the companions, except Thorin, expected the mountain's corridor to be stale with a somewhat mildew smell to it, but instead were surprised when the air was actually fresh and clean. An elaborate, natural venting system brought the outside oxygen to the subterranean passage causing even the strong, pungent odor that had engulfed the atmosphere back within the goblin's lair to be gone now. It had been dissipated by the constant flow of new air arriving from the surface. All the party's members were relieved to be rid of the terrible stench.

In front of the adventurers, a thick, stone parapet wall stood with a shut portcullis halting any type of advancement. The defensive structure following the boundaries of the tunnel's walls so close that it almost looked like it and the mountain were one. The only space between the ceiling and the rampart was above the only entryway blocked by the structure's barred grating.

"This is the hall's second defensive barrier," the dwarf informed the knight after taking a puff from a cigar and removing it from his lips.

"Second? What was the first?", puzzled Calvin.

"A set of large, stone doors that close off the hall's entrance back at the cave."

"But I didn't see any doors," reflected Moric while scratching the side of his head.

"Exactly gnome. Where'd they go?", questioned Thorin.

The rest of the line all coming together to discuss the corridor's obstacle that lay ahead.

"How are we going to get past this here?", queried the big man.

"Levitate the gnome up the wall," came Faith shooting forth her idea. "When he reaches the top, Moric climbs over and raises the gate allowing all of us to walk through."

"Good idea!", excitedly complimented the gnome moving towards the wall. "Go ahead, I'm ready."

"I can't," dejectedly admitted the young magic-user.

"What do you mean you can't?", questioned Moric.

"I was just a novice when the lady I told you about died. I never learned how," she explained bowing her head almost shamefully.

Placing a hand on her shoulder, the leader seemed to support the young woman with only his words. "Do not trouble yourself Faith. We are all young and like you we will learn."

The young woman gazing into his face and smiling at his words of inspiration.

"Speak for yourselves lad," interjected Thorin seeming to be smiling.

A couple of the companions sharing in a brief smile as well as they had a hunch that the dwarf was the oldest amongst them.

"Well Faith it is your idea, but I think I can help," advised Jhessail glancing from her to the wall and back to the young magic-user. "When this escapade is over, if we are in accord, then I can also be of some aid to you by assisting you in picking up with your studies in the arts where you left off," he added with a smile.

The half-elf's words causing not only the woman to smile again but also nod her head in affirmation.

Stepping forward and calling upon a spell to aid him, Jhessail magically guide the gnome up the side of the wall. Everyone watched as Moric climbed over the top and disappeared from sight.

Within moments the portcullis began to rise.

⚜

Katherine along with the other slaves had just returned to their holding pen for a night's rest. The little girl was run down and felt extremely exhausted from the lack of sleep the day's toil had caused along with the limited amount of food and water they had been given. She moved in slow motion like a zombie and Thomas, who just about mirrored her state, held his sister's hand.

Both siblings were concerned and worried about their older brother all last night and today as the two made their way over to where the boy laid near his overseer, Drü Slopewalker. Katherine and Thomas' weariness was rapidly overcome when they saw Junior laying on his side talking with the dwarf. Both zombie-like children started a mad dash for their older brother.

"Junior!", simultaneously cried his siblings, their tears of happiness already beginning to run from their eyes.

Looking over to the only family the boy had left, an instant smile dressed his face when he heard his name called. "Kat! Thomas!", he yelled while sitting up.

Little Katherine fell into his outstretched arms. "Junior you're alright!", excitedly stating the obvious. "I missed you! I love you!"

"Hey Junior, you're back!", excitedly remarked Thomas while throwing his arms around both his embraced siblings.

"I missed and love you guys too," proclaimed the oldest of the three.

Drü smiled while watching the family reunion.

The happy moment was suddenly interrupted by four, drow guards accompanied by both a dark elf priestess and wizard entering the slave's pen. One of the sentries approached the three children and the rising dwarf. Behind him strolled the woman causing a look of fear to mask Junior's face as the recovering boy was engulfed with terror. The memories of their pain-filled meeting washing over him.

"You! Come with us!", ordered the snarling guard pointing at Slopewalker.

"For what?", pridefully inquired the dwarf.

"You dare show insolence to your superiors?"

"I only hold the Forger and his brother the Quarrier, along with my king, as my superiors. Not some…"

The crack of the drow's whip sent the captive reeling back from its strike. Fear radiated from the three children as the guard lashed the dwarf a second time followed by a third. Everyone in the cell withdrew in terror.

Fresh blood on Drü's bald head and face began to flow from the whip's lashes. Dazed, he fell to a knee.

"You will be an example for anyone else who dares rebel against your masters!", the sentry announced as his whip lashed out at the dwarf again and again.

Scared for the fallen cleric, Katherine, who was witnessing the horrible act, rose to her feet and tried to shield the one responsible for helping her older brother. The little girl was not aware of his direct involvement in Junior's better health but knew the dwarf had been watching over him and nursing him. "Stop! You're hurting him!", she yelled.

The dark elf cracked the whip against the floor beside the little girl causing Katherine to flinch and blink her eyes, but the small child stayed rooted in her place. An anger-filled snarl creased the guard's face. The drow sentry pulled his arm back preparing to strike Katherine punishing her for her insubordination while the child knew what was about to come. Shutting her eyes and raising her little arm as if trying to block the whip's lash, Katherine heard her brothers cry.

"No!", both shouted out as they fumbled to gain their feet.

The drow, leading with his elbow, was caught by surprise when the forward progress of his arm was stopped by a hand seizing his wrist. Snapping his head around to see who held onto him, the guard looked into the one face he never expected. Standing behind him was the dark elf slave.

❧

Zolktar had sat off to the side out of the way when the six drow had entered the large holding pen. The dark elf's thoughts were lost as they wandered aimlessly around in his bound mind seeking for answers, but no matter how hard he tried to remember who he was, the drow's memories always ironically seemed enslaved themselves. The girl's doe-like eyes dominated his own absorbed thinking.

Zolktar was broken from his own silent deliberation by the cracking of the guard's whip. His punishment directed on the dwarven slave. The priestess stood in the sentry's vicinity and seemed to enjoy the beating the bald captive was receiving. Zolktar thought the woman looked familiar but he just couldn't place where he had seen her before.

The other three drow guards stood scattered amongst the cavern. Just their presence and the whipping the dwarf was receiving seemed to be sending an appropriate message to the terror-stricken prisoners. The black-robed wizard stood only half a dozen feet away from him watching in amusement. Just the notion of the wizard seemed to bring unanswered questions to Zolktar's mind.

Turning his attention back to the whipping, Zolktar witnessed the child, who had to be around nine or ten winters old he guessed, rise to defend the kneeling and blood-covered slave. Memories from earlier today with the little girl ran through his mind's eye calling to memory how she had brought him a mug of water when no one, not even his kind would offer him a drink, and how the young child, despite what the others said, gave him a bowl of food as he starved. She had gone out of her way to be nice to him but the dark elf could not figure out why.

The guard cracked the whip on the ground near her, but still the child held her shielded position between the attacker and the wounded dwarf. Zolktar still knew that his dark race would show the child no mercy and she would be the next example to be lashed and lashed good for her insolence. The dark elf felt like the child not only deserved him to show her a favor due to her acts of kindness towards him, but the feeling he had of her being the key to his rediscovering who he really was ran deep in him.

With the speed of a striking viper, Zolktar was up covering the short distance and seizing the guard's wrist ready to strike the child causing the sentry to snap his head around.

"Enough," Zolktar growled the statement. "She is only a child trying to defend her fallen friend. Her crime is not one of insolence nor disobedience but rather compassion."

Before Zolktar knew what was happening, he dropped to his knees and the veins in his neck bulged as he fought against an invisible, downward pressure. A hissing filled the air and the lashing accompanied by its biting pain returned to the shirtless slave. Priestess Xarna had loosed her snake scourge. Both the sight and the sound caused Junior to scurry backwards across the stone floor.

"Do not tempt me on this night," warned the drow woman. "Guards take both of them to the dungeons and chain them up. I'll be paying them a visit later," she addressed the sentries with a devilish grin.

Turning her attention to Katherine, who slightly cowered at her glance, Priestess Xarna spoke scornfully to the little girl. "That was a brave thing you did child and I commend you on it, but if you ever do that again I will personally enjoy whipping you myself," she threatened making a point to show the child her snake scourge.

Katherine swiftly backed further away by the sight of the three, viper heads writhing and striking but biting nothing but air. Fear washing over her.

"Ask your brother how he felt while I whipped him."

Junior pulled his little sister into his arms while Thomas attempted to shield them both with his body.

"Let's go," ordered Xarna slightly amused at the boy's heroic act.

Two of the drow guards together dragged the bodies out of the cell's entrance. One set pulled Zolktar while the other two took Drü. Wizard Zebbulas was the last to leave the pen closing and locking the gate behind him.

For several minutes all the horrified occupants of the holding cell sat quietly. Their terrified panic still housed in their bodies.

Finally glancing up to her brother's eyes, Katherine softly stated to Thomas, "See. The wizard stuck up for me again."

Changing her gaze to where Zolktar had sat, the little girl added, "I hope he's going to be alright."

CHAPTER 25

Jericho helped Moric remove the stone weights filling the basket that counter-balanced the raised portcullis. Every time one of the hard minerals was taken away, the wall's barred gate lowered until finally it closed shut separating the companions from the rest of the tunnel they had just followed. The passageway's floor littered with dark stains from dried blood. Its ceiling inclining up-wards into the darkness ahead.

Calvin had decided to form two separate lines on opposite sides of the hall's corridor instead of a single-filed one down its center.

"Dwarf, I want you up ahead in the lead followed by myself, Jhessail, Faith, and Devis on one side while on the other wall I want Moric followed by Jericho, Harold, and Edward," he informed the party. "People stay close to the walls and look alive. I do not have to tell you where we are now."

The leader of the party also decided to get an update from the group's two magic-users regarding what spell-casting abilities were left in their arsenals. "Faith. Jhessail. Where are we at as far as magical aid goes?"

"I have one spell left along with three cantrips," advised Faith.

"I still retain the ability to cast several more including the clerical ones that I need to pray to Guerra for," updated the wizard-warrior.

Nodding his head, Calvin perplexed on Faith's earlier words. "What do you mean by cantrip?"

"It is just a small spell that a magic-user knows allowing he or she to cast it without the need for the spell's components."

"But elves seem to never use any items and speak only words to cast their magic," questioningly pointed out Edward recalling an elven mage, who had once before visited Oakhurst's mid-summer festival and made coinage performing tricks of magic.

"That's because they are part of the magical web of life. It is like elves are one with the art," explained Faith. "Do you understand what I am trying to say?"

"Yes, I think so," the McKinley hesitantly replied.

Looking amongst all in the group, Calvin came forth with another question, "It is getting late outside of the mountain. Do we need to rest for the night, so you can study and replenish your spells?", glancing between the two casters.

"If we can find a safer place it might be a good idea for Faith," the halfelf responded. Jhessail had received both abilities to cast spells with no daily studying and no need of components from his elven father. Unfortunately he had not inherited the "Reverie" of the elven people, but needed sleep like that of his human mother.

"Up ahead is a small chapel that's used during the times needed to man the tunnel and its wall," Thorin interjecting the possible beneficial information. "We may be able to stay there for the night undetected."

"It is worth a shot," hopefully stated the knight. "Take the lead dwarf and the rest of us shall follow."

In minutes the armed companions were back on the move down the passageway. Their destination; the chapel to the dwarven gods the Forger and his brother the Quarrier known as "The Iron and the Rock."

⁂

The two lines of party members against each side of the tunnel's walls followed the rocky corridor for another four hundred and fifty feet. At a couple of spots along the way, the passage snaked and wound but for most of the distance it had run a straight course. The wall's recesses were still spaced exactly the same and the light coming from the almost burnt out torches was dimmer now than before. The only difference in the underground hallway was the height of the ceiling.

It had risen to the point where one could only see darkness now, but every once and a while, the tip of a large, rocky stalactite could be seen by the human eye. Only the group's demi-humans could still somewhat make out the appearance of the rough, overhead lining. Located on the wall up ahead, before the tunnel took another left, was a set of wooden doors. The dying light from the torches could barely be seen reflecting off of iron bands decorating both solid, oak portals. "That's the chapel up ahead," softly informed Thorin glancing back over his shoulder to Calvin.

The adventurers swiftly, but as quietly as they could move while searching the passageway high and low, started for the doors.

Upon reaching the two solid, oak portals with three iron bands running across them for reinforcement, Thorin reached out for the decorated, metal latch. He was surprised when the gnome suddenly smacked the dwarf's hand away from the opening device.

"What did you do the for you runt?", asked the irritated dwarf around the cigar butt protruding from his mouth. A scowl dressed his face.

"It may be trapped!", justified the self-proclaimed locksmith.

"Now why would dwarves go and trap their own chapel door lock?", inquired Thorin perturbed with the gnome while rolling his eyes towards the surface above ground.

"They wouldn't, …", obnoxiously replied Moric, "…but if you remember right, from what we know so far, the dwarves don't run this place anymore.

Glancing to the party and then back to the so called lock expert, Thorin slightly lifted his brows as his facial expression changed to one of acknowledgment. "Good point," he softly added.

Moric glanced back to the cavalier, who met his gaze with only a nod.

"Everyone fall back ten feet," ordered the knight. "Go ahead gnome. Do your thing."

When Moric was satisfied that everyone was back far enough, the gnome scanned the other side of the tunnel looking to see if anyone was coming down it. The coast was clear. Dropping down to a knee and laying his sword on the ground next to him, the gnome took a minute to inspect the locking mechanism while softly talking to himself, and at times appearing to the others to be speaking to the device. Moric removed a stiff, leather, case-like pouch from his hip underneath his pot belly and laid it open on the tunnel's floor in front of one of his knees. The locksmith stuck his small, stubby digits inside it searching for something particular.

Rummaging around until he found what he was seeking, Moric withdrew three lockpicks and held two up at eye level comparing them for a brief time before putting one back. The gnome took hold of the remaining two tools, one in each hand, and once again closely inspected the door's lock. The locksmith seemed to play with the mechanism for a minute before turning back toward the anxiously waiting party glancing all about.

"No traps," Moric advised the group waving them to him. Turning back towards the device, he started to fiddle with the picks again.

"Can you open it?", inquired Faith as she and the others approached their kneeling companion. His tongue slightly hanging out of the side of his mouth.

"Does a dragon have wings?", he answered her question with one of his own causing the young woman to just shake her head at his query.

The thief finally twisted both picks together at the same time as his small, stubby fingers worked nimbly on the lock.

"Click." "Click." "Click."

The gnome withdrew the two tools and put them back in their proper places. He buckled up the straps to the case-like pouch and retrieved his short sword while rising to his feet. Replacing the case back to its location on his hip, the self-proclaimed locksmith turned to the others. "Ta dah! Who said you have to be a mage to perform magic?"

Again, Faith just shook her head at the question and rolled her eyes.

"Good work my friend," complimented Calvin accompanying it with a pat on Moric's shoulder.

"Good job little buddy," added Jericho.

The little locksmith took a step back so Thorin could begin to push open the heavy door.

Slowly the dwarf opened the door ajar giving him a chance to peek into the chapel's room. The chamber was completely black and with the dull lighting from the corridor, Thorin's eyes couldn't adjust properly causing him not to see anything.

Pushing the door open enough he stuck his head in to have a better look. The dwarf's vision began to adapt to the room's pitch darkness and moments later he could tell that no heat forms stood anywhere in this area of the chapel.

Thorin drew his dagger while uttering the command word calling upon its magic. Starting softly and slowly picking up its intensity, the sapphire housed in the dagger's pommel began to glow casting a bluish light. The dwarf's vision adjusting to the gems illumination allowing him to make sure the room was completely empty.

"Hurry up everybody. Get in," he suggested relieved there was no one present.

The others followed Thorin into the room, and after the last companion slid through the doorway, he shut it barring it from the inside with a six by eight inch wooden beam. The hallway torches slowly faded to black dousing the tunnel in complete darkness. Not even the sapphire's bluish light shone from under the double doors.

Surveying the worshiping room of The Iron and the Rock, the party of companions found over a dozen and a half pews in the chamber beautifully carved from stone. Looking closely at the ends of the seats, one side had a dwarf forging an axe while the other side possessed a dwarf hammering a block of granite. On the backs of each pew ran a series of iron strips holding what appeared to be dwarven hymn books, and only Thorin, Moric and Devis seemed to know exactly what the songs read. It was obvious to the group's others that they spoke the dwarven language.

In the front of the room was a dais large enough to hold a three to four foot wooden table and a wooden lectern with a carved emblem of an anvil on it. Cut inside the image were a pair of forge tongs crossed by a hammer one way and a pick axe facing the other. Several feet behind the table were three chairs made from stone. The high sides to the chairs were also decorated with the same designs found on the pews.

Directly behind the places where obviously the hall's priests sat, but not on the raised platform, was a wooden door with iron bands running across it. The solid portal matched the set of double doors leading into the chapel.

"That door leads to the clerics' bed chamber," the dwarf pointed out.

"This is more your home than ours, Thorin, and as I have said before, you have the lead," confirmed the knight.

Going over to the entryway while still carrying his illuminated dagger, Thorin gently opened the door and pushed it in. The sapphire's radiance sliced through the sleeping quarter's darkness revealing a figure sitting on one of the three beds in the chamber with his back leaning against the wall while two more bodies laid about on the floor. The three, dwarven clerics had been dead for some time now and their corpses had already started to break down and decay. A foul odor wafted through the air eliciting some of the party members to cover their noses.

The room also contained two, wardrobe closets and a writing desk. On the desk appeared to be an ink bottle, a quill, parchment, and an open book.

"Looks as if the three were murdered," regretfully came Calvin.

"Looks that way to me also," painfully retorted Thorin throwing his cigar butt down and stepping on it.

"Grab some candles and light them up. We should be alright out in the chapel's main room for the night," advised the dwarf pointing to the room's candelabra. "Knight remain here with me while I check and see if there are any magical elixirs stashed about."

❦

The time had passed and three of the twenty two candles had already burned halfway down. During the search of the clerics' sleeping chambers, Thorin was able to find a wall stash they had kept in case another dwarf had gotten injured out here away from the center of the hall. The cache contained ten, four inch long beakers all labeled as healing potions, ten glass tubes marked as elixirs to neutralize poison, and four potions of regeneration. The hidden cubbyhole also held two, gold necklaces attached to onyxes, and a gold ring decorated with a small emerald. Thorin automatically knew that the jewelry was all magical when the gem in his axe's pommel began to glow and he could feel the weapon sheathed on his back vibrate. The dwarf closed the door behind him when both he and Calvin left the bed chamber turned holy tomb.

Both companions stood at the table on the dais located in the chapel. The group's leader inviting the rest of the party to join them on the raised platform.

"Everybody to me," requested the knight. "Thorin has some stuff he wants to hand out to everyone."

The others left their resting spots and gathered at the dais awaiting the items the dwarf wanted to pass out amongst them. Their eyes fixed on the objects sitting on the wooden table.

"All of you lads and lass,..." -the dwarf addressed the group gathered around him- "...I've got some potions that I believe will come in mighty handy when all hell breaks loose. Wrap these beakers up in something soft, or if you need a piece of that blanket I pulled out of the priests' room, tear it up and use that," he advised while pointing to the bed dressing laying on the floor in front of one of the three chairs on the platform.

Pulling the potions out of their test tube stands, the dwarf offered a brief explanation on the beaker's contents while handing one to each companion.

"This here amber-colored liquid one is a potion of healing. It will cure all wounds and repair any type of inflicted damage save for a severing strike or a death blow," he continued after everyone received one with Thorin keeping the extra potion to add with the one he already had given to himself.

Next he dispensed the creamy-colored, milky-textured beakers. "These here are antidotes used to neutralize poison. If anyone gets bitten or struck with a blade that causes you to become envenomed then this here little puppy will offset the poison's affects," his glance going around the table and meeting everyone's eyes for a second or two before adding, "And these will all come in extremely handy against the drow. Them buggers like to play with their toxins!"

"Finally, these four here I'm going to give to the half-elf," -pointing to the last ones that held a sparkling, blue liquid- "He's our cleric and we're going to be counting on him to heal us if need be."

"What are they?", slightly puzzled Jhessail trying to call to memory what type of potion sparkled.

"These here are the dwarves' version of potions of regeneration."

"What about those there?", inquired Moric pointing to the three pieces of jewelry.

"I know only that they are magical gnome," replied Thorin unsure of their properties. "I would lean towards them not being cursed, but I really don't know what they do," -he shrugged before adding- "I'll hold onto them for now."

"Everyone, put the potions in a safe place and get some sleep. The next day or two are going to get pretty hairy," tensely stressed Calvin.

"What about a watch tonight?", Harold questioned paranoid of a future encounter so soon.

"Since no one will be able to spot any light coming from under the door then we shall leave at least two to three candles burning for the night so everyone has light and can see," revealed Calvin. "I shall volunteer for first watch while the rest of you get some rest. I believe one person each shift shall suffice."

"I'll take second," came Devis.

"Since I'll be up studying, sign me up for third," reported Faith.

"I'll get up with you so you can concentrate more on your studies," Jericho's deep voice tolled in.

"Very well people. Everybody try and get some rest," advised the knight. "We have a long day tomorrow."

৵৶

An hour had passed since Devis was awoken from the Reverie and began his watch. The others all slumbered strewn about the dwarven chapel. A few of them slept on the pews, while the rest found spots littered on the chamber's floor. All three candles were about to burn out so the elf decided to replace them, but instead of lighting three new ones he only brought one to burn. Now the room's illumination darkened quite a bit.

His attention had been focused on the door leading in to the clerics' sleeping chambers ever since Thorin had called for the little gathering so he could hand out the magical potions that he had found, not to mention the three pieces of jewelry the dwarf had put in his own bag. Devis wanted badly to know if anything magical still laid hidden in the other room.

Taking a peek to make sure everyone still slept, the quiet elf skulked towards the wooden portal. Before disappearing into the space behind the chairs on the raised platform, Devis took a look back one more time checking on his sleeping companions. Everyone slumbered peacefully. With the coast clear, the stalker checked the door, but unfortunately for him it was locked.

"Son of an orc!", he thought while dropping to a knee.

Reaching his right hand inside his cloak, the elf slipped it into a hidden pocket near his left side. Grabbing the rolled up leather cylinder and pulling it out, Devis once again looked over his shoulder and then back to the contents in his hand. Two leather straps tied it up.

Laying the cloth-like object on the floor in front of him and untying the straps, the elf unrolled the cylinder pouch open. It was not unlike the gnome's set of lockpicks. Devis located the two tools he needed to accomplish the job and stuck them into the lock's keyhole. With the elf's naturally slender and nimble fingers working, he listened for the sound he wanted to hear. His acute hearing picking up the three, soft clicks of the mechanism's tumblers.

Putting the lockpicks back in the unrolled pouch before tying and rolling up the leather cylinder, the thief placed it back into his cloak's concealed pocket. Sneaking a second peek over his shoulder, Devis opened the door and entered the room. Inside, he quietly shut the wooden portal behind him.

The place was as black as a starless and moonless night, but his elven vision adjusted to his surroundings quickly causing all of the objects to appear more as forms of cold blueness.

Pulling his dagger from its sheath on the outside of his lower right knee, Devis uttered a word in elvish and within seconds light illuminated the room. Placing an ear on the door and taking a minute to listen for any noise, the elf heard nothing from his slumbering companions in the other room. Satisfied with their lack in knowing he was sneaking around, the thief went to work seeking both high and low for any type of treasure. Coins, gems, or other items of interest made no matter to him. Several times during his search Devis put an ear to the door, and like earlier the elf heard no movement only leading to him continuing his microscopic observation of the place.

The elf laid on his stomach checking under the last bed in the room where the body of the dead cleric sat on it leaning against the wall. It took him a couple of minutes of staring followed by running his hand over the minute cracks in the wall, but Devis realized he had found a hidden cache. The elf pushing it in and trying to slide the small eight by sixteen inch section until finally it worked and a small, hidden door opened. Inside was a small, iron box.

Sliding himself with the box out from under the bed, the elf placed it on the floor in front of him. Devis carefully checked it for any traps and found none, so he slowly opened its cover taking a look inside. The small, metal case held silver and gold coins along with four rubies, a white, gold ring with a black onyx, and a matching neck chain decorated by a jet black stone.

"Well, well, well. What do we have here?", softly asked Devis to himself. "Looks like the dwarf didn't get everything in here."

Getting up and once again putting an ear to the door, the satisfied thief returned to the box and opened a small, concealed pouch on the right inside of his cloak where he dropped all four rubies into it. Taking a look at the ring, he let that slip in right after the gems.

"I'll wear this under my armor," he remarked to himself before donning the white, gold necklace with the onyx. His leather armor concealed the piece of jewelry.

Closing the iron box and putting it back into its hidden cache, Devis secured the cubbyhole's hidden door leaving it just as he found it. Making his way over to the chamber's portal, the thief softly uttered another command word that dispelled the magic causing the dagger to light up the chamber and leaving it in total darkness again. For the last time, Devis placed an ear on the door and listened for any type of noise. Still the other room was silent. Opening the door, the elf quickly exited the room shutting it ever so quietly behind him.

The secretive thief peered around the three stone seats on the dais before returning to the wooden portal. Quickly he retrieved the two proper lockpicks from their pouch and secured the door. Within minutes Devis was joining his sleeping companions in the chapel.

The sly elf used the half burnt candle to light three new ones before extinguishing it and breaking the used one in half again. Surveying the unaware slumberers, Devis was confident in knowing none of them had any inclinations of what abilities he possessed or of what exactly had just taken place. The mysterious elf took up a seat on an empty pew watching over his sleeping companions while his mind was full of thoughts and ideas on how he would use his newly acquired items to procure the goods he wanted to attain in the upcoming future. Being one of the longest living races on Kanaan and only a century old, Devis with a content smile creasing his lips knew his future consisted of a lot of years to go.

CHAPTER 26

Drü Slopewalker cried out in pain again as Priestess Xarna's snake scourge lashed and the three viper heads bit into his hairy back for another time. The dwarf had been taking a beating that had begun back in the holding pen, and after being practically drug to this cell, had continued for a couple of hours now. The sadistic, drow priestess had already healed Slopewalker a couple of times securing that he wouldn't perish any time soon from the beating he received, so she could continue to brutally punish the last of Bright Star Hall's clerics. Blood stains spotted the floor around the dwarf, and Drü's hand shackles were suspending him from a hook that hung in the center of the chamber. House Wizard Zebbulas stood off to the side in one of the cell's corners. He was not about to get too close to the writhing and striking weapon.

"So, you wish me to believe that you are the only cleric left?", she snarled. "Is that correct dwarf?"

The beaten prisoner could only nod his head thanks to a cloth bit that had been stuck in his mouth muffling his words. The dark elves making sure Drü Slopewalker wouldn't be able to call on his gods for aid. His offered prayer for the boy's healing, his last spell granted him.

Taking a glance towards the wizard nodding his head in the affirmative seeming to confirm the truth of the cleric's answer, Xarna whipped the dwarf one more time. The fangs from the three snakes sinking into his skin. "I enjoy inflicting my wrath on you dwarf and I believe I might heal you again that way I can keep you amongst the living a little while longer," calmly spoke the priestess raising the prisoner's face with a hand under his chin. "I think the moral of your people will be lost when they see their beaten and destroyed cleric along with their battered king."

Putting her snake scourge back in its place on her hip, the viper heads became lifeless and the hissing died in the small room. House Wizard Zebbulas moved to open the cell's only door.

"Let's see how that traitor is doing?", demanded Xarna.

Before leaving the chamber she looked back to the prisoner, "By the way dwarf,…"

Drü Slopewalker raised his weary head to meet her gaze.

"Where are your gods now?", she asked arrogantly before laughing and strolling out of the cell. The house wizard followed closing the door behind him.

❦

The gate to the holding pen opened and the two drow guards tossed the bloody, unconscious Zolktar into the slaves' cell. His body hitting the ground hard. The dark elf was covered in blood and the sight of pink-colored meat caused by ripped and torn flesh appeared more than his ebony-colored skin did. The sentries laughing as they closed the barred portal behind them and left.

Katherine rose from her seated position next to her two brothers and went over to the dark elf's side. A gasp escaped the little girl when she noticed the drow's torn and mangled flesh. "That is what happened to him for sticking up for me again," she thought as the child began to kneel next to Zolktar. A tear beginning to form in the corner of her eye.

"Get away from him Kat! He's no good!", shouted Junior. His warning causing his sister to turn and glance at him for a second before returning her attention back to the unconscious drow.

"He saved me again," she yelled back over her shoulder.

"I wish I could help you but I'm stuck here with nothing and I can't. Thank you for sticking up for me again just like you did with those mean goblins. Those ugly creatures needed to be slapped," she informed the motionless Zolktar. "I'm sorry that my brother Junior is being mean to you, but he blames you for killing mother and father. I don't think you did and please don't be mad at Junior though because he's a really nice boy."

Playing with a small rock on the ground that she looked at, Katherine's gaze went right back to the fallen captive. "Anyways, I don't know why those people are being so mean to you. Don't they know you're a wizard and could probably kick their butts?"

"Come on Kat, really come over here!", begged Junior.

"Please!", cried Thomas.

"My brothers are calling me so I have to go for now, but I hope when you wake up you'll speak to me," the little girl rose from the spot. "Bye," she added before leaving his side.

The dirty, doe-eyed child started to return back to her brothers but stopped and turned to the unconscious drow. She added one more thing before leaving. "How silly of me," she giggled, "My name is Katherine, if you're wondering."

❧

Thorin peaked his head out of the chapel's door looking one way and then the other down the tunnel's dark passageway. "Coast is clear," the dwarf informed the others. "You might as well cast those spells of yours now before we're in the corridor," he added.

"Please allow me," cordially offered the half-elf before calling on the aid of his magic. One at a time, two candles flared into brightness as Jhessail imbibed the sticks of wax with light spells allowing the humans the benefit of sight as they ventured down the tunnel. The candles would radiate their glow for at least the next five hours, and if the group needed to douse the light rays all the holder would have to do is hide them in something or cover them with thick cloth.

"I want a single, zig-zag line moving down the passage," sternly requested Calvin. He knew everyone would need some room to swing and use their weapons. "Thorin, you still have the lead followed by Moric and then I. Next will come the rest of us humans; Jericho, Faith, Harold, Edward, and then Jhessail with Devis will guard our rear." The group's leader finished by giving his usual order, "Everyone look alive."

245

With their weapons in hand, the companions looked to be a force to be reckoned with as they started down the stony hallway. The cigar-smoking dwarf carried his two-handed maul followed by Moric, who was armed with both daggers, one in each hand. In the third position of the zig-zag line walked the knight carrying his shield in his left hand and his sword in his right. Jericho armed with his staff, and on an angle away from him was the magic-user carrying both light sources in her left hand and her bull whip still rolled up in her right. Then came Harold toting his javelin with the other McKinley brother behind him carrying his loaded crossbow. Finally the wizard-warrior stalked slowly and ever vigilant of his surroundings armed with his sword, and the elf constantly searching the darkness behind them with his bow and a half-nocked arrow at the ready.

The party of rescuers followed the tunnel always getting closer and closer to the main area of Bright Star Hall. The mountain's corridor remained the same with its smooth walls arched on both sides and the passage's ceiling out of sight. Thorin had led them for at least two hours now and only the dwarf could tell that the floor slightly continued to slope downward for the last half of that time. He wondered if the gnome had any clue of the decline.

His cigar had burnt out a while back, and after a slight smoke break, Thorin had used a different magical property of his maul to light up another. Small, white waves of smoke rose from it as he puffed on its other end several times while the dwarf had a quick thought cross his mind. The group had not encountered anything yet, but little did the lead companion know that that was about to change. Suddenly without any warning, a giant spider fell from the ceiling landing right on top of the unsuspecting gnome. Two more descended from out of the darkness above. One landed near Faith while the other hit the ground directly behind the group. Venom dripping from their large fangs.

Moric had no time to react as one of the spiders crashed down on him and quickly drove the gnome onto his back. The air stolen from his lungs left them burning while the gnome desperately sought the oxygen his body badly needed. The arachnid's two, short sword length fangs dripping venom on both sides of Moric pinned underneath it. The spider's surprising attempt at its piercing strike failed to hit its struggling target.

⟟

The giant, black, hairy spider missed landing on Faith by only mere feet. Its stabbing fangs thrusting downward but only meeting with air. The arachnid's eight legs starting its advance towards the startled woman.

⟟

Both the elf and the half-elf witnessed the attempted attack on Faith along with the one on Moric. Like the rest of the party, the two were not only caught off guard but also surprised by the sudden appearance of the two spiders. They never saw the arachnid that had dropped behind them, but thanks to their elven trait, Devis and Jhessail spun towards the wall on their respective sides of the tunnel. The spider's fangs finding nothing but empty air.

⟟

Being caught by surprise for a moment, Calvin finally seemed to realize what was happening. Orders flew through the air after he rapidly assessed the situation seeming to snap a couple of his startled companions from out of their stillness, "Jericho, Harold, assist Faith!", the knight shouted. "Edward aid the rear! Thorin help me with the one on the gnome!"

⟟

Again the fangs pierced downward at the gnome, but this time air had begun to flow into Moric's lungs and for the second time in a row he was able to barely dodge their attacks. "I need some serious help like yesterday!", Moric anxiously yelled to no one in particular while struggling under the heavy weight of the giant arachnid on top of him. "Helloo!", he shouted.

Hearing the gnome's cry for help, Calvin was already closing the distance between him and the spider. "I am coming my friend!", assured the knight raising his shield and tucking his shoulder behind it as he ran toward the creature. The leader rammed the spider's side behind its front leg jolting the beast towards its right and almost into the wall.

Thorin's axe began to vibrate and the emerald in its pommel started to glow. He could feel it shaking because it was sheathed on his back. The dwarf with his two-handed maul over his head charged the arachnid. Swinging the hammer down, he missed as Calvin's shield ram was enough to move its body clear of the dropping hammer's head.

Caught initially by surprise and trying to swiftly step back, Faith tripped over her own two feet causing her to fall to the ground. The magical candlesticks flew from her grasp as the young woman's eyes widened for a split second.

Witnessing the magic-user trip, Jericho desperately tried to cover the distance between him and her rapidly. The big man swung his staff like a club hoping the placement of his hands on the end of his weapon would give the extension he needed to at least graze the spider stealing its attention away from the prone woman. The strike not even coming close.

Harold was on his way to Faith's aid when a small, needle-like dart found its mark piercing his neck. The stinging prick caught his attention as he instinctively smacked the lodged missile away from him. Looking down to see what had hit him, Harold's eyesight was already becoming fuzzy.

It was a McKinley brother that saved the fallen woman, but not Harold. Edward was about to turn around and lend his assistance to both Devis and Jhessail when he saw Faith fall backwards surprised by the attacking beast. At the instant, he took a quick moment to aim and fire his crossbow. The bolt flew through the air and hit the spider in one of its six eyes. The arachnid reared back screeching in pain.

Coming out of his spin, Devis fully pulled the bowstring back and let the nocked arrow fly. The fletched missile hitting its mark pushing the attacker a step or two back. Quickly, the elf reached over his shoulder and pulled another arrow from its quiver.

Jhessail started uttering the spell incantation when he began to spin towards his left. Doing a complete three hundred and sixty degree turn, the half-elf pointed his open left hand at the spider upon the completion of the last word and three magical, golden arrows sailed into their target.

Squealing in pain, the arachnid hastily retreated backwards.

Calvin's shield ram had done more than just jolt the arachnid and prevent it from sinking its fangs into Moric. It had provided the gnome, who had lost both weapons from the initial impact of the spider falling on him, the opening he needed to crawl out from under the black, hairy attacker.

"I'm coming out Calvin!", the gnome yelled his plan so he wouldn't catch a sword slash in the mouth. Moments later, Moric was helped from underneath the spider by the knight's gauntlet-covered hand pulling him free of imminent danger. Noticing what he thought to be was one of his lost daggers on the ground at first, the gnome picked up and looked at a dart with a bent tip.

The leader had just heard Moric's intentions and glanced down to see the small hostage trying to get free. Calvin, with his weight still against his shield trying to push the beast off of his companion, reached down grabbing the gnome and pulling the little guy out of harm's way. The knight thought he heard something deflect off his shield, but for all he knew it was probably one of the spider's eight legs.

Thorin raised is warhammer high in the air and for a second time brought the weapon down. This time however, the dwarf hit the bulbous, rear half of the spider. Instantly it squealed its pain while thrashing its eight, hairy legs.

Faith was trying to rise to her feet while still attempting to back away before fully upright. The woman, magic-user uttered a spell's incantation and moments later, a greenish, liquid orb flew into the face area of the spider. The floating globe ruptured on impact and the sound of hissing along with smoke rose from the screeching beast. Instantly the spider started to back into and slightly up the passageway's wall. "Be careful, I just hit it with acid!", warned the young woman.

Hearing Faith stating her forewarning and witnessing the smoke rise accompanied by the hissing sound, the big man decided to swing at one of the spider's four legs closest to him. The strike hit solid on the creature's second leg joint of what would be equivalent to its knee, and Jericho not only heard the snap but felt the joint give way to the blow from his staff. It seemed to him to help being muscular because when he landed a shot something almost always broke.

Loading his crossbow, the long-haired McKinley watched the arachnid take three hits already. He glanced over his shoulder to see how both the elf and the half-elf faired against their opponent. The two seeming to have the upper hand.

Turning his attention back towards the spider taking a pounding presently, he noticed Harold go down hard out of the corner of his left eye. Instantly, Edward looked in that direction.

Devis released his second arrow, and like the first one, it hit its target. The arachnid could barely move now and its steps were both shaky and slow. The elf drew another arrow from its quiver and suddenly noticed something whiz by the back of Jhessail, as the half-elf charged forward ready to strike at the spider with his sword.

Seeing the beast ready to die, Jhessail rushed at it slashing at the terminally troubled creature. The wizard-warrior finally cleaving into the side of the spider's head causing the black, hairy arachnid to drop and twitch a couple of times before going completely limp. Jhessail never noticing the dart that flew behind him.

The knight took two steps back giving himself enough room to take a swing at the creature, but the spider had other plans as it pushed it bulbous body away from the wall. The arachnid lashed out with its front leg closest to Calvin, and the hit struck the leader's shield square launching him into the air and across the tunnel. The knight smacking the rocky wall hard and bouncing off of it before landing on his face.

❧

Smoke rose from the burning acid covering the face of the black, hairy spider while still screeching its pain. The three companions had appeared to have knocked the fight right out of it as Faith and Jericho watched the eight-legged creature try to climb up the passage's wall.

❧

"What's this?", Moric asked himself stealing a brief second to look around while rising to his feet. Before the gnome could thoroughly give the tunnel a once over he watched Calvin get thrown across the mountain's corridor and hit the wall hard before hitting the ground even harder. Drawing his short sword, the freed gnome rushed to position himself between the spider and his downed leader, who had charged in and helped Moric to get free from his predicament.

The gritty warrior was becoming ornery by the second and he had had enough of the arachnid. Thorin witnessed the spider throw the knight through the air, and knowing the gnome was clear, decided to really get the creature's attention. Calling upon the magical aid from his maul, the dwarf pointed the top of the hammer's head at the arachnid. The ruby in the weapon's pommel glowed red bathing Thorin with a devilish appearance as a sphere of fire shot forth from the enchanted, dwarven weapon blasting the rear half of the spider's body apart. Smoke rose from the simmering carcass.

❧

Edward peered into the blackness above after witnessing his brother fall to the ground. His crossbow loaded and at the ready. Harold had not been involved in any melee with an opponent so he must have been struck down from something shot from above, the young farmer reasoned. The light from the magical candles did not illuminate enough area to clearly see the tunnel's ceiling, but Edward just knew that something was up in the darkness.

Faith had regained her feet and the young woman was not happy. She let the rolled up whip in her hand unravel to the ground while still holding the leather weapon's handle. "It's going to be coming towards you Jericho," she angrily announced before lashing out at the spider, which still faced her on its left side.

The weapon cracked against the smoking creature's side and it stepped right towards the party's big man. Another forceful blow from him caused the giant arachnid back a step left.

Jericho had just knocked the smoking creature back a step setting it up for another lash from Faith's whip when a needle-like dart stuck into his tricep on the back of one of his tree trunk arms. The prick causing the big man to swipe at the stinging area. A second hit to his hamstring brought Jericho crashing to the ground like a tree having been chopped down. His staff rolling a foot away from his fallen body on the corridor's stony floor.

Edward had seen the area where both small darts had flown out of the darkness. Taking a second to aim in the direction where they had come from and estimating the path of the bolt's trajectory, Edward fired his crossbow sending the bolt up into the area. The ceilings blackness engulfed it. Without wasting a second by watching the missile-fired weapon disappear into the darkness above, the farm boy had already began to reload.

～⁂～

The elf was able to see the figure on the tunnel's ceiling in between a cluster of stalactites fire its hand-held crossbow as he witnessed Edward fire a bolt skyward into the blackness above. The farmer's shot into the dark meeting with luck as it struck the thing above in its upper arm. Before it could move to a different location and set up for another attack, Devis let loose the nocked arrow he had ready. The missile-fire weapon struck the abomination's bulbous body causing it to mishandle the dart it was loading.

"On the ceiling!", yelled the elf addressing the rest of the companions. "It's a drachnid!"

Turning his attention quickly to the ceiling, Jhessail's ability to see in the darkness did not exactly rival that of Devis'. Because he was only a half-elf instead of a full-blooded elf, Jhessail's capability to see in the dark was hampered and his sight in both the blackness and at night was half that of an elves' vision. Lucky for him the tunnel's ceiling along with its fleshy addition was at the edge of his range to see.

The half-elf spoke the words to the spell's incantation and three, magical, golden arrows shot forth from his fingers. All of them found their target and for a quick second briefly illuminated the drachnid. Everyone; but the fallen knight trying to shake out the cobwebs from his head, along with the two, unconscious companions, and the woman magic-user, whose undivided attention was locked on the spider engaged in battle with her, saw the monstrous foe.

The drachnid yelled out its pain.

⤫

"I need some help here!", shouted Faith while striking out with the whip at her black, hairy adversary. Its crack missing the foe by only inches, but succeeding in pushing the arachnid a step to the right.

With the defeat of the spider by the dwarf that had originally landed on Moric, the gnome rushed to the knight's side. The party's leader still on his knees trying to regain his wits about him.

"Calvin, are you alright?!", he asked concerned for his friend's welfare.

"I shall be okay," he confirmed rising to a knee. "Aid Faith," ordered the knight scanning the corridor's floor for his sword.

Nodding his head, Moric ran to the woman's aid.

"Get some light up there!", advised the ornery, cigar-smoking dwarf. "I can't see em in that darkness!"

Unknown to Thorin, the drachnid had used its limited magical ability and cast a supernatural darkness in the area around it.

Devis spun quickly when he heard Faith's cry for assistance. The spider she faced alone looked to him as if it was preparing to spring and try to pounce on her. The elf pulled the string of his bow passed his pointed ear and took a couple of moments to aim his shot before letting loose the arrow. The missile flew passed the back of Edward's head sailing straight into the side of the arachnid's head piercing its brain. Instantly the foe dropped.

Not being able to see into the darkness, Edward could only stand at the ready to fire. He constantly scanned the blackness anxiously awaiting an attack to come.

Once again Jhessail called upon his magic and pointed his left hand to a stalactite he envisioned in the magical orb of darkness. "Watch your eyes!", he warned as the ceiling's rocky, mineral deposit instantly bathed the tunnel with a sixty foot radius of daylight. The half-elf's spell negating the drachnid's magical darkness.

Staring up at the ceiling all the companions, except for both Harold and Jericho, who were both laying prone, saw the monstrous abomination. Clinging to the side of one of the rocky ornamentations dotting the tunnel's roof was the drachnid.

Legend behind the existence of one of these half-spider, half-drow creations was known by many on Kanaan. As the lore went throughout the lands only a favored of the Goddess Thaisia would be bestowed her divine privilege to walk the subterranean realm as one of these creatures. From torso up, a drachnid was a dark elf warrior with long, flowing white or black hair, and their sinew muscles were ripped and hard as stone. From the waist down was that of an eight-legged, black, hairy spider with a large, bulbous body. A drachnid possessed the combined attributes and characteristics of both mixes of its godly creation.

This particular abomination had a man's naked torso with long, flowing, white hair over its ebony-colored skin and the creature's lower half was that of a black spider. Blood slowly ran from two pierce marks caused by a crossbow bolt and an arrow protruding out of its bulbous body. A pouch holding the darts hung from its hip and a spear was strapped to the drachnid's back. A hand-held crossbow filled its left hand as it used its right to cover its eyes from the bright light.

It took everyone in the passageway several brief moments for their eyes to adjust to the magical illumination.

Edward's shot was the first attack to be made after what seemed like an extended duration of time. He aimed the crossbow and fired watching the bolt soar upwards finding its mark and sinking into the foe's body. Edward obviously did a lot of hunting.

Snarling its pain, the drachnid pointed at a stalactite that hung from the tunnel's ceiling in the center of the McKinley brother, the half-elf, and the elf, firing a black arrow highlighted with a purplish aura at it. The magic missile struck the mineral deposit causing a loud crack to echo down the tunnel as the rock spear dropped from the ceiling. Devis and Jhessail dove towards where they had just come down the tunnel while Edward laid out over his brother's fallen body. The stalactite crashed down into the floor throwing rocky debris in all directions while the drachnid moved across the ceiling attempting to get away.

Thorin was the first companion to react as debris and a cloud of dust washed over him. The dwarf took aim with his hammer's head pointing it in front of the fleeing creature and triggered the maul's power. Its ruby, glowing red, as a sphere of fire shot into the air. The blazing orb catching the goddess' creation with a direct hit.

The drachnid screamed in both pain and horror as it began to plummet towards the ground. Somehow letting a last shot from its crossbow go.

"Got the bug!", excitedly claimed the dwarf as the dart it had fired nicked Thorin's cheek as it flew passed.

The drachnid landed awkwardly, both smacking and crunching the stone floor as the abomination's body burned from the magical fire.

Thorin could tell some of the sleep poison that had made contact tried to have some affect on the dwarf, but with his naturally, strong constitution he would not be succumbing to its effects anytime soon.

Suddenly, another stalactite fell landing on the drachnid's smoking corpse. Debris accompanied by a second cloud of dust bombarded the corridor and its occupants.

Gazing back to the others, the dwarf proudly confirmed his claim from earlier around the cigar sticking out from his beard, "Yup, definitely got the bug."

CHAPTER 27

Clouds of dust slowly flowed their way throughout the tunnel, and stony debris from the two fallen stalactites littered the corridor's rocky floor. The dwarven hall's complex, venting system that supplied air, not only to this passage but rather the whole stronghold, would eventually clear the billow of smoke running both ahead of the group as well as where they had just come down the mountain's conduit.

Like the fiery phoenix rising reborn from the fire and ashes on Calvin's shield, the companions seemed to rise from the wave of dust rolling over them. Coughing and wiping their eyes, all the members of the group, except Jericho and Harold, responded to the roll call from their leader. Both had been victims of direct hits from the hand crossbow's darts and laid unconscious on the passage's stone-littered floor.

"Calvin!", Edward excitedly reported. "Harold must have been hit from something above. Probably one of those darts."

"Jericho also," came Faith moving towards the fallen oak.

"Sit em up," instructed the dwarf pulling the half-smoked cigar from his mouth and walking towards where the magic-user and Jericho were.

"They'll need those neutralize poison elixirs poured into their mouths and down their throats. Both took a hit of drow sleeping poison."

Edward dragged Harold's rubble-covered body over to the tunnel's wall and leaned his back against it. The long, wavy-haired McKinley dug into his own pack searching for the creamy, milky-white liquid. Finding the cloth it was stored in, he removed it from his gear and unwrapped the material extracting the vial. Uncorking the stopper and opening Harold's mouth, Edward poured the liquid cure into it.

The smooth-textured liquid flowed passed the unconscious brother's lips and down his throat. Edward had to slow to a stop when Harold coughed a couple of times appearing to have slightly choked on the substance, but the short-haired twin ingested all of the tube's elixir. Now the companions would have to wait a bit for the antidote to work.

Thorin and Calvin helped Faith with the big man while the gnome found and retrieved his daggers. Moric sheathed his sword and went to retrieve the two, magically-lit candlesticks. In between his assistance, the group's leader double-checked on everyone's status.

"Devis. Jhessail. You two alright?"

Both acknowledged their wellness with a nod as they remained ever vigilant and kept guard over the other.

It took the two sleeping, party members around ten minutes to start coming to and at least another ten to fifteen minutes to shake off the effects of the poison's grogginess. Helping the two up to their feet, both Harold and Jericho needed a little more time finding their legs. After roughly a half an hour the party made sure they collected anything dropped in the fight with the drachnid and its three, monstrous comrades before beginning back down the passage moving in the direction of Bright Star Hall.

Both House Wizard Zebbulas, and Priestess Xarna followed the drow messenger through the corridor's of the dwarven hall, now under the dark elves control, towards the mining cavern. The three walked with no alarm in their steps, but it was more than obvious that both the wizard and the priestess were determined to get where they were heading. Only the clicking from her stiletto-heeled boots making contact with the passage's stone floor offered any type of sound in their advancement to their destination.

It was still mid-morning when the messenger had reported that the slaves had discovered what was believed to be another area full of gems within the mountain's belly. A field of stars is actually what the dwarves called such a discovery, and both Zebbulas and Xarna knew that if this dig had uncovered such a vast amount of precious and valuable stones then it might actually be enough to pay for the expenses accrued from this mission, along with the possibility that it could also help to prepay any future costs that came the dark elves' way.

For years now, the drow have been working on a plan to use a section of the Border Mountains as a type of bridge or canal that would connect the realms of Kanaan with the evil lands known to all as the Separate Lands. This channel would make whole the two divided parts of the continent allowing a chaotic wickedness the ability to spread out and over the relatively lawful and peaceful domains. Of course, the dark elves having total control of this conduit between the two lands would definitely receive a major kickback, whether it being coins or another type of benefit, from anyone wanting to cross. One would have to admit the scheme was sound, but the steps and actions taken were diabolically spun out of a pure hatred and evilness. Not only was there an opportunity for a constant flow of income, but the chance to oppress centuries old adversaries proved another major bonus in their wicked plan.

The three drow finally rounded a bend in the corridor leading to the extremely, large cavern that the human and dwarven slaves toiled in. The dark, rocky walls littered with unpolished, precious stones still had a dull shine to it giving off the appearance of a star-filled night sky thanks to the bright lights in the mountain's chamber. Even House Wizard Zebbulas and Priestess Xarna were taken aback by their initial gaze upon the area. After only moments, the two's looks of surprise were replaced by devilish grins.

The party stopped for a late lunch in the tunnels and a brief rest. All of the companions only had a couple of handfuls of trail mix in their packs, and even though the war god, Guerra, would most likely bestow a complete meal on them if Jhessail prayed to him, Calvin didn't want the group to be taken off guard while they ate nor be slowed by a full stomachs. The knight figured the group could eat good later provided they found a safe place, but as for now, the companions were exposed out here in the open passageway.

Moric kept going further down the corridor for another forty feet setting up a spot to look out for any oncoming trouble. He was at the outskirts of the magical candlesticks and sat in the darkness alone allowing his visibility to adjust. Digging into his pack, the gnome pulled out the last of his trail mix beginning to finish it off. Around his neck hung a signal whistle.

"How much further dwarf?", inquired Calvin before popping a handful of mix into his mouth.

"By the end of the day we'll reach a bridge over a flowing river," informed the dwarf. "Then a little after the crossing we'll be at the hall."

"Wow! That long?", amazingly queried Faith.

"About a day's travel, and this is actually the shorter of the three tunnels leading in," chuckled Thorin.

"Have you got a plan yet?", questioned Jericho.

"Not a full one, but I think we are all going to have to do our best and improvise," Calvin replied more hopeful then determined in everyone's ability to think and react at the moment. "Right now I can honestly say that at least four or five of us are a bit more seasoned to battle than are others. However, I do believe that everyone of us here will give it their all," he confidently proclaimed.

"Let's move out people and meet up with the gnome," advised the group's leader.

The party once again was on the move.

"Pick up the pace you mutts!", came the drow taskmaster yelling the order while cracking his whip for the second time in a row. "You're not leaving today until we're done here!", he added.

The dirty, smelly slaves kept their work up even though they were tired and rundown. Hunger pains consumed most of them and all the prisoners were parched with their dry mouths and throats desperately in need of water. A couple of villagers from Oakhurst fell out from total exhaustion, and unfortunately the whip would be the only taste they would receive.

Being such a young child, Katherine, who was covered head to toe with dirt, was given the job of collecting the gems and sorting them out according to size and color. The slaves had found diamonds along with sapphires in this cavern, and the number of gems was incredibly promising in the monetary support of the dark elves' scheme. Two-wheeled carts were strewn about the place each containing the different stones.

Both the little girl's brothers worked together taking turns to dig with a pick or pulling a full cart by its extended handles. As for Zolktar, beaten and bruised, he worked by himself due to none of the other slaves wishing to be his partner because they all knew his race was the cause of this wicked atrocity, and the fact that he was responsible for being in charge of the goblins that brought most of them here to this hellish place.

Several more of the laborers dropped as the day continued to march on and at least three of them wouldn't be getting back up. Their captors literally working them to death. The dead bodies only moved by others and thrown in a mass grave to be burned at the end of the day.

It was late in the afternoon when the taskmasters finally called a break to barely feed and water their human and dwarven livestock. The captives relieved at the brief rest. Four more people and two dwarfs succumbed to the touch of death so far making the total of deceased nine for the day. There was still plenty more work and more could be joining that number.

The two brothers and their little sister sat huddled with each other eating and drinking. Their soil-covered hands used to spoon out a thick, grayish gruel from a small clay bowl. Earthen-covered mugs filled with water containing a floating film of dirt sat on the cavern's floor next to them.

"Do you think anyone's found the stuff you left back in the forest?", quietly inquired Katherine.

"Not now Kat. Just eat," Junior replied wearily.

"Well do you?", pushed the little girl without meaning to.

"Let it go for now Kat," he replied with a little anger in his voice.

Katherine happened to notice Zolktar for the first time staring at her and offered the drow both a smile along with a small wave. The dark elf's eyes only slightly squinting at the girl.

Without even realizing what she was doing, the child asked her question again. "Junior, you think we'll be saved by someone?"

Before a tired Junior could answer his sister, Thomas cut into both the conversation and Katherine. "He said, let it go Kat because probably not! Somebody would have been here by now," Thomas growled at the little girl. "Besides, you need to stop doing and thinking whatever it is about that dark elf over there. He's the one that brought us here and he's one of them. They're all no good and they're the ones who killed mother, father and Veronica!"

"Thomas!", snapped Junior.

Katherine shocked by her brother Thomas' angry outburst at her began to tear up. Soon a droplet ran from her eye flowing down her cheek and the little girl's half-filled bowl dropped and smashed on the rocky, cavern floor as she abruptly got up to flee from her brother's hurtful words. Katherine's vision blurred as her tears flowed faster now. The little girl seeking solace in an empty corner of the mined chamber.

"No wait Kat!", concerned Junior shouting after the girl.

"I'm sorry Kat!", cried Thomas. "Come back!", the boy pleaded.

Disgustedly looking at his younger brother and giving him a bop with his backhand on the side of his head, Junior sharply proclaimed, "Smooth move King Stupid!"

❧

The worn down and beaten slave Zolktar sat on a small pile of dirt and rubble watching the little girl eat with her two brothers. Her face seeming so familiar but the dark elf could not remember where he knew her from. Every time he tried hard to think and recollect, Zolktar's memories would also lead to a dead end. He knew his name; He knew he was a drow; but what he didn't know was who she was and who he was. The trail of answers always starting to go cold as the dark elf's mental responses were bound up with a knotted blackness that Zolktar's mind could not penetrate. He noticed the small child smile and wave at him, but shortly after, the drow witnessed her run away from her siblings in tears.

"How do I know her?", he thought.

CHAPTER 28

Moans escaped her throat and sweat beaded on her forehead along with the priestess' chest right above her firm breasts. Xarna's arms fully extended supporting her weight above the desktop. Her fingers balling up and scratching against the papers littering the piece of furniture, as Zebbulas stood behind her plunging into the depths of her womanhood exhaling breaths onto her hair-covered neck.

The discovery of all the gems earlier put the dark elf woman into the mood, and the two lovers had spent most of the day copulating off and on in every part of Wizard Zebbulas's office. The fact that the drow male had no say in their sexual exploits took away from his total enjoyment. Work needed to be done and now the wizard looked at the coupling like it was more of an unwanted distraction than a time of pleasure. Zebbulas knew not to say anything that opposed Priestess Xarna's desire or it would only bring him punishment, death, or both.

As the wizard's thrust grew harder and faster, the priestess rocked back on her heels to match every drive impaling herself further and deeper on his manhood. In the throes of their dance, Xarna moved and shifted the papers strewn across the desk's top until, breathing heavy with ecstasy, she dropped her head accidentally gazing at the writings.

One particular, unfinished letter caught her attention even though her climax rapidly approached. It was addressed to her mother the Matriarch of House Zexthion, House Mother Xanthiaz, causing her to discreetly read it considering she had planned of disposing of the house's head. Priestess Xarna could not hold back her satisfying culmination any longer, but she was unable to contain her curiosity either.

Dear House Mother Xanthiaz

Matriarch of the House Zexthion,

I pray to Thaisia that this letter finds you in good health and well being upon its arrival. Upon receipt of this note, you should be receiving the second shipment of gems from our newly acquired outpost. I hope like the previous goods you are both happy and satisfied with their conditions and amount.

I would also like to put your mind at ease with the news that your daughter, Priestess Xarna, seems competent in our pursuits unlike your original thoughts. She is still ignorant and unknowing of the sexual pleasures we have shared in the past. The priestess has a lot to learn and I think you should know that she wants...

The letter abruptly ended there, and it was obvious to the dark elf woman that somebody, probably her, had walked in on Zebbulas before he had finished the work. Quickly, Xarna slid it back under the scattered batch of others dressing the desk before the wizard had any idea that the priestess knew about it.

Thoughts of treachery and betrayal ran through her mind as the woman got dressed. Xarna could only speculate what Zebbulas was going to add to the letter. The fact that her mother and the wizard had laid together in the past only deepened her suspicions of his loyalty should she attempt to remove the matriarch from the picture. "Whose side would the house wizard be on?", she wondered. Priestess Xarna had exposed not only her body but her plans to him as well. Now the only move she could make towards any type of damage control was not to let him know she knew about the letter, along with beginning to plan for his opposition should he take her mother's side. The fire of rage silently ignited in Priestess Xarna when she thought about her actually being played the fool in a plot focusing on her. Still she held her tongue, but now her mind raced.

❧

With the tears flowing from her eyes beginning to slow, Katherine made her way over to a deep, dark chasm located in the northwestern corner of the mining cavern. A small, stone bridge crossed the gap allowing one to access the other side. Through her watery-filled eyes, the little girl took two steps up and started across the structure never glancing back to see if anyone was following her through the crowd of seated slaves.

Hurrying to cross the bottomless gorge, Katherine stopped at the last stone stair on the other side and sat down. The bridge's side walls hid the little girl from anyone trying to find her, as the child wiped away her blurry vision the best she could with her soiled, nightdress' sleeve.

Katherine had seen the bridge several times throughout the day working in the area and her curiosity finally got the best of the little girl. She had never noticed anyone coming even remotely close to it earlier and considered it might be a good spot to hide out for a while. Especially since Thomas and Junior seemed to be mad at her.

"What are you doing child?", asked the voice causing the girl to jump in surprise. She never heard anyone crossing the bridge or approaching her from behind. Katherine's heart seemed to leap out of her small chest as she whipped around to see who the owner of the voice was. The question coming from the dark elf gazing down at her.

❧

The noise in the passage was deafening and no one tried to talk knowing that none of the other companions would be able to hear their words anyways. It was lucky for the group that the knight had taken the time to give the dwarf a lesson on how to communicate using only hand signals while they had spent the night for the first time together back at the cave in the valley. Now Thorin crouched down hidden by a stone bridge spanning the wide gap caused by the

266

flowing river below running through the mountain. The roar of the water echoed off the tunnel's walls and ceiling. The structure was wide enough for a small cart. He currently waved the group's leader and the gnome to him, and moments later both Calvin and Moric took a knee next to the dwarf.

Thorin pointed at both of them before placing two fingers near his own eyes. The hand signal used to keep your eyes open and remain ever vigilant for danger. When both the party members nodded their understanding, the dwarf started his hunched over crouch across the bridge carrying his maul by the center of the weapon.

Within the next two minutes, that actually felt more like an hour to the party, the dwarf was across. Calvin tapped Moric on his shoulder signaling him to go and then summoned the others to his side. They all watched the gnome make it safely to the other side. The knight motioning for Jericho next.

Turning to the remaining five companions, Calvin signed the order to cross the expanse two at a time. He and Faith would go next followed by the McKinleys with both Devis and Jhessail crossing last. The knight and the magic-user both watched the big man make it before they began their journey. The two would only get halfway over the river when Moric threw up a closed fist signaling the duo to "Stop." Calvin and Faith squatted low trying to hide against the solid, stone rails of the bridge.

❧

Keeping an eye out for any trouble, Moric just happened to look back towards the structure when he noticed a pair of hairy, black legs coming out from under the crossing. The two were followed by another two and the first bulbous half of a giant spider's body. The gnome holding up a closed fist before pointing in the direction of the danger.

❧

Jhessail watched as his two companions making their way across the stone structure quickly lowered themselves to a squat. The half-elf taking notice of Moric pointing in the opposite direction from where the two had stopped on the bridge. He slowly leaned toward his left to see a large, black spider crawl out from under the stone crossing and begin to head up its side towards the top. Jhessail quickly offering a prayer asking for his god's aid and pointing in the direction of Calvin's sword.

The gnome watched the knight slide over to the side of the bridge where he had pointed out the danger. Calvin sat with his back against the solid railing waiting on the first sign of trouble. Faith letting her whip unroll beside her.

Calvin sat and watched two black, hairy leg tips fold over the rail, each on either side of him. Faith's eyes widened when she saw the two just miss the seated knight. Calvin quietly placed his shield down, so he could use both of his hands for more power, and positioned his sword for an upward drive hoping it would score a direct hit ending the encounter before a skirmish broke out. His eyes widening a bit as a red aura surrounded his weapon.

Within moments, the arachnid's head was birthing over the bridge's side, and the knight drove his blessed weapon up into the exposed spider. His glowing red blade erupting from the crawler's crown. Calvin twisted the sword one way and then the other before he removed it.

Faith was prepared to lash out at it with her whip, but the arachnid just slid from the railing plunging into the rushing waters of the river underneath. The current sweeping it downstream.

The group's leader took a second to collect his shield before tilting his head towards Faith in the direction of the other side of the bridge. Together they finished the crossing.

Making their way across the structure two at a time with no more further encounters, the remaining four joined up with the rest of the group and continued on.

Fear washed through Katherine's little body and her red eyes widened witnessing the drow standing behind her. She swiftly rose to her feet stepping down off of the bridge's stone stair.

"I'm not doing nothing," shakiness in her voice as she answered.

"I said child, what do you think you're doing?", the snarling guard asked moving towards her.

"I'm going back to my brothers," she nervously responded.

Katherine climbed up the two stairs on the stone structure and tried to hurry by the taskmaster, but the drow pushed her back forcefully launching the child in the air, over the steps, and crashing onto her back. The little girl both hurt and definitely scared attempted to crab walk backing away from the dark elf. Katherine's doe-like eyes never taking their gaze from his whip.

The guard followed the frightened girl's line of sight right to the weapon of punishment in his right hand. "Oh, this is what scares you child," he menacingly rasped. "How come it frightens you now, but you knew not fear while you were defending that dwarven scum?"

Tears began to fill her eyes as she looked back up to the sneering drow hovering above her. Engulfed with fear, she desperately begged while shaking her head. "No. Please just let me go to Junior and Thomas. I promise I'll be a good girl!", she swore as her tears began to flow faster and faster.

"No. This time you'll feel the whip's bite, and I guarantee the next time you will never show a sign of disrespect to me human child," wickedly snarled the taskmaster moving his right hand intimidating the crying girl.

Before the dark elf could raise the whip to lash out at Katherine, he lurched forward dropping to a knee from a bladed kick in the bend at the leg's joint. The drow taskmaster's head almost spinning from his shoulders as Zolktar broke his neck. The corpse falling forward on the bridge.

"No one whips Zolktar fool," he said to the lifeless body.

Katherine sat on the ground still not fully aware what just took place. Her body so surprised, the little girl didn't know if she should keep crying or feel relieved. Her shock only broken by her savior's question after she watched him toss the body over the side of the bridge and into the blackness of the chasm below.

"Are you alright child?", inquired Zolktar. "Can you stand?"

The little girl softly responding after the second query. "Yes. I'm okay," she answered while beginning to rise to her feet. "Thank you mister. You helped me again," she pointed out wiping her eyes dry with the back of her dirty hands.

The puzzled drow took a knee lowering himself closer to the child's height. "Who are you?"

"I am Katherine," she tried to smile while introducing herself. "What's your name?"

"My name is Zolktar. Your face looks familiar to me. Have I seen you before child?", he asked squinting at Katherine trying to place where he knew the little girl from. "You said that I helped you before, but I don't remember."

The girl giggled a bit. "Remember, you came to my aid with the goblin."

"Goblin?"

"Yeah, my brothers Junior and Thomas said you were the one who led the goblins who killed mother and father along with my sister Veronica, but I don't believe it because I didn't see you there," she informed him.

Zolktar thought as hard as he could but he couldn't call to memory when, or even why, he would be leading a pack of marauding goblins.

Changing the subject, Katherine asked Zolktar, who had been lost in his thoughts a pair of questions. "Why do these guys keep whipping you? Don't they know you could kick their butts?"

"What do you mean?", perplexed Zolktar. "You speak in riddles child."

"Don't they know you're a wizard?"

From the instant the word "wizard" left her mouth, Zolktar's memories, which were bound up and forgotten, began to come back to him. Somehow that one phrase untied the binding magically placed in his mind. Like flood waters running over a dam, his recollections flowed fluently and his thoughts that had been bound up came rushing back to him.

Gazing over Katherine's shoulder at nothing in particular, Zolktar growled out the name of the one responsible for the trespasses against him. "Zebbulas."

⁓℈

The party of rescuers had followed Thorin the rest of the way through the mountain's tunnel and now hid against the set of eight, stone stairs leading upward before the entrance into the main cavern of Bright Star Hall. This primary chamber of the dwarven stronghold was both vast and expanse, and none of the companions could even see the other side from where they hid. The great areas ceiling, which was hidden by the darkness above, also eluded their vision. Stone buildings and shops, built as one with the mountain's interior stretched beyond everyone's line of sight, while wooden booths littered the colossal room's center. Only a soft, purple glow radiated any type of light throughout the cavern.

The entrance passageway along with the stairs leading into the gigantic area were wide enough to accommodate all of the party's members a look into the dwarven home while hiding behind the steps. Nine pairs of eyes surveyed the area for any movement from the occupying enemy and within the next several minutes, the group had already seen over a dozen dark elf warriors go by. Only four lookouts seemed to be posted to this tunnel's entryway.

"Where do you think they are holding the dwarves and the villagers?", inquired Calvin.

"My guess would be over that way in the cell area," responded Thorin pointing to the first tunnel on the left.

"How far away do you think that is?", questioned Harold.

"I'd say roughly a hundred or so feet lad," estimated the dwarf. "It's not that far, but we've got these fellas here who ain't about to let us just stroll right by. They'll be more willing to bring the place right down on our heads," he tensely remarked pointing at the four drow guards talking amongst themselves roughly seventy feet away from them.

"We need a diversion," revealed Calvin. "I believe I have a plan."

The companions dropped from the steps to the bottom run completely hidden from the four sentries so the party's leader could explain the details of his plan.

"We need to go left, but we also want the dark elves to head off in the other direction," the knight started. "Devis shoots an arrow ricocheting it behind them causing all of them to turn and take a look."

"But why behind them when we need them to run off to the right?", interrupted Harold.

"Because that will buy enough time for someone to leave this spot without any of them seeing where he came from. Then using live bait, they will run off to the right drawing the four sentries with them. I would never ask anyone to do something that I would not so I shall go and get them to follow me," explained Calvin.

"You can't do that!", shockingly reasoned Faith.

"Why not?"

"Because we need you, and you could be killed!", she warned him.

"Faith's right, Calvin. You're the one who's got us this far," interjected Moric remembering how the knight saved him from the spider attack after swearing a promise to defend him from any form of harm back at the inn. "It's too dangerous."

"They're right. Because of you and your strategies we're here and still alive," Edward pointed out what most everybody, if not all of them thought. "Besides, I know you're armor and shield are dirty, but you don't have the look of a prisoner. On the other hand, I'm from the village and with this dirty look I would pass as an escaped prisoner before you would," the long-haired McKinley making a very good point. "I'll do it."

"Edward wait! Do you know what you're saying?", surprisingly asked his twin.

"I do…" -he confirmed- "…but we have to at least give it a shot or this here is going to keep going on until there is no more Oakhurst Village."

Harold sat quiet looking at the ground pondering his brother's words. After a quiet moment of silence, the short-haired twin glanced up at his brother, "Let's do this for our village."

A smile creased both the McKinley's faces.

"Are you guys sure?", inquired Calvin looking back-n-forth between the two.

"Yup!", was their one word answer in unison.

෨෩

Both McKinley brothers crouched on the top of the steps ready for their turn in the leader's plan. They had decided to leave the javelin and crossbow, along with its quiver of bolts, behind. The presence of both weapons would have alerted the drow guards to what was really going on and could end up throwing a wrench into their plan. The two needed to buy the rest of the group the time they desperately required for this scheme to work or it would be all for not.

On the ground, with the stone stairs hiding him, Devis drew back the bow's string and loosed the nocked arrow. It flew through the air in an arc before skidding across the stony floor of the mountain's cavern. The missile had the affect on the dark elf guards that everyone was hoping for. They quickly turned around in the direction of the sound while both Edward and Harold were off and running towards the right.

A second sound near to where the two, rushing brothers were captured the four drows' attention. Spinning back around, they took in the sight of the McKinleys dashing behind some of the buildings.

"Over there!", cried out one of the sentries pointing out Harold's disappearing backside. The dark elves started after the two. The chase was on as the guards ran around the corner of the building and out of sight.

Calvin held back the group of seven for three or four more moments making sure the coast was clear. Satisfied, the companions dashed a hundred feet towards the left tunnel's entrance. Soon the elf was the last to disappear down the rocky hallway leading to the cells.

None of the group saw the hand-sized, furry, black spider hanging from a web on the upper level of the stone building near the hall's entryway. Its multiple pairs of eyes watching their sprint into the tunnel.

CHAPTER 29

"I can't keep this up for too much longer!", advised a winded Harold in between breaths.

"Quick, we'll duck in here!", a tired Edward replied.

The McKinleys had been running for at least twelve or thirteen blocks now and were beginning to tire. Sweat passed from their brow stinging their eyes causing them to constantly keep wiping their faces. The two had done their best in getting the drow guards to pursue them, and this diversion had worked. Both knew they were not city people trying to get away from someone chasing them, but Harold and Edward tried to use the buildings and shops to their advantage while running this way and that.

Checking a door to what looked like some kind of bakery, the twins were in luck when the unlocked door opened. Quickly they rushed inside closing and locking the door behind them. Neither one of the young farmers saw any signs of the dark elves.

Scanning the room for a place to hide, Edward and Harold passed the handful of dwarf-sized tables and chairs. A couple of the wooden seats knocked over in their haste to reach a stone counter next to four long, glass cabinets used to display fresh pastries and breads. Only now the food occupants were green with mold. The brothers quickly hiding out of sight behind the counter.

An exhausted Harold and Edward breathed in and out rapidly trying to catch their breaths. Taking another scan from their seated position, the two noticed racks lining the wall in front of them mostly filled with molded baked goods. To the right of both the stone counter, where they hid behind, and the racks was a curtained doorway, obviously leading to the back where all the work was performed. Stealing a glance through the glass showcases and seeing no signs of the four pursuers, the brothers swiftly made a bee-line behind the curtain.

This room was at least twice the size of the shop's front and contained three stone ovens, four tables, a wheeled metal rack holding half a dozen baking pans, and six wheeled racks used to cool finished products. Mold covered all the goods left out. Suddenly the brothers heard the door to the shop rattle. Both Edward and Harold knew who was outside.

"They're trying to get in Edward," acknowledged his brother in a relatively calm tone. "What do you want to do?"

"I wish I kept my crossbow on me now," Edward regretted leaving it behind. "I would have least got one of them with a shot."

"I have an idea Eddie!", piped up Harold. "Give me a hand with these racks."

"What do you want to do?", asked a puzzled Edward.

The locked door banged from the other room as it received its first of several shoulder blows.

"Hurry up!", Harold cried excitedly while pulling a rack and positioning it in front of the curtain. Its wheels extending passed the opening of the wall.

The McKinleys put two racks, one in front of the other, on their side of the curtain. The hanging cloth hiding the metal shelves and the wall hiding their wheels from view.

"This should buy us some time," explained Harold. "Quick find a way out."

The brothers didn't have to look far for the back door to the place.

The front door began to bang louder and faster now as the drow guards were intent on gaining entry into the shop.

Dashing to the rear door, Edward opened it ajar taking a peek around to see if anyone was out there. The coast looked clear, and luck seemed to be on their sides as they darted out of the bakery when they heard the front door smash to splinters.

Without warning both brothers were surprised as a large, circular, purple web smothered them from behind, entangling them, and pulling them to the ground. Its stickiness pinning them down. The trapped McKinleys each witnessed a pair of black-booted feet walk up around the area of their heads.

"Going somewhere?", a voice asked with slight amusement in its tone. "We have them back here!", it yelled after the initial question.

"Oww!", cried Edward.

Without any type of warning something sharp pierced Edward's neck and within moments his vision blurred and his eyelids began to feel heavy. He thought he had heard Harold express his own sudden shock from pain, but the creeping blackness of unconsciousness swallowed him whole.

Harold's last thought was how both he and Eddie's luck had run out seconds before joining his brother in the realm of slumber.

❧

The light in the tunnel was very dim but thanks to the soft, purple glow radiating from torch brackets every ten feet, the party's humans were still able to see even though Faith had covered the magically lit candles in a piece of cloth from her pack. The seven companions keeping close to each other while always on the lookout for any signs of trouble stopped only feet away from the "T's" intersection at the passageway's end.

Thorin crept forward looking down the right side of the crossing's tunnel as far as he could. When he saw nothing, the dwarf decided to stick a little bit of his head out and have a peek for himself. The corridor was clear that way, but stealing a quick glance down the left side where the single holding cells were, the dwarf saw two drow guards posted in front of one of the room's doors roughly twenty five feet away from where the two tunnels met. Pulling his head back, Thorin relayed the finding to the others.

"What's the plan knight?", questioned the dwarf warrior. An ornery tone beginning to invade his voice.

"Take it easy dwarf," Calvin tried to calm him down a bit.

277

"I've got this one Calvin," informed Faith looking from the knight to the half-elf. "With Jhessail's assistance," she added with a brief smile.

"What do you have in mind?", interestingly asked the wizard-warrior.

"How about casting a couple of flare cantrips near them causing the light to steal their sight long enough to take them out?"

Jhessail's lips spread in a wicked grin. "Are you sure you don't worship the war god?"

"I knew you'd like that idea," she smiled again.

Both magic-users remained hidden behind the wall as they started to call on the aid of their magic. Stepping more to the right side of the intersection when they cast their cantrips, the young woman and her half-elf companion allowed clear access around the corner so the rest of the others could charge the two guards.

❧

The two sentries stood in front of the heavy, wooden door and neither of them heard the party of seven down and around the corner of the corridor. They seemed to have most of their interest on a conversation between them. Suddenly, movement at the "T" intersection caught the peripheral vision and they turned when a woman and a half-elf stepped into the tunnel. Both dark elves started towards the two drawing their scimitars, but abruptly stopped when the magical flares blazed in front of the their faces. The drow sentries cried out in pain as the instant flash of bright light blinded them momentarily. The two would never get enough time to recover or see death swiftly rush at them.

❧

Within seconds, the one-sided onslaught was over, and unfortunately for the two drow, they never stood a chance. Everything happened so fast, and now their dead bodies laid in the corridor.

"Grab that set of keys there lad and let's have a look at who's important enough to guard," pointed Thorin to the ring on one of the dark elf's hip.

278

"Faith take out one of those candles and cast some light into the cell so we can take a look," ordered Calvin.

Moric handed Thorin the ring of keys while the woman removed one of the magically bright sticks. Its radiance casting throughout the passage and into the prisoner's room revealing a bloody and beaten, red-haired dwarf shackled by his wrists and ankles on the far wall. The captive's head dropping down leaving his long hair hanging over his face.

Thorin found the key to the room's door and opened it.

"Jericho post up in the entryway. Moric. Devis, keep a lookout in the passage," ordered the party's leader. "You two, come with us," he added to Faith and Jhessail.

The three followed Thorin to the far wall where the secured hostage hung.

The group's dwarf recognizing the prisoner's face when he slowly looked up towards the four coming through the doorway.

"Fireheart!", surprisingly exclaimed Thorin.

"Hammerstone," the wounded softly stated behind an effort to smile.

Rifling through the key ring, Thorin found the ones he needed to unlock the shackles. "Help me get him to the floor lads," he requested the knight and the half-elf for their assistance.

"You know him?", Faith inquired.

"Yeh lass. This here be the chief of this hall," Thorin informed her. "Chief Fireheart."

"Leave one of those candles with us and take either Moric or Devis with you and check the rest of the cells for anybody else," Calvin sternly instructed Faith while handing over to her the key ring that Thorin had given him.

"You've got it," she acknowledged while handing him a candle before exiting the cell.

"Jhessail, can you help the chief here?", asked the knight.

Laying his hands on the chief's body, the half-elf offered a prayer up to his god asking for Guerra to find it in his interest and grant the wounded dwarf the god's touch of healing. Jhessail's hands and body began to take on a dim, blue aura and within minutes the azure glow radiated from Chief Fireheart's body as well.

Calvin and Thorin watched as open cuts and lacerations, along with dark purple bruises, began to mend and fade. The chief's health rapidly improving by the moment.

"Remain still for a few more minutes," Jhessail advised the dwarf when the aura faded away. The half-elf looking over to Thorin offering him a nod.

Reaching up from the room's floor and placing a small but thick hand on Jhessail's arm, Fireheart gave him his gratitude. "Thank you half-elf. I already feel like I did over two centuries ago. What is your name and the name of your god?", he asked.

"I am Jhessail, worshiper of the War God, Guerra."

"I shall not forget that," smiled the newly healed clan chief.

⁊৲

"Back to work you lazy dogs!", shouted one of the other drow task-masters. His order being repeated by several others throughout the mining cavern.

"Go child back to your brothers before anyone else finds us here," Zolktar advised the little girl. "You must keep up the illusion that we never met here."

"Are you going to keep working?", asked Katherine crossing the stone bridge.

"For now, but I have other ideas."

"What are you going to do?"

Zolktar had left the conversation for a brief second staring at nothing particular before returning his gaze back to the little girl and speaking with apprehension in his voice. The drow's mind beginning to formulate a plan of revenge and freedom, at least for himself. "Now hurry child! Remember, do not speak a word of any of this with no one."

Katherine gave Zolktar a nod accompanied by a smile before starting her run back to Junior and Thomas. The newly aware Wizard Zolktar headed off in another direction. Vengeance on his mind.

"Faith and Devis found a second one," came Jericho helping a bald dwarf into the cell.

"Where are they now?", questioned the knight lending the big man a hand with the wounded dwarf.

"Both went to finish checking the remaining cells," the big man replied assisting the newly found prisoner to the floor.

"It's Slopewalker!", came Chief Fireheart beginning to rise from his laying position.

Upon the mention of his name, Drü Slopewalker looked over at both his friend and chief. Just the sight of the clan's leader brought relief to him. The dwarven cleric noticed the other dwarf standing off to Fireheart's right and instantly a smile formed on his dirty, bloody face as Drü let out a small chuckle.

The drow priestess' question reverberated throughout his mind over and over. Returning his gaze to the bewildered looks from the other occupants in the room, Slopewalker reiterated the dark elf woman's query, "She asked me, where are my gods now?", he laughed. "It's obvious they were out looking for Hammerstone. Just the sight of you my old friend gives me hope."

"You are right Slopewalker, but this time Hammerstone isn't alone," agreed Chief Fireheart. "He brought some friends with him," he informed gazing in the direction of the others presently in the cell.

"Here drink this," Thorin offered the dwarf cleric a tube with an amber-colored liquid in it. "It'll heal you up."

"My thanks," smiled Drü.

"Calvin, sorry to break up your little introductions, but we have got four drow coming down the passage!", excitedly informed Moric rushing into the room. "They'll get to the intersection at any time now."

"Quick, get in here and close the door!", he quickly replied. "We shall douse the light and surprise them when they arrive. Now everyone ready yourselves."

Devis was the first to walk out of the large cavern being used as one of the slaves holding pens. Both him and Faith had made a clean sweep of the cell making sure no one occupied it, and with it being the last one that needed checking, they had only found the two dwarves. Instantly, four drow guards dragging two unconscious bodies rounded the intersection's corner seizing his attention. He swiftly stepped back into the cell raising his closed fist. Faith automatically knew there was trouble. Lucky for the elf, they were going the other way and never saw him.

"Four guards dragging two people just rounded the corner and they're heading the other's way," he informed Faith. "We might have to create a diversion or the group in that cell are going to have a serious problem."

Standing in the dark cell with only the soft, purplish glow from the light in the corridor shining a bit through the small, barred, peek window in the door, Calvin noticed the error of their way. On the passageway's floor still laid the two, dead guards. The knight closed his eyes for a second in frustration but it was too late. He heard the drow's question when he noticed the bodies.

"What's going on there!"

This mistake would cost them the element of surprise.

Devis pulled the bow string with the nocked arrow past his ear. He hoped to get two attacks off before the guards rushed at him and the magic-user. Faith was on stand-by with a spell in case the elf needed some bought time to draw his sword.

The elf let loose his first shot when he heard a guard question, "What's going on there?" The arrow flying straight and true finding its mark. The missile's target; one of the closest drow. Devis went to draw another arrow from the quiver on his back.

The front two guards had just dropped the unconscious man to the floor and started to draw their weapons. One brought both scimitars from their sheaths while the other raised and cocked his hand-held crossbow.

One of the last two, drew his scimitars, but the ally on his left side lurched forward before he could loose his swords and fell to his knees. An arrow shaft sticking out of his back. The one rear guard left standing spun on his heels yelling. "Behind us!"

Automatically the others hiding in the cell knew both the magic-user and elf were attempting to get the guards undivided attentions. The two were diverting the heat away from them. The knight prepared to open the door, and rush into the melee, but before he could and arrow flew down the hallway. Calvin quickly stole a glance at the door's peek-hole before informing the others of his intent.

"Watch for any flying arrows!", he warned.

Opening the door, the knight, with shield raised in defense for any flying missile fire, charged out of the room followed by Jericho and Jhessail. Both Thorin and Moric remained in the room guarding the chief and cleric.

The dark elf guard, who was now turned and ready to fire the poisoned sleeping dart at the defenseless elf drawing forth another arrow from the quiver on his back, fired the shot while Calvin used his shield and rammed him from behind. The surprise attack causing the dart to bounce harmlessly off the wall a few feet in front of him. The knight driving his sword into the captor.

The drow next to him was also caught by surprise when the blunt blow came up in between his legs striking him in the groin. The shot robbing him of his breath for a moment and leaving him stunned for a thrusting sword strike hitting him directly in the upper back. The weapon's blade tip bursting out of the stunned directly under his throat. The guard fell into the tunnel's wall.

The last drow, who was closest to the elf, turned around and began to charge down the hall right at Devis. His scimitars twirling menacingly. The elf had no time to nock another arrow leaving him open to an attack.

Acting without hesitation, Faith stepped out of the cell. Uttering words to the incantation of a cantrip, the woman magic-user cast the small spell that hurtled an orb of green liquid at the charging foe.

The dark elf tried his best to slow and cover up but ran into the orb smashing it all over his face and arms. The drow gave an ungodly cry and backed away, as the burning acid splashed in his eyes.

Faith had bought Devis enough time, and the elf put an abrupt ending to the wounded when his arrow shot pierced the blinded guard's throat. Dropping his swords, and then his arms, he followed his weapon's lead to the corridor's floor.

"Thanks," offered her relieved companion.

She just smiled at him and patted him on the shoulder. "Anytime for my favorite elf."

They both shared a small laugh before starting back towards the other companions.

The two unconscious bodies on the passage's floor were the two McKinley brothers. Near one of the dead drow bodies was a web sack carrying their belongings.

"Hit with sleep poison no doubt," offered the half-elf.

"Let's get them up and on their feet," advised Calvin. "We need to get out of here and free the others."

"Let me get my armor and weapons," requested Chief Fireheart coming out of the room.

Calvin turned to address him after sending both Devis and Jhessail to guard the tunnel leading to the "T" intersection. "I don't know if that's such a good idea right now. This place is crawling with drow."

"You go to the mining cavern with Thorin, meanwhile Slopewalker and I will go get my stuff."

"But chief the hall...", started Calvin before Fireheart interrupted him.

"I know! It's mine!"

"Forget it knight. You'll never win with a dwarf, especially a clan's chief," chuckled Thorin.

"Alright dwarf, but meet us at the mine," agreed the group's leader. The chief winning the war of wills.

A short time later the twins were up and ready.

"You two did a hell of a job boys!", bellowed Jericho.

"He's right. Good work," praised the group's leader. "Are you guys ready to move?"

Both Harold and Edward nod their affirmative.

"We shall meet you at the mining cavern. Safe journey to you both," wished the knight addressing the clan's chief and healer. "Let's move people!", he ordered as the nine started down the original corridor at the intersection and out of sight.

"Let's go Slopewalker," Fireheart said while walking back up the passage from where the two had come. Both dwarfs passed the cell's they were kept in and continued on towards the end of the corridor.

"We're going to use the secret door my chief?"

Fireheart turned with a grin parting his moustache and beard. "I'm the one who designed Bright Star Hall, remember? Now lean against the wall."

The two dwarfs leaned their backs against the end of the tunnel's wall.

Finding the plate and pressing it, a section of the stone partition started to revolve.

Both Chief Fireheart and Drü Slopewalker disappeared out of the corridor and out of sight.

CHAPTER 30

The thick, wooden door with the three metal bands to the chamber that House Wizard Zebbulas occupied, seemed to vibrate from the pounding on it. The dark elf sitting at the room's table going over some projected figures that he had brought back with him from his office, looked up startled by the first of the loud beatings. Before the drow even had the chance to invite the one responsible for the hammering blows into the room, the door swung open and Priestess Xarna entered in an angered haste.

"We have a problem wizard!" angrily she stated.

Noticing the priestess's scowled face and recognizing the seriousness in her voice, Zebbulas rose from his chair. "What is it priestess?", he asked.

"Two intruders were captured and brought to the dungeon," Xarna informed him. "My spy has also informed me that shortly there after both along with other trespassers were seen leaving the cell area heading in the direction of the mining cavern."

"That is an issue, but our guards will catch them putting an end to their shortly lived heroics before we even get there," Zebbulas confidently advised the drow woman as he headed for the doorway. "After you," he offered sweeping his hand to the wide open portal.

Thinking of the half-written letter she discovered earlier in the wizard's office, Xarna tried to steal an inconspicuous glance at the papers on his room's table, but the dark elf couldn't get a decisive look at them. The priestess wasn't ready to give the house wizard the notion that she knew about his correspondence so she started for the entryway. Zebbulas' loyalty in question.

The flaming sphere of fire from the dwarf's maul engulfed the drow's head. The hammer's magical attack dropping the last adversary from the second group of the three enemies the companions had encountered already as they made their way through the underground city.

Even though the party had overcome this second obstacle of dark elves, their attacks had slowed the group down. Devis, who had drawn his sword, and fought in the two melee's, bled from a cut on his upper arm along with a nick on his right cheek. Harold slowly jogged with a limp, and Jericho bled from a flesh wound across his stomach. Even the gnome seemed a little woozy from a blow to his head from the stony street when he dodged an attack, but fell down slamming his skull against the hard surface.

"How much further dwarf?", inquired Calvin.

"A little more than halfway," Thorin revealed yelling over his shoulder.

The party pressed on.

The door to the wardrobe closet opened ajar very slowly, as the red-haired dwarf stole a peek into the large chamber making sure the coast was clear. Viewing only the carved dragon table and chair set while hearing no sound throughout the room, he opened the furniture's portal a little more cautiously sticking his head out of it making sure his bedroom held no occupants. Satisfied it was empty, Chief Fireheart jumped out landing on the floor.

"It's clear. There's no one here," he informed the other dwarf peering through the secret door in the wall behind the closet full of robes. Fireheart scampering to bar the room's only regular entrance.

Drü Slopewalker separated the royal clothing as he climbed out of the furniture. "I really do despise that rail system you installed,…" -the bald cleric revealed while leaping the rest of the way down- "… but it was a good idea, I must admit!"

"Well don't make yourself too comfortable because we'll be taking another ride on it."

Hurrying over to the last wardrobe closet and opening it, Fireheart revealed his suit of plate mail armor.

"Help me get this stuff on!"

"Of course my chief," came the cleric who was looking through the documents left on the table by House Wizard Zebbulas. Glancing up to the other dwarf, he quickly scrambled over to his aid, but even with the cleric's assistance, it took the clan's chief roughly twenty to thirty minutes to dawn the armor.

When Fireheart was finished, with of course Slopewalker's help, the red-haired dwarf, wearing no gauntlet, stuck his hand back into the wardrobe seeking the proper panel that would trigger a section of the closet's sidewall to open. Finding it, he firmly pressed in on it and it lifted. The secret cubbyhole revealed his hidden armory; a double-bladed axe, a dagger, and a spiked, square-headed mace. Reaching for and taking hold of the fearsome looking bludgeon, he gave it to the cleric.

"Take good care of this baby," handing him the blunt weapon. "It's caved in a lot of goblin's noses over the years."

Fireheart sheathed the dagger on his left hip and lastly withdrew his long time favorite, bladed companion. Closing the panel, the chief put on his spiked knuckle gauntlets and held the golden-crowned helmet under an arm. "Let's go Slopewalker back to the cart. We've got to catch up with Hammerstone."

"What about the door?", questioned the cleric pointing over to the barred room entryway.

"What about it?", queried the befuddled chief.

Realizing it was an inquiry that never should have been asked, the bald dwarf climbed into the closet, "Nothing."

Its door closing behind the armored chief.

❧

House Wizard Zebbulas appeared out of thin air in the tunnel leading to the mining cavern a split second after Priestess Xarna did. The drow magic-user using a piece of chalk to draw a circle on the floor outside of Chief Fireheart's chambers only moments after him and Xarna had left the room. The wizard teleporting both her and himself here. Zebbulas stood watching the dark elf priestess peer into the large cave where the slaves toiled.

"Are they in there yet?", he softly asked.

"Not yet," the drow woman responded. "We need to set up a trap for our visitors."

"What do you have in mind preistess?"

Xarna offered the dark elf a sly grin before entering the cavern. "We'll invite the flies into the web and then pounce on our unsuspecting prey," she revealed before a sinister laugh escaped from behind her lips.

A stone slab shifted to the side as four, stubby, armored fingers slid the thick, flat piece located in the city's alley behind one of its shops. The landing of the store's rear steps located in the narrow passageway in between the buildings, which also doubled as a portal for a secret rail system running under the city, slowly moved until it was sloping off its foundation. Cautiously a helmet adorned with a golden crown rose from the hole. A set of eyes surveyed the surroundings.

"The coast looks clear," the chief silently spoke while scanning the area.

Delaying his movement for another several moments, Fireheart placed his axe on the ground and started his climb up from the darkness. The clan chieftain moving with a spring in his step that he hadn't seemed to have in awhile.

Taking another second to make sure they weren't walking into a trap, the dwarf's chief offered a gauntlet-covered hand to the cleric helping him up and out of the hole. The two replacing the slab when Slopewalker was back in the city.

"Come on, this way!", the armored dwarf informed the cleric with determination in his tone. "The corridor to the mining cavern is just on the other side of these shops."

Both the clan's leader, and its holy man cautiously heading to free their people and the human captives.

Thorin secretly surveyed the mining cavern from the passageway right outside the room's entrance. The dwarf's eyes trying to take some kind of count of the enemy's force while hundreds of diamonds and sapphires sparkled within. He stepped back giving a quick assessment to the group.

"Looks like these guys here found a field of stars," he reported while throwing a thumb over his shoulder.

"A field of what?", puzzled Faith.

"A field of stars," stated the dwarf. "Means a lot of gems lass."

"Like how many?", queried Moric with a twinkle in his eyes matching that of the precious stones inside.

"Don't worry about that gnome," scowled Thorin. "They belong to the Fireheart clan."

The elf's heart seemed to brighten when he heard the words "gems" and "a lot", but he kept his cool and none of the others ever noticed his moment of internal excitement. Devis was well aware that there were riches to be had as long as no one was watching.

"Anyways, I count over twenty two armed drow in there. One's even standing on a ledge and has his back to the entrance," informed Thorin. "There's a path on either side of it," the dwarf added.

"What's the plan Calvin?", anxiously asked Jericho. Saving his friend's children the only thing on his mind.

The knight shaking his head. "There is no plan people. All we can do is go in there hoping to start a revolt."

"Do you think they'll fight Calvin?", questioned the elf.

"I cannot say, but if they do, then we will definitely outnumber the dark elves."

"They'll fight!", excitedly offered Thorin.

The companion's leader quickly formulated a plan and relayed it to the rest of the group. "Dwarf. You take out the one on the ledge. The rest of us will split up into two groups of four and charge down either path."

Everyone listening intently to his orders.

"I will take the right side with Faith, Moric, and Jericho. Jhessail, you, Devis, and the twins on the other side," Calvin was sure to meet everyone's eyes as he spoke. "Now all of you, watch your back and your friend's back. It will be pure chaos and hell in there," he stressed. "Keep your eyes peeled for the wizard. This is it people. For the pursuit of freedom and Jacob's children!"

Looking to Thorin, he added, "You have the lead."

Thorin nod his approval.

The dwarf looked back into the cavern one more time taking a quick inventory before starting his count down. "Is everyone ready? One. Two. Three!"

The companions erupted through the entrance to the extremely, large cave following the dwarf. Thorin stayed his course charging towards the drow taskmaster standing on the rock outcrop while the rest of the group split flowing around the stone ledge. No one in the party had any clue that they were running into a trap until it was too late.

Thorin, with dwarven maul in his hand, lowered his shoulder preparing to ram the drow, who had not turned around yet, in the back launching the taskmaster. The dwarf was taken by surprise as he ran through the illusion of the dark elf. Attempting to stop his committed charge, the warrior flew over the small ledge. His magical battle axe still sheathed on his back vibrated while the emerald in the weapon's pommel glowed trying to warn him of the false image, but Thorin made the assumption it had alerted him of the dark elf's evil presence. Lucky for the dwarven warrior the drop to the ground was only about eight feet. He landed hard causing his dwarven warhammer to bounce across the stony floor as he lost his grip on the maul.

Calvin never saw the purple, magic arrow that slammed into his shield as he held it in front of him rushing into the cavern, and down the sloped path on the right side of the ledge. Its impact throwing him backwards through the air past the other three companions following him. The knight slamming into the ground.

Jhessail watched as a purple, magic arrow caused the defensive magical globe around him to instantly light up and brighten red when it absorbed the surprise attack. The half-elf experiencing too many previous battles was relieved with his preparation.

Edward crashed to the ground entangled in a purple web cast from the companion's rear. The origin of the magical attack was a dark elf warrior clinging to the rocky wall above the entrance. The drow's spider climb spell gave him the advantage of the surprise attack. The long-haired McKinley found himself incapacitated at the time.

Over a dozen drow guards, dropped the facade of unsuspecting and charged across the cavern towards the intruders drawing their weapons. Others stayed where they were controlling the dwarven and human slaves. Both House Wizard Zebbulas and Priestess Xarna stepping out from behind carts where they were hiding. The captives in surprise and shock.

❧

Slowing down for a quick second with a look of horror on her face, Faith saw both Thorin run off the ledge and fall hitting the ground hard, along with Calvin being thrown through the air past her. The magic-user's attention quickly returned when a dark elf charged straight at her. Faith kept hold of the whip's handle while she let the roll fall to the ground. Her focus on the closets approaching enemy.

The gnome moved to the woman's left with both his daggers drawn ready to taste drow blood. Moric's eyes on the scan for the nearest resting gem-filled cart.

Jericho stood off to Faith's right side, far enough to allow the woman to use her whip to lash out and strike but within close enough distance to aid her if the situation demanded his assistance. Due to the giant size of the big man along with his notable face throughout the village, a soft acknowledgment of, "It's Jericho!", passed through most of the crowd.

❧

The half-elf, who had just been saved from the surprise attack thanks to his defensive globe, watched as over a dozen dark elf warriors rushed forward approaching the companions. Words escaped his lips as Jhessail recited the incantation to one of his spells. The wizard-warrior pointed to the rocky ground fifteen feet in front of the oncoming drow attackers and let loose his magic.

Devis, with long sword in hand, placed himself on the left of the half-elf. Uttering a command word for a spell, he summoned his magic. Suddenly, four magical images of the elf popped into existence out of thin air. Devis knew this wasn't the time to be discreet with his magical abilities anymore.

Rushing to Jhessail's right, Harold looked wide-eyed when he saw the multiple images of the elf pop into existence. "We didn't know he could do that!", he shockingly thought. The short-haired twin had no idea that his brother lay behind him trapped on the ground entangled in a magical web.

❧

"Just be patient and wait priestess," Zebbulas advised, as Xarna kept walking forward. "Our guards should be able to handle this group of fools. When they do the survivors will join our little ring of slaves."

Stopping her progress, the priestess turned on the wizard with a snarl. "Never tell me that I can't have fun. I am the one, who makes the rules around here!", she rasped.

Turning back around to watch the upcoming battle Xarna added, "You would be wise to remember that House Wizard Zebbulas!" The memory from the discovery of the unfinished letter running through her mind. Priestess Xarna placed a hand on the snake scourge's handle hanging at her hip.

❧

Cracking whips from the remaining drow taskmasters not in melee with the intruders yet lashed into the huddled up packs of slaves. Their intentions of causing fear and intimidation working at this present time. No one noticed the shirtless, dark elf crouching behind a half-full cart of sapphires watching the house wizard's every movement.

❧

Two of the fourteen dark elf warriors rushing towards the companions reached the area where Jhessail had just pointed at. Their feet coming in contact with some type of greasy substance causing them to lose their balance slipping and sliding. Before the two could try to make any kind of adjustment helping them to regain their balance along with their footing, both dark elves fell head over heels. Their momentum carrying them towards the left side companions. The other dozen just about closed the gap between them and the party.

The one spider climbing, dark elf dropped to the cavern's floor. Drawing his two scimitars, he started to stalk over to the downed Edward stuck in the purplish web. Saliva dripped from his snarling mouth.

***

Thorin slowly raised his head off the ground and looked around to see what had taken place after he had bounced twice off the hard ground. Witnessing the onrushing enemy line, the dwarf rose to his feet and moved to retrieve his maul. The warrior's pace and his actions began to pick up speed as the initial blow from the fall started to wear off. Thorin prepared for the attack.

***

Calvin shook off the initial blow from both the magic missile and the crashing fall on his upper back. With his shield a little dented from the strike and his arm already throbbing from the attack, the knight got to his feet grabbing his sword. Calvin knew the group would be run down if they just stood there letting the drow attack. For this rescue mission to succeed, the party needed the slaves to revolt, but importantly, the companions needed to bring the fight to the dark elves. The leader roared a battle cry rushing forward. "For the children and each other!", he yelled running past Faith and Jericho.

The magic-user heard Calvin before she saw him rush by and just the sight of her leader compelled her to follow him into battle. Cracking her whip in the air, Faith started forward.

Jericho needed little reminding why they were here but after hearing the knight and witnessing him bringing the fight to the enemy, the big man bellowed a loud yell reminiscent to a bell tolling a midnight. Its tone seemed to reverberate off the cavern's walls. The party's giant oak rushed towards the oncoming enemies.

Moric knew he was a better fighter when doing it stealthier compared to when battling an adversary straight on. There were dozens and dozens of carts along with dirt and rock mounds. Watching his friends run at the charging foe, the gnome instead sprinted away from them to his right. Moric needed to hide in the cover of either a two-wheeled wagon or one of the cave's piles of soil or stones.

The five Devis's all took off forward at the same time. Their swords swinging in the air above their heads caused a questioning look from the drow approaching on the elf's side. Devis's defensive mirror images helping the companion's group to look a bit larger at first.

Harold, waving his studded mace in the air, started forward more in the direction of the drow's center to help assist Thorin. He still had no idea his brother was trapped and being stalked.

The half-elf began his rush to meet the wave of foes. His lips moving as he quietly offered a prayer to Guerra.

The crowd of slaves began to jostle about as they took in the sight of the eleven party members engage in battle. Their captor's methods of punishment and intimidation caused their irrational thinking, and even though some of the huddled slaves held onto picks or hammers along with outnumbering their captors, they still were too frightened to act.

Whips cracked not only in the air but actually struck some of the prisoners pushing them back and huddling them closer together. "Get back you mangy animals!", a taskmaster screamed. The slaves seeming not able to comprehend exactly what was happening.

Edward had been yelling trying to get Harold, or anyone else's attention, right after he was ensnared by the magical web. With the loud noise throughout the room no one heard him, and now his friends had met the dark elves in combat. The entangled McKinley could hear the sounds of swords clashing along with the shouts of battle. Desperately he tried reaching for his dagger when the realization that none of the others were aware of his predicament. Edward knew he had to free himself.

" We'll put an end to this resistance before it starts!", snarled Priestess Xarna. Freeing her snake scourge from her hip, she issued her orders to Zebbulas before rushing into the battle between the companions and the dark elves. "I want you to crush this display of insolence!", she hissed rivaling the hissing caused from her weapon's viper heads filling the air.

House Wizard Zebbulas began preparing to cast a spell as he watched Xarna starting towards the fray. Minutes later a bolt of lightning shot across the cavern on its way to the battle line.

The drow exposed his torso for a brief moment by spreading his arms out wide to either side. With one swift movement, he swung both scimitars aimed at Calvin's neck. The knight reacting quickly to the rapid attack dropped down into a squat, dodging the swings. Both of the dark elf's weapons came together in the empty spot where Calvin once stood.

Trying to take advantage of his position, the group's leader started to stand back up while thrusting his sword upwards, but the dark elf took a step back, bringing both his blades down. Crossing each other to form an "x", that blocked the counterstrike.

Jericho feigned a right swing but instead tried to come up low on his left side with his staff. Unfortunately, the drow was more fluid a fighter. With no great size or even muscles like the big villager, the dark elf fashioned his style of melee combat on speed. Side stepping the attack, so he was inside Jericho's guard, the drow connected with an elbow to the big man's nose. The bone crunching strike sent the oak reeling backwards. Blood flowed from the villager's broken nose.

Faith's adversary ran at her twirling both scimitars in his hands. His snarling lips and menacing gaze displayed that he meant serious business. The woman striking out with her whip aimed low on the dark elf. Lashing one of his ankles, she managed to wrap the body part and yank her weapon tight pulling the attacker's leg slightly farther on his next step. Instead of an oncoming attack, the drow lost his balance and fell to the ground. Glancing back up at her, as she released and reeled in her whip from his ankle, the adversary growled while starting to get back up. In moments, he once again started towards her.

❧

Committed to his charge, the drow warrior had no time to dodge or pull up as Thorin called upon the magic aid of his maul. Pointing the head of the hammer at his oncoming foe and letting loose the fiery magic, the drow's face and head were engulfed by the flaming sphere. The dark elf's full head of white hair was now red and orange burning from the fire. Soon a stink rose from the blazing head of the fallen corpse. Two more enemies engaged the dwarf.

A slight murmur rose from the dwarf slaves as they all watched the gritty warrior. They all knew of Hammerstone.

❧

A lightning bolt shot across the cavern straight into and through Devis' chest slamming into the rocky ground behind him. One of the mirror images disappeared.

The real elf moved with a fluidness that rivaled his opponents continuous movements. They danced the steps of death striking and blocking each others attacks. The drow's two swords against the elf's one.

❧

The dark elf's scimitar quickly slid off the half-elf's forearm leaving a gash across it. Already blood began to run from the cut. Jhessail backing away briefly before pressing his attack.

Moving with the agility inherited from his father's family, the half-elf caught his foe across the stomach. Now it was the drow's turn to step back leaking from the slash. "I'd say we're even," stated Jhessail with a smile crossing his face. The slight pain and blood that accompanied the wound seemed to send a feeling of exhilaration through the war god's disciple.

The enemy growled before rushing at him. His blades held high.

❧

One of the fallen warriors, a victim of Jhessail's grease spell, was halfway up when he noticed Harold swinging his mace overhead approaching him. The drow quickly uttered an incantation and pointed at the oncoming McKinley. A purple, magic arrow shot into the young man's upper chest blowing him backwards causing Harold to hit the ground with such force that he lost hold of his mace. The McKinley's shoulder felt to him as if it were dislocated.

❧

Approaching the battle, Priestess Xarna watched the gnome from behind his charging companions make a wide birth attempting to get behind the drow's line. She offered a prayer to Thaisia asking the goddess for the divine power to smite her enemy. Pointing her palm at the gnome a purplish, black flame shot forth from it heading directly at him.

Just catching sight in time of the onrushing, weird-colored flame, Moric; pot belly and all, was nimble enough to dive out of the holy magic's way. Dirt and rock debris showered him, as the attack slammed hard into the cavern's floor.

❧

"Tsk. Tsk. Tsk", sarcastically came the dark elf, who had caught the McKinley in his web. "Don't bother struggling now it's too late. At least know that your death was delivered to you by House Zexthion," the drow stated standing over the trapped Edward. His sword pointing down preparing to plunge it into the young man. The McKinley couldn't do anything to help himself. He knew his time had come.

Ready to drive his scimitar's blade into the villager, the dark elf offered a grunt and his eyes widened. Blood started to trickle from his mouth as he faltered and dropped to his knees next to Edward's head. Releasing the grip on his weapon, the sword fell forward followed by his headless body. A river of blood began to flow from the separated carcass and the dark elf's head rolled on the ground beside him.

"Cut the boy loose," a voice ordered obviously to another, who was already slicing at the purple web.

Edward watched as a small, gauntlet-covered hand picked up the drow's head by it's long, white hair.

"Are you hurt son?", asked another mysterious voice.

"No. I'm alright."

Within minutes the McKinley was free of his bonds and his eyes got their first glimpse of one of his rescuers. In front of him stood a bald, dwarven cleric.

༺၉༻

The voice grew louder and louder eventually causing the combatants a brief rest as they separated for a few moments. The drow of House Zexthion stood almost in a trance gazing in amazement at the plate mail, armored dwarf wearing a helmet adorned with a gold crown standing on the ledge located near the entrance into the mining cavern. The red-haired clan chief presenting the decapitated head of the dark elf by holding it slightly out in front of him. His voice seemed to grab a hold of everyone in the room. Just the sight of his presence stirred a feeling of inspiration in his people.

"My people!", pausing a brief moment, as the chief gazed around the room before starting up again. "My kinsman, we are not a weak and feeble people to be beaten and whipped nor be used by others to perform their bidding while we hand them our home and our riches. Our race does not run and cower from fear. We are dwarves! The same people who take a dragon's treasure as the beast roars its protest." Fireheart looked over the crowd. "The same people, who stand and fight while others rush to hide. This is the face of our enemy!", the dwarf held up emphasizing the dark elf's severed head. "And this is what we do to the evil that opposes us. Dwarves will never live under their rule and we will never toil for their benefit. So as your chief, I command each and every dwarf to fight now and take our riches back, take our home back, and to win back our freedom from our dark enemy!"

Chief Fireheart threw the decapitated drow head into the cavern. Raising his battle axe over his head, the clan's leader issued a roar to fight.

❦

"Fireheart!", growled the drow wizard when he saw the dwarf standing on the rocky outcropping. Zebbulas witnessed the room fall silent, as the clan's freed chief addressed the dwarven slaves. The house wizard knew to witness Fireheart fall in front of their eyes would rob them of any notion to rebel against their drow captors.

Quickly, Zebbulas began to recite the words to a spell, but lost them when his defensive sphere protecting him against energy attacks brightened as it absorbed the power from the lightning bolt just shot at him. Off to his left, rising from behind a cart stood a shirtless, drow.

❦

Rising from behind a cart, Wizard Zolktar gazed at the astonished look on the house wizard's face. His bolt absorbed into Zebbulas's defensive globe.

"How is this possible?", the overwhelmed drow asked. "You couldn't have figured out your potential without someone to help you. My binding spell is flawless."

"Was flawless," snarled Zolktar. "You should have never placed me in a cell with those I brought here as slaves. Didn't you think that someone would recognize me?"

Still wearing a stunned look on his face, House Wizard Zebbulas knew he better act quick and called on the magical aid from a ring he wore. Thrusting his right hand forward, he spoke the jewelry's command word activating its property. A cone of ice shot forth from it. The blast heading straight for the shirtless, dark elf, but the magical attack disappearing as it was absorbed by a protective globe surrounding Wizard Zolktar.

Smiling the drow slave stated the obvious to the house wizard. "Looks like two can play this game."

Priestess Xarna stood in quiet amazement listening to and seeing the dwarven chief. She even lowered her snake scourge caught in the grip of Fireheart's words. Her anger building inside her until finally the pure rage erupted from within. "No!", she screamed when the mass of slaves inspired by their leader's call to battle turned on their captors using whatever was in their hands to rebel. Chaos broke out in the cavern.

After watching one of her dark elf taskmasters get bludgeoned to death under multiple hammer blows from the mining tools, she rushed forward. Her destination; Chief Fireheart.

Calvin pressed his attack by following his upward thrust with a bash from his shield. The strike catching the dark elf in his chest knocking him back another step. The drow quickly recovered from the blow and counterattacked swinging his left sword followed by his right in a downward motion. The knight, using his shield to steer and guide the strikes away from him, side-stepped to his right. The leader's enemy made the crucial mistake of over-extending his forward step putting him almost past the parrying knight. Calvin thrusts his blade into the back of his foe's neck severing the dark elf's spinal cord. Momentum carrying his adversary's body forward as he dropped to the ground. The knight's head instinctively on a swivel looking left and then right.

Jericho's eyes filled with tears from his broken nose, as he dodged another sword swing from his adversary. The drow warrior would not stop coming, and the big man knew that he could not stay on the defensive or he would fall to the fighter's two scimitars. Still he could not find an opening in his enemy's flawless attacks.

❧

While Faith kept the dark elf at bay with her whip she discreetly tried to untie the pouch at her hip. Inside was the component she needed to cast her last spell for the day. Unknowing to her, the drow was uttering words preparing to cast his own spell. Beating her to the punch, he tossed one of his swords at her. Nimbly the woman dodged the hurled weapon, but as she looked back to the dark elf, her sight was stolen by the purplish, magical web that struck her from point blank range. The force of the blast driving her backwards causing Faith to trip over both the web and her feet. Her enemy advancing on the struggling woman engulfed by the sticky trap.

❧

Thorin was confronted by two drow warriors twirling and swinging their scimitars. As the closest of the two rapidly approached, the ornery dwarf spoke the command word once again activating the hammer's magic. A globe of fire shot from the maul's head blasting the dark elf back several feet slamming him to the ground. The agitated dwarf commented to the other one of his enemies, "You just saw me do the same thing to your buddy! I swear thick as a stone giant." Thorin just shook his head. The other drow stepping back trying to get out of point blank range.

❧

Two more images of Devis disappeared, as the dark elf warriors sliced through them with their swords. Surprise housed on their faces when the realization that their enemy was only an illusion meant to distract them and the fact that it had worked only made them angrier. Scanning the area for the real adversary, both drow fighters witnessed a human with an armored dwarf followed by a bald dwarf running from the direction of the paths around the ledge towards the small battle line. On the other side a hoard of rushing slaves yielding picks and hammers came fast. In the cavern's background magic spells flared in and out.

The real Devis had just been sliced again making the count three to two, his enemy's way. The elf had had enough and began to recite the incantation to a spell while keeping up his fluid dance of death with the drow. When he was done, Devis waited for the opportune time. Seeing a brief opening he spoke the command word and pointed at the dark elf. Two green, magical arrows shot forth striking his foe in the chest. Both of the drow's swords seemed to hang in the air for a moment by themselves, as their wielder's body was blown backwards.

⤙෨⤚

Grimacing in pain, Harold held his limp arm close to his body.

"Harold!", cried his brother coming up behind him with the two dwarfs. "What's the matter?"

"I think it's separated or broken," he responded looking at his shoulder.

"Slopewalker, heal the boy!", Chief Fireheart ordered. "Then you two stay with the cleric and guard him. I feel your gonna be needed!"

The armored dwarf charged towards the line.

⤙෨⤚

The half-elf's sword skidded across the stony floor of the cavern as he laid up looking at his enemy hovering over him. The drow feeling the companions end was near drove one of his swords into Jhessail's upper arm, but the fallen half-elf moved just enough that the blade only pinned him to the ground by his cloak. Menacingly laughing, the dark elf stated before preparing to skew Jhessail with his other sword. "Ain't going nowhere now half-breed. Tell your god, whichever one it may be, that House Zexthion arranged the meeting between him and one of his followers."

As he prepared to bring his second weapon down, the wizard-warrior reached up across his body with his free hand and grabbed the drow's wrist of the hand holding the sword he had used to pin the half-elf down. Jhessail finally spoke the command word for the spell from his earlier prayer.

The dark elf's eyes rolled up in his head as his body began to softly shake building its way up to a violent movement. Blood began to flow from the drow's eyes, ears, and nose. Lacerations and cuts appeared on his face and hands.

"No, tell your bitch queen that one of Guerra's followers has sent her a new subject to torment," proclaimed Jhessail letting the dark elf's wrist go and kicking him backwards.

Pulling the sword that had been pinning him down from his cloak, Jhessail swiftly rose to his feet and retrieved his own sword. "There are many more subjects to send to their queen on this day," he thought scanning his vicinity.

⁓❧

Faith struggled in the web that had taken her by surprise. The magic-user knew that her foe was still in the area and she feared for her life. Not succumbing to the panic, the woman tried to free her dagger so she could cut her way out of her trap when she suddenly heard a wet, sickening sound above her.

Faith gasped from surprise as the drow's limp body fell to the ground beside her. His dead stare meeting her gaze.

"Now hold on and don't move," a voice said out of nowhere as she felt the web's grip began to loosen as it was being cut apart. Faith never had been so relieved and so happy to hear that obnoxious voice.

Sitting up in the sliced remains of the spell, the woman's eyes fell upon her rescuer. Crouched near her armed with two daggers was the group's thief.

"Thanks Moric!"

"Don't thank me yet. Jericho's in trouble!", pointing in the direction of the big man with a dagger. "Do you have any spell's left that with aid him?"

Faith loosened her pouch that had helped distract her before she had gotten webbed. She reached in it pulling out some type of glittering dust before calling upon her magic to aid her.

Throwing the spell's component into the air, she issued the command word activating her magic. Within moments, Moric and she watched the drow fall to the ground as it was put into a sleep.

Rising to their feet, the two witnessed a bloody and beaten Jericho squat down and break the slumbering drow's neck.

Both companions got a quick breather as they prepared to meet a new foe and witnessed the slaves now taking the fight to their captors.

CHAPTER 31

The mining cavern took on a chaotic scene as pandemonium broke out between the captives and their outnumbered captors. Just the sight of the dwarves' chief, along with his accompanying words, rose the spirits of his people and rallied the slaves to action. Even the villagers seemed compelled by Fireheart's speech, inspiring them as well. In the midst of the rebellion, a wizard's duel between two hated rivals took place. Sparks of magic flew in the cave's air.

House Wizard Zebbulas dove to his right landing behind a cart full of diamonds. A bolt of lightning exploded a pile of stone when it missed the drow causing rock debris to rain down on him as he tried to quickly take cover. The dark elf counting his fortunes as only minutes before his defensive globe against energy attacks faded out of existence. Zebbulas snarled at his enemy from behind the two-wheeled wagon.

"Come out Zebbulas and fight me like a real house wizard, you weasel!", shouted the shirtless drow. His body still beaten and bruised from his previous whippings.

Suddenly, it was Wizard Zolktar's time to dive and roll away from the black ray shooting from behind the cart where the other drow took a moments refuge. It struck the cart Zolktar had been standing near and within seconds the object was disintegrated. The dark elf coming out of his roll to witness the seven images of Wizard Zebbulas standing roughly forty feet away. He knew that it would take at least seven shots to destroy the mirror images before the real Zebbulas would be vulnerable to attack.

Still on a bent knee and beginning to prepare a casting, Wizard Zolktar was caught off guard by the phantasmal fist that flew at him with great speed. He tried to use his own quickness to dodge the fist but was only half successful. The ghost hand's knuckles glancing off his shoulder. The magical strike lifted him into the air slightly knocking the dark elf over and onto his back.

Retaining a knee, Zolkar began reciting the words to his next spell, as the fist flew closer closing in on its target again. Waving his hands and casting the dispelling magic, the one time slave witnessed the phantasmal attack fade before it had reached its kneeling target.

House Wizard Zebbulas, along with his seven images, diabolically laughed. "Since when did you think that you could ever rival my magic?"

Snarling his rage, Zolktar prepared another spell. He knew he would have to get rid of the fake Zebbulases if he was ever going to stand any type of chance against the real one. The dark elf issued the command word and five, purple arrows shot forth from his raised hand. Unfortunately, he never got to see more than half the false images disappear from the attacks as a human slave swinging a shovel snuck up on him and made a glancing blow to the back of Zolktar's head. Instantly, unconsciousness consumed him even before he hit the ground.

House Wizard Zebbulas broke out in a laugh before rewarding the rebel with a barrage of four magical, purple arrows himself. Blood sprayed everywhere on impact.

The drow with his two remaining copies made their way over to his one time pupil. "You were always weak and a fool, but how did you figure out the binding spell that I placed within your mind?", he softly asked himself while gazing at his slumbering foe.

Zebbulas tried to think of what aided his fallen student but still an enigma remained. "Who helped you Zolktar?", he wondered letting the query escape his lips.

The house wizard was trapped in his thoughts for a moment but when one of his false images disappeared he quickly looked around to see where the attack was coming from. Zebbulas was taken aback at first when he realized the missile fire had come from the small child throwing a stone at him.

"Get away from him and leave him alone!", shouted Katherine.

"You are the one!", realized the drow. "It was you that helped him."

Flashbacks of the child from the slave's holding pen ran through his mind. The laughs and jeers she had given the guards whenever the child attempted to be nice to the dark elf. The little girl was the key that had unlocked Zolktar's blocked memories. The house wizard yelled out, "You!"

Junior and Thomas were both afraid from the anger on Zebbulas's face and cried out their warning, "Kat, run! He's going to hurt you!"

The drow wizard turned his full attention from the fallen Zolktar to the one responsible for breaking his binding spell on his punished student and prepared the casting of a new spell. His words rising in decibels as Zebbulas waved both his hands to and fro.

Junior knew what the drow was about to do. He was going to kill Katherine just like the rest of the boy's family. "Thomas, he's going to kill Kat. We have to stop him!"

"What are we going to do?", questioned his brother with his voice cracking from fear.

"You take one of them and I'll take the other."

"And do what with them?"

"We'll give Kat some time to get some help," reasoned Junior looking to Thomas. "Get him!", the older sibling yelled.

The little girl's older brothers ran as fast as their legs would carry them. Closing the distance to Zebbulas in a hurry, the wizard had to decide quickly who would be the recipient of his prepared spell. Instantly, the drow made the choice and a command word caused a purplish web to shoot forth from his hands devouring both onrushing brothers. Their momentum carried them along with the magical trap ensnaring them into and through the last fake Zebbulas leaving only the real drow's image.

"I'll be back for you two,..." -he advised the two brothers who were kicking in the web- "...but now I've got a meeting with your sister." Zebbulas took off after the fleeing child trying to catch up.

❧

Katherine ran as fast as she could. Dodging fights between drows and the rebels, she dashed to an area of the cavern where the little girl broke free from all the chaos surrounding her and the wild uproar it produced. The child's little, bare feet slapping against the stony floor and her breath starting to become labored. She was frightened and knew only one place she would be able to hide and get away from all the trouble. The child swiftly ran towards solace. Katherine headed for her hiding spot. She dashed for the bridge.

❧

Priestess Xarna's snake scourge lashed out again, it's three viper heads sinking their fangs into another slave's flesh, as she hurried towards the dwarfs' leader wearing his plate armor and dawning a golden-crowned helmet. The rebel screaming out his pain while venom dripped from the wound. She was closing in on the clan's chief battling another drow in the efforts to free his people. Priestess Xarna offered up a prayer to her goddess as she approached Fireheart. Petitioning Thaisia to lend her aid in defeating the chief.

Xarna looked on as the dwarf seemed to slow for a moment and just blocked a sword strike from his face with his double-bladed axe in the nick of time. Again, the drow woman prayed and within minutes a wall of spinning and slicing daggers appeared out of thin air in front of her. Motioning with her free hand, the bladed barrier slowly advanced on the two enemies locked in combat.

The dark elf priestess was almost taken by surprise by one of the rebelling slaves as he instantly appeared behind her carrying a pick. Raising it above her head, the captive slung it downward from an overhead position, but Xarna was much faster than his attempt and side-stepped the blow. The tool digging into the cavern's floor.

Swiftly the priestess whipped out at him and the deadly weapon bit into his flesh causing the rebel to reel backwards from the blow.

The priestess grabbed the tool's handle on its way up and drove the pick into the human's chest. Its point just breaching the underfed man's back and dropping the rebel with a thud.

Turning back to the drow and the dwarf already engaged in melee, she watched the floating, blade wall slice and dice the surprised drow from behind to pieces. His blood splattering the air and painting the ground.

Chief Fireheart and his dark elf adversary traded blows and parries in their fight to the death. The dwarf seeing the wall of spinning daggers approaching the two combatants had an idea to end the melee. The clan's chief led with a swing from his battle axe and followed the strike with a bull rush. The drow not expecting the charge from the dwarf was caught off guard. Fireheart lifted the dark elf off of his feet and sent the enemy backwards into the oncoming bladed barrier. His adversary screaming in pain as the daggers shredded him apart.

The drow priestess began to whisper a silent prayer, but not for the dead, dark elf. Within minutes her snake scourge began to glow a purplish hue as she propelled the blades forward towards the armored dwarf through her magical control of them. A diabolical grin spread across her face.

"Time to meet your makers Fireheart," she confidently stated.

The wall of bladed death advanced on the chief, all he could do was step back trying to keep his weapon in between him and the barrier. The clinging of contact between the daggers and the dwarf's axe rang in the air until suddenly Fireheart's double-bladed weapon flew from his hands back over his head. Xarna's grin turned into a laugh.

The dwarf scrambled backwards all the time looking for his axe. Locating it about three feet away from him, the chief looked up to see the wall of daggers gone and a lash from the woman's weapon coming right at him.

Drü Slopewalker noticed his long time friend and clan chief in trouble. The drow priestess' spell advancing on the weaponless leader. Having just dispatched an enemy, while the two McKinleys dropped another, the dwarven cleric prayed to his gods. Hearing and answering his appeal for help, the Forger and the Quarter, bestowed the spell he would need to give his friend a fighting chance. With his palms extended in the direction of the bladed wall, Slopewalker spoke the words dispelling the drow's magic.

༜

Fireheart grunted in pain when the blessed magic bit into him. The viper's fangs piercing through his armor sending him to a knee. Another strike landed across the chief's back causing his body to arch in pain. The scourge's biting attacks meeting no defense from his armor. The fangs puncturing the metal plates like needles through cloth.

"Remember the feeling dwarf?", angrily yelled Xarna. "Kneel before your master!"

Fireheart took another lash as he stumbled towards his axe. The blows repeating one after another, but still the dwarf; falling to a knee, reached his weapon. He could hear the priestess uttering words but they were indistinguishable to his ears at the time.

Xarna had been praying to Thaisia asking the goddess to grant her divine power so she could smite her foe. Drawing back the woman's elbow preparing for another lash from her blessed, magical whip, the snake scourge's purplish hue began to glow a deeper color. It's radiating outline taking on a supernatural, violet-colored fire.

Priestess Xarna gave one last animalistic growl as she dropped her elbow, swinging the weapon down at the dwarf for the final blow. The three viper heads, mouths wide with fangs exposed and highlighted in a violet fire, came at the kneeling chief shaking in pain. Purplish-colored venom dripped from their hypodermic syringe-like weapons.

Fireheart wrapped his thick, stubby, gauntlet-covered hand around the shaft of his axe, and in an act of desperation, brought the weapon up across his body adding his other hand near its pommel.

311

The double-bladed weapon meeting the scourge's strike causing the axe's blade to sever all of the viper's heads from the whip.

Everyone in the cavern jumped at the loud explosion that rocked the mountain's stone. Pieces of the cave shook loose dirt clear from the place's walls causing clouds of dust to form in more than two dozen places, and some panicked thinking the whole mine would collapse from the shock wave.

The explosive discharge consumed the snake scourge and sent both the drow priestess and the dwarf chief head over heels in opposite directions. The two landing hard roughly fifty feet apart. Xarna unmoving and clothes torn, laid in an awkward position on the cavern's floor. Part of her face and her hand blown off.

"No!", cried the dwarf cleric starting for his old friend. Harold and Edward following Slopewalker.

Skidding to a halt, Drü quickly dropped beside the chief. Fireheart appeared in bad condition. The dwarf's armor saved him although his right shoulder and its arm were broken in several places. Smoke rose from the chief's plate mail protected chest and the right side of his helmet was missing. Blood flowed from a head wound along with several cuts on his face. Instantly, the dwarf cleric checked for any signs of breath coming from his clan chief's nose. The slight feel of air against his finger brought with it hope to Slopewalker.

"Hold on my chief!" the bald dwarf cried while laying his hands on the remaining part of Fireheart's helmet. Drü Slopewalker bowed his head and spoke the words to what was his most important prayer for almost two centuries. The cleric not only trying to save his clan's leader but also one of his best friends.

Time seemed to drag and the three lost track of it, as the dwarf kneeled next to the chief and both McKinley brothers stood guard over the two. Fireheart finally opened his eyes slowly.

"Welcome back," a relieved Slopewalker greeted breaking into a smile. "How do you feel my friend?"

❧

Calvin had fought his way through the skirmishing crowd, as the captives had gotten the upper hand on their captors. The drow seemed to be falling at a much faster rate than the outnumbering mass of rebels. The knight had been on the search for Jacob's children when an explosion rocked the mountain's cavern.

Surprised gasps filled the vast room but cries for help seemed to grab and take hold of his attention. Scanning the area around him, Calvin saw where the pleas were coming from. On the floor, roughly twenty five feet away from him, lay a purplish-colored web. Whoever was trapped inside was responsible for the shouts of distress. The party's leader started for the object.

Reaching the web, Calvin kneeled near the magical trap. "Who is in there?", he asked not being able to make out its unfortunate guest.

"It's Junior and Thomas," responded a voice.

"Jacob's children?"

"Yes, that's us!"

"I will have you out of there in a couple of minutes," assured Calvin ready to use his sword to start cutting the web. The knight on the lookout for danger. "Be still children. I have got to cut this stuff."

"No. You have to help Kat!", cried the scared boys.

"Where is the girl?", inquired Calvin still slicing the spell's remnants but having cut enough that both the web's inhabitants could sit up.

Pointing to the northwest direction of the cavern, Thomas answered. "She went that way!"

"Please get Kat!", pleaded Junior while working his way out of the trap's stickiness.

Calvin nodded his head before starting off in that direction.

⤳⤶

"So you're the one that ruined my work!", shouted House Wizard Zebbulas yelling at the child, who ran on ahead of him. "You will pay dearly child!", he warned. The drow's attention stolen away from the little girl running towards the bridge by the loud explosion. Looking back in the direction the sound originated in, the wizard figured he had some idea what was going on back there.

Turning back to start his pursuit for the little girl, Zebbulas was caught by surprise from the blunt strike to his stomach. The blows force backing him up a step or two. His eyes fell on a curly, red-haired dwarven woman. Her dirty face covering her freckles.

"Where do you think you're off to?", the woman asked.

Wizard Zebbulas quickly called on his magic.

Bouncing the hammer's handle in one of her palms, the dwarf came at the drow. "Time to,…" but her words cut off when she took five purple arrows in her face. The shots blowing her head clear from her body.

"I know. Die," chuckled Zebbulas. "You should have remained out of the way dumb bitch," he added leaping over her fallen body and continuing his pursuit of the child.

❧

Katherine reached the bridge and her little feet slapped the stone structure as she ran across it. In seconds, she was on the other side hiding behind its walls. The child breathed heavy trying to catch her breath while her heart felt like it was pounding out of her small chest. Tears streaked her dirty cheeks.

Katherine tried to stay quiet as she hid. The time dragging from both fear and anticipation. The little girl refusing to look and see if the evil elf was still searching for her. Katherine almost leaped out of her skin when the drow stood at the beginning to the bridge. He had found her.

"There you are child," growled Zebbulas looking down the crossing at her before taking a moment and surveying the place's surroundings. "Looks like you won't be getting off to nowhere now," he sinisterly laughed.

Katherine's body involuntarily shook from fear washing over it. The scared child rose to her feet. There was no sense in trying to conceal herself any longer now. She knew she had been found.

"They'll be coming for me," the little girl trying to bluff the drow.

"Who your brothers?", asked the wizard. "They're all tied up waiting for me to return so I can keep them as my personal pets."

"He'll be here, and when he does...", the child started. Her words coming to an end as Zebbulas offered another loud laugh.

"Who? Wizard Zolktar?", the drow asked with a snarl starting to form on his face. "You and him seem to have become real friendly as of late."

"That's right!", confidently stated Katherine. "And he's going to kick your butt when he gets here! The little girl trying to suppress her fear.

A smile crossed the house wizard's face. "He won't be coming to save you any time soon. Besides he was the one responsible for killing your family."

"That's not true!", defiantly yelled Katherine.

Zebbulas laughed again finding the little girl's bravado much amusing. "Than who child? The goblins?", he sarcastically inquired.

"That's right," she responded with her hands upon her hips. "Wizard Zolktar came to my rescue..." -Katherine stopped to think. Her head slightly tilting up as she brought the times back to memory- "...four times so far, and he'll be coming again soon."

"He won't be here because I've killed him," the drow informed the child wearing a menacing look upon his face. "Just like I'm going to kill you."

Suddenly, a silent warning from the alarm spell the wizard had cast went off in his head. Zebbulas did not want any surprises, like the one with the dwarven woman and her hammer, to catch him off guard and delay this child's death any longer.

Glancing inconspicuously over his shoulder when he spoke, the drow saw something or someone coming at him fast. Waiting till the last second, House Wizard Zebbulas rolled to his immediate right. An armored man trying for a shield ram rushed straight past where he once stood. The passing knight taken by surprise by the move.

Calvin almost fell forward but caught himself as he came to a halt between where Katherine stood on the bridge and where the drow wizard positioned himself.

"It is over wizard!", proclaimed Calvin. "Stand down, and I will make sure you at least see dwarven justice."

The dark elf breaking into a laugh. "And if I don't foolish knight. What then?", again laughing at the absurdity of the party leader's statement.

"Then you shall fall at my hands!", decreed Calvin. "As long as I live you will never harm this child!"

Zebbulas broke into laughter which eventually grew into a roar. Instantly he stopped and began to recite the incantation to a spell.

Knowing he couldn't just stand back and wait, Calvin gave a battle cry and charged. He knew he would not be able to go sword strike versus spell cast with a wizard. The knight's only hope was to hit the drow and foil his casting.

The child's defender got within ten feet from the wizard when the drow pointed his hand at the knight launching five purple magical arrows. Calvin only had enough time to raise his dented shield. The blast hitting it hard and propelling him through the air and onto the two steps of the bridge.

Calvin's arm burned as if it was on fire. He knew the instant the five magic missiles hit his shield the knight's arm had shattered. The man grimaced and moaned in pain, but Calvin slowly rose to a knee.

Katherine's little feet carried her across the stone structure to the wounded knight's side. Her own face seemed to grimace just from hearing him moan in pain. "He's going to kill us, isn't he?", the child asked.

"Not as long as I can still breathe," replied a grimacing Calvin rising to his feet. "Now get behind me."

Zebbulas laughed at the two before beginning the casting of a new spell. He had had enough of the delay. The child was going to die. The drow figured he would be receiving a bonus killing the knight along with her. The dark elf spoke the command word to his spell and a giant, phantasmal hand materialized in the air.

The drow directed the ghost hand to a large boulder resting on the cavern's floor. Closing its five digits and grasping the huge rock, the phantasmal hand lifted it from the ground hurtling it at the two on the bridge. The flying, two ton object spinning end over end.

Calvin knew he was no match for the boulder. He also knew that the launched rock would drive through him and strike the child

316

killing both of them unless the little girl laid flat at his feet. Calvin believed it might fly over the little girl leaving her untouched if she laid down and stayed low.

"Child!", Calvin yelled while throwing his sword to the ground and using his free hand to raise his dented shield. "Lay on the bridge at my feet. When the stone flies over you run back to the others. Jericho is there with friends that will aid him."

"What about you?"

"Do not worry about me. Run and do not stop until you find Jericho," Calvin advised Katherine.

As the boulder flew through the air closer and closer to the two, Calvin said a prayer to his god. Tucking his head into his shield, the knight waited for the hurled attack that never came. The air around them filled with a loud sound from the flying rock exploding against the unseen wall protecting the two on the bridge. Debris flew through the air around them plummeting into the chasm. The shattering of the boulder caused Katherine to look up. The little girl's eyes widened with surprise.

⁓❧⁓

House Wizard Zebbulas smiled at the knight's futile attempt to try and protect the child from their oncoming doom. He watched as Katherine laid at the knight's feet and even the drow thought maybe the boulder would fly right over her missing the girl. The dark elf being so caught up in Katherine's demise flinched with startled amazement when the large rock shattered in the air. Zebbulas had made a valuable mistake by somehow being so consumed with the child's imminent death that he never paid any attention to his alarm spell going off in his head.

Suddenly, Zebbulas was propelled forward by the three magical, purple arrows that crashed into his back. The slightly stunned drow looked in the direction the attack had come from. House Wizard Zebbulas froze for a moment when his eyes met the sight of the four images of his new adversary on this field of battle.

"I don't believe we were done," came the dark elf he recognized as his one time pupil.

Before Zebbulas could react a bolt of lightning shot forth from the dark elf's hand heading directly for the drow on the ground. The house wizard made an attempt to roll out of the spell's way but the bolt caught his trailing hand blowing it off at the wrist. Zebbulas screamed in pain.

⁓❧

"Zolktar!", excitedly shouted Katherine. "You came."

Calvin kneeled down to retrieve his sword helping the child to her feet first.

"Get out of here Katherine!", the dark elf yelled. A split second later he followed it up. "Lead the child out of here now knight."

"Let's go!", ordered Calvin.

"But what about Zolktar?", asked the concerned girl.

"This is his battle," responded Calvin knowing not to trust the dark elf but also realizing this was the chance to save Katherine. He was too wounded with a lame arm to do anything else if the window of opportunity shut. "Just keep me between you and them."

The two ran from the bridge. Katherine couldn't help but to keep her eyes on the four images of her savior once again.

⁓❧

Calling on his magical aid with much haste, Zebbulas fought to recite the words to the spell's incantation. Without the aid of his magical ring, he would have to pull it together to leave this battle alive. The house wizard pointed at the four images, and five magic arrows rocketed through the air hitting the multiple Zolktars. Three images disappeared when they were hit, but their caster was preparing another spell as he started to rush at the rising drow. Moments later a ball of fire flew through the air. Zolktar following his hurled attack.

House Wizard Zebbulas began to speak the words to his next spell while attempting to rush out of the fireball's area of attack. The ball smashing into an area of the wall behind where he once stood. It's concussive force launching

Zebbulas into the air towards the chasm. Realizing there wouldn't be enough solid ground to land on, House Wizard Zebbulas knew he would be falling for a while.

The air borne drow couldn't change over to another spell fast enough to stop what was about to happen. Instead he altered the words to the spell's incantation and shot forth a purplish-hued web. It engulfed Zolktar entangling him from head to toe. The dark elf was stuck. Zebbulas' modification was the attaching web line from his grasp to the bundle trapping the other dark elf. As he fell over the cliff, and into the chasm, Zebbulas held the line causing the bundle entangling Zolktar to follow him into the deep, black gorge. Both wizards disappearing from sight.

❧

Katherine, followed closely by the wounded knight whose shield arm hung limp as he jogged behind the child, weaved their way through the vast cavern. The place littered with bodies of the dead human and dwarf freedom fighters along with the overrun drow. Blood stained the rocky ground and in some spots, the dark, red liquid formed small pools that both had to dodge.

Katherine scanned the crowd of rebels looking for her two older brothers, but it was her father's best friend that she noticed first towering over the rest. The little girl's heart and soul filled with excitement when she saw him. "Uncle Jericho!", she shouted, and her pace quickened a bit running for him.

"Kat!", answered back the oak when he gazed in the direction his name seemed to come from. The man recognizing the dirty, little girl approaching. Jericho's tree, trunk arms swallowed the child up, as she leaped into his grasp. Katherine's small twig-like arms wrapping around her uncle's neck.

"You're safe now peanut," he assured her.

Staring into Jericho's smiling face, the little girl smiled back at him when she heard the reassuring words.

"Junior! Thomas!", excitedly expressed Katherine when she saw the two. Jacob's three children rejoicing over the ending ordeal. Their sister telling them all about what took place at the bridge.

Sheathing his sword while witnessing the family reunion, Calvin triumphantly addressed all the companions standing within the vicinity through pained words. "Every one of you has done a good thing here today and have performed above what was expected of us ever since we left the village. Thank you all for your full efforts."

"No, thank you knight," came Jericho. "We all voted you this group's leader back at the tower. You have kept us all alive and because of that we have now got back our fellow villagers." The big man looked down placing a hand that covered the crown of Katherine's head. "Along with this peanut."

The little girl smiled.

"Your hurt knight," the half-elf broke in.

"My arm has sustained serious injury and I believe it to be broken in more than just one place," grimaced Calvin. "Right now it's so swollen the thing is stuck in the straps." The knight looking to the shield.

"Come on let's fix you up and make what was once broken whole again," suggested Jhessail.

The group's leader offering a pain-filled smile before following the half-elf to an appointed gathering spot for those in need of healing.

CHAPTER 32

The party and the villagers all remained in Bright Star Hall, guests of the dwarven people, for ten more full days. The one time slaves were treated for any wounds and healed. Slopewalker and Jhessail were extremely busy during that time and their three gods responded to all their requests for healing magic. The dwarven people also making sure the people of Oakhurst received the desperately needed intake of food and proper nutrition.

Chief Fireheart sent out patrols throughout the gigantic stronghold with the orders to seek out and destroy any remaining drow or other type of evil creatures that had taken up residence since the beginning of the hall's problems. He had also dispatched dwarven engineers to work on and come up with a solution to prevent any further access the dark elves had to the clan's water flow. Fireheart never wanted the river to be spiked with anything in the future.

Already a crew worked on the body disposal in the mining cavern, and no matter how much the little child from the village spoke about some type of hero drow named Zolktar, his body was never found. As for the other dark elf wizard, only a hand with a ring was discovered lying on the room's floor not far from the chasm. The drow believed to be dead due to a dwarven patrol searching the western entrance tunnel with the assistance of both Calvin and Devis and finding nine Oakhurst patrolmen instead of morphed goblins. Their spell's broken by the death of House Wizard Zebbulas.

"My people and I are indebted to you all," graciously offered Chief Fireheart to the group of companions at a banquet held in their honor the night before they would all be returning to the village with the people. He rose from his throne motioning to several other dwarves approaching the party's individuals and Thorin. Each companion was presented a small, brown, leather pouch.

"In gratitude of what you all did here I give to you all a pouch holding three diamonds and three sapphires," smiled Chief Fireheart before continuing. The clan leader now formally presenting a gift of his appreciation to each one of them personally.

"For you knight, I have had my smiths working day and night on this gift," he informed Calvin while handing him a new shield and bastard sword.

"This is not necessary chief," humbly spoke the companion's leader.

"Please accept it. Without your help my people may be under the rule of the bitch queen and her evil minions."

"Thank you," the knight graciously accepted the gift with a slight nod.

"They are sturdy and strong bestowed with magical properties. The shield will give you the defensive ability to protect you from all types of arrows both regular and magical. While the sword will cut clean and never dull."

Chief Fireheart gave a nod and moved to the next in line; Faith.

"For you lass, a magical necklace that absorbs all types of energy attacks," he handed her a gold necklace with an onyx stone.

"To the elf, I give him this white, gold ring with a diamond. Speak the command word inscribed on the inside of the band and a cone of ice shoots forth."

Fireheart stepped in front of Moric. "It is my understanding that you are a locksmith gnome," he slyly smiled.

Both the jesting chief and the acknowledged locksmith looked down the line at Faith trying hard to contain the rest of her laugh.

"For you, a gold ring housing a magical emerald. The jewelry will vibrate and the gem will glow if it detects any type of magical trap."

"Gee thanks!", excitedly expressed Moric.

"For you half-elf, the same kind of necklace as the young woman wears. It will absorb all types of magical energy."

Jhessail nodded his thanks.

The dwarven chief addressed the three farmers from the neighboring village as one. "To all three of you, I give you these three silver necklaces housing amber-colored gems. Wear them in battle and the yellowish aura will outline your body protecting you from evil."

"Thank you Chief Fireheart," tolled Jericho.

"And finally to my friend. What do I give you Hammerstone?", queried the clan's leader.

"I don't want anything Fireheart."

"But I have something for you my loyal friend," revealed the chief. "In fact, you already wear it."

Thorin looked himself up and down a few times but still couldn't figure out what the other dwarf was speaking about. Puzzled he inquired, "What is it?"

The chief pointed to the bandolier he wore across his chest.

"This is a never ending supply of cigars. Remove one and another magically appears."

Hammerstone giving it a try by selecting a cigar and watching another take its place. A touch of happiness as he shook his head approvingly.

"How did you get it?", he astonished.

"That's a talk between you and Slopewalker."

Thorin looked over to his old friend, and Drü met his gaze with both a nod and a smile.

&

"Fitzgerald go get the captain! He needs to come and get a look at this for himself," one of the wall's guards yelled over his shoulder.

Minutes later, Captain Woodrow joined the soldier on the stone barricade. Gazing out to the road leading out of the Border Forest, Woodrow took in the sight of a cigar-smoking dwarf riding a cave bear leading a procession of the missing villagers of Oakhurst. Located on the parade's perimeter were the eight companions and nine of the missing patrol.

"It's Sergeant Piner sir!", shouted the guard.

"By all the gods!" -Woodrow exclaimed- "They did it!"

The captain spun on his heels and ran down the stairs of the wall. "Fitzgerald, raise the gate!"

"Yes sir!"

Captain Woodrow stood outside the entrance to the tower's wall. A smile spread from ear to ear.

⁓⧆⤻

It was late in the day and all of Oakhurt's villagers had left. The original seven had squared up with the captain and the McKinley brothers returned to their farm with the promise to meet their other companions at the tavern on the morrow. Jericho had taken Jacob's children home to live with him, his wife, and their kids. The big man planned on taking the whole family to Carl and Martha's place also tomorrow so all could meet up. The time had now come to not only mourn his childhood friend's fallen family but to celebrate the return of the townsfolk and the aid Oakhurst had received.

After Thorin sent the bear into the depths of the forest, the six companions followed the road back into the small town.

"I can't wait to take a bath," offered Faith to no one in particular. Just the thought of washing away all the dirt and grime from the adventure seemed to bring a smile to her face.

Looking towards Calvin, Moric asked a simple question that had been on his mind since they started back. His stomach giving a loud rumble. "Do you think Martha's made biscuits?"

Calvin, Faith, and Devis all looked to one another before breaking out into laughter. Unfortunately, both the dwarf and the half-elf were lost at not only the outburst but the inside joke as well.

The hungry gnome glanced amongst his laughing companions for several moments before offering the others a shrug of his shoulders. "What?", the self-proclaimed locksmith innocently perplexed.

CPSIA information can be obtained
at www.ICGtesting.com
Printed in the USA
FFOW03n1035211117
43599190-42395FF